I0586023

More books by Scott Stoll

For adults

- *Falling Uphill: One Man's Quest for Happiness Around the World on a Bicycle*

For children

- *Feel Your Feelings*
- *Dream It!: A Playbook to Spark Your Awesomeness*
- *Falling Uphill: The Secret of Life.* (The children's edition of Scott's bicycle ride around the world.)
- *Cayendo Hacia Arriba: El Secreto de la Vida.* (The children's Spanish edition of Scott's bike ride.)
- *Ruby the Red Worm's Dirty Job*
- *Mirabella the Monarch's Magical Migration*
- *The Cupcake Boy*

Upcoming books

- Scott continues his exploration of life in *Going Nowhere*, the sequel to *Falling Uphill.*
- *I Didn't Know I Loved A Cat.* A picture book for kids and adults.

BREATHLESS
The Oxygen Apocalypse

∘ A NOVEL ∘

Argonauts Press

BREATHLESS
The Oxygen Apocalypse
By Scott Stoll

Copyright © 2023 by Scott Stoll. First edition.

All rights reserved as per international and United States copyright law. No part of this book may be reproduced or distributed in any form without written permission from the author, except for brief quotations. For permission requests or other information, please contact the author via the website below. https://scottstoll.com/

Disclaimer: This novel's story and characters are fictitious. Any resemblance to actual persons is entirely coincidental. However, historical events, like the Permian Extinction, are true, and the author has made every effort to ensure that the information and science were correct at the time of publication. (Scientific research and understanding are always improving.) That being said, the author has taken some artistic license, and oxygen depletion is his own hypothesis.

Published by Argonauts Press. Palo Alto, CA. https://theArgonauts.com/books/
Printed and distributed by Ingram in the United States and various countries.

Library of Congress Control Number: 2023947693

ISBN: 978-0-9827842-9-7 (paperback)
ISBN: 978-0-9827842-5-9 (ebook)
ISBN: 978-1-971967-00-4 (audiobook)
ISBN: 978-1-971967-01-1 (audiobook library edition)

We must learn to live together as brothers
or we will perish together as fools.

~ Martin Luther King, Jr., 1964.

Table of Contents

Preface

I sharpened my quill on my travel memoir, Falling Uphill, an award-winning story about my quest for happiness around the world on a bicycle, but I've always wanted to write a science fiction novel. I've been fascinated with the idea of the Earth running out of oxygen since I was a young teenager. I remember polling people: "How do trees make enough oxygen for all the cars?" The consensus was: "Obviously they do." But I worried that we were cutting down the trees. The idea has haunted me ever since, so I thought a story about a world running out of air would be horrifyingly entertaining.

I may have had the idea in the 1980s, but it wasn't until 2007 that I committed to the book, and it took another 16 years to finish. Back when I started, climate change and global warming weren't widely accepted concepts, and there was no mention of oxygen depletion. So, I spent years doing research. I love science, and great science fiction is based on creating a believable world for the reader to step into, preferably a world only one step removed from our own. To me, that meant writing about the genesis of the apocalypse rather than the common post-apocalyptic stories, where some mysterious calamity has befallen humanity, and it becomes a soap opera of people eating people.

When I began this project, I didn't realize that mass extinctions due to oxygen depletion is a reality the Earth has already experienced several times. As my research took me down the rabbit hole, I expected oxygen levels to be declining, but I didn't realize that it was worse than I thought and that humanity really is at risk of reaching a tipping point. Though that possibility is very small, my book didn't seem like science fiction anymore.

As I extrapolated several theories and began writing a novel to give these ideas life, several interesting things happened:

First) Climate change awareness began to accelerate. So, reading the everyday news sounded like reading my book. As a result, I've thrown out many chapters because, now, even casual observers of the news are aware of many dangers that we face.

Second) Some of the events that I predicted as precursors to catastrophic climate change began to happen. Hurricane Sandy flooded lower Manhattan. Methane deposits in the Arctic exploded like bombs. Pollution runoff created giant, hypoxic dead zones in the ocean. The Great Barrier Reef suffered not one but three mass bleachings. Entire cities in China became so polluted people couldn't breathe. The coronavirus, which had similar characteristics to an anaerobic virus in my book, put uncountable patients on ventilators because they couldn't breathe. The sixth major mass extinction became widely accepted to be occurring now and caused by humans. Scientists corroborated that, indeed, oxygen levels are declining and that it represents an existential threat… It was an eerie feeling, like being stuck in a Twilight Zone episode, where I am not just predicting the future but creating the future as I write. My partner suggested that maybe I should stop writing. And, I nearly abandoned my book thinking it was too late—we had already entered the apocalyptic world.

In addition to being believable, my favorite science fiction is also thought-provoking and inspirational. So, though my main goal is to tell an entertaining story, I don't think I'm spoiling anything by saying I hope to inspire change. It's one of the consequences of cycling around the world. I saw the damage humans were causing to the planet firsthand, and I lived among the poorest of the poor who had to scrape a living out of the filth and barren lands. It wounded my spirit.

But don't worry, my book isn't really about the environment or oxygen depletion. In storytelling, as the screenplay writer William Goldman teaches, you have what appears to be happening and what's actually happening. What appears to be happening is the characters in this book are struggling to survive in a world without air. What's actually happening—the subtext of this book—is for you to discover.

Whether the events in this book continue to come true or not, one thing is for sure: the world will change. So, I hope you enjoy the end of the world as we know it.

Scott Stoll
Cincinnati, Ohio
2023

PS. For more information about this book and some fun bonus material, please visit my website:
ScottStoll.com/breathless/bonus/

Part I:
The beginning of time

The breath of life
2.4 billion years ago

There were many times in Earth's history when she remade herself. Some voluntary, others not, like the passing of an interstellar object so dense that it sucked a great glob off the ocean, which temporarily—meaning some thousands of years—was a frozen moon, until it crashed back into the Earth, creating many famous monuments and landmarks in the Southwestern United States.

If one were to witness time on the scale of the Earth herself, glaciers would put one foot in and take one foot out. Entire continents would flow like water and be shaken out like a rug. Lakes would form across the continents and then evaporate suddenly like raindrops falling in a dusty desert. Rivers would perambulate across the plains seeking safe passage, carving valleys and filling oceans with the debris of their sculptures. Mountains would rise and fall with the winds. Species of all kingdoms would scurry from one niche to another—evolving, devolving, blossoming and dying—sometimes painting the Earth with a rosy glow, and sometimes leaving a dry and cracked skin.

The first species to blossom was born in the boiling soups of the Earth's primordial oceans. It was an anaerobic form of life—meaning it *did not* breathe oxygen—that fed off the heat and nutrients of hydrothermal vents. The byproduct of its existence—its flatulence—was methane, a potent greenhouse gas that percolated into the atmosphere and warmed the Earth. Anaerobic life ruled the planet for about 1.5 billion years, proliferating and evolving until their success led to a new form of life, an aerobic organism—meaning it *did* breathe oxygen. Classified as cyanobacteria or what might be fondly referred to as algae, this primitive organism used sunlight to power photosynthesis. Like a miniature chemical factory, it combined water and carbon dioxide to create its own food while simultaneously excreting a few oxygen molecules as waste material.

Except for the Earth's iron heart, oxygen is the most abundant element, almost half of the Earth's crust, but until the evolution of algae, it was locked into unbreathable forms, like water. Though the algae proliferated, it took a billion years to saturate the oceans with oxygen and another billion years to fill the atmosphere. Eventually, the algae terraformed the planet in splashes of green and blue, driving many of their anaerobic ancestors—the first Earthlings—into extinction.

But the algae were victims of their own success. Their byproduct of oxygen burned out the methane in the atmosphere. The reaction formed more greenhouse gases—water vapor and carbon dioxide—but paradoxically, it had the opposite effect of global warming: the algae vacuumed up the carbon dioxide to make food, and the water vapor shrouded the Earth in a cloak of thick clouds that reflected the energy of the Sun. The temperature plummeted, and the oceans froze over for 300 million years. Thus the First Great Oxygen Crisis triggered the greatest global climate disaster ever known—Snowball Earth. This double whammy, essentially two sides of the same coin, wins multiple awards for the first, longest and largest mass extinction in history.

What life remained survived on the warmth of the Earth's core radiating off the deep ocean floor. As the millennia ticked past, ancient glaciers began to melt and release bubbles of air that oxygenated the ocean waters like an aerator in a fish tank. New forms of life evolved to thrive on oxygen, and when the frozen skies fell to the ground, once again allowing the Sun's rays to reach the surface, they sprang forth. Eventually, the oxygen-rich atmosphere would support the evolution of multicellular animals, trillions of times bigger and more complex than bacteria. Instead of feeding off the Sun, they fed off their competition. Over time, the prey grew fleet of foot while the predators grew fearsome in tooth and nail. In tandem, their game of hide and seek encouraged them to grow smarter, always seeking the most reward for the least effort.

During the Carboniferous Era, a name which reflects the modern era's reverence for their bountiful wealth of coal, oil and gas, the atmospheric oxygen reached its highest peak of 38%, almost double the modern era. This extraordinary level gave evolution and diversification a jumpstart: bizarre sharks, giant amphibians, millipedes three meters long, dragonflies as big as hawks, and plants in uncountable forms. It was a lush paradise.

But, once again, life was the victim of its own success. Again, the cost of this golden age was methane gas, the byproduct of the decomposition of plants and animals. For millions of years, the methane had been slowly accumulating, frozen deep in the sea and tundra. When the methane began to thaw, it caused a feedback loop—this time, instead of ice, it was fire. The more that thawed, the higher the temperature rose. When the Earth reached a tipping point—an era of intense geothermal activity—pockets of methane exploded round the world. Temperatures skyrocketed, and the oceans grew so hot that the oxygen boiled out and most forms of marine life—both plant and animal—asphyxiated. Once the ocean, the source of oxygen, was destroyed, life on land lasted little longer. It was the Second Great Oxygen Crisis, the Great Dying. About 83% of all species were lost. It would take over ten million years for the oceans to recover and life to reemerge, though the biodiversity and oxygen levels would never reach more than half of their previous record.

It is a scenario that has repeated itself many times. When the Earth reaches a tipping point, all it takes is an asteroid, a volcano, the hiccup of an earthquake, or just the proverbial flap of a butterfly's wings to drain the air of sustenance.

Mass extinctions happen regularly—about every 64 million years—and minor extinctions are happening all the time, the vacant spaces giving rise to entirely new species—oftentimes arguably superior species. From the point of view of Earth's neighbors, she pirouettes around her Sun, blinking from red to blue to white, then red again. The atmosphere churning, breathing in and breathing out. It is the circle of life on the grandest scale.

Inhale—life flourishes.

Exhale—life perishes.

Inhale.

Exhale.

It has been 66 million years since the Earth last breathed a sigh of relief. A new modern-day extinction has begun. It will not be the first time the success of a species spells its own doom, but it will be the first time a species knowingly runs into the abyss. On a positive note, to the Earth, the occasional mass extinction is little more than a bad cold.

Part II:
The short-lived era of Heaven on Earth

Warning signs
30 years ago

Mykelti, a precocious boy from Cameroon, might have saved the world had he become the poster child for the apocalypse, but first, he would have had to die, second, the world would have needed to notice, and third, someone would have needed to care. Nothing tugs at the heartstrings more than a child dying a needless death; unfortunately, humans had become immunized to tragedy. A viral photo, a virus, climate change, an impending apocalypse—it was all the same, just another blip in the endless scroll of news. It was hard enough for the average person just to survive the day.

§ § §

Mykelti unravels his fishing line from a block of wood and baits the hook with a beetle. When his hook hits the water, the lake bubbles, and a fish floats to the surface, belly up. His brothers laugh. "Look, Mykelti finally caught a fish." He thought they would be proud. They all use his beetles now. The fish love beetles. Mykelti had discovered how to lure the beetles out with the inedible bones and sinew from their meals.

Mykelti wades into the muddy periphery of the lake to gather the fish.

"You would save yourself a step if you ate your beetles instead," they laugh.

Mykelti picks up a smooth rock and slings it towards his brothers, not to hit them, but as a statement of displeasure, and a warning that he is bigger than he looks. The stone soars over their shoulders and plops into the lake. A ring of circles echoes out from the impact, followed by a fizz of bubbles.

Before his brothers can retaliate, Mykelti scurries back to the road and loads his bicycle with their harvest. He is so tiny that he must straddle the bar to reach the pedals. His brothers laugh again. "He's going to win all the bicycle races, too."

Mykelti pedals his bicycle barefoot down the rutted dirt road, cursing his brothers underneath his breath. Each bump of the wheels puffing red dust, smacking the bar into his groin, and rattling the basket of fish. It's his job to bring the fish to market. It isn't as idyllic as fishing the lake and bragging about the hunt to the pretty girls like his brothers, but there is much prestige to be had from owning a bicycle.

He grows short of breath, and his legs burn; it is hard work to cycle over the hills every day. He coasts around the crater of an extinct volcano, which now cups Lake Nyos. Looking back, he notices the lake still bubbles where his stone had sunk to the bottom.

The humid air fans his sweaty body as he cycles through the fringes of the thick and straggly jungle, which is unusually quiet. *The hunters take too many birds,* he thinks. *Someday, they will all be gone, like the fish.* His brothers undoubtedly took too many fish, yet despite the law of supply and demand, bringing fewer fish to the market seldom meant more money. The village fish-mongers held no sympathy. They, too, had to survive and bargained as if fish fell out of the sky. Lucky for Mykelti, some days are better than others. After an hour of bargaining—"This is fresh meat. Not like yours. Half died of old age, and the other half were run over by a car."—and pitting one fishmonger against another, he sells all his fish for a good profit. So much so that he thinks his brothers wouldn't miss a few centimes for one of Tanginika's sweet and sticky rice treats.

It is the heat of high noon when Mykelti arrives at Tanginika's restaurant, which is little more than a shack with a wood-burning stove, some chairs, and a broken mini-refrigerator that does little more than trap some of the cool night air. Instead of a sticky treat, Mykelti upgrades to a Coca-Cola. It is the most luxurious food most poor villagers in Cameroon ever taste. It costs him a week's worth of profit for one bottle. Tanginika sets the bottle down on the table. "Your secret is safe with me," she says. When Mykelti reaches for the bottle, his hands fumble with feelings of guilt and excitement. The bottle rolls off the edge and hits the ground with a thunk. He doesn't know to wait a few moments for the contents to settle, so when he pops the cap, the hot soda foams like a volcano and spews out between his fingers as he fails to staunch the flow. Mykelti is aghast as his small fortune runs away, so he slurps the carbonated sugar water off his hands and out of the dirty cracks of the table. *My brothers would really be laughing now,* he thinks, *but they would have done the same.*

As Mykelti slurps up the sugar water, the sky echoes like a thousand thun-derclaps, knocking Mykelti to the ground. Seconds later, a foaming wave crests, breaking among the treetops and falling to the ground like heavy rain. Suddenly, the air is drained of oxygen. Mykelti gasps for breath, but the air's foul smell makes him choke. His vision swirls and dims as he grows faint. His terror propels him towards the safety of Tanginika's motherly figure, but he collapses, and his world swirls into darkness as a hurricane wind tears apart the village.

When Mykelti regains consciousness, he sees Tanginika sprawled across the floor. Her arms outstretched in her last attempts to protect Mykelti as if he were her own child. He wants to speak, but his mind is as muddy as Tanginika's dress. Mykelti crawls towards his friend, hoping she is asleep, but as his hand grazes her arm, it is evident that life no longer animates her. Aghast, he stumbles outside. The village lay in pieces. Dizzy and not able to get his feet under him, he teeters to the next hut. The neighbors are sprawled in awkward positions—dead. The next hut is the same. And the one after that.

With a muddy body and horrified mind, Mykelti manages to balance his bicycle and return home with sticky fingers. Dead cats, chickens, and goats are strewn alongside the roads. Even the beautiful wild birds and antelopes had not escaped. Witchcraft is banned in Cameroon, but he cannot help thinking this is terrible witchcraft. He fears for his own life because, even in the turmoil, he had filled his pockets with sticky sweets. Mykelti's ever-present hunger made many decisions for him. *Tanginika would understand. She doesn't need these anymore,* he had thought, but now he worries that he has angered the spirits of the lake. "Please, forgive me," he whispers, "I didn't mean to do it."

§ § §

The few survivors fled the village to a hilltop, abandoning Mykelti to wander among the dead. For days, his hunger demanded he steal more, but his upset prevented him from touching anything. Rounding the corner to the village center, he is startled by strangers from a tribe he doesn't recognize. They are covered head to toe in colorful garb, bright like a sunset, their headdresses transparent like a plastic bottle. Though Mykelti speaks Pidgin English, their accent sounds like a foreign language to his ears.

"What do you make of the situation? Chemical? Biological? Worse?"

It had taken days for the French and American disease prevention teams to reach the remote village of Nyos, and when they arrived, it looked more like a scene from a science fiction movie than a rescue effort. About 1700 people were dead, twice as many cattle, and countless smaller animals.

"Baffling! There's no evidence of disease or physical trauma. No signs of radiation or chemical burns? I would have guessed poisonous volcanic gases, but there are no indications of carbon monoxide poisoning—these people would be red as lobsters. If it were hydrogen sulfide, they'd be showing some significant eye and throat inflammation. Decomposition and arthropod colonization seems to be progressing normally."

Mykelti, partially hidden behind a tree, quietly observes the strangers until one turns towards him. Mykelti retreats behind the tree. Moments later, when he peeks out, the stranger is leaning forward and offering a hand. "Hello, little one."

Mykelti realizes it's a woman hidden in the costume. Bewildered by these strange people—yet hungry, tired, and with nowhere to go—he takes a tentative step forward. He holds a deflated soccer ball—filled with plastic bags instead of air—like a rag doll. With his family gone, it is his only comfort.

The bigger, louder man steps forward, scaring Mykelti. He seems to be the leader by how everyone jumps into action when he speaks—everybody but the woman. She waives him back.

"Are you hungry?" She kneels, removes food from an interior pocket, and offers it in her outstretched hands like a bowlful of food.

Mykelti trusts this gesture more than he trusts the person. He is drawn to the comforting hand, offering the bounty she presumably scrapped from the Earth, like his mother, who would labor to grow and harvest the food and then labor to prepare the meal. Sometimes—too many times—at the end of the day, there was nothing more than a handful of food.

"Do you know what happened?" the man asks. "Did you see it?"

Mykelti takes a step back.

"Shush, Jonathan. You're scaring him." She removes her hood.

"Pearl! Don't!" Jonathan shouts.

"He needs our help."

"Following your heart is going to get us all killed one of these days... if it hasn't already."

Mykelti, not understanding their words, slowly walks forward, his need for safety outweighing his fear. He takes the food and feels instant relief. Tears glistening with the colors of the rainbow flood his eyes.

The woman sweeps him up into her arms and speaks in a soothing voice, squeezing him tight like his mother would have done if she were still alive. Mykelti averts his eyes in shame, as if his brothers still watch him, and sobs. When he stops to catch his breath, she holds hers, afraid to disturb him. When he sobs again, she releases her breath. An intense feeling catches Mykelti in the chest. With every synchronized breath, the feeling grows larger and larger until it wraps him in a womb of overwhelming emotion. Mykelti takes one last fearful gulp of air before relaxing into her arms, falling fast asleep.

§ § §

At the bottom of Lake Nyos, a pocket of magma left over from an extinct volcano had slowly been releasing carbon dioxide gas. Over the years, as the gases percolated through the lake, it became supersaturated. When the lake reached critical mass, it required nothing more than a grasshopper's misplaced landing to ripple the surface, much less a careless boy's stone. The dissolved gases exploded, clouds of vapor rising high into the air. So much gas was released that it lowered the level of the lake by a meter. The heavy carbon dioxide fell back to the Earth and created an invisible tsunami of gas that filled the caldera and ran down the valleys. It knocked over trees and flattened shacks, displacing the oxygen and asphyxiating almost every animal within a 25-kilometer range.

The discovery of oxygen
1772

There will never be more oxygen on Earth than there is now. The oxygen was created in the intense heat and pressure of a supernova explosion of a long-dead star whose remains seeded the Solar System. Those seeds coalesced to form a new child star and all of its planets. The Earth was fortunate to form in the Goldilocks Zone with all the ingredients of life: hydrogen, carbon, nitrogen, sulfur, phosphorus and oxygen. Even if the Earth were struck by asteroids or comets containing oxygen, it would not be enough to compensate for the loss. The gravity of the Earth is not strong enough to prevent the gaseous elements, like helium, hydrogen and oxygen, from bleeding into space.

Like a fish is unaware of the water it swims through, most animals are unaware that they live on the bottom of an ocean of air that nourishes their existence. Often, life is referred to as being carbon-based, but carbon comprises only about 18% of the human body, compared to oxygen at 65%. Oxygen is an invisible, colorless and odorless gas, so for most of history, humans lived life breathing air with only a vague understanding that air represented a kind of energy flow or mystical life force, which led to superstitions like cats stealing the breath of babies while they slept, when, actually, the cats, curled atop the infants, were accidentally suffocating the object of their affection. It also led to what chemists called the theory of phlogiston. Flammable materials were thought to contain phlogiston, so when objects burnt, they dephlogisticated, meaning they released their excess phlogiston into the atmosphere. When a person exhaled, it was thought they lost their phlogiston, or *élan vital*, to the atmosphere; eventually dying of old age when they ran out of breath.

Another theory was that life was considered to be composed of the four elements: earth, wind, fire and water. So the first scientist to isolate oxygen during experimentation, Carl Wilhelm Scheele, described it as *fire-air* due to the sparks it created. His contemporary, Joseph Priestley, concluded this new gas was about 5-6 times better than regular air to keep a mouse alive inside a jar, meaning the mouse lived 5-6 times longer before asphyxiating. Now, in the so-called modern era, humans subscribe to the theory of oxidation. Instead of exhaling phlogiston, humans inhale oxygen. The average person inhales about 10,000 liters of air per day to extract the 600 liters of oxygen needed to survive. This is equivalent to about 0.84 kilograms of oxygen. The byproduct of oxidation is water and carbon dioxide. Surprisingly, the lungs excrete more waste material than sweat, urine and feces combined.

Oxygen is important because it is one of the most reactive elements. It is an unhappy, free radical running around trying to make friends with everybody. Combined with hydrogen, it forms water. Combined with iron and water, it forms rust. Combined with sugar, it is used for respiration and powers all life on Earth—from microbes to plants and animals. Combined with hydrocarbons, it is used for combustion to power machines, and as a byproduct, it forms carbon dioxide, carbon monoxide and a myriad of other pollutants. Combined with itself, it forms molecular oxygen (the breathable form), and three molecules of oxygen make ozone. Combined with other elements, the list is almost endless.

Once oxygen makes friends, the bond is difficult to break. One exception is water. Photosynthesis is one of the few processes that can break the bond of water. But the power of plants is limited. Oxygen that gets bonded with fuels, glass, plastics, paints, cement, man-made chemicals, and pollution are effectively permanent under Earth-like conditions and essentially subtracted from the circle of life. Even the oxygen that is inhaled to oxidize sugars into energy is essentially lost forever, being converted into a myriad of forms like bones, shells, coral, limestone and fossil fuels.

Since oxygen can only be recycled—not created on Earth—there is less and less breathable oxygen available every day. Indeed, when the oceans run dry, like on Mars, and photosynthesis shuts down, there will be no more air to breathe—no élan vital. In the meantime, an orchestra of life plays a great symphony that rises and falls throughout the eons.

A sleeping giant
Over 2 years ago

The snowmobiles are impressive Russian-made machines that hop, skip and plow through snowdrifts like ships in a stormy sea. Ahead of Mykelti, a lake glimmers in the sunlight. When it becomes apparent the snowmobiles are heading straight for it, he reflexively shouts, "No, Stop! What are you doing?" If the driver heard, it made no difference. The snowmobiles hit a snowdrift at the edge of the lake and launch into the air. Everyone screams, even the Russian guides, but they scream in delight as the snowmobiles make hard landings— *CRACK!*—on ice. The water was an illusion, a reflection of the sky. Looking down, Mykelti sees rocks on the bottom of the lake. The ice is so clear it appears as if they are flying.

"A shortcut. You are getting your money's worth now, no?" Mykelti's guide laughs.

After many arduous days, their destination looms on the other side of the lake: the snow-capped plateau of an ancient volcano, the highest point in central Siberia, and the heart of the Putorana Nature Reserve. The Russians circle the snowmobiles like wagons as if it will shelter them from the elements. High atop the massifs, the Sun and wind disintegrate the ice, and the particles fall several kilometers, blasting into their exposed skin. It is like still being on the back of the snowmobile.

"Careful with that. You've probably broken it already. Give it to me." Mykelti yells at the Russians unpacking the gear. "Brandon, give me a hand with this. Daylight is half gone." They unpack the drone and examine each piece before assembly.

"I'm freezing my you-know-whats off. Tell me again why we are in the middle of Siberia in the middle of winter," says Brandon.

Brandon is being sarcastic, but Mykelti explains for the benefit of the eaves-dropping Russians, hoping to inspire them. "The plants are dormant. There's no oxygen being produced anywhere near here. Also, the atmosphere is denser in winter. And at this latitude, the ceiling of the troposphere is about half that around the equator. Think of our atmosphere as a fishbowl. Inside the fishbowl is where all the weather happens. Down here, on the bottom, all the gases are equally mixed, and the atmosphere is thick, warm and wet. Nice and easy to breathe."

"It's not feeling that way to me," Brandon says.

"Oxygen is the most important nutrient in life, yet you don't even need to think about it. It's not until we get to the top of the fishbowl—above the water vapor—that the composition of the atmosphere changes. Denser gases, like oxygen, tend to sink to the bottom. If I'm right—and we're about to find out—the fishbowl is getting lower and lower."

"Yes, yes, yes, we're running out of air. But why us? Didn't we hire a bunch of Sherpas to do this for us on K2?"

"Not air. Oxygen." Mykelti fires the engines on the drone. "Are you getting a readout?"

"All systems check."

The drone buzzes louder before zooming into the sky. "This is why. Let's see how high this thing can go."

"What do you mean? Doesn't that thing have a limiter?"

"I made some adjustments." The group gathers around the monitor and watches as the altimeter blurs. Within a minute, the drone reaches a height of 1500 meters. Another minute passes. 3000 meters. The drone's cameras show the whorls of the lakes and valleys below, like a white fingerprint underneath a dazzling blue sky.

4500 meters.

"What are you doing, Mykelti? I'm pretty sure this isn't FAA regulations. Sergei, do they have an FAA in Russia?"

"You crash drone, you stay here till you find it," Sergei says.

Around 5000 meters, the signal weakens. Pixelation distorts the image.

5500 meters.

The image on the screen shows the horizon line swinging wildly as high-altitude winds batter the drone. "Just a little further."

6000.

The drone flips over, and the screen shows a blizzard of interference. "Shit. Shit. Shit." Moments later, the signal comes back and the drone rights itself. "Dang! That was close."

"Careful! Have you no respect?" Sergei exclaims. *"Blyat! Tak eto je zapovednik."*

"What?"

"He says, I paraphrase," says the translator, "'This is sacred land, you asshole!'"

"Neither of you are helping."

6500.

The numbers on the screen are nearly unreadable now, and the drone is swinging wildly.

7000.

"Almost there. We gotta be close."

"Give me dis. I'll bring it down myself." Sergei swipes for the control.

Mykelti fumbles the controls while dodging Sergei, and suddenly the drone stabilizes, and the screen is blindingly blue. "Aha! We made it."

"Made where?" says Sergei.

"The tropopause. There's no weather up here. Wait a minute until I get a measurement. Altitude. Check. Nitrogen. Check. Carbon dioxide. Check. Ozone. Check. Most importantly, oxygen. Check. And double-check. Just a few more bonuses. Carbon monoxide. Nitrogen dioxide. Sulfur dioxide. Particulates. Lead. Gotcha."

"And, I thought *lead balloons* was just an expression," says Brandon.

"Okay, I'm bringing it down." After a few more minutes of maneuvering, Mykelti lands the drone atop a nook on the highest peak of the massifs. Charges in the drone's landing pads detonate, and spikes drill themselves into the earth, anchoring the drone against the winds. "Wait a sec. Yes. Okay. We have secured a landing. Sensors are online. We have a stable connection. Everything is a go!" says Mykelti.

"Ladies and gentlemen, we'd like to thank you for flying Mykelti Airlines. Please be careful; luggage may have shifted in the overhead compartment," jokes Brandon. "Now, let's head back and celebrate."

"We not going back," Sergei directs the crew to unpack the tents. "It is too late to make it back. We going to camp here."

"Are you serious? How do you expect us newbies to survive the night?"

"Don't worry. Is like vacation to a Russian. I brought you nice warm blankie. You want?" says Dimitri.

"People pay for this?" Brandon groans.

"Snowmobiling. Ice-fishing. Starry sky. New friends. What not to love?"

"Ah, jeez," Brandon heaves and groans dramatically, slinging camping equipment off the sled. "Just tell us pack mules what to do."

"We have hired help for that," says Mykelti. "What I need is a climatologist with some passion for their job. Come, take a look at these numbers."

Mykelti sets up an impromptu office using crates of gear. Brandon peers over his shoulder. "I'm glad to see any numbers whatsoever after your flying."

Mykelti raises an eyebrow. "These readings are incredibly low—lower than I expected."

"Okay, serious moment. You could have taken down an airliner with that stunt. For the sake of our toes and fingers, why didn't we stay home and analyze the data from the satellites and weather balloons?"

"You've spent too much time in a classroom, my friend. The satellites can only measure the whole column of air. As for the balloons, I figured out why our readings haven't fluctuated much. The balloons are governed by the density of the atmosphere, not altitude. If there is an anomaly in the weather patterns, the balloons are getting blown out of the way. If the oxygen drops, the balloon drops. I figured this was my one chance to get samples of the air column from top to bottom. I needed a baseline. Now, with the drone in place, as long as the solar panels are functioning, we'll be able to measure the oxygen levels— the real oxygen levels, not those—" Mykelti makes air quotes— "*theoretical* numbers everyone else is using."

"You might have mentioned this."

"And if you had said no? Never mind. We're here now. Where are the air samples?"

"Safely stuffed away."

"We'll need to double-check this back in the lab and ensure our machines are calibrated."

"Well, until then, let's have some fun. Look, the guides have finished setting up camp. And there is a nice cozy fire."

"Fire good for keep bears away," says Dimitri.

"See, Mykelti, I'm not the only one with a sense of humor."

"No joke," says Dimitri matter-of-factly.

"C'mon, put down your gadgets, Mykelti. There's enough pop-up chairs for everyone. Let's kick it, as you Yanks say."

"I'm not American."

"Take it from this ol' Brit. At this point, you're more American than not, ol' pal. Except for that singsong cadence of yours. Which is beautiful, by the way."

"Being an American is not a compliment in this world."

"Aw, mate, snap out of it. I'm just providing a bit of levity," Brandon tries to placate his friend, "You're always so serious with this doom and gloom stuff. I know. I know. The sky is falling—"

"Literally, falling."

"Take it from me. You're missing life while there's still life to be had. And, if the world does come to an end, all you'll have left is your sense of humor. Well, and me. I'm not going anywhere."

"Ah," Mykelti exhales, trying to reset the brain, "Did you remember to bring the marshmallows?"

"Now look who has a sense of humor. I wish. But I did bring beer. I don't know about you, but I'm so cold I'd drink a hot pint of beer like soothing tea. Maybe, I'll start a new tradition. It's been ages since the Brits came up with a good drink. I think the last one was the gin and tonic. But the ol' G and T is a sailor's drink. We need a mountain man's drink, don't you think? Watch this. I'm about to go down in history."

Brandon holds his beer over the fire until the flame sputters. His hands are painfully cold, and the beer slips from his fingers into the fire. He tries to grab the can from the coals. "Ah, dang. That's hot. Ouch!"

The can warms rapidly. Inside, a thousand bubbles begin to form and expand. Trying to roll the beer can out of the fire with a stick, Brandon inadvertently inverts the can. The top, its weakest point, bulges under pressure. In less than a minute in the hot coals, the top pops off. Beer explodes out of the bottom, showering everyone with sparks—singing some beards—and sends the can rocketing off into the Siberian wilderness.

"Wow, who would have thought a few burps worth of beer could have done that?"

Sergei guffaws, "You two are better than the YouTube. Sit down. Sit down. Look, Russians have already invented perfect mountain man drink. Try this." He leans over and hands Brandon a flask.

Brandon takes a swig and coughs out, "Vodka? That's stereotypical, isn't it?"

"If it works, it works. Like these beards. Your plain faces are no match for Siberian winter."

"Not much flavor, but it is nice and warm. How'd you do that?"

"You don't want to know," Sergei guffaws again. His laughs are like the beer can—pressure released.

"Your sense of humor has found its match, Brandon," Mykelti says.

"You forget," Sergei looks like he's chewing on a cud, thinking about what to say, "I am scientist, too. You Western scientists come here all measuring the air. 'Too much this,' they say. 'Too little that,' they say. No one asks me my opinion. Nobody ever says, 'Sergei, what do you think problem is?'" He drinks from his flask as if preparing to tell a story, but says nothing.

After an uncomfortably long silence, Mykelti asks, "Okay, Sergei. What do you think the problem is?"

"Okay, now, this is my theory. You must give poor Sergei credit in your fancy scientific paper that no one will read," he laughs. "Have you ever heard fable of swan, pike and crab? It speaks to heart of many problems of Russian people... and I think your people. You see, the three of them agree to haul a cart. They pull with all their might. The swan pull towards the sky. The fish swims towards the sea. And the crab pulls backward towards the shore. You see the problem?"

"The cart didn't move."

"No. No. The problem is, who to blame?" He guffaws again.

"Are you telling me humans aren't the problem?"

"Maybe. Maybe not. They don't help, that's for sure. If you ask me..." He pauses expectantly.

"Yes, we're asking you."

"The problem is not in the sky. It is below your feet."

"Care to explain?" asks Brandon.

"Come. I show you."

The group follows Sergei through the snow and out onto the frozen lake. The Sun has melted the surface, and the winds have reformed it into a sheet of glare ice that makes progress slow and treacherous.

"Methane locked underneath Siberia's lakes and underneath the frozen soil has been seeping out for thousands of years," says Sergei, voice as grizzly as his beard. "In past decades, as planet warmed, the permafrost has been thawing more quickly, accelerating release of gases. There are millions of lakes like this in the Arctic. Methane is most abundant organic compound and twenty-three times more powerful greenhouse gas than carbon dioxide. Here—" he gestures towards the horizon and the vast expanse of ice— "the total carbon storage in permafrost is equal to all rainforests on planet—"

Brandon whispers to Mykelti, "Is it me, or is Sergei getting more fluent the more he drinks?"

"—and more than all the coal and oil reserves. If this permafrost thaws, it will release 1.6 trillion tons of carbon frozen in the earth since the last ice age, perhaps since the Cretaceous era. Teratons of methane, these numbers so big they are hard to measure—"

"Let alone comprehend," Mykelti concludes, beginning to understand.

Sergei gestures grandly, "You are looking at the epicenter of a climate time bomb—Arctic Armageddon."

"That was poetic," says Brandon. "Can we go back to our warm fire and warm vodka now?"

Sergei is looking for bubbles in the black ice. "Da, here," he says. "Watch closely. Make your camera ready."

Sergei bends over, illuminating the ice with the flame of his lighter and polishes the lake's surface with his glove. Satisfied, he drops the lighter, raises his ice pick over his head, and plunges it deep into the ice. He levers the handle sideways. The ice cracks open, and methane whooshes out, erupting into a fireball amongst the men. Mykelti and Brandon cry out, stumbling on the ice and falling backwards.

The Russians laugh. "Now, you are believer, no?"

Stunned, Brandon and Mykelti watch a geyser of methane melt the surrounding ice.

"But, the permafrost is not predicted to thaw for hundreds of years," says Mykelti. Despite his eyes, his first instinct is cynicism.

"Maybe. Maybe not. You are standing on a mirror—the ice. When this mirror melts, sun will penetrate deep into the muck. The problem will—how do you say, snowball?—out of control."

"More like *hotball*," Brandon laughs. "Hot balls."

"Great," says Mykelti. "Now we have two problems."

"No, no problem," Sergei says.

"How can Arctic Armageddon not be a problem?"

"Problems can be fixed. This is just fact. The damage was done long ago. You only seeing the after-effect. There are plumes of methane bubbles in Siberian sea a kilometer long. And, not just here, another bomb hides beneath Canada's tar sands. You Americans stick your straws into it, not even noticing."

"Since we're speaking theoretically, what if everyone stopped driving their cars tomorrow, stopped contributing to global warming?"

"Bah! Global warming isn't problem. Global warming is story we tell babies so they sleep at night. So, you can ride bicycle to work and think you are saving planet."

"It sounds like you're predicting the end of the world."

"Not end of world, just humanity."

"Are all Russians this skeptical?" asks Mykelti.

"No. I'm optimist. Most of my countrymen think world has already ended," Sergei guffaws louder than ever.

"Humanity is overrated, anyway," says Brandon.

"What are you going to do about it?" asks Mykelti, realizing his brilliant research project was no longer brilliant and no longer relevant.

Sergei chuckles, pulls out a cigar and lights it on the methane geyser, which has diminished to the size of a large blow torch. "Enjoy the show. Care to join me?"

"I'm with Sergei. Hotballing it," Brandon laughs.

That night, while Mykelti drifts off to sleep, the local guides play broken pieces of ice like drums. The haunting melody vibrates the lake and the campsite sitting atop it and echoes into the night.

A bump in the sky
A few days later

Brandon and Mykelti return home on a jumbo jet, sucking up oxygen at a rate to sustain thousands upon thousands of animals, like a car with a 250-horsepower engine would need 250 horses constantly eating, drinking and breathing to do the same amount of work. Mykelti does a rough calculation on his laptop. The plane consumes about one gallon per second, and each gallon would require almost four times as much oxygen by weight. By the time they land, the airplane will have burned about 675 tons of oxygen. Even he has a hard time believing that number. And that's only from Beijing to Los Angeles International Airport. The total round trip from the middle of nowhere Russia to Chicago will probably consume 2500 tons of oxygen. He consoles himself by thinking that his research—when it finally convinces people to change—will conserve millions of times more fuel and oxygen.

"Do you need anything, sir?" a flight attendant interrupts Mykelti's idealistic plans to save the world.

"Seltzer," Mykelti says absentmindedly.

"And for you, sir?"

"I'll have a single malt whiskey on the rocks. Oh! And—" Brandon gestures to Mykelti— "he's paying. He promised me all I could drink if we survived a Siberian winter."

The air pressure in the cabin is much lower than sea level, so when the flight attendant breaks the seal on the seltzer, it fizzes loudly. She places the drink in the cupholder on his tray as the plane begins to rumble and shake.

Watching the bubbles in the seltzer get knocked loose, Brandon asks, "What happens if we land and our ice core samples are nothing but a puddle of water, and the air bubbles all went poof?"

"We go back and get more," says Mykelti, too preoccupied with the data processing on his laptop to pay attention to Brandon, much less notice the orange clouds rising before the plane like a wall.

A storm has been brewing for days. Not a storm of wind and rain visible to a radar, but an invisible storm of dust and pollution. As it passed over Europe, Asia, and cites, like Chengdu and Chongqing—which are each more populous than all of Australia—the storm sucked up the smog composed of the pollution and byproducts of cars, factories, fertilizers, and household cleaning products, like sulfuric acids, nitrogen oxides, carbon monoxide, carbon dioxide, and many more volatile compounds. Most of these pollutants are gases heavier than air, so they fall to the bottom of the atmosphere, suffocating and poisoning the plants and animals. However, in this case, the storm vacuumed them into the upper atmosphere, along with hitchhiking anaerobic bacteria that are learning to thrive in this new environment. The storm would spread the particulates across the Northern Hemisphere—even on lands never trodden by human foot—but for a few days, the citizens of Eurasia would breathe easy.

Mykelti's plane lurches into the backend of the storm, hitting a pocket of dead air—a doldrum lacking oxygen—and spilling his drink.

The "Please fasten your seat belt" sign lights up with a double ding.

The shaking grows until the plane is rising and dipping. Panicked parents are yelling at their kids. Others are screaming in artificial delight as if on a roller coaster. Another double ding announces the captain, "We're encountering an unusual amount of turbulence. Please return to your seats. Flight attendants, secure the cabin."

One glance at the burnt orange cloud rising high—too high—into the atmosphere tells Mykelti a different story. "This isn't just turbulence," he says.

As passengers and crew panic to secure their belongings, there is a moment of reprieve when the turbulence stops, but moments later, so do the engines. Jet engines are designed to compress the thin air at high altitudes in order to gather enough oxygen to burn the fuel, but even this is not enough to compensate for the doldrums. Everything is deathly quiet as the plane free falls. It doesn't do a nosedive… it simply drops straight down. The oxygen masks pop out of their hidden compartments when what is really needed is oxygen for the engines. They dangle uselessly as hands are busy clutching the armrests or loved ones. For a few seconds, there is no gravity. It's like a slow-motion scene. Drinks, books, cell phones, and even people—their mouths agape with fear—are rising into the cabin. One passenger expels the contents of their stomach midair. Mykelti's cup floats up in front of his face, the seltzer water trailing behind, looking like gelatin.

None too soon, the plane bottoms out on a dense patch of air. All the people and paraphernalia crash back down. A Sikh falls to the floor head first. His turban saves him from trauma, but a flight attendant is not as lucky when their head cracks open on the edge of the drink cart.

The plane has fallen into fresh air full of oxygen, and the engines sputter to life. The wings grab hold of the thick air, and the pilot slowly reverses the tailspin. When disaster is no longer imminent, the pilot announces, "If there are any medical professionals onboard, we have an emergency. Please, make yourself known to the nearest flight attendant." And trying to restore a sense of normalcy. "Folks, in my thirty years of flying, nothing like that has ever happened. The engines cut out. We suspect we were struck by lightning. Luckily, we were able to bring them back online in time. We'll be putting down at the nearest airport with a runway big enough to accommodate us. We're first in line. Again, ladies and gentlemen, we're very sorry."

"I failed that test," Brandon says.

"What test?"

"I was once told that if you jump out of an airplane and forget your parachute that you have two options. One, panic all the way down. Or, two, enjoy the view. And, well…"

Mykelti follows Brandon's gaze. He's wet himself.

"Excuse me. I need to get myself cleaned up." Brandon stands.

"Is everyone okay?" Mykelti asks.

"Looks like they are getting the help they need. Stay put. I'll be back in a jiffy."

Mykelti's laptop dings. The first batch of data is done processing. The results are worse than Mykelti had anticipated. The troposphere is dropping, which means oxygen levels are dropping, too. Mykelti begins a new batch of data to calculate the rate—how much time is left. But he pauses. "If Sergei is right, none of this matters. We may have years or decades left, but the damage has been done."

Brandon returns with the drink cart as the new self-appointed flight attendant. His charm is putting everyone at ease. "Nothing like a near-death experience to give you a new appreciation for the simple things in life," he says to one passenger, and to Mykelti, he asks, "You look knackered, sir. May I get you something? Drinks are on the house. I happen to have some Russian vodka. Apologies if I didn't have time to warm it up, if you know what I mean. And here—" he tosses Mykelti a bag of peanuts. "You might want to save these for winter."

As the realities of their situation soak in, along with Mykelti's vodka, he feels a personal turning point has been reached. Like all things you can't see—God, love, the future—oxygen deprivation is hard to believe and easy to forget. Mykelti can no longer pretend that the world, as he knows it, exists anymore. Even though Mykelti is trained as a rational scientist to ignore suspicions in favor of evidence, there is a bad feeling in the air. Society is sick with anxiety, like a viral meme. Even under normal circumstances, people are a fearful race of beings, always looking over their shoulders.

The white noise of the engine and the vodka work their magic. Mykelti is about to fall asleep when his drink begins to vibrate violently once again. *If God exists,* Mykelti thinks, *This must be his sense of humor.*

The missing piece to the puzzle

A week later

Brandon enters the lab at the Chicago Institute of Sustainability with a young, fashionably bookish woman. "Mykelti, I'd like to introduce you to Natalie. She's a prestigious journalist that caught wind of your work."

"Wow, it's good to have you." Mykelti rushes over to shake her hand. "It's about time the media took an interest. This is life-changing—"

"Actually, I'm from the school newspaper."

Mykelti tries to hide his disappointment. "Yes, great. In that case, prepare to be famous. You are about to scoop the world. Do people still say that? *Scoop?*"

"Um, no."

"Okay, well, get prepared to wow your audience."

"Take it down a notch, Mykelti," says Brandon. "Natalie, look around. Feel free to ask questions."

"I'm more the quiet observer type."

Mykelti's lab has a central light table surrounded by countertops with books, papers and miniature experiments. In one aquarium, two candles burn. Connected to the tank in a makeshift construction are bottles of oxygen and nitrogen, tubes, valves and pressure meters.

"What kind of steampunk science is this?" asks Brandon, trying to prompt a conversation.

"We don't know a lot about the history of the atmosphere. Would you believe the oldest sample of bottled air is from 1968?"

"An Australian scuba diver filled a tank and forgot about it," Brandon elaborates for Natalie.

"Right. So, I'm using beeswax candles to estimate the levels of atmospheric oxygen in the sixteen hundreds. The candles are replicas that ship captains used before the invention of a seaworthy clock. Calculating a ship's latitude is easy using the stars, but the only way to estimate the ship's longitude was by knowing the time of day. The candles were made to exacting standards, ensuring they burned for the same period of time. So, by lighting one candle at dawn, the captains always knew what time it was. Now, I'm calculating the burn time at different oxygen concentrations to see if I can find a match."

"How's it going?"

"I believe I have duplicated the candle recipe. I'm even using Italian beeswax. The burn times indicate that oxygen levels haven't changed much, if at all. Maybe something's wrong with the candles. Could be the bees?"

"You're blaming the bees!?" says Natalie.

"Well, pollen, monoculture, pollution… who knows? My numbers are way off my estimates."

"No surprise there. Good thing we have a backup plan." Brandon takes a bottle out of the refrigerator. "How about some fresh mountain air?" He rolls it across the table, exposing the label K2.

"Did you bring the rest of last year's bottles? I want to double-check them all. I've been recalibrating our instruments with the data from Siberia."

"How many times are you going to do that? Besides—"

"As many times as it takes."

"—I thought you were all gung ho about Sergei's explanation?"

"There's still something missing."

"Well, you're in luck that I'm so understanding." Brandon unloads a box of canisters. "Our latest adventure, good ol' Russia. The tallest and most isolated mountains in the world: Aconcagua, Denali, Kilimanjaro, Mount Elbrus, Mount Everest, Mount Kosciuszko, Puncak Jaya, Vinson Massif… Hey, what's this?" He holds up a bottle labeled: "The Middle of Nowhere."

"That's our baseline."

"No, I mean, where is it?"

"Nowhere important."

"Are you holding out on me?"

"You'd hate it there," Mykelti smirks.

"C'mon. I've been traipsing all over the world."

"Waikiki."

"Hawaii! You got me traipsing over dead bodies in the Himalayas while you're drinking mai tais on the beach!?"

"See, I said you would hate it." Mykelti laughs and gives Brandon a friendly punch on the shoulder. "Seriously, we need a measure at sea level as far away from civilization as possible."

"Far away from civilization… Are you kidding me, mate?"

"Well, it's upwind of civilization. C'mon, we got work to do."

"How much more evidence do we need!?" Brandon says, feigning exhaustion. "It's common sense. Look," he turns to Natalie, "Here is your whole article: If carbon dioxide is formed by burning fuel and oxygen—driving cars, for example—then the more carbon dioxide, the less oxygen there is to breathe."

"Yes, that's the theory. But the numbers don't add up. With the exponential increase in burning fossil fuels—in particular, the industrialization of China and India—there should be a dramatic decline in oxygen levels. If we want people to take notice, we need the science to prove it. We sound like crackpot conspiracy theorists."

"Yeah, kinda," says Natalie.

"It's difficult to measure oxygen," defends Mykelti. "First, the atmosphere is constantly changing temperature, pressure, density. Obviously. But not so obvious, it's difficult to separate molecular oxygen—the kind we breathe—from other gases containing oxygen that we can't breathe, like ozone and other pollutants... And industry is causing permanent changes to the composition. In short, the percentage of oxygen can remain the same while the actual number of molecules goes down. I could go on."

"Believe me, he does."

"Well, burning oxygen is only half the problem. The other half is—"

"By the way—" Brandon opens a soda— "found these in the back. You Americans may have lousy beer, but your fizzy drinks are quite nice."

"And, not to sound full of doom and gloom—"

"Trust me, mate. You might as well be standing on the street corner wearing a placard that says: 'The end of the world is near.'"

"The plants are dying."

"That was melodramatic," says Natalie.

"The environments that produce the oxygen are dying. Humanity is bulldozing, paving over and poisoning the ground, and then it all runs into the ocean, killing the coral reefs and phytoplankton. By my estimates, the atmospheric concentration should be down to 17–18% oxygen. People should literally be passing out in the streets. I just can't figure out where I'm going wrong."

"A dilemma indeed. There is nothing more deceptive than an obvious fact." Brandon imitates Sherlock Holmes and, with a grandiose gesture, knocks over his drink. Ice cubes and soda flood across the glowing light table. The carbonated water warms rapidly on the surface of the table. As it does, the dissolved carbon dioxide gas quickly expands into bubbles. "Oh, shit, sorry. Damn, there's a whole ocean inside one of these cans. Ah, global warming. The icebergs are melting," he flicks a cube off the table, and it leaves a trail of bubbles in its wake that pop and shower fizz.

"A whole ocean," Mykelti repeats, mesmerized. He leans close. The bubbles burst, and tiny droplets tickle his face. He even notices bubbles trapped in the ice cubes. "It's so obvious."

"Have you gone mad, mate?"

"How could I have missed it? I'm not measuring anything wrong. There's extra oxygen being added to the system. And... I know where it's coming from."

"Okay, here's me waiting, holding my breath in anticipation."

"The ocean."

"Are we talking coral reefs again?"

"There is a record-breaking dead zone in the Gulf this year—the size of Wisconsin. It gets bigger every year. I thought it was the pollution runoff, but it's more than that. The oceans are running out of oxygen at an even faster rate than our models predicted. We—scientists everywhere—have only been thinking of the ocean as a carbon sink, meaning it's like a sponge. It soaks up the excess carbon dioxide in the atmosphere, which becomes things like limestone and seashells. But the ocean is also an oxygen sink. In fact, for about a billion years, all the oxygen produced was absorbed by the ocean. It wasn't until the ocean became saturated with oxygen that it began accumulating in the atmosphere."

"I'm waiting for the *but*."

"*But* the sponge can also be wrung dry. Change the temperature, and the carbon dioxide gets released back into the atmosphere—outgassing. But not just carbon dioxide. Oxygen, too. And with global warming comes—"

"Ocean warming. And warm water can't hold as much dissolved gas."

"Right! The ocean is letting out a big sigh. It's releasing all the oxygen we've been burning back into the air. But—"

"*But*, how long can it last?" finishes Brandon. "And—*Blimey!*—glaciers. They have an enormous amount of dissolved gases and air pockets trapped inside them, as well. We need to send teams to get samples."

"No," says Mykelti, brow furrowed, hand over mouth.

"What do you mean, no? This is a major breakthrough. Nobel Prize, here we come."

"There's no time for science anymore," says Mykelti. "Sergei was right. It's too late. The oceans are on their last breath. We need to take action. Natalie, what do you think?"

"Sounds like a pretty good story. I don't know. We'll see what my teacher thinks."

The population bomb
1870

Humans have been around for millions of years in one form or another, and the so-called modern humans, Homo sapiens, have been around hundreds of thousands of years. However, they are not as sapient as they give themselves credit because it was only 30,000 years ago that they learned to make tools and paints, which, for the first time, differentiated them from all the other hunting and scavenging animals. About 13,000 years ago, when humans invented agriculture, their success was all but guaranteed—that is until they discovered fossil fuels and soon thereafter invented the steam engine. In a geological wink, humans not only became the dominant species on the planet, they also changed the ecosystem of the planet. The face of the Earth changed from the green and blue of organic life to the brown and gray of city life.

After the success of the steam engine, there came an evolutionary boom of machines. Inventions like the adding machine, circular saw, cotton gin, watches, batteries, flush toilets and sliced bread inspired humans to revolt against their handmade life. The invention of the internal combustion engine was hailed as a modern miracle and destined to become mankind's single greatest creation for transforming the face of the Earth. Suddenly, humans were capable of moving more dirt than quadrillions of ants, who had previously held the record.

The shackles of slavery were dropped in favor of machines that could produce faster and better products without complaint. But the machines were thirsty. Mankind inserted their straws into the ground and extracted free energy—free labor—in the form of oil. And, for every drop of oil, 1866 drops of oxygen are used to ignite the fire of the combustion engine. Both oil and oxygen are a byproduct of photosynthesis. Over 200 million years of the Sun's energy was trapped in organic material and compressed into fossil fuels, and billions of years of the Sun's energy were captured and stored in the atmosphere as oxygen. But in less than two centuries, the Earth's bounty was sucked dry and the atmosphere depleted.

Humans primarily used their machines to increase their safety and comfort, which meant inventing ways to grow more food. Not only did they use petroleum to fuel their agricultural machines, but they also used the derivative petrochemicals to make pesticides and fertilizers, which resulted in the average American's body being composed of approximately one percent of petroleum byproducts. Humans did not even need the Sun anymore. Greenhouses with lights powered by fossil fuels and oxygen grew delicate foods that could be harvested year-round.

Human ingenuity transformed oil and oxygen into the pieces and parts of houses, clothes, tools, vehicles, roads, toys, paint, plastic, medicine—an abundance of wealth in every form. Advertisements were invented and promised a life of luxury and convenience: modern appliances would fully automate life, cigarettes would cure the common cold, beer would create super strength— any conceivable virtue was available for purchase. To suit their needs, humans changed the surface of the planet faster than any other event except an interstellar disaster.

There has never been a species more successful, more safe, more content, or with more opportunities. By the late 20th century, the average human had more food and more choices than any ancient king or queen could command. With this practically free food and wealth, the population swelled exponentially, like the phenomena known as the Rat Flood in northeastern India. Here, an exotic species of bamboo flowers and fruits once every 48 years and is accompanied by a plague of rats that quickly multiply with the abundant food source.

By the early 21st century, there were more humans alive on Earth than all the deceased humans that had ever existed combined. Despite their ingenuity and success, humans are still animals. Their unlimited wealth and energy did not satiate their desires. Not only was the population expanding but also their needs and, more so, their expectations grew proportionate to their successes. It was estimated that the ecological footprint of the average person in a developed country was seven times bigger than sustainable—it would take seven planet Earths to feed the hunger of humanity. The electric lights of this artificial desire were so great, they bedazzled the astronauts orbiting above as they performed experiments to sustain life outside the dying womb of the Earth.

Though humans knew better, they could no more control their greed than the rats could control their gluttony and lust. Like any instinct, greed is a virtue bred into humans by evolution. Greed encourages long-term thinking and hoarding to survive winters. Without greed, humans would have gone extinct long ago; however, greed left unchecked by some other virtue is like the Rat Flood of India. Once the rats had devoured all the bamboo seeds, they swarmed the farmer's fields, eating not only the fruits and vegetables but the entire plant down to the root. And when the fields turned to dust, the rats cannibalized their infants and flooded over every other living thing.

Intergovernmental Panel on Climate Change

14 months ago

It took Mykelti over a year to organize his research and prepare for his presentation halfway around the world in Geneva, Switzerland, among the world's elites. He begins with his catchphrase, "Have you ever wondered what goes into your car besides fuel?" After a dramatic pause, Mykelti prods, "Does anyone want to venture a guess? No? I'll give you a hint: We're all aware of what comes out of the backend. Water vapor. Carbon dioxide. Carbon monoxide. Not to mention hundreds of pollutants. In other words, your car exhales greenhouse gases. But have you ever wondered what your car breathes?"

The room remains silent except for coughs and the shuffling of paper and shoes. During the awkward pause, Mykelti notices the smell. A smell unlike any in his home country. In his village, a stranger, a conman, could disguise themselves in fancy clothes and a fancy walk and talk, but they still smelled dirt poor. The nervous sweat fermenting in their armpits was a telltale giveaway. Here, money could not only disguise a person in fancy clothes, it could buy them a shower, deodorant, perfume, hairspray... It made their intentions hard to penetrate.

"I'll give you a hint: Gasoline—petrol—is the carbon in carbon dioxide, but what else goes into your car?"

Mykelti gets nothing but disgruntled looks. The members of the United Nations are accustomed to rhetorical questions. Or perhaps they are unaccustomed to thinking.

"Anyone?" He pauses again, and the shuffling of impatience grows.

When he can bear it no longer, Mykelti blurts, "What is oxygen? Oxygen is the other component of carbon dioxide. Your car breathes air—just like you do. The difference is that you burn glucose—sugar—instead of gasoline to power your body. The point I'm trying to make is that we are focused on the wrong end of the equation. We are subtracting oxygen from the atmosphere at a much greater rate than we're adding carbon dioxide."

Despite unimpressed expressions from his audience, Mykelti continues to deliver the most impassioned speech he can muster, filled with the best soundbites of wisdom from his last twenty years of research, and examples to personalize the issue, like: "It takes 456 mature pine trees constantly producing oxygen for the average car to travel 25 miles per hour. By the way, I have all my boring math online for you to double check..."

At the end, he looks out at a sea of faces, the full spectrum of humanity: different genders, cultures, religions, countries... This is perhaps the most diverse group of humans ever gathered and, purportedly, the most well-intentioned human beings, the ones that see the big picture. They realize how small the world is and how the actions of one human can indirectly affect another human on the opposite side of the planet.

Mykelti had visited the leading university researchers, the National Oceanic and Atmospheric Administration, the Scripps Institute, the President's Council of Advisors on Science and Technology, and more. There is no shortage of institutions, organizations, committees—or whatever they prefer to call themselves—but the hurdles are always the same. Nobody listens. If they listen, they don't care. If they care, they don't want to do anything about it. If they want to do something, they have no money—no power. If they have power, they don't need to listen. It was an endless loop. He just needed one credible organization to support his findings so the real work could begin.

The UN is his last hope. They have all the pieces of the puzzle, but what remains to be seen is whether they dare to take the necessary steps to save the world, even if it means trying to convince the rich—including the very people in this room—to be average, and convince the poor that they will forever remain poor. He has no doubt that eventually, the poorest of the poor will slip through the cracks as society tries to save itself. Mykelti feels lousy about that. He was born the poorest of poor, himself. His village, a literal footnote in history. It was dumb luck that rescued him. He intends to repay that luck, here, now. But, as he looks across this gilded room of experts—politicians, scientists, philanthropists, the best humanity has to offer—crickets. That's the expression they use these days in America. Nothing. Not a flicker of emotion. Many are staring at their papers or gadgets. Some are even asleep.

"May I take any questions?"

"The chair recognizes Delegate Van de Berg of the Netherlands."

"Thank you for your enlightening presentation. Given this theory to be true—"

"The evidence is overwhelming. I have years of research. But don't take my word for it. Analyze the data for yourself."

"As you've explained, the problem and the solution are the same. Whether we have too much carbon dioxide or too little oxygen—it doesn't matter. The problem is burning things. And the solution is to stop burning things. I see no further cause for action here. It is two sides of the same coin, is it not?"

Mykelti had anticipated this argument and has reserved his best rebuttal. "Millions of years ago, the arctic was filled with swamps, giant sequoia trees and insects the size of drones. The North Pole itself wasn't an ice cap, but rather floating mats of ferns, temperatures rarely dropping below freezing. The continent of Antarctica was a lush forest filled with giant dinosaurs. The Earth is actually at the *end* of an ice age now. We are due to get hot again. Climate patterns will change, but humanity will adapt. We will simply move north to greener pastures. Once, where there was arctic tundra, now there will be fertile fields and eventually temperate weather. That's where our farms and cities will be. And perhaps we will wait there for thousands of years, but we would survive. Humanity would survive. Global warming isn't the problem. Consider it a side effect. The actual problem is much worse—

"What I am saying is that oxygen depletion is the problem. And that is *not* something we can adapt to. And, it is not something that can be fixed in a few hundred—or even a few thousand years. Huge amounts of damage have already been done. It could take a million years—yes, a million—to repair. Our forests and oceans are dying—the things that make the oxygen are dying. Already, oxygen levels are dropping faster than the Earth can replenish them. I believe the Earth may no longer be capable of regenerating itself. And, every day, more and more machines burn more and more oil. At some point, we will hit a wall where we can't recover. On that, we all agree."

A man rises abruptly. "And when do you think we will hit that wall?"

Mykelti's heart sinks when he hears his father's gruff voice.

"The chair recognizes Delegate Doctor Jonathan Adams of the United States of America," the Chairperson says belatedly.

"About 2700 years if all the variables remain constant," Mykelti says.

"2700 years seems like quite a long time… No one here believes we'll be driving gas-guzzling cars forever."

"I said *if*. If the world population doesn't increase. If developing and undeveloped countries stay undeveloped. If we don't invent new toys everyone must have, like the iPhone. If the phytoplankton doesn't die. If there isn't a black swan event. However, people always want more—bigger and better. I estimate with current trends that the average person will be short of breath in as little as fifty years. In fact, I believe we are feeling the effects now. The missing oxygen— call it a global cooling gas—explains why climate change is many times worse than our current models predict. Too much CO_2 and too little O_2 makes the problem doubly bad—maybe exponentially bad. We need to address both sides of the equation."

"What do you think will happen if we tell the citizens of the world, 'Oh, never mind global warming, the real problem is oxygen depletion?' Seriously, take a moment. What do you think will happen?"

Now it is Mykelti's turn to be on the defensive. "The frog would reach out of the boiling pot and turn the burner off."

"Yes, of course, you think of us all as unwitting victims. If only we would wake up." Like Mykelti, his father pauses to let his words resonate—to increase the drama. "I'll tell you what will happen. Mass confusion and denial. It will take years to penetrate the noise and rewrite the narrative. Think it through to the end—what would happen if you convinced everyone your doomsday prophecies were true? They didn't have warmer winters to look forward to but, instead, they were going to slowly suffocate to death!? Be honest with yourself. What would happen?"

Mykelti knows he's been led into a rhetorical trap, like the one he tried to set. Whereas his question was diffused among the crowd, the focus of all the members compels him to speak.

"Fear," Mykelti regrets the word before it leaves his mouth.

"And what happens when fearful people try to run?"

"We need to do something," desperation creeps into Mykelti's tone, undermining the authority he worked so hard to establish.

"What makes you think we don't already do as much as we can do?"

The room is in silent agreement.

"There is no more time for science and debate. I'm advocating a call to action."

"Agreed. We have science coming out of our ears. Hundreds of research papers are published each day, and what does it amount to? Nothing. Nothing but gossip and opinions and arguments on the talking-head stations and fake memes. But creating mass panic? No, mass panic is not the course of action."

A grizzled man stands and shouts, "So, our decision is *no* decision!?"

"Order. Please. Order."

Mykelti shields his eyes from the lights. *Is that Sergei?* he wonders.

"Do you have any useful solutions?" delegate Adams continues. "Or did you just come here to tell us to plant more trees?"

"I've drawn up a new UN resolution. My aide is handing them out." He gestures to Brandon, who has turned his charm up so high he's glowing. "We can vote on this and sign it into international law right now. This resolution will make a statement to the world that time is running out. It outlines how we can form strategic partnerships, develop new technologies, and—"

"As you may know, a resolution, treaty, international law—whatever you want to call it—is nothing more than a recommendation—a gentleman's agreement at best. And, even if nations agree, usually, they do nothing. Does the Paris Accord or the Kyoto Protocol sound familiar? I am not demeaning the work of our esteemed colleagues. We all find it frustrating. But, I assure you, we are working on practical solutions to become carbon neutral—solutions that don't require the world to agree. Consider this a win. You've gotten your fifteen minutes of fame, which is more than we grant most."

A less passionate person would have realized they reached the point of diminishing returns and walked away. A lesser person would have convinced themselves they had done everything possible, that it was time to live their own life—the rest of the world be damned if they didn't know any better. But to Mykelti, happiness is not a priority. His only joys are the rewards of his work. He didn't even allow himself pleasures of the body. "Many years ago, the Secretary-General warned us not to sleepwalk past the point of no return. I'm afraid we have done just that. I want to help." Mykelti's final plea shifts the power back to the UN to either agree or disagree, and it is always easier to say no—to do nothing.

"These are problems that only diplomats can solve. If you want to help, we advise you to stop panicking people. Stay on point: global warming is the problem. Why don't you go home and find a practical solution? Start by riding a bicycle."

"I already do."

"Well, you didn't ride one across the ocean to get here, did you? Or did the butterflies carry you here? Have you thought of the environmental cost of this meeting?"

"Yes, of course. I thought it would be worthwhile," Mykelti says despairingly, knowing he had fallen for the final trap.

"That's the problem. You see, no one is *trying* to destroy the world. We all think our actions are worthwhile. Nobody has the time to weigh all the pros and cons of every decision. Not everyone is an expert, or even educated. Nor should they need to be. That's why we're here. We process the information and make the big decisions, so the average person can go on living their life. We thank you for the tidbit of information you've brought us as an expert in your own field. We'll be in touch if we need you," Delegate Adams' final perfunctory sentence concludes the present moment and takes control of the future.

Dead end
A few hours later

As Mykelti leaves the Palais des Nations, above the door is an enormous relief sculpture. Like Michelangelo's painting, God touches Adam's finger, giving him life. The figures are surrounded by chiseled words:

Thou mastering me

God! giver of breath and bread;

World's strand, sway of the sea;

Lord of living and dead;

Thou hast bound bones & veins in me, fastened me flesh,

And after it almost unmade, what with dread,

Thy doing: and dost thou touch me afresh?

Over again I feel thy finger and find thee.

God, Giver of breath, taker of breath, Mykelti thinks as he continues down the stairs, past the monolithic courtyard and all the flags of the world's nations. With nowhere else to go, he crosses the street towards the fountains and contemplates a giant sculpture of a chair. It's ironic. The world's elites, in one room, unwilling or unable to do anything. They sit there day in and day out. They listen. But they do nothing but keep their chairs warm. The chairs have a greater purpose for existing than these world leaders. The chairs, at least, serve their purpose.

A friendly hand reaches out and touches his shoulder.

Surprised, he turns. "Mother!?" Pearl has aged beautifully since she first scooped up Mykelti in her arms.

"We tried, Mykelti." She takes his hand in hers in lieu of a hug.

"He roasted me in front of the world—the literal world."

"You are both on the same side. You just have different ideas about the solution. It's like our marriage. Our display of love didn't always look like what the other thought it should."

The differences between Mykelti's adoptive parents—one raised by genteel people, the other a self-made man from a broken family—somehow strengthened their front against the world. He tried to be a partner to his father to team up against the injustices of the world, but his father didn't tolerate his point of view. In fact, all his relationships are strained. Maybe being African, he would never fit into the Western World. "They didn't listen. They didn't even try to understand. I was just wasting my breath."

"Your father didn't want to appear to be playing favorites. He gave you a chance to defend your ideas."

"His rhetoric was an embarrassment."

"But did you hear their response, Mykelti?"

"Of course. They said they would do nothing. We could have taken our first step right now."

She gestures to the ten-meter-tall chair. "This broken leg on the chair symbolizes people losing their legs to landmines, but it has a double entendre, don't you think? The delegates are chosen because they, presumably, hopefully, know best. They occupy those seats of power, thinking they are making decisions for you. They do not sit at a round table facing the world; they sit in broken chairs, facing their leader. A leader of the world, no doubt, but one of many thousands, if not millions. Come, I need a bit of a rest." She guides him to a park bench. "They *said* they tried to convince the world to change, and it didn't want to. Did you hear what their proposed solution is now?"

"There was no plan given."

"There was no specific plan revealed yet, but they did reveal the strategy. Care to take a guess, or do I have to do all the work?"

"They are no longer giving the world a choice," Mykelti finally realizes. "And the world will rebel," he says as the idea slowly sinks in.

"Not so much rebel. More like, they won't be able to participate. Their fate will simply be handed to them. You've been playing the same game, Mykelti. You are trying to force the UN to force the world. Perhaps it's time for a different strategy."

"You are full of wisdom today."

"A mother's job is never done," Pearl laughs lightheartedly. "Humor an old woman. My wisdom is all I have left to give."

"You have so much more," he reassures her. "But if they—if the world— won't listen to science... and they won't listen to anyone but themselves... What's left?"

"You are no longer in the arena of fact. Public policy is governed by public opinion."

"Ha! Public opinion is going to save the world. We're doomed."

"Think of it this way," Pearl says. "Everyone is trying to save the world. They are just starting with themselves. Each and every person needs to realize they play a part in the bigger picture. The problem is bigger than any of us, bigger than any nation, bigger than all the nations. We can start with public opinion and, eventually, public opinion becomes the cultural norm. Why do you think your father is a Chicago Bears fan?"

"Yes, I know this one."

"I suggest that you don't."

"Because he was born in Chicago," Mykelti says begrudgingly. "And, if he were born in Milwaukee, like you, he'd be a Packers fan."

"The point is: most people don't even question the culture they are born into. The good news is that you don't have to change the people; you can change the culture, and then the people will change themselves. First, we need to seed the culture with an idea. The idea must be big, passionate, and rewarding enough that people choose to change."

"Sounds so simple," Mykelti says facetiously. "Perhaps you should have told me this ten years ago."

"I did. You didn't want to change either. I had to plant a *lot* of seeds."

"And what makes you think the world will *want* to change? That could take generations."

"It might. It's never too soon to start. What is needed now is a leader with a vision and passion. Those that choose to follow, follow the passion, not the person."

She lets Mykelti digest her words before continuing. "There is another reason I'm here," she says ominously. "There's something you need to know. There was a reason I was blessed with you as my only child. I have been diagnosed with ovarian cancer. I'm going into treatment. Your father, he's a man of action. He's convinced modern science will find a cure. Maybe he's right. I'll follow his passion. I don't have the energy to question things anymore. But, don't worry, everything—"

"Everything is not okay," Mykelti finishes.

"Everyone gets their ticket stamped eventually. Yes, it's a bit of a surprise. Yes, there are better ways to go. But I've lived a good life. Mykelti, I don't want you to worry. There's nothing you can do, and the stress will ruin your life, too."

Mykelti stutters, "I— I—"

"There are no words." She hooks her arm in his. "Take me for a walk in the park. There aren't many beautiful days left."

The new normal
The not-so-distant past

The Qin Shi Huang, the new aircraft carrier sailing under the flag of the People's Republic of China, was a pleasure to behold as it sliced through the seas. It was on a routine mission of pomp and circumstance, which disguised an even more routine mission of espionage.

Oil not only fueled machines, but it also fueled the power structure of the Middle East and, to a great extent, the entire world, making humans—at least, those in charge—territorial and unwilling to change. Though most avoid change, the background energies of life never cease to flow, making change an inevitable encounter.

As the world's oceans warmed and polar caps melted, it left more surface waters exposed to exchange gases with the atmosphere, which changed the wind patterns; likewise, as the glaciers melted, the frigid runoff changed the ocean currents. Throughout the years since the Second Industrial Revolution, as humans continued to burn oxygen and change the density of the atmosphere, the oceans of air and water stirred themselves with greater force as Mother Nature tried to correct the imbalance. The pressures exerted on the surface of the Earth began to vary tremendously. Storms that were once annual events now became commonplace. Two generations of children had never experienced what was once considered normal.

The gargantuan weight of the atmosphere acts like a cork in a bottle, pressurizing land and ocean, but as a low-pressure storm—a superstorm of superstorms—rotated across the East China Sea, it was like someone popped the cork. The pressure difference was like a Midwest tornado, which could explode barns and toss cows into the next county, but on a scale never recorded. As this invisible pressure cyclone passed over the ocean surface, it caused the ocean to boil as the dissolved gases could no longer be contained in solution, nor could the methane hydrate remain frozen and undisturbed in the ocean bed.

As the Qin Shi Huang cruised the East China Sea, it passed over an area rich from millennia of rotting sea life and their byproducts of methane. The ocean gases reached a critical mass, and the Earth belched beneath the relatively toy-sized warship. The bubble rose in a great torrent, and the Qin Shi Huang did not sink so much as fall to the bottom of the ocean. As the aircraft carrier fell, the cigarette of a petty officer ignited the methane. And when the ship's fighter jets returned from patrol, the pilots were surprised to find they had no place to land. It did not matter, there was too little oxygen to power their engines, and they plummeted to the bottom of the ocean to rest near their mother ship, but not before reporting that the Qin Shi Huang had been engulfed in a giant fireball, undoubtedly from some unknown enemy.

The storm left many vessels adrift. One ghost ship arrived in port perfectly intact except for the crew and mascot, found dead in the tracks of their daily routines, which sent the superstitious fishing village into a panic of prayers. Nations blamed their usual suspects—suspects for no more reasons than the lingering feeling of malcontent passed from father to son to grandson. Nationalists and fundamentalists of all sides reached a fevered pitch to prove their version of God in an increasingly godless world.

A war may have benefited mankind if they would have been capable of learning a lesson and changing their ways, but one war to end all wars has always led to the next war to end all wars. Likewise, it would have been beneficial if the storm had been slightly bigger, a miniature global catastrophe, one big enough to thin out the herd and unify the tribes of humanity against a singular enemy, but small enough that it would not create a devastating feedback loop.

Smooth Move
13 months ago

The hot pink hair of the barista catches Mykelti's eyes. Her artful tattoos—thorny rose branches—trace the lines of her physique, dragging his gaze further down. Eclectic jewelry hugs her curves and sucks his eyes into the black hole of her bosom. Her outfit is dazzling, but it wouldn't have helped her survive a Third World village, except maybe her earrings could have lured a fish, or her brassiere, a husband. But in American culture, you're not even supposed to think those thoughts. Mykelti can only guess what kind of woman she advertises herself to be—a contradiction, to be sure.

"Welcome to Smooth Move. May I take your order?" she punctuates her sentence with the corporate smile needed to get the job done.

"Nice day for a smoothie," Mykelti says, in an awkward attempt to reconnect with humanity after too much time gathering and analyzing data. Data doesn't have emotions or require civilities.

"Every day is a good day for a Smooth Move, if you ask me," she says.

Mykelti laughs. "Do they tell you to say that?"

"Believe it or not, that was an original."

"Nice." He laughs awkwardly while searching for a way to keep the door open to their conversation. The smoothie shop grows herbs and spices; unlike the barista, they are yellow and wilted. "Your basil is in dire need of watering."

"Ooh. *Dire*. Look at you, Mr Big Vocabulary. It's not the water. They get plenty of water. They just don't like where they're sitting?"

"How so?"

"They don't get enough sun."

"Seems like there's a simple solution to that."

"Corporate dictates where everything goes in the store."

"Well, corporate isn't here right now."

"You see this hair!? This is the only control I have over my own life."

"I'll buy one. Maybe they'll enjoy sitting in my apartment."

"Only one? You're going to leave the rest to die?"

Mykelti thinks she's right; they will all die. "Okay."

"I'm joking," she says.

"Are you?" he laughs nervously. "If you don't mind me asking a loaded question…"

She draws an imaginary gun from her hip, points her finger and pops her thumb. "Shoot."

"What are you doing working here?"

"Where else is a vegan girl going to work these days? I don't even like depending on corporate 'Merica this much. But, let's face it, if I walked out into the woods Thoreau-style, I'm not going to last long. I can't do anything practical, like build a house or bake bread."

"You've read Thoreau? I'm impressed."

"Well, I'm not. Do you think I'm a savage or something? What'll ya have?"

"I meant, I like Thoreau, too."

"And…"

"I'll have the usual."

"Which is…?" she intones condescendingly.

"I come here every day." He's surprised. Of course, Chicago isn't a village, but he still expects the people he sees every day to know who he is and care. "I just thought…"

"Look. You seem like a nice guy. But save your breath. I try to forget this place so I can go home and binge TV in peace."

"What's your favorite?"

"Raspberry sherbert."

"I'll have that."

"Great."

Mykelti heads to the patio to get away from the television tuned to the 24-hour infotainment channel. As the talking head describes the day's news in a hypnotic voice, "...latest bleaching of the Great Barrier Reef indicates the collapse of..." the announcements scroll along the bottom, "...algorithms accidentally assigning sperm whales more value dead than alive..."

As he watches people walk by, the data no longer processing in the back of his mind, he begins to relax. But, all too soon, he's back to thinking about how his life's work hasn't amounted to anything. *I should have retired long ago. No one cares what scientists say anymore. People simply don't want to listen. They prefer being stuck in their own echo chambers.*

The pink-haired barista walks past, smoking a cigarette.

"Hey, Raspberry Sherbert, is that a vegan cigarette you're smoking?"

"Hey, asshole, my name is printed on my tag. Not only do you feel like you're getting personal service, it makes filing a complaint a lot easier."

Mykelti attempts to look at her name, but she comes to a quick stop and her breasts jiggle in their brassier. He quickly averts his gaze. "Sorry, I was trying to be funny. Why don't you sit down?"

"No offense, but do you think I want to hang around here for fun?"

"We can go somewhere else if you like."

"Ah. Screw it. I might as well sit down and enjoy my cigarette. Besides, don't need you stalking me home. You realize you're mumbling like a crazy man? And—yes—better believe it. All-natural. None of the million chemicals those corporate assholes use. Would you believe they put chocolate and formaldehyde additives in cigarettes? How about that for a smoothie of the month?"

"If you don't mind me asking, smoking but not eating meat seems like a contradiction."

"If you don't mind me saying, you sound like a judgmental prick."

"It's just scientific curiosity."

"'Folks who have no vices have very few virtues.' Abraham Lincoln. Words to live by. Anyway, before I lose all my respect, what am I supposed to call you?"

"Mykelti."

"That's a mouthful. Can I call you Mickey?"

"Like the mouse? Funny, my mother always used to—"

"Where you from, anywho?"

"Cameroon. And. No."

"Wow, all the way from Africa to drink the 'Merican Dream Kool-Aid. No, it's great. Really! We're going to make a great pair. Raspberry Sherbert and Mykelti Mouse."

Science is dead
1 year ago

Mykelti feels guilty sitting in the restaurant filled with formal costumes and forced gaiety, but his mother's parting words had sunk in deep. "Enjoy yourself for once, Mykelti. What if the world *does* end tomorrow?" He's been in this country for decades, and it still hadn't eased his fears that someday there wouldn't be a fish on the plate; and if there were a fish, thinking it might be the last. Nobody knew how old he was when they found him. Maybe four, probably six, possibly a malnourished eight-year-old, but his character had been formed and frozen into place the day his village died. You mature fast in Africa. You have to. Unlike here, in the so-called First World, people hang on to their youth for as long as possible. In Cameroon, the elders wore their wrinkles and scars like badges of honor and the weight of their years like a bank vault. Anything less was a sign of immaturity. It must be a nice luxury—*privilege* is the word they use these days—to invest so much energy into appearances and to command so much power wearing an unused but beautiful body, a body without enough reserves to survive a plague of locusts or a drought.

Internally, Mykelti is arguing against his attraction to Sherbert. He's jealous of how much power she commands as the heads of men steal glances in her direction when she struts past their tables like a peacock. Mykelti always marveled at birds and the miraculous colors their bodies somehow manufacture out of dry and dull birdseed—an advertisement of strength and fertility. Mykelti thinks nature could have made a better investment in survival than spending energy on lush plumage and exuberant mating dances, but apparently, even in the animal kingdom, wastefulness is a virtue.

"Sorry, I'm late," says Sherbert. I was trying to get a smoke. And then this lady needed help. Ugh! My life is complicated."

"Patience is a virtue. I was getting good practice," Mykelti laughs to emphasize the joke but falls into old habits with his next comment, "If you haven't noticed, it's getting hard to breathe even without cigarettes. You might—"

"If you haven't noticed, it's safer to smoke cigarettes than breathe all the shit big corporations are pumping into the air."

"Sorry, that wasn't a criticism."

"Oh, I see. That was Mykelti-speak?"

"Well... I guess it's my way of saying I care. Anyway, thanks for coming."

"You're so sweet, looking out for me like that. Anyway," she mimics, "I had nothing better to do."

Up close, Sherbert's warmth and scent are breathtaking. Mykelti can't help but admire her, but her sarcasm buries her intentions. "You polish up nice," he fishes.

"Hey, if you got it, why not flaunt it? I enjoy seeing you men do impersonations of bobbleheads."

The *maître d'* escorts Brandon to the table. No heads turn to follow his progress. "Your guests have arrived. *Bon appétit.*"

"Boy, you sure do feel like you are getting your money's worth when they treat you like that," Brandon says. "Oh, who is this? I heard you had big news, but this isn't what I was expecting?"

"It's not—" begins Mykelti. His words and seemingly important thoughts being lost in Brandon's banter.

"Call me Ishmael," Brandon jokes.

"Call me Sherbert."

"Put down that water, Mykelti. I'll order a real drink. *Garçon*—" Brandon flags a passing waiter.

"Sir, this is not my table."

"That's okay. I don't discriminate."

"I'll send your server right over."

"Save them a step and put in an order of Champagne."

"I'm afraid we're all out of Champagne. May I offer you some Californian sparkling wine?"

"*Merci beaucoup.* You are too generous with your time. I'll leave it up to your impeccable taste. As long as it has bubbles—we're celebrating."

"We're not—" Mykelti tries to interject.

"Since you're being so accommodating, perhaps, to accompany our *apéritifs,* you'd be so kind as to add an *hors d'oeuvre*?" The waiter rolls his eyes, already trapped by his concession to order wine. "The lobster *canapé* sounds fantastic."

"And the country salad. Minus the goat cheese," says Sherbert.

"I'll have whatever is in season," says Mykelti. "Even better if it is locally produced."

"May I interest you in the *provençal* vegetable tart?"

It doesn't seem appetizing, but after hearing Brandon's order, Mykelti feels obligated to offset Brandon's carbon footprint. "Sounds local to me," he says.

After the waiter leaves with the orders, Brandon leans in to whisper, "If you know five words of French in a place like this, they'll give you the keys to the Eiffel Tower," he laughs. "So, doctor, what's the big news? Geneva went well? Did we win that Nobel Prize, yet?"

"Oh, a doctor," Sherbert fails to hide her surprise and tries to recover, "And, here I thought you were just another wannabe author at the smoothie shop."

"I research—used to research—the oxygen flow. Where it comes from; where it goes. How it affects climate and respiration..." Mykelti tries to shrug off the conversation. "That's not what I wanted to talk about."

"I'm waiting with bated breath."

Brandon laughs, "I see what you did there. If you haven't noticed, the good doctor doesn't have a sense of humor."

"Oh, but he made a joke earlier. He said he had patience." Brandon and Sherbert laugh.

"It's no joking matter. I have been correlating prehistoric levels of oxygen with the Industrial Revolutions to confirm my theory—"

"See, no sense of humor." They laugh again.

"No, it's scary. Every day my predictions—"

"What he's trying to say is that he's a climate scientist with all kinds of new-fangled ideas about the end of the world. It gets quite boring. Fortunately, I am paid to listen."

"You mean the end of life as we know it," says Sherbert.

Brandon and Mykelti are taken aback.

"Sorry. Pet peeve of mine: people talking about saving the world. The world isn't going anywhere," Sherbert clarifies. "The planet's probably better off without us."

"Ah, a budding scientist," Mykelti says, excited there is more to her than peacock feathers and sarcasm.

"More like a budding therapist. You wouldn't believe how many egos I have to soothe just to sell a smoothie." She winks at Mykelti.

The appetizers arrive quickly. "Since when do the appetizers arrive before the bubbly?" asks Brandon.

"Lobster?" Mykelti has been watching the plates of uneaten food being shut-tled back to the kitchen. There seemed no point in ordering more when the trash is being filled with delicacies from around the world. But people are en-joying themselves... or at least putting on a good show. Their self-indulgent chatter filling the room, taking turns sharing their clever observations. Mykelti imagines that after their intellectual mating dances, many would return to their rooms to make love and fall asleep without a care in the world.

"Hey, it was your idea to 'live a little.' Give me a break. I just got off the boat from Tibet. Trust me. There are no lobsters anywhere near the Himalayas."

"There are no lobsters anywhere near here."

"Yes, there are. Flown in from Maine yesterday. Look, I deserve a treat. Care for some?"

"I haven't been eating meat lately."

"My dear boy, you haven't been raised by proper Catholics, have you? Meat only comes from land animals. Whatever we can fish out of the ocean is fair game."

"I haven't been eating anything that can crawl," Mykelti amends.

"Sherbert, care for a taste?"

"Eww. Underwater spiders! Seriously?"

"She's a vegan," Mykelti says chivalrously.

"I don't have to explain my decisions. And, I don't need you to either," she says with contempt.

"Well, I, for one, am offended that you are eating that green stuff." Brandon gestures to her salad. To emphasize his point, he picks up a glistening chunk of lobster, its segmented body like an anatomical lesson. He sucks it into his mouth as if giving birth in reverse and mops the juice from his chin. "Where do you think our breathable oxygen is coming from? All those poor, hardworking plants. I'm feeling faint. Is anyone else finding it hard to breathe? The fanciest restaurant this side of town, and I'm being starved of the most valuable nutrient of life—air!"

For a moment, it appears dinner will come to a crashing halt as Sherbert's senses are assaulted, and she digests his comments. But she smiles. Then laughs. And everyone joins her, laughing heartily.

"Ah, finally, the bubbly. Did you have to go all the way to California?"

"I'm sorry, sir. There was—" the waiter pops the cork and pours three glasses— "an oversight and the wine needed to be chilled to the proper serving temperature."

"Thank you, Garçon. That will be all," Brandon says pretentiously. "So, mate, how long are you going to keep us in suspense?"

"I'm retiring," says Mykelti.

"Wow! Giving up on planet Earth? That's a surprise."

"No, I'm giving up on science."

"Join the club. Half the world doesn't believe in science anymore." He raises his glass. "To Mykelti's retirement." Brandon clinks their glasses too enthusiastically, and they erupt into bubbles, pouring over rims and hands, and puddling on the table. "Stop the presses. This just out. Greenhouse gases released from sparkling wine causing climate change," he says in a newscaster's voice. "For the good of the planet, I must drink this and use my own body to absorb the excess CO_2. Call me a martyr." Brandon upends his glass and pours another round. "Quick, we mustn't let these bubbles escape."

"To saving the planet," Sherbert toasts.

"To the planet," Mykelti says, not wanting to be left out.

"Looks like I'll have to accept that ol' Nobel Prize without you, dear chap. So, doctor, what are you going to do now?"

"I can't sit behind the desk anymore. And politics. Ugh. I need to do something! Maybe I'll start a non-profit. Maybe I really will try to save the world," he laughs.

"Go easy on yourself. You can't do it alone, mate."

"Change always starts with one person."

"That's cute. Is that a meme or something?"

"I could start small. Plant trees. Build bamboo bicycles. Something like that."

"Planting trees is great," says Sherbert. "But, you don't look to me like the Johnny Appleseed type."

"The world needs ten-thousand Johnny Appleseeds," says Brandon. "Why don't you be the one to inspire them?"

"Yes, if you believe in it, you need to spread the message."

"Ah! I don't know. I tried. Governments, corporations—they're machines. It could take years to replace the parts."

"Go to the people," says Brandon. "You Americans are all about power to the people."

"Yes, better to be the herd of angry bulls than the hungry lion."

"You need to make a grassroots effort," says Sherbert. "Be the apple seed."

Brandon refills everyone's glasses.

"To being an activist," Mykelti raises his glass.

"Only problem is, the last I checked—and that was, like, yesterday—being an activist doesn't pay very well," says Sherbert.

"To being a martyr," says Brandon.

"To being a martyr," Mykelti echoes, reluctantly.

The blame game

2 days ago

— The Doomsday Clock stands at fifty-nine seconds to midnight. We don't have much time, so let's get right to it. Today we have a special guest on the show. His podcast, "Warm Beer, Cold Showers," has been trending in the top ten. Please welcome Doctor Mykelti Adams.

— Glad to be here. Glad to talk to anyone who will listen. [Polite laughter from the audience.]

— **Mykelti, your podcast has catapulted you to fame. How so? Doom-and-gloom stories about the environment are so commonplace they're barely newsworthy.**

— I understand the fatigue, but climate change is not a theory anymore. It's affecting our daily lives. People are finally wanting to change. And none too soon. The Doomsday Clock is just a guesstimate by our best scientists. No one knows what or when the tipping point will be. What we do know is that we're on the edge of the sixth great mass extinction event, and that, eventually, there will be a correction.

— **Right, and you're hoping that humanity will make the correction before the Earth does.**

— If you ask me—and I assume you are because I'm on the show—the dominoes are already falling. That being said, it's not too late to prevent an entire collapse of the ecosystem.

— **So there is hope for humanity?** [Audience laughter.] **Before we get too far ahead of ourselves, in a nutshell, what is the problem?**

— We are running out of air to breathe. Humans are burning oxygen in their machines, and the plants that make the oxygen are dying.

— **Most of our viewers aren't scientists, so skipping the fancy names and big numbers, what can you tell our audience that will convince them beyond a reasonable doubt?**

— Ask yourself this: Why isn't the Earth greener? If we are experiencing a greenhouse effect, why aren't there more plants? Plants love warm, wet weather. They eat carbon dioxide. But do you see a lush paradise? Do you see heaven on Earth?

— **Spoiler alert—I live in an urban jungle. There's not much green to begin with.**

— And that's the problem. Less plants. Less oxygen. Look, you don't have to be a climate scientist to gather some empirical evidence. Are there more roads, more parking lots, more buildings in your neighborhood? Are there more or less cars? Do you use your heating and air conditioning more or less? Are your gardens as productive as they used to be? For those of you living at higher altitudes, have you noticed the tree line? Has it moved up or down? Trees need oxygen, too. So, if there's less oxygen, the trees would be at lower altitudes, and vice versa. We could also look at the infection rate of respiratory diseases—this is harder to prove due to pollution—but are there more cases of lung disease: asthma, emphysema, COPD, bronchitis… or less? The coronavirus pandemic of the early twenties required ventilators for critical care patients. In other words, patients couldn't breathe. Coincidence? Are you, yourself, experiencing any symptoms of hypoxia: tiredness, faintness, shortness of breath, headaches, numbness or tingling of extremities…

— **Aren't we all?** [Laughter.]

— Bottom line. Whether or not you believe me, if we're worried about what's coming out of exhaust pipes and smokestacks, shouldn't we be worried about what's going in them?

— **You have some impressive credentials. You have a doctorate in both paleoclimatology and paleontology. For over a decade, you were trying to reconstruct a picture of prehistoric Earth and compare it to where we stand now. But you gave all that up. Now, you're an activist. Why?**

— Simple. I've done the math. The results are in. We don't need more science. Now is—

— **This brings us to your philosophy. It's catchy. Warm beer, cold showers.**

— Every little action counts. Imagine the energy needed—the oxygen burned, or if you prefer, the carbon dioxide released—for nine billion people every day taking a hot shower and drinking a cold beer? I believe humanity has come so far down this road of overpopulation and overconsumption that we can't afford simple luxuries anymore. Think of the oxygen reserves as a bank. We've been withdrawing free energy for over two hundred years; eventually, we'll have to pay back the debt.

— **You seem to be contradicting yourself. If you're an environmental activist—some would call you an alarmist—why are you telling everyone there is a global warming conspiracy? Doesn't that defeat the point of getting people to take action?**

— Let's be clear. I'm not saying that global warming isn't happening. Or that mankind isn't making the problem worse. What I *am* saying is that global warming—I prefer the term climate change—is the symptom of a much larger problem. A problem that requires immediate action. A problem some people at the highest levels don't want you to know about.

— **Why the conspiracy? I mean, what do they have to gain?**

— There are two types of conspirators. First, the profiteers. As everyone knows, people profit from the carbon industry. They aren't motivated to change. They have enough money to insulate themselves from any foreseeable disaster. And, many don't think they will live long enough to inherit any problems. The second group of people are what you might call benevolent protectors. They don't think we can handle the truth. They believe we live in an immature society. They're thinking— Let me put it to you this way: it's easier to tell children to reduce, reuse and recycle than it is to get them to grow up and be conscientious adults.

— **So, why tell people the truth? You said it yourself; aren't you risking a backlash?**

— I have faith—I have to have faith—that people want to and will do the right thing. There's no time to beat around the bush anymore. Anyone that is part of the system is part of the problem. Anyone that owns stock, even if it is just a traditional retirement plan, is a profiteer. Anyone that drives a car or has a car deliver items to their door is a mass consumer. Anyone that has a cell phone. Anyone that doesn't grow their own food. Everyone watching this show, sucking up energy, is part of the problem. People are the problem. It's too late for bandaids. Society needs to change. We—individuals—need to change.

— **Now?**

— Yesterday!

— **We have a caller on the line. Welcome to the show. You have a question for our guest.**

— *Do you take us all for idiots because we use a light switch at night, wash our faces in the morning, jump in the car, train, or on a bus to get to work to put food on the table for our families? You should be held accountable for the rubbish you are shoving down our throats. If you think my words are cynical, you're right. They are. I'm seventy-eight years old. People like you have been crying wolf my whole life. But I'm still here. I've built a good life and never did nobody a whisker of harm. Now you, hiding behind books your whole life, hammering into my head how to live. Shame on you. Get this on your spoon and swallow it, you bunch of no good, do-gooders.*

— **Thoughts, Mykelti?**

— I'm sorry to be the bearer of bad news—

— **Let's put a pin in that. I hear both your parents work for the United Nations. In fact, your father is head of the UN's Intergovernmental Panel on Climate Change. Do you think he would be proud of your work?**

— Everything I am, everything I have done, I owe to my parents. So, yes, I hope so.

— **Well, let's find out. I've just been told we have a special guest appearance. This may come as a pleasant surprise to you, Mykelti. Please welcome your father, Doctor Jonathan Adams. Good to have you, Jonathan. Are you—**

— *Please, call me Doctor Adams.*

— **Doctor Adams, are you proud of your son?**

— *My son is an adult. He shouldn't need to cater to other people's opinions. I do hope he enjoys his life and finds his work fulfilling. I wish the same for everyone, but there are those who enjoy the struggle.*

— It appears your son is accusing you of a cover-up. Care to explain?

— *I appreciate the melodrama you are trying to create for ratings, but the truth is we're on the same side. Everyone here—including yourself, no?—agrees we have a problem. We just differ on the necessary solutions.*

— What would your solution be?

— *The subject of climate change is as broad as it's long. They didn't build Rome in a day, and we're not going to fix climate change overnight. As we heard our caller say, people can't stop driving their cars tomorrow; they have families to feed. I'd like to reassure people that the IPCC has several subcommittees working hard to implement a broad range of solutions.*

— Like…?

— *I'm excited to tell you that we are in the preliminary stages of building carbon dioxide reclaimers in strategic locations across the globe. These factories, through a complex but cost-effective process, capture and sequester as much CO_2 from the air as 80 million trees—*

— Why not plant 80 million trees? I'll tell you why—

— *Alongside this initiative, we are working on international legislation to ensure that all industries must offset their carbon dioxide emissions by purchasing greenshares with our carbon reclaimers. Furthermore, to offset costs, we'll be ushering in a new Diamond Age. As you may know, diamonds are crystalized carbon molecules made under intense heat and pressure. With improvements in technology, we can take the carbon dioxide out of the air and make artificial diamonds, which have many industrial uses like drill bits and sandpaper.*

— What my father fails to mention is that though these methods may reduce atmospheric carbon dioxide, they will actually escalate the problem by consuming even more oxygen. These facilities use massive amounts of energy, and our energy comes from burning oxygen. By the way, who's going to profit off these carbon taxes? You know what they say: follow the money.

— *A strange thing to say coming from someone who has made a living perpetuating myths using grant money and, now, advertising and product placement.*

— I don't contaminate my message. The only one profiting off our misery is you. I hope members of our audience have enough money to buy a hermetically sealed house! Because that's what they'll need to survive.

— *My apologies for my son's outrageous remarks. He has good intentions, and I appreciate that the world needs a spokesperson, but he has resorted to fearmongering and rabble-rousing.*

— Is that your solution, Mykelti, creating mass panic?

— I call it raising awareness. I've tried everything else. Governments are dead-locked by public opinion. Corporations deadlocked by profits. Media stuck in the echo chamber of likes and shares. No offense.

— **None taken. By the way folks, don't forget to like and share.** [Laughter.]

— We can't buy our way out of this problem. And science can't save us. The cows are already out of the barn. The only thing that will work is massive social change—getting people to see the benefit of making a change and taking immediate action.

— **What do you recommend our listeners do, specifically?**

— Unfortunately, we need to pay for the sins of our fathers. Severe austerity measures are in order.

— **Do you really believe cold showers and warm beer will save us?**

— We need to do this and much more. If not, Homo sapiens will be joining the thousands of animals on the endangered species list.

— **I think our audience is tired of doomsday prophecies. We could all use some hope. Dr Adams, what do you recommend? What can people do right now to help?**

— *If you can drive one less mile in the car, put one less degree on the thermostat— you've done more than most. I agree. We are running out of time, but there is no need to panic. We have a full spectrum of long-term solutions in place. In 40 years, our oil reserves will run out. There will be nothing left to burn... Not fuel. Not oxygen. Humanity will have to invent some new technology long before then. I, for one, am optimistic about the future of nuclear fusion—unlimited clean energy. In the meantime, we must mitigate the problem by achieving net-zero carbon dioxide emissions. As you heard my son say, he gave up science. So he may be unaware that our leading research and cutting-edge tech prove we can beat this. We're working on your behalf to make the world a better place.*

— **Mykelti, final words?**

— We can't assign this problem to future generations and magical technolo-gies. Rain does not fall on one roof alone. We all need to take action now. Do anything and everything you can to minimize your impact.

— **Unfortunately, we can't simply stop driving our cars tomorrow... And, with that, we really are out of time.**

The first wave of deaths: Malthusianism

2012

Humanity was like a grand experiment being performed. The End of Days, the result of the experiment, has been foretold since the dawn of civilization. The world's most infamous seer, Nostradamus, prophesied it. John recorded his vision of Armageddon in Revelations: the Earth will be "tried by fire." The Chinese I Ching and Hindu Vedic texts make similar predictions. The ancient Greeks described the decline of man from the Golden Age down to the Iron Age. Halfway around the world during Pre-Columbian times, the Hopi Tribe of Native Americans predicted that the Great Purification would occur soon after men brought back pieces of the Moon, a great web crisscrossed the sky, and the sea turned black. Thousands of years in advance, the Mayans used the precession of the Earth and the revolution of the Solar System's orbit around the arm of the Milky Way Galaxy like a celestial clock. They calculated the exact astronomical event that would coincide with the End of Time: the alignment of the winter solstice Sun with the center of the galaxy—a celestial phenomenon that happens every 26,000 years. Ancient astrologers, persecuted by the church, left hidden clues: Sagittarius' arrow points towards the black hole in the heart of the galaxy, alluding to the same ominous galactic alignment the Mayans observed.

Modern history saw many people hopping on the doomsday bandwagon. Some religious sects, like Armageddonists, believed it was their right and duty to reap the Earth of everything she had—God gave men rule over the fish and birds and every creeping creature on Earth—thinking that once the Earth was harvested of all her goodness, mankind would ascend to Heaven. Scientists cautioned that global warming and the rampant degradation and pollution of the environment could lead to the Domino Effect and the global systemic collapse of civilization. Sociologists like Malthus predicted that the congenital need to survive would drive humans to eat themselves out of house and home. And as evidenced, archaeologists discovered that mankind's hunger, even without machines, turned the Fertile Valley, the Cradle of Civilization, into a desert. And paleontologists discovered many species had evolved themselves to extinction. Geologists unearthed the fingerprints of multiple cataclysmic upheavals. New Agers said the Solar System was entering a location with a different composition of the primal chakric energies; and, therefore, a slightly different set of physical laws would govern nature, meaning the delicate balance of Mother Earth's ecosystem would be tipped askew, and pushed over the edge by mankind's meddling...

There were so many doomsday prophecies that humans invented a word for the study of the end of the world: *eschatology*. But, one did not need to be a scientist, prophet, or religious fanatic to predict the destruction of the human race—all one needs is a little common sense.

It cannot be ruled out that the apocalypse was a mass-induced, self-fulfilling prophecy. Still, it is an odd fact that these disparate cultures, separated by unnavigable spans of time and space, therefore effectively unknown to each other, claimed humanity would face a crisis somewhere around the year 2012 of the Common Era, now known as the Anthropocene Era, the era of mankind. Indeed, humanity, as a species, has what might be called a collective ability to predict the future. They could sense the disaster like waves splashing off the prow of an oncoming boat. Indeed, the average person panicked at the slightest sign of danger, sweeping clean the stores in less than 24 hours. This instinctual fear stripped many of the ability to survive and even more of the will to survive. People filled with terror and insanity would figuratively and sometimes literally run naked through the streets. School shootings, mass suicides, financial meltdowns, genocidal wars, terrorism, conspiracies, anarchy, and much more were symptoms of society's immune system inducing a fever—a panic contagion— to burn out the disease of greed and corruption from the sociopathic species.

Not everyone was a skeptic. It's interesting to note that the original Latin definition of *apocalypse* means *revelation* or *to uncover;* in other words, a time would come when the veil of blindness would be lifted, ending an era dominated by falsehoods and manipulations. Nostradamus' predictions were meant only as a final proof of his greatest warning—that humans were the architects of their own destruction. Nostradamus urged people to change the course of humanity's fate. Spiritualists heralded that humanity was entering the Age of Aquarius, where humanity would be spiritually transformed if—and only if—they could make the leap to a global consciousness, or to paraphrase the modern Mayans, "If we can dream a new dream." Though most records were destroyed by the conquistadors, historians believed that the end of the Mayan Long Count Calendar, the End of Time, was really the beginning of a new time, a new era of enlightenment and prosperity. Even laypeople agreed everything happened in cycles and hoped that humanity was just experiencing growing pains.

Twenty-twelve came and went. However, when the Earth passed the dense gravitational and electromagnetic plane of the galaxy, it did not light the skies on fire, and the tidal effects were minimal. The Sun did not emit any solar flares to destroy the electrical grid. No comets arrived bearing carnivorous plant seeds, terraforming microbes or alien viruses; though it has happened in the past, the bubonic plague for example. Nemesis never arrived to rip away the atmosphere, like it did when leaving a gash in the side of Mars, or shatter the Earth in its gravitational wake, like it did the fifth planet, now known as the asteroid belt. No divine intervention from a god or alien arrived, nor, alas, mass ascension into heaven or spaceships. The Earth's magnetic poles did not flip. Mankind kept its fingers off the nuclear button. In fact, there were no global cataclysms of any sort, except a few smaller man-made varieties, which seemed dramatic according to the media frenzies.

Human ingenuity prevailed—mankind had conquered the natural world. Their success was almost guaranteed, except the population bomb kept ticking. Not only was the population growing, but so was their appetite. The heat of their frenzied activity, like sandpaper on wood, warmed the Earth, unlocking diseases trapped in the arctic ice for tens of thousands of years—zombie pathogens, they are called. One such virus that normally would have bloomed and faded away almost unnoticed found a new home in humans and quickly leapt from person to person until it circled the globe—a pandemic was to be the price of sin. The death toll was high, but the panic was worse, and the collateral damage was immeasurable. The population bomb had exploded.

Humanity woke up and realized they were in the future. Life was now like the science fiction novels and television shows they had grown up watching: they were living in artificial environments, insulated from the dying world, and distracted by electronic gadgets and manufactured foods, a synthetic world that overstimulated mind and body. Humans realized, among many things, that they had enslaved themselves. They built a society forced to keep the never-ending supply chain moving. For example, when the restaurants were closed, even though people still needed to eat, billions of animals were "euthanized" because there was no way to get the animal from farm to slaughterhouse to market. People not only needed to feed their families, they needed to feed the economy. If one sector could not perform its job, it created a cascading effect far down the line. So people floundered for jobs even if their jobs were obsolete or detrimental to the environment. In a practical sense, food shortages turned into job losses; job losses turned into bankrupted businesses; bankrupted businesses turned into a worldwide recession; recession led to starvation and hopelessness; and, hopelessness caused wars, both within a person and without.

Ironically, the pandemic gave the Earth a chance to heal a few wounds, and it gave humans a chance to pause and reflect. For a moment, after feeling lost in a sea of billions, individuals regained hope: *we are all connected; small things matter; together, we can make a difference.* It seemed that the ravaged planet gave humans no choice but to cooperate and that human consciousness had reached critical mass and made the evolutionary leap forward. Humanity decided to upgrade its software. Society finally prioritized providing everyone health and happiness and a dream for the future. The air improved, and the birth rates declined.

Unfortunately, the damage had been done during their adolescent years: the industrialization, the pesticides, the deforestation, desertification, mass extinctions, mono-speciation, ocean acidification… and so much more was still eroding humanity's foundation like mutinous cancerous cells. And, there were still many individuals that clung to their old beliefs with more force than ever. The winds of society blew with a gale force.

As history has concluded, 2012 was not the end—it was the beginning of the end—the end of the era of mankind, and the end of most lifeforms inhabiting ecological niches alongside mankind. It was all too late and too little. The Age of Heaven on Earth and the foretold 1000 years of peace on Earth began and ended before humanity had a chance to notice.

Unintended Consequences
Yesterday

Dr Jonathan Adams walks into the smoothie shop with a bang of the door and a blast of hot summer air. "Your mother told me I'd find you here."

"Every day is a good day for a Smooth Move," Mykelti says with a cheery voice, hoping to lighten the mood. He is more disappointed than surprised; he's used to his father's surprises.

"I see you are fully Americanized now. Is this what your mother and I dragged you out of that shit-hole African village for? So, you could sell slushies over the counter during the day and frighten people late at night on the radio?"

"Podcast."

"Same shit, different name."

"That's very Shakespearean: 'A rose by any other name…'"

"Take a break and meet me outside." His father walks away.

Sherbert turns to Mykelti and says, "That was your father?"

"That's not where I get my good looks."

"Obviously."

Mykelti's father sits on the patio, people-watching. He still has the angular physique, ropey neck and short hair, from his time in boot camp when they broke him down and built him back up to the man sitting before Mykelti.

"Another surprise visit?"

"I was doing damage control. Your mother told me about your television debut."

Mykelti sits down and slides a roast beef sandwich across the table. "I assume you still eat meat."

"Somebody has to keep the population under control."

Mykelti sits down with his avocado toast. "It's popular right now," he justifies, "seasoned with our own peppers and onions. Did you notice we have a garden? That was my idea. Corporate fast-tracked it in all their stores."

"You really are effecting change on a global scale," Jonathan scoffs.

"Somebody has to..." he echoes his father's words. "But, people are starting to change."

"For the better?"

"Of course."

"By whose definition? Yours? Are you enjoying your notoriety? Does it make you feel important to see everyone running around doing your bidding? Re-tweeting. Re-liking. By the way, have you checked your drones lately? Or, has our grant money all been shot to hell?"

Mykelti averts his eyes. "That's Brandon's job now."

"I'll give you a hint. It's getting worse."

"Funny, you didn't mention that on the show."

"I have a present for you." He clunks down a heavy aluminum canister. "Do you know what that is?" The label is illustrated with a picture-perfect woman smelling a handful of fresh strawberries and the slogan, "As refreshing as a walk in the garden."

"Breezy!?"

"Yes, that's right. Goddamned, fucking, strawberry-flavored, Breezy Breathe Easy. People are now buying and selling bottled oxygen. Do you know who I blame this on?"

"Corporate American greed?"

"You! I blame this on you and your save-the-world shitshow. You've undone half of what I've worked for... But, I have to give you credit. You persevered just as I taught you. It took years, but your cute little meme—Have you ever wondered how much your car breathes?—finally got into the mainstream consciousness. But did you factor this—" He picks up the Breezy and slams it down on the table in front of Mykelti "—into your equation? What's the environmental cost of this? It was bad enough people buying their own water, enough bottles to stretch to Mars and back. Now you got them buying air."

"At least people are listening."

"They aren't listening. They're panicking."

"Why are you telling me? You had a national audience."

"Giving people bad ideas is your job. You give away bad ideas like little viruses every time you sneeze a sentence. You and your do-gooder followers have been driving the planet into a hole. It's not just this—" he waives a dismissive hand over the Breezy. "People are throwing away everything they own to go—" he makes air quotes "—green. They're trading their perfectly good cars for battery-powered electric vehicles as if they are recycling a beer can. They're tearing down their houses and building green-certified buildings. People are replacing the entire infrastructure, replacing it with parts mined, manufactured and transported by fossil fuels. Green energy is another scam. Solar panels are made from plastic. And plastic is made from fossil fuels. And hectares of natural habitat are leveled. Worse, people are building bunkers and hoarding decades worth of supplies. There's even a goddamned TV show about it now. Does any of this sound environmentally friendly to you?"

Mykelti is used to his father's rants. His logic is hard to argue. "Unintended consequences."

"Unintended but not unforeseen."

"People are starting to wake up. Starting to change." Mykelti is as surprised as anyone. For over a year, he discussed every aspect of the problem, and though his listeners acted as if they understood, they still chose their creature comforts over the environment. And those that didn't listen accused him of being the one with the hidden agenda. But, now, finally, he has a following and people are changing.

"Not fast enough. There are another nine billion idiots out there. Mykelti, the average person is just that—average. They don't know what's good for themselves, much less the world. They aren't capable of thinking about the big picture. And, even if people are of above-average intelligence and well-intentioned, they don't have the time to think through all the pros and cons of every decision. All your fans are mindlessly following the latest trend that you helped create."

"We're talking about people, not sheep."

"People are sheep, and we need to herd them in the right direction, not cause a stampede. Rabble-rousing is not the change we need. Commitment is not about how many *likes* you get. Why don't you tell your fans to do something useful like unplug themselves from their twenty-four-seven drain on the power plants," he mocks. "Or move to the woods and eat grass. Better yet, I suggest you all castrate yourselves. That would work. It would take about fifty years before enough of you die off to make a difference. But that would work!"

"You call it fearmongering; I call it educating. As for you, you are a hypocrite. What are you eating that for if you believe in what you say?"

Jonathan picks up his roast beef sandwich and throws it on the ground in front of a Labrador chained to the fence, waiting for its owner. In two gulps, the sandwich is gone. After Mykelti's shock disappears, Jonathan says, "Do you know why I did that?"

"I'm sure you have some point to prove."

"You made me angry. I don't like to be told what to do. I wanted to prove you wrong. And it felt good." He takes a calming breath. "People aren't ruled by logic; they are ruled by emotions. And, when driven to extremes, there's no telling what they will do. That's why we need to take the decisions out of their hands."

"You want me to outright lie?"

"The truth has consequences. It's time to put a bandage of white lies on this mess and move forward before you unravel all my good work."

Mykelti has run out of arguments. He can't deny that the consequence of his activism has made many things worse. He had hoped it was a temporary setback. "I'm doing the best I can."

"You know what they say about the road to hell…" Jonathan sighs. "I didn't expect you to agree. The main reason I am here is so that we are both on the same page tomorrow when we visit your mother. I'd like you to put on a happy face. Not this doom-and-gloom thing you've been doing your whole life. Contrary to what you might think, I still love your mother. And we're still married. Un-fucking-fortunately for me, she saved the *happily* part of being married for you. The only reason she's still alive is because of her love for you—her pretend child. So, pretend you've done something with your life. I'd like your mother to pass with some peace of mind. That's what she wanted most in life—to be a good mother. She gave up her career; she gave up me; she even gave up herself—all for you, all so you would have a place to stand in the world."

"Everything I do has been to pay back mother for saving me. For you saving me. To prevent it from happening again. Like you said, we're on the same side. We're both trying to save the world."

"You could have fooled me," his father says. "I need to return to the hotel.

Meet me here tomorrow, and we'll go see your mother together."

Sherbert clears Mykelti's table for the next customer. "I can see where you get your sense of humor."

"My father doesn't have a sense of humor."

"Exactly."

Sherbert slumps into a chair. "Shit, I could use a cigarette if it weren't for all your nagging... Look, it's not your fault. The world will be fine with or without us?"

Mykelti laughs. "That's uncharacteristically optimistic."

"Sometimes denial is a good thing—I call it hope."

Part III:
The end of the
Anthropocene Era

The second wave of deaths: The tipping point
Last night

The point of no return was passed many decades ago, and under normal circumstances—if there is such a thing as normal—mankind, left unchecked, would have slowly suffocated itself, much like the allegorical frog in a pot of boiling water; however, mankind's slow march towards the cliff of extinction was accelerated when the Siberian Traps Supervolcano was stirred from her 250 million year slumber when a disturbance in the weather patterns tickled the indigestion growing in her belly.

It may seem unlikely that a decrease in the weight of the atmosphere, especially when measured by a few grams difference per square centimeter, could awaken such a monster as the Siberian Traps. But extrapolate that small difference to millions of square kilometers, an area the size of Europe, multiply that by an additional drop in the barometric pressure of an unseasonable thunderstorm, and compound it by a decrease of the relatively dense and heavy element of oxygen… The result is that the magma chambers were relieved of trillions of metric tons of pressure as if someone removed 13 boulders the size of Manhattan Island from the chest of an asthmatic giant.

When the methane hydrate, the product of millions of millennia of rotting vegetable matter trapped within the permafrost, was suddenly exposed to the great heat of the volcano and the reduced pressure of the atmosphere, it was instantaneously vaporized. By geological standards, it was not a full-fledged eruption, more like a flatulent husband rolling over in bed, but the explosion dwarfed Hiroshima by many orders of magnitude.

The giant bubble of methane rose high into the atmosphere and was pushed forward by the polar jet stream at unprecedented speeds exceeding 500 kph. The ionized particles caused the storm's leading edge to sparkle like Frankenstein's lab, igniting the methane and creating a firestorm that spread like liquid. So, as the doomsday prophecies foretold, the skies burned, but only momentarily as the storm front passed, because immediately thereafter, the excess methane snuffed the fires as it consumed all the oxygen. Nothing, not wood, gasoline, or even the highly flammable methane, can burn with less than a 16% concentration of oxygen in the atmosphere. The internal combustion engines that power most machines ceased to burn fuel; likewise, the internal combustion engines of animals, which also burn oxygen to fuel their bodies, shut down. Carbon dioxide rose to toxic levels. Even water vapor became a hazard as it displaced what little oxygen remained. Though the excess methane may not burn, many other chemical reactions formed poisonous gases; one byproduct being hydrogen peroxide, which created a toxic rain that fell like a whitewash.

As the event rippled across the planet, it swept through the unpopulated areas of northern Russia along the Arctic Circle, through upper Mongolia, mostly missing Japan and then flooding across the Pacific Ocean. At first, the event went largely unnoticed—there has not been a day in Earth's history that some natural disaster has not befallen something somewhere—except by some seismologists that suspected Russia was advertising her superiority by doing more underground nuclear bomb testing.

Due to the atmospheric inversion layer preventing the dispersion of gases, the storm slammed into the United States' western seaboard like an immense tsunami, breaking upon the skyscrapers, blowing out the windows, flowing through the streets like rivers, washing over any obstacle, and drowning both cars and people in unbreathable gases. The storm piled up against the Coastal Mountains until the pressure from behind caused it to surge forward once more, rolling over the Rockies, speeding down the other side, flattening the corn of the Great Plains, and causing North America's lakes to erupt their stored gases like a string of firecrackers. The Sun did not rise on the storm until it reached the Midwest, and until that point, most animals, including humans, died quietly in their sleep.

Doomsday
Present day

Chicago is the third largest city in the United States and is primarily composed of concrete. The concrete has displaced both flora and fauna and acts like a sponge for ultraviolet radiation. The Chicago metro area, over 30,000 square kilometers, is essentially its own ecosystem with forests of buildings and rivers of roads that create its own pressure systems (weather) and migration patterns. Chicago is known as the Windy City, but that moniker refers to the politicians blowing hot air rather than the weather. Today Chicago is a windy city in all respects, and the weather is hot! On bad days, the stagnant heat of summer, without a fresh wind or cool forests, can cause the oxygen to drop 3–6 points. It is not unusual for dozens of elderly people in their claustrophobic, outdated, high-rise apartments to die; it is typically blamed on the heat. Today the hot, low-pressure, hypoxic megapolis acts like a magnet for the oncoming super-storm.

§ § §

Mykelti has the television tuned to one of many non-stop news stations. Now that he has a podcast, he needs to get his daily dose of gossip to stay informed on public opinion, and, as always, he's hoping that oxygen depletion is creeping into the mass consciousness. But today, he is distracted. Today he must console his dying mother. He tried calling her, but the phone lines are busy. If he were listening more closely—if the newspeak wasn't generally so melodramatic as to turn deaf ears—he would have heard:

> *"Unprecedented reports of mass deaths in several US cities. As of now, there is no known cause, but the authorities are ruling nothing out. Many speculate a resurgence of terrorist activity. Perhaps a biochemical attack or genetically engineered super—"*

It's a hot, but beautiful day, so Mykelti decides to walk to the smoothie shop to meet his father. *It will be nice to get some fresh air,* he thinks. *Before I get caught between my parents.*

In the background of his existence, the news anchors continue to narrate; however, the news is many hours delayed to appeal to the breakfast crowd, and they are unaware that the disaster continues to march forward.

"We have just received exclusive footage. What you are seeing here is an aerial view of Seattle. No ground crews have been able to get within twenty miles of the city due to the extraordinary amount of abandoned vehicles clogging the arterial roads."

Images of the skyline scroll across the television. Buildings sparkle against a brilliant sky. The news anchor heaves an unprofessional sigh of relief.

"Nothing appears out of the ordinary. It goes without saying, we are glad to see the city is still standing. We're getting a closer look now. I must warn viewers—the images you are about to see are graphic—"

Mykelti feels like he is sleepwalking to the smoothie shop. The streets haven't been this quiet in Chicago for years. *Maybe I'll have a coffee,* he thinks. Coffee is the only luxury he allows himself in this world. Coffee is shipped long distances. It has no calories or vitamins. And it goes against his podcast mantra. *I'm still human. I need something to live for!* Mykelti sighs. His father is right: everybody believes what they are doing is for the greater good, even if it is to buy a moment of peace. That's part of the problem; on some subconscious level, the entire world knows something is wrong—billions of people are trying to buy a moment of peace. Despite preaching to millions on his podcast, exposing their fear to their conscious minds, and despite more and more people changing every day, their positive effect, if anything, is immeasurable. It seems hopeless. If anything, the recent pandemics have taught Mykelti that the world will never agree on a cause nor a solution. *How many people will it take before the world reaches a critical mass of agreement?* he wonders. *Fifty percent? Two-thirds? Eighty? Certainly, a large percentage of the population—easily recognized by their lifeless limbs and dull eyes, like real-life zombies—has effectively checked out. Can the remainder of the population make up the difference? Carry their dead weight?* Mykelti laughs at his accidental pun.

Outside the smoothie shop sits a cosmopolitan woman in a wide-brimmed hat with a white toy poodle tied to her chair. She appears as serious as any lawyer, doctor or business person, but she is just posting a photo of her breakfast sandwich, smoothie and coffee. In Cameroon, any one of those things would've been a luxury. *Maybe Father is right,* he thinks again. *What is the purpose of telling the common person of impending doom?*

Mykelti wants to enjoy his coffee at a table until his father arrives, but a group of elderly people from the nearby assisted living facility form a long queue. Mykelti can't even see if Sherbert is working. Just then, a stiff breeze knocks over half-empty cups and ruffles the umbrellas. Distant explosions echo off the sides of the city's artificial canyon. Mykelti follows everyone's awestruck gazes down the road. Pyrocumulus clouds tower over the city, while below, billowing orange clouds overflow Chicago's skyscrapers like meringue frosting pushed over the edge of a cake. As the wall of meringue approaches, it is heralded by exploding windows, fire hydrants erupting, and sewer caps popping off in rapid succession. *Boom. BOOM. BOOM!!!*

The straight lines of traffic suddenly go crooked. Some cars hop the curb and plow through pedestrians and storefronts. Behind Mykelti, a woman loses her balance, falling into the elderly group, toppling them like bowling pins. Their bones pop and break when they hit the ground. Mykelti turns to help. Feels faint. Stumbles and tries to recover his balance, but his legs have no will left to cooperate, and he collapses on the pavement. A cry of pain escapes his control. Around him, people fall to the ground like rag dolls.

Nearby a girl wearing pigtails and a pink dress plastered with her blueberry smoothie lies askew on the road. Her outstretched hand trying to find her mother. For a moment, Mykelti is transported back to his village amidst the broken trees and crushed huts. His hand desperately seeking Tanginika. The nightmare he had been trying to outrun has finally caught up with him. He was given a second chance but failed, and this time he has lost not only his village but the world. "Not again!" he cries but doesn't recognize his own voice because the density of the air has caused his vocal cords to resonate in a deep timber, the opposite effect as inhaling a balloon full of helium.

In the buildings above, office workers stare down with horror. The automated ventilation systems of the high-rises give the office workers a few more minutes of fresh air, but soon the buildings become towering death traps as the machines pump methane and carbon dioxide into their rooms and lungs. As if it is a towering inferno, the office workers hurl chairs at the windows attempting to let fresh air in. Windows shatter, but it only hastens their death.

A jumbo jet pinwheels out of the orange meringue into a high-rise apartment building several blocks away, showering the city with broken brick, shards of aluminum and unburnt jet fuel. At any moment, there are dozens of airliners circling O'Hare Airport. The tsunami of dead air swats most planes out of the air like flies. The rest simply fall to the ground as their engines run out of oxygen. Planes, helicopters and drones bombard Chicago like a blitzkrieg, but the bombs don't explode.

Suddenly, of its own accord, Mykelti's body spasms, banging his limbs painfully into the concrete. He is surrounded by the death throes of people as their bodies spasm like beached fish gulping air. They are drowning in an ocean of dead air—asphyxiating. Ironically, it isn't the lack of oxygen, but the excess of carbon dioxide in the bloodstream that the body senses as pain. They have a chance to survive, unlike some neighborhoods caught in low-pressure, micro-pockets of the storm. At lower pressures, a person can asphyxiate no matter how much oxygen is in the air. But these residents didn't have time to asphyxiate; they died as their blood boiled like a diver rising too fast from the depths of the ocean.

I'm too late, Mykelti thinks as he lies cooking on the hot summer concrete. *I saw this coming. I tried to stop it, but I just made things worse.* Helplessness and desperation brew another storm within him, but sudden fatigue overwhelms him, tempting him to fall into eternal sleep. *Life is hard. I'm tired. I deserve a rest.*

As Mykelti lies on the sidewalk gasping for breath, he watches the skies, mesmerized by the beauty. It is true that your life flashes before your eyes right before you die; however, it wasn't the life he lived, but the life he wished he had lived. Perhaps it was a revelation or epiphany, but not the kind that would give his life a last-minute sense of purpose. *Well, Mykelti, you tried...* his spirit sighs, trying to justify this as the end result of his life.

As Mykelti's consciousness fades, a ghastly figure, backlit in orange clouds, hobbles towards him and wraps a gnarly knuckled hand around the back of his head. The figure leans closer and uses its other hand to force open Mykelti's mouth. *Has it come to this already?* He wonders if he is about to be robbed. Or, perhaps, humanity had already degraded into mindless cannibalism. Or...

§ § §

Humanity did not come to a grinding halt as much as a slow-motion, quiet bump of crushed metal and stifled screams, as most people simply fell asleep before tragedy befell. Others, whose hearts labored frantically to pump blood to the brain, had their last thoughts cut short by heart attacks and strokes. And, still, others thinking, "I'm going blind," as their world shrank into a pinpoint of light as they fainted into the arms of their lover. Many tried to shout or whisper profound last words, but they had no air left in their lungs. And, many died never hearing those words deemed more valuable than any others: "I love you." Worse were those who died alone. And worst of all were those that lived with sights that could not be unseen and screams that could not be unheard. Perhaps the most surprising thing about the apocalypse was how many people welcomed death as it released them from their routines and self-imposed, first-world problems, like not drinking when all the drinks are free, or not needing to work yet being restless with boredom, or having the world at their fingertips but being distracted from what really matters.

The Great Purification and Trial by Fire were no longer metaphorical myths. There are many prehistoric and ancient personifications for this diva of destruction like Thanatos, the Greek daemon of death, the Four Horsemen of the Apocalypse, the Hindu deity, Shiva the Destroyer—all of which have diplomatic immunity to purify the Earth of evil. If one were to examine the storm objectively as a scientist, the Great Grandmother of Superstorms—if one were to honor her with a name and gender like humans are fond of doing—was neither good nor bad, but the Earth restoring homeostasis. She had loaned humans their bodies and their buildings; now, it was time to collect rent.

If time travel were possible and history buffs stood by to observe the onset of the apocalypse, their impression would be how peaceful it was as the birds fell out of the trees like autumn leaves and the people collapsed like puppets without strings. However, if emotions are a physical energy, the death cry of Earth's children would echo into the universe like a piercing beacon of distress.

The children of the storm
Ongoing

When the Great Grandmother of Superstorms reached Lake Michigan, it unleashed a great storehouse of carbon dioxide and methane in the rotting sediment. The lake exploded into bubbles, flattening everything near its shores, contributing its latent power to the storm, which gobbled a breath of fresh air and leaped forward to inhale all the Great Lakes. It flowed over the Eastern Seaboard, sucked more life out of the Atlantic Ocean, drowned all of Europe, and arrived back in Asia.

In a geological instant, the superstorm transformed the surface of the planet and forever changed the global weather patterns. However, the storm did not end after one circumnavigation. In the Northern Hemisphere, superstorms fringed by tornadoes repeatedly raked across the continents, snapping trees and flattening houses. They melted glaciers and spawned hurricanes that drowned islands. The Southern Hemisphere was temporarily spared, but soon the deoxygenated wind engulfed the Earth and spawned cyclones that, due to the Coriolis effect, rotated the opposite direction, like water going down a toilet bowl, and ravaged coastlines that had never seen a cyclone before and penetrated deep inland. In turn, the low-pressure zones spawned more earthquakes, which caused more volcanoes to erupt, which triggered tsunamis and avalanches. Every natural disaster known—and some unknown—befell mankind in a few dozen rotations of the Earth. If certain lands were missed by the immediate impact of the changing weather patterns, they would eventually suffer. Deserts would be flooded, and rainforests would dry up and blow away.

Had conditions been slightly different, had mankind not been slowly burning its methane, reducing the storm's potential, had the Earth not been scheduled to leave its current Ice Age, had the global firestorm blanketed the Earth in clouds, it would have been the onset of Snowball Earth again. Instead, it was the Runaway Greenhouse Effect; enough methane and enough sunlight remained to melt the North Pole. Now, instead of reflecting sunlight, the Arctic absorbed the Sun's energy, and, as the Arctic warmed, it released more methane, thus more warming. This caused more ice to melt and more water to evaporate, which is also a greenhouse gas… and so the Earth spiraled out of control.

The aftermath
Moments later

Except for the pouring rain, silence has befallen the city—there are no sirens, no one coming to the rescue. Mykelti's vision slowly swims back into focus. Looming over him appears to be Thanatos, the figure of death himself. He panics and squirms on the streets of Chicago, trying to shrug off the hands wrapped around his head, but they tighten their grip.

"Hold on, son. You're okay. Take a deep breath."

Through the fog of his thoughts, Mykelti realizes that the undead don't console their victims. As ridiculous as this may seem, it is the best rationalization that his mind—the product of too much pop culture—can deduce. It takes a concerted effort to stop squirming and breathe. The world sharpens as if dialing the focus ring on a camera, and he realizes that a man, a very old, haggard and gray man has a plastic mask cupped to his mouth and nose.

"There you go. You'll be okay. Just breathe." Mykelti sucks in the air greedily, clamping down on the man's wrist. "Okay, okay. Hold on, my turn."

The old man removes the medical breathing apparatus and inhales deeply before returning it. "We seem to be the lucky ones," he says. "If it weren't for this here iron lung—" he indicates a green canister of compressed oxygen on a two-wheeled dolly— "we'd both be like all these others." He gestures widely.

Mykelti follows his hand. It's a peaceful scene, except everything is slightly out of order. The cars are no longer filed in law-abiding queues. The streets are strewn with bodies. Most lay motionless, yet in positions as if they were still trying to walk or run or scream. Some twitch with irreparable brain damage, alive but not for much longer. While life on the ground fades away, the atmosphere rages: orange clouds boil and roll east, steam billows from broken radiators all around, and a nearby building smolders from the impact of a helicopter.

"Hold on, my turn again. I ain't what I used to be," the old man's sentences deflate as they go.

"What...?" Mykelti croaks.

"Looks like we missed the last boat to the rapture. If you can get your legs under you, we should go."

Mykelti props himself up on an elbow. If it was the rapture, no lucky souls bodily ascended to heaven; instead, they lay rotting where they fell. More likely, the event was the result of mankind's foolishness. Either way, doomsday has arrived. *It's quiet—deathly quiet,* he thinks... except for a baby's soft cry. "Did you hear that?" He levers himself to a standing position, but stumbles and falls to the ground again. There is barely enough oxygen in his bloodstream to power his brain, much less his muscles. He crawls forward, desperate to rescue the baby and accidentally drags himself through a puddle of scalding water that recently poured out of a broken radiator. Mykelti rolls to the side, burnt and gasping for air.

"Slow down, there. Take a deep breath. There ya go. Easy now."

As soon as Mykelti is able, he stands and stumbles towards the muffled cry. He opens the door of a car that ran up the curb. Had it not been caught on a telephone pole, it would have shattered Mykelti's body like a glass bottle. The limp body of the driver rolls out the door until the seat belt catches. Mykelti lifts her back into the seat and shakes, harder and harder. "Wake up, lady," he commands. But when her head lolls to the side, he sees her eyes dull, lips blue, hands curled, the veins in her neck soft, motionless—dead. Mykelti remembers the look well from long ago when he scrambled from friend to friend, trying to shake them awake. It ignites the helpless feeling he had as a child.

The baby's cries grow softer. Mykelti throws open the back door to reach the baby seat. He's shocked at the baby's blue visage. Mykelti's research required working at high altitudes, so he recognizes cyanosis. It means the baby is critically low on oxygen. It's one of the first warning signs of altitude sickness. Working at high altitudes also forced Mykelti's body to acclimate to low levels of oxygen, which meant his lungs grew more robust, his veins and arteries grew more copious and red blood cells multiplied. It's the reason that many athletes will train at high altitudes, because when they return to the lowlands, their bodies are supercharged with all the extra oxygen they can digest. This training helped Mykelti survive. "Give me the oxygen."

The old man hesitates.

"C'mon," Mykelti urges.

"Stop! You can't save them all. If you want to be a hero, you have to save yourself first."

These words would echo throughout the rest of Mykelti's life, but, for now, the only thing Mykelti understands is the need to save the baby, to finally make a difference, regardless of the cost.

Seeing Mykelti's resolve, the old man shrugs, takes a deep breath and gives up the mask. Mykelti takes a quick breath before putting the mask over the baby's entire face. He palpitates the chest and doesn't stop until the baby takes a deep breath and screams.

"Let's go," says the old man. "There's more air in the old folks' home."

Mykelti unbuckles the baby and grabs the diaper bag. The old man scowls.

It's a slow walk with many stops, making him burn with pain and feel as old as his savior. They pass no more living humans; even the pigeons are dead at the feet of their coffeeshop crumb givers.

In the lobby of the old man's assisted living facility, the elderly people and their aides appear asleep in their chairs. The only apparent clue that anything is out of the ordinary is that everyone is a ghostly blueish-gray, especially their lips. As Mykelti approaches, he says, "Hello? Are you okay? Can I help?" but gets no response. One elderly lady's arm hangs awkwardly beside her wheelchair. He grasps the hand. It's cold and lifeless. Her veins are prominently blue, and her shriveled fingertips are purple like raisins. After a quick check, he discovers they are all dead.

"Don't worry about them. They were half dead to begin with. Here—" the old man disconnects the mask and oxygen tank from a person with their face resting on a stack of pancakes like a pillow— "She won't be needing this."

But, as the old man yanks the cords off, the woman comes back to life with a fright, "Fitzpatrick, what are you doing? Help! He's trying to kill me. I always knew you had it in for me."

"Mildred, relax! You're okay. We thought you were a goner."

Mildred sees Mykelti. "Who's he? What's happening? Ah…" she gasps for air. Fitzpatrick tries to reattach her mask, but her flailing arms prevent him. "Stop," she tries to shout but has run out of air. Mykelti rushes over and holds her arms down until Fitzpatrick can get the mask on.

The effort leaves them all faint and short of breath. Mildred is hyperventilating, her eyes opening wide with each inhale. The old man collapses on the musty couch. Mykelti slumps hard into a chair, and the baby whimpers in a way designed by God or evolution to tug on the heartstrings. The small group of survivors are surrounded by elderly people slumped over their breakfast and games and nurses lying on the floor as if taking an afternoon nap.

As they catch their breath, Mykelti tries to fill in the blanks. "How did you know what to do out there?"

"I've been using this thing so long, being out of breath and turning blue in the face comes between shaving and breakfast," says the old man. "You're lucky saving that baby didn't get us all killed."

"Then why'd you save me? Isn't—" Mykelti runs out of air before he can finish.

"You're breathing wrong. Watch. Inhale deeply. Hold. Let your lungs soak it up. Then exhale your sentences to make room for the next deep breath."

"Isn't your philosophy that we need to all save ourselves first?"

"It is, and I did. Look, don't take it the wrong way... You're no one special. Saving old Bernice or even that baby would be like tying myself to a sack of potatoes. Hell, if you want the truth. I needed help. I chose you because you're a strong lad."

Another person rounds the corner using a wheeled walker and oxygen concentrator. "I thought I heard something. Am I missing the party?"

"Agnes, you're alive."

"Fitzpatrick. Mildred. Ooh. Who is this handsome young lad?" she says with wry humor.

As Fitzpatrick deflects her banter, Mykelti takes deep breaths until suddenly, the oxygen jumpstarts his thought process. Fitzpatrick isn't the only one alive. Everyone that had supplemental oxygen is alive. That means—

"My mother." Mykelti jumps up and immediately becomes woozy and slumps back into the chair.

"Now, hold on there. Let's get our bearings. Make a plan."

"I have to get to her before it's too late."

"I understand, son. It won't hurt to check the news first. Don't ya think?"

Hearing that causes Mykelti to reactively check his phone. He has no messages, but a quick check of the news apps shows them all blinking red.

Fitzpatrick finds the remote, and surprisingly, the TV flickers to life. "Behold! Our window to the rest of the world."

The television floods the room with visions of Chicago, not the Chicago of today, but the idealized stock footage of a thriving city of culture and commerce. A newscaster narrates:

...reporting to you from our Atlanta headquarters. This just in: reports indicate that the same fate has befallen Chicago that has afflicted Seattle, San Francisco, Los Angeles, Denver, Houston, Phoenix. I'm sorry, we don't have more information at the moment. Our local crews have not been able to report. It may be an equipment malfunction. Authorities have declined to comment. The possibility of a terrorist attack, however, does—

Just as Mykelti marvels that his survival depends on the infotainment industry, the screen goes blank and then flashes as the station gets commandeered by the Emergency Alert System. Teletype scrolls across the screen, and after the ear-splitting warning sound, an artificial voice narrates the text:

```
We interrupt this broadcast with the following vital
emergency message from the Midwestern Department of
Military Affairs Division of Emergency Management,
Civil Department of Defense, and the Emergency Alert
System. The following is a Civil Danger Warning that
presents a significant and immediate threat to the
civil population. First and foremost, we urge you to
stay calm, and remain where you are. Second, follow
the instructions of any emergency personnel, including
ambulance, fire, police and/or military. The respond-
ing emergency personnel will determine what emergency
protocol is required. Stay tuned to this station for
further information and instructions. If you hear a
wailing siren (rising and falling in pitch), please
seek shelter immediately, and take necessary precau-
tions as directed during any emergency broadcast. Stay
tuned. An Immediate Evacuation (EVI) or Shelter in
Place Warning (SPW) order may follow.
```

The message is repeating on all channels. Fitzpatrick mutes the television. Outside, wailing sirens grow louder. It becomes clear to Mykelti that his worst fears have come true...

"Looks like the safest thing to do is get the hell out of Dodge," Fitzpatrick says melodramatically, his bulldog expression and wrinkles adding to the effect.

The scientist inside Mykelti calculates that if this weather system has affected everything between the West Coast and Chicago, then it will affect the entire world. "There is nowhere to go," he says. "I need to find my mother."

"No offense, she might be gone already."

"As long as the power is on, she's alive."

"What about the rest of us?" Mildred says.

"My mother worked for the United Nations Climate Council. She'll know what happened. What to do." Mykelti had been so single-mindedly trying to save the world that he had hardly considered what to do if it actually ended.

"And what might that be? Wave a magic wand? Turn back time?" says Mildred.

"Even if the rest of the country still exists, waiting for help could take days, maybe weeks or months," says Mykelti. "I doubt FEMA is capable of managing a disaster of this magnitude. I— We can't wait for help. I need to go to them. I'm sorry." He hopes that he doesn't sound disingenuous.

"You're leaving us here to die."

"You'll be okay," Mykelti says. "You must have a week's worth of food and water; more if you raid your neighbor's apartments."

"What about that baby!?" says Fitzpatrick sternly.

Mykelti had forgotten about the baby. He won't have time or energy to stop every minute to give the baby air. "It's better off here."

"Mildred's right. Leaving that baby here—with us is like a death sentence," says Fitzpatrick. "How many more miles do you think this old jalopy has left?"

In the background, the television continues with its near useless information: "—and we'll forward your call to the appropriate Dispatch Center—"

"What can I do? Like you said, I can't save you all."

Fitzpatrick is quieted by his own words. "So, who are you going to choose?"

"I need to find my mother. She may have a solution to save us all. I'll be back before you know it."

"And, if not…"

Mykelti doesn't have an answer. All his life, he has run headlong towards his ideals, failing again and again…

"You're leaving us all to fucking die!" Mildred's volume increases with her anger. In her time, it was forbidden to even utter *damn;* now, her more taboo words give her curses extra poison.

"We all have to make our choices, Mildred," Fitzpatrick says.

"Do you want to die, Fitzpatrick? Agnes?"

"I've had a good life," says Agnes. "Maybe my time has come. What's left anyways?"

"Look, kid. When it all comes down to it, we're all just people," Fitzpatrick says. "It doesn't matter if you choose your family or a stranger; we're all the same in the eyes of God. You've made your choice. I hope it makes a difference to you."

"I'm not thinking of myself; I'm thinking of my mother—of humanity."

"Look, you want some words of wisdom!?" says Fitzpatrick. "I'll boil my life lesson's down into one simple sentence for you: You can perform miracles, and there's no guarantee anyone will give a rat's ass except you. Maybe your mother's worth saving… Maybe not. Humanity? God only knows. How about you? Are you worth saving?"

Mykelti looks downtrodden.

"Okay. I didn't mean to hurt your feelings. Look. If you're going out there, you'll need a lesson in how to use this equipment," Fitzpatrick says, referring to some supplies he ransacked from the nurses' station. "Now, this here is an oxygen concentrator. A portable oxygen therapy machine, that's the fancy name. Everything's gotta have a damn fancy name nowadays. It takes the oxygen out of the air. It's small and convenient, but since there doesn't seem to be much oxygen left, it probably won't do much good. So, you'll have to go with the old iron lung variety—condensed bottled oxygen. Problem is they're heavy, and there's no telling how many canisters you'll use. But you're young. You'll only need a breath here and there, just enough to keep you going. Now, this here is your alarm. It's an oxy-something-or-other. It measures how much oxygen you have in your blood. The saturation. It goes on the tip of your finger like this," Fitzpatrick gives a clumsy demonstration. "Wait a few seconds, and you'll get a readout. Now, every time that number dips down into the low nineties, stop and take a breath. Don't let it get too low, or you'll pass out. And watch your heart rate. Can't let that get too high."

"Why are you all so calm? So rational?"

"I don't have much left but my name and my dignity—that's one of the benefits to getting old. It strips away everything you hold dear: your youth fades; your children leave; your loved ones die; your body begins to fail; your accomplishments are forgotten. For some, like George, here—" Fitzpatrick points to a man that Mykelti thought was dead but whose chest moves slightly and eyes stare unblinking at the wall— "you don't even remember your own name, just a mouth to be fed and an ass to be wiped. It's all good practice for when there's nothing left to lose but to meet your maker. It puts things in perspective. This, too, shall pass. All that crap."

"What do you have left to live for?"

"Same as anyone; I'm enjoying the show. And, it's getting really interesting."

Mykelti remembers Sergei's words; maybe there's not much left to do but *enjoy the show*. On the other hand, if there's any chance whatsoever, he must keep going. "Here." He hands the baby to Fitzpatrick. "There isn't much time. I have to go. Maybe it's not too late…"

"Sure, kid. I'll watch your sad sack of potatoes. Thanks for asking," he says sarcastically.

"I'm sorry," Mykelti says.

"Let's be honest with each other. Times are changing, and we owe ourselves honesty. In desperate times that's all we got—our integrity. Do you understand me?"

"I'm not sure I do," he says, fearing he's being criticized. Leaving may well be Fitzpatrick's death sentence.

"I reckon it's a lawless world now, so the only law is a man's word. And you won't be able to give him but one chance to show his salt. Take this from an old man who knows better—that bit of advice goes for yourself as well. You won't have the luxury of pulling the wool over your own eyes anymore. Be true to yourself. That's all ya got."

"I'm sure help will be here soon," Mykelti says, but realizes he's lying already, more to alleviate his guilt than reassure a dying man.

"If this ill wind blows again, there won't be anyone can save me. Don't worry, son. One more death ain't but a grain of sand on the heap. Do what ya gotta do. God speed."

Mykelti squeezes Fitzpatrick's papery hand goodbye. "Thanks for the advice."

"Come back if you want some more. I'm full of it." He winks.

Mykelti tries to sneak out, but not before Mildred curses him, "You're leaving us to die! You'll have to live with that!"

The race to save mother
Hours later

Mykelti stumbles and bursts through the doors into a surreal world. A suffocating miasma from the firestorm hangs in the air. The mirrored windows of the skyscrapers reflect the orange skies like a beautiful sunset. It is strangely peaceful, as if the hand of God reached down and flipped off the switch. Corpses and cars litter the streets, but as if sleeping or parked in haphazard arrangements. Nothing moves except the smoke from smoldering cars and buildings. The city would be an inferno if enough oxygen were left for combustion.

Mykelti pauses, inhales deeply several times before racing forward. Even with the bottle of condensed oxygen Fitzpatrick gave him, Mykelti feels woozy. It takes all his stamina to maintain a fast walk, sucking oxygen greedily. His surging adrenaline helps keep his feet moving. The whole world may be dead for all he knows, but that concept is currently too far from reach to comprehend. He's motivated, like most people, by the immediate concern and solution to his happiness, which, in this case, is to save his mother.

It will take me hours to reach the hospital, he thinks. *She might not have that much time.* He had always taken a taxi. Now, the world is at a standstill with cars as far as the eye can see. Most with the keys still in the ignition, but there is no way through the traffic jam. Around the corner, Mykelti finds a scooter. The owner is sprawled on the ground nearby, seemingly uninjured. Mykelti kneels beside her. "Ma'am, are you okay?" He rolls her over. Her eyes are wide open, but dry and dull—unmoving. He takes her helmet. "I'm sorry," he says. It is the only thing he can think to say or do to soothe her soul. He sets the scooter back on its wheels and turns the key. The starter whirrs and clanks. Inside the engine, the spark plugs spark the gas vapor, but without enough oxygen, the fuel won't ignite. He could have thrown a book of matches into a lake of gasoline and nothing would have happened.

Mykelti notices a nearby bicycle. He untangles the messenger from his bike and pulls him up onto the sidewalk out of harm's way, as if the traffic will suddenly start moving. Already, Mykelti is realizing how meaningless his actions are. He had spent years of his life learning the rules of this society, and suddenly they are gone. Nonetheless, he obeys the invisible rules as he rides toward the hospital, wearing his helmet, staying on the right and swerving around cars and up onto the sidewalk, if necessary. Often he carries the bike over broken glass or piles of cars and bodies.

Nothing appears alive in all of downtown Chicago except some fleeting shadows and disturbing sounds, possibly looters lurking. Mykelti heads for the open trails on the lakefront, only to discover that cycling is even more difficult. The lakefront is a frothy mess of sand, mud, garbage, trees snapped in half, and broken boats strewn helter-skelter, some thrown up on land. It appears like a tsunami had erased the lakefront. It is difficult to cycle through the mud and around the corpses of joggers, sightseers and their dogs, or birds that lay in clumps of feathers where they had fallen out of the sky in mid-flight, and squirrels that dropped out of the trees like the acorns they chase. Mykelti gasps for air, trying to go faster, trying to outrun the faces—the death mask, is it called? So many faces of surprise and anguish, but the ones etched into his memory are those frozen in the dreams of a lost future.

As Mykelti arrives at the hospital, the sliding glass doors open automatically. He doesn't stop and cycles inside. When he can coast no further, he jumps off his bike. The bike, severed from its soul, falls to the ground in a disrespectful heap like the other bodies strewn in the lobby.

He gets on the elevator and punches the thirteenth floor. Halfway up, the lights flicker and the elevator shudders. "C'mon." He bangs on the panel hitting more buttons. It's just a hiccup in the power, and the elevator lurches forward. The doors open to a scene that is becoming familiar: bodies draped over furniture, littering the floor, and some seated in their chairs, still staring at the phones in their laps. Mykelti turns left and is surprised to hear moans. A bedridden man reaches towards him, "Help," his feeble voice cries.

Mykelti enters the room, unsure how to help. This person doesn't have long to live, but neither does his mother. He is wracked with indecision. Fitzpatrick's words echo in his head, "If you want to be a hero, you have to save yourself first." And, by extension, that meant saving his mother, their lives long ago intertwined by fate. Mykelti hopes she will know what to do. "I'm sorry. I'll be back," he says to the stranger and races down the hall. Moans and pleas for help echo out of many rooms. The patients on their supplemental oxygen and ventilators have ironically outlived their caregivers.

His mother lay motionless, looking out the window. She isn't in a hurry to turn around and doesn't seem surprised that he is there. "It's been quite the climactic ending to an old lady's life, wouldn't you agree?"

The television shows the firestorm rolling over Chicago. In the foreground, more outstretched hands film the oncoming disaster on their cellphones. "—deemed uninhabitable. A humanitarian emergency has been declared in the following cities—"

She turns off the television. "They hardly say anything new anymore. It's mostly the Emergency Alert System on repeat. I think everybody left alive has gone home to their family. Like you, Mykelti. I knew you would come. It's poetic, isn't it? I found you among the ruins of your village. Now you find me among the ruins of mine."

"I'm sorry. I was too late."

"You're not too late. You're here."

"No, I mean the world. Nobody listened. I failed." His thoughts spin in disbelief. His life's work, gone—not just gone—useless. Worse than useless.

"Oh, Mykelti, what more could you have done? You didn't fail. The world didn't want to succeed. Not by your definition of success, anyway. People listened, but they chose differently. They lived their lives until the end: birthday parties, job promotions, picnics in the park, first dates, vacations and retirements. Had they listened, they wouldn't have had lives worth living. Admit it, Mykelti, you haven't been living your own life. You haven't been living for a long time."

"What's there to live for now?"

"It's not too late. It's the same reason as always."

"Well—" he gestures outside to the smoldering buildings with broken windows. "There is no more world left to save."

"The world needs you now more than ever."

"Does that mean— Please tell me there's a plan. The United Nations has a plan!? We have a plan!? Don't we?"

"Oh, Mykelti, what do I know? I'm a diplomat. That's your father's department. But I'm sure he—"

Mykelti notices her oxygen monitor is blinking red. The flickering power is disrupting the air supply. "You're almost out of air. Hold on."

"No, Mykelti. Let it go."

"What are you talking about?" Before she can answer, Mykelti runs down the hall knocking boxes over. It takes a long time to find the nurse with the keys and longer to find the room with the oxygen. The whole time moans from the dying patients are pinging him like cell towers every time he passes within range.

Mykelti rushes back to his mother. She's barely conscious. He rolls in an oxygen tank, cranks the valve open and places the mask over her face. "Breathe deep, mom. You're going to be okay. C'mon. There's plenty more where this came from," He says, squeezing her hand, pumping life back into her.

"Mykelti, you've always had a big heart. But, it's time to learn how to look out for yourself."

"That being said—" he squeezes life into her hand one more time— "the other patients need air, too." He rushes out of the room once more to bring bottles to all the other surviving patients. But the effort is obviously futile except to buy another hour of life. Fitzpatrick was right: he can't save them all.

When he returns, his mother asks, "Your father. Where is he? Is he okay?"

"I don't know, mom. He was supposed to meet me this morning."

"Have you tried calling him? If he was alive, he'd be here. Try the phone."

Mykelti tries his father's number. "All lines are temporarily busy. Please try your call again later." He tries the hotel with no better results.

"Maybe he's hurt. You'll need to go to him. He's still your father. He loves you."

"It's always been conditional love, mom."

"He only wants the best for you."

The phone rings. They look at each other expectantly. Mykelti fumbles to turn on the speaker as the exciting emotions that his father is alive conflicts with years of chastisement:

```
The following is an urgent message brought to you
by the Reverse 911 Emergency Notification Service on
behalf of the U.S. Department of Homeland Security's
Federal Emergency Management Agency (FEMA).

A severe threat has been detected in your area that
involves probable airborne chemical contamination
and imminent biological hazards due to inadequate
sanitation. The person or persons receiving this
phone call are ordered to evacuate the area imme-
diately following designated routes. Repeat. You
are ordered to evacuate your area and proceed to
the nearest government-designated safe zone. If you
cannot evacuate, you are advised to shelter-in-place
by remaining indoors and sealing all exterior doors
or windows. The capabilities of the authorities are
limited to immediate life-threatening situations.
The time for action is now. Do not delay.

Instructions on evacuations procedures to follow…
Citizens are required to render assistance when—
```

Mykelti hangs up.

Disappointed, his mother puts her hand on her heart, "Promise me, Mykelti, you'll look for him."

"I promise. But, I'm here—now—with you."

"It's time to say goodbye."

"Yes, it's getting late. Perhaps I should find some food and a place to sleep."

"That's not what I mean."

"Mom!"

"Your father wanted to treat the cancer aggressively. I may be alive, but it's become unbearable. I should have let nature take its course."

The tears well in Mykelti's eyes. "But, mom, I have no one else. There is no one else."

"Oh, sweetheart. What are we going to do? Go to dinner and a show? Be practical. You need the air for yourself, Mykelti."

"We need to make a plan."

"Is it my wise council you're after?" she teases. "Mykelti, I've taught you everything I know. Given you everything I have, except perhaps your freedom. I always kept you too close to home. I should have kicked you out of the nest a long time ago."

"We need to rebuild. I can't do it alone. I don't know how. I don't know if it's possible. I can't go on alone."

"It's not too late, Mykelti. It's never too late to begin again. You thought you could fix a broken world, but what you really wanted was to make the world a better place. It's never too late to make the world a better place."

"It's too late for you." Mykelti can't hold his tears back anymore.

"It's not the end of me. The soul is eternal. It's just onto the next life. In the meantime, my body will fertilize the soil for the next generation of flowers. And my ideas will live on in you, and you can seed the next generation of people. Give the future generation a message for me. Tell them our legacy is not the monuments we leave behind but the hope and dreams we pay forward, like wisps in the winds of humanity."

"You still have things left to teach," Mykelti grieves.

"Have you heard this one? A dying person gets their last wish. My wish is to die with dignity and grace, surrounded by my loved ones," she says sternly.

Mykelti is reminded of his biological mother and her tickles and big Cheshire grin. He still feels the pain of never being able to say goodbye. Mykelti musters a brave act. "Your wish is my command," he says with a bow.

"Good, I'm glad to hear that. Now, we can spend some quality time together. Think of it as a date. Not our first, but our last. We still have time to make one more memory. That's all life is about in the end." Her eyes well with tears. "Remember the time we first saw each other? I had never seen such a pathetic thing. You looked like a kitten that had been dragged through the mud. You broke my heart—or should I say?—mended my heart…?"

They reminisce through the night. His mother was right. Everything else being stripped away, their life and time together is nothing but the emotions then and the memories now.

Mykelti replaces her bottles of oxygen, one after another, as they talk through the night. In the morning, before the Sun rises, when the birds usually begin to sing, he doesn't replace the bottle. "I lied," she says softly, running out of air. "I have one more wish. Tell me—promise me—you'll be okay when I'm gone." She passes away as if falling asleep.

§ § §

Mykelti was an idealist and a daydreamer, even in Africa before the disaster. His birth mother couldn't satisfy his curiosity alone, so she raised him to be a friend to all and encouraged him to go out into the village and learn from others. Mykelti's dreams—to catch his first fish, laugh with his brothers, own a bicycle repair shop, and maybe someday, to be the tribal elder with handfuls of wisdom, like candy for children—were all erased with his village. Even the shadow of those dreams was lost when he arrived in his new home, the United States of America. Mykelti understood the word *united,* but he didn't see any tribes, just an endless flow of people in the streets. The promises of an education and modern amenities that his new parents spoke of had no meaning to him. All he knew was that he had been happy, and now he was not. Even the magical television seemed empty to Mykelti. He could not step into the picture to talk with friends or swim in the rivers and lakes. And, if he thought about his friends, it was only to see their bodies sprawled across the ground, camouflaged in mud, as if Mother Earth had cast a comforting blanket over her children before taking them home. In short, Mykelti discovered the emotion of loneliness for the first time.

Pearl, his adoptive mother, saw that Mykelti's emotions ran wild. "What is your favorite animal, Mykelti?" she asked the child.

Mykelti shrugged. His accent was still thick and vocabulary limited. To Mykelti, all the animals had a special role. He liked fish for eating and birds singing...

"What about badgers or foxes?" Pearl suggested as a lesson on the local fauna.

"I don't know."

"What about the mighty elephant? With that big trunk of theirs, they can—" she reached out with an arm and wrapped up the big-eyed boy until he giggled—"hug all their friends. And giraffes. I've always liked giraffes. I bet they can see everything from way up there. They're so pretty with the puzzle pieces on their fur. They all look so different. Not like lions. Lions look all the same to me."

"Lion. Lion is my favorite."

"Why the lion?"

"The lion is the strongest. The lion is the King of the Jungle. It protects the family. Eats the bad people."

"Ooh, scary. Being eaten by a lion. I have an idea. Why don't we eat a lion?"

"You can't eat a lion!" he giggled.

"Yes, we can. We'll make lion cookies—cookies in the shape of a lion—and then eat them up."

Mykelti, reminded of Tanginika's sweets, readily agrees.

Pearl shouts, "Dad, can you get us a step stool for Mykelti?"

"I had to improvise," Jonathan says, bringing a wooden box. "Soon, you won't need any help, will you, son? You'll be big and strong," he patted the boy on the back, his display of fatherly love more for his wife.

Pearl measured and handed the ingredients to Mykelti to pour into the mixing bowl. "Emotions are like animals. You have lions. They can seem big and scary. They can chase you. And eat you. Just like you said. But you have other emotions. They are small and friendly, like a mouse. But most people don't notice a mouse. All they can see is the lion. Do you know the story of the Lion and the Mouse?"

Mykelti shook his head.

She handed him a spoon. "Give that a good mix. No, well… Once, while a lion was fast asleep, a little mouse thought it would play a game—mice love to play games—and run around on top of the lion. This soon woke the lion, who promptly caught the mouse in his big paws and opened his jaws to swallow him whole. 'I beg your pardon, King. I was just having a little fun,' squeaked the little friendly mouse. 'Forgive me this once, and I shall be forever in your debt.' The lion laughed." Pearl held up the wooden mixing spoon like a scepter and said in a deep voice, "'I am the King of the Jungle. What could you ever do for me that I can't do for myself?' The mouse, dangling by his tail above the lion's jaws, said, 'Only a mouse can do a mouse's job.' The lion was amused by the friendly mouse. 'Well, you never know,' said the lion, and he let the mouse go. Sometime later, the lion was caught in a hunter's trap. As strong and mighty as he was, the lion couldn't break the ropes. He roared in anger, he roared in pain, he roared a warning to all the other lions and lionesses, mostly he roared for help. But, even though he was King of the Jungle, all the other animals were scared that if they let the lion go, he would eat them up." Pearl took a pretend bite at Mykelti, "Grr. As the lion grew weak, the little mouse happened to walk by. Seeing the lion look so sad, he quickly gnawed off all the ropes with his sharp mouse teeth. 'Now I know,' said the grateful lion, 'you'll never know when you need a mouse to do a mouse's job.'"

As they shaped the cookies into animals, "What happened next?" Mykelti asked. "Are they friends?"

"Great friends," Pearl ad-libbed. "The best of friends. You see, the mouse was the only animal in the jungle that wasn't scared when the lion roared."

When the first batch of cookies cooled, Pearl picked one up like a puppet and joked, "Oh no. Scary lion. He's going to eat me. But not if I can eat him first," she chomped the cookie, sending crumbs flying. "Nom. Nom. Nom."

Mykelti laughed and grabbed a lion cookie. "Nom. Nom. Nom."

His mother reached for the mouse cookie. "Ooh, shriek. A mouse."

Mykelti put a gentle hand on his mother's arm. "Not the mouse. Don't eat the mouse, mother."

Hearing "mother" for the first time brought tears to her eyes. "No." She put the mouse back. "Not the mouse. He's our friend."

"Damned Cheeseheads are winning," Jonathan said, making a dramatic return to the kitchen. "We got a new coach, a new quarterback, practically a whole new team, and we're making the same damn mistakes as last year and the year before and the year before that. How is that even possible? It's like losing is in our DNA. How am I supposed to root for a losing team year after year?"

"It's called team spirit, honey."

"God-damned Bears." *Bang!* Jonathan slammed the refrigerator door shut, causing cans to rattle and grabbed a plateful of cookies on his way back to the couch.

"No, not the mouse," cried Mykelti.

"You have to fight for what you want, kid." He offered the cookie to Mykelti.

His brothers often did the same thing. When Mykelti would try to accept the offer, they would snatch it away and laugh. He waited to see what game his new father was playing.

"Not worth the trouble, eh?" Jonathan said and then bit the head off. "You have to fight for what you want. Remember that, Mykelti."

"You're not a drill instructor anymore," said Pearl. "Besides, he's just a child."

"We all have tough life lessons to learn."

"Come, Mykelti. Let's watch the game and root for the Packers. Then we can be the winners. How is that for a life lesson?"

Mykelti giggled at the idea.

§ § §

Mykelti is jerked awake, gasping for air. He had sobbed himself to sleep, and his oxygen has run out. Fortunately, he stockpiled more bottles nearby at the expense of the other patients.

Mykelti rolls his mother's bed downstairs. The elevators are still functioning despite the flickering power, but the exterior doors have automatically locked. Habit causes him to hesitate before going through the emergency exit, which triggers the alarm to scream into the dead quiet streets. *Dead quiet,* his thoughts echo. *Yes, another cliché proven true.* The stormy skies are turning to rain.

Mykelti buries his mother in the nearest park in a bed of flowers. It seems pointless to bury his mother—he could spend his life burying the dead—except that laying her to rest is the only thing that brings comfort. It's a new day for her soul—if she was right about that. It's a new day for all the souls in the hospital. Mykelti has many messages to deliver to the future.

The search for father
24 hours

It's pouring rain now as the atmosphere purges itself of the firestorm's vapor. The hydrogen peroxide being washed out of the atmosphere is bleaching Mykelti's hair and clothes.

Where once the hustle and bustle of cars and people flowed down the street, now the only traffic is the garbage being washed down the gutters, the cups and papers that had fallen out of dead hands the day before. *Chicago is a ghost town,* Mykelti thinks. *Overflowing with ghosts.*

Mykelti alternates between giving the bike a few robust pumps with his legs and coasting. Coasting the bike saves oxygen and gives him time to think. But thoughts don't come easily. It's too difficult to process what has happened, much less make a plan. He continues to check his phone reflexively, but there are no messages, no texts. The social media feeds are filled with chatter, but it could just be bots. Even though Sherbert and Brandon's safety weighs on his mind, Mykelti heads towards his father's hotel room. His father is the only person who might know what happened. And, no doubt, he already had a plan of action.

It is an agonizing bike ride pulling the tanks behind him. Even at a slow pace, supplemented with oxygen, he overexerts himself. His body aches from the anaerobic workout. He checks his oximeter. The number has dropped into the eighties. "What did Fitzpatrick say I'm supposed to do? I can't remember."

Fortunately, his destination is within sight. The hotel glows in the early morning light, promising hospitality. The taxis, with open doors, wait for new passengers; the bellboy and his luggage cart are nearby; and the automatic doors whoosh open, inviting him in. There's a line at the counter and couches full of people waiting for their tour of the city, and the café is full of breakfasters. It's like any other day, except everyone has fallen over dead, including the concierge, which means Mykelti has no way to find his father's room.

He steps behind the counter and, as gently as possible, moves aside the worker, but the chair spins, and they fall onto the floor in a heap. He attempts to access the guest list on the computer, but the system has timed out and requires a password. What to do? He can't search every room? He rifles through the papers for names. Nothing. In the back room, he finds the mail cubicles. Half of them are stuffed with letters and messages. It's only a matter of luck that he finds a letter addressed to his father. It's from the television station where they had their interview. He rips open the envelope—*There's no harm in reading it now,* he thinks—and discovers that the "surprise guest," his father, had been staged long ago.

His father is in room twelve on the twentieth floor. *Damn!* The power is still on, and the elevators are working. *Is it worth the risk?* he wonders, *If the power goes out, I'll die in that elevator. But I might die trying to walk up twenty flights of stairs.* He's undecided. He pushes the call button. The doors open. A family lay dead, heaped on top of each other. That settles it. He commits to the stairs.

Rolling the oxygen tank up the staircase requires extra effort. *Thump. Thump.* By the fifth floor, his body burns with pain, his vision sparkles, and his chest is weak from labored breathing. He's forced to take frequent breaks to let the burning subside. By the time he reaches the twentieth floor, he feels like he has summited a mountain. After another deep breathing exercise, he continues down the hall to room twelve. He swipes the keys he took from the maid until he finds one that turns the light green. Eventually, when the power fails, the locks will stop working.

Mykelti opens the door slowly. Probably, he should have knocked, but he assumes the worst. Though he's already passed thousands of dead people, he's fearful to see what death has in store for his father. Death is cruel and unforgiving; its last act to leave everyone humbled, their flaws naked to the world. But the room is empty. A suitcase lies open on the bed. Mykelti searches the suitcase, but there are no papers, tickets or clues. The closet holds his suit and dress shoes. In the bathroom, empty bottles of medicine and canisters of Breezy. Mykelti wasn't aware his father was sick. He pockets an old bottle.

Most likely, his father is lying dead in the street or in the back of a cab somewhere between here and the smoothie shop. But where? There could be a thousand cars and miles of alternate roads. He would have liked to give his father an honorable burial, like his mother, to put closure on some of his grief. *Forgive me,* Mykelti thinks. *I tried.*

Worse than his grief is not knowing what to do next. His father always had plans and backup plans. But now what? Even though Mykelti imagined a day like this might come, he thought the changes would be slow and incremental. He thought he'd have time to prepare. At the most, he thought he might have to retire to a farm off the grid, forced to live the agrarian lifestyle. It would have been like his childhood again. But this is much worse—devastation beyond his ability to comprehend.

"What to do? Okay, first things first." Mykelti checks his oxygen level. He's running very low. Climbing the stairs took too much energy.

He has little choice but to take the elevator. It arrives filled with guests, piled on the floor, smelling of urine and feces. It's not a figure of speech, he learns, that a person can be scared shitless. He tucks himself into the corner, trying hard not to look at anyone's face—he already bears too many memories of despair—and pushes the button for the lobby.

As he feared, the power flickers, and the elevator lurches. Then the power goes off, and it coasts to a stop. A moment later, dim emergency lighting goes on. It must be the backup generator. No, that can't be right. There isn't enough oxygen for a diesel generator. It must be battery-powered.

"Now what?" he asks himself for the umpteenth time that day. He tries the open button. Nothing. It's no use even trying the alarm or call button; no one is left to come to the rescue. He picks up an umbrella and tries to leverage the door open as if using a crowbar. The umbrella snaps without budging the doors. Quickly becoming desperate, he looks around for another solution. A trapdoor in the ceiling leads to the shaft for the maintenance crew. Can he crawl out like he's seen in the movies? Or is that just movie magic? He tests the trapdoor with the umbrella. It pops open. He tries jumping, but can't reach the opening, so he hooks the umbrella around the upper corner and tries pulling himself up. But the plastic hook snaps before he can get even a few inches.

There is only one other option. He begins stacking the bodies, starting with the biggest and fattest ones. He lays two more adults on top in a crisscross to make a pyramid of humans. He climbs up their squishy bodies like a ladder. The people may be dead, but inside each one, trillions of bacteria are still thriving, producing foul-smelling gases, which get squeezed out with each of Mykelti's wobbly footsteps. Standing atop the pile, he still can't reach the trapdoor. He dismounts and, with regret, drags the bodies of two children to the top of the pile. "I'm sorry," he says, as if God watches and cares. He tries again, and just as he reaches the top, the elevator shudders back into motion. Mykelti falls on top of the heap and rolls down into the puddle of urine and intestinal juices.

The search for friends
30 hours

As Mykelti passes a corner tavern, he hears shouts and laughter, and the windows flicker with light. Excited, he parks his bike—city habits still cause him to worry that someone will steal it—and swings the door open. Inside, an array of televisions illuminates bodies slumped over the counter and tables.

His spirits fall once more until a man sitting in the back corner of the bar shouts, "Look, the second to last man on Earth! Come, let's have a drink. Celebrate the end of the world." His mouth and limbs move slow and heavy, dulled by alcohol. The televisions are like windows on the apocalypse. The great cities of the world are in disarray. "Come, sit your ass down. It's prime time Armageddon," the man laughs and pounds a beer bottle on the bar like a gavel. "Humanity zero. Mother fucking nature: one and done."

Mykelti has a bad feeling about the disheveled man. "Just looking for some friends," he says defensively. *How is this man even alive?* he wonders.

"What? I'm not good enough for you? Come sit. I insist."

Mykelti tentatively backs out of the tavern. A week ago, he might have caved to peer pressure and tried to console the man; yesterday, he might have tried to save the man; now, he is forced to choose who is worth saving. He can't blame the man for being drunk and belligerent, but he doesn't have time to wait for him to get sober. He has already made his choice; he needs to help Fitzpatrick and the baby.

"C'mon. It's the end-of-the-world party." The man throws his empty bottle at a television. The glass cracks, and the pixels scramble.

Mykelti walks out backwards. When the door swings shut, he wastes no time getting on his bike. Abandoning the man is the same as a death sentence. It's easier to leave knowing that the electronic eyes of cellphones are no longer watching him and that no anonymous figures are passing judgment on social media. But he doesn't get far. A bottle whizzes past his ear and crashes down in front of him, flattening his tires. "Damn you!" cries the man.

Mykelti drops the bike and runs off as fast as his oxygen-depleted bloodstream allows. When he's out of sight, he stops to catch his breath. "That was close!" he wheezes and realizes the rules of the world have changed. There are no more police. No firefighters to rescue him from elevators. No doctors or nurses. *One tumble off my bike, a broken collarbone, even a tiny scratch left unattended could be the end of me. I'm on my own. There's only one rule left: survive! Maybe that was the only rule all along.*

He's forced to walk, and the effort depletes his oxygen fast, so he hurries, taking long, smooth strides to the assisted living facility to find more. But when he arrives, George is dead. Fitzpatrick, Mildred, Agnes and the baby are gone. Also gone are all the spare oxygen containers. Panic causes his heart to race and his body to demand even more air; fortunately, he finds two oxygen concentrators in a supply cabinet. They are not as effective as having a supply of pure oxygen. Mykelti tests the machine to see if it can pull enough oxygen out of the air. It's slow but seems to work, and should work as long as the battery remains charged.

Mykelti's obvious next step is to go to the nearby smoothie shop and look for Sherbert. When he arrives, a sleeping dog wakes and rushes towards him until it's throttled by its leash. It's the same Labrador from a few days ago. It gives him hope that Sherbert is still alive. He rushes into the shop. He sees Sherbert's pink hair. She's slumped over the counter in an awkward position that could only mean one thing—she's dead. He rushes to her side, wheeling his oxygen cart over corpses in the process.

But it's not her. It must be a new employee. Relieved, he absentmindedly wipes the tears streaming down his cheeks. He laughs. It's an odd thing to do. Laughing over another person's empty shell. *It must be the stress,* he thinks.

He steps over her body to brew a fresh pot of coffee. This also seems ludicrous and makes him laugh. *Is this the new normal?* he thinks. *I've always hated that expression. When has my life been normal?* But now, he is climbing over people's backs to get what he wants. *Is this what civilization has come to? How fast I've fallen.* He warms a banana muffin in the microwave and grabs a roast beef sandwich. On the patio, he sits down at the only table unoccupied by bodies. The dog is running back and forth, straining on its leash. Mykelti unwraps the roast beef sandwich and tosses it to the dog. "It's your favorite." He remembers his father doing the same. He was making a point that humans aren't ruled by logic. Mykelti wonders, *What's the point of anything now when no one is left to care?*

He picks up his phone to try calling Sherbert again. He pauses a moment to try to think positive thoughts, as if his emotions have some control over the event. It seems easier not to make the call. If he doesn't, there is always hope that she is alive. But if he calls, and she doesn't answer, then she is most certainly dead. He cradles the phone in his hand as if it's Schrödinger's box. The event—whether Sherbert is alive or dead—won't be decided until he opens the box—makes the phone call. He pulls up her contact info and waits until his emotions align and he feels certain she is alive, then he pushes the button.

He lets it ring four times and then, avoiding voicemail, hangs up and tries again. The second time, it goes straight to voicemail. "Hi. I'm off fighting the machine. Leave a message."

He talks fast in case her batteries are drained or voicemail full. "It's Mykelti. I'm fine. Call me back. Don't go anywhere. I'll come to you. Be safe," he says, feeling too deflated to be the hero. He wishes someone would rescue him.

He doesn't have the heart to call Brandon. He can't take another disappointment. Brandon might be the only friend he has left in the world. It wasn't easy for Mykelti to make friends. He wasn't sure if people found him off-putting as a foreigner or because he buried himself in his work. He often overlooked pleasantries—people don't like it when you get straight to the point.

Mykelti settles into a chair on the patio. The rains have stopped, but the sky remains cloudy and a surreal orange. He wishes he had a newspaper to read about what happened. Instead, his only source of information is what he can observe in his surroundings and his imagination. He didn't think it would ever be this bad. Something must have disturbed the methane deposits in the arctic or the deep sea. An earthquake? A meteor strike like the Chelyabinsk Event? Could it have been intentional? Terrorists? Would anybody be foolish enough to risk killing us all? *Yes*, he thinks. *Yes, they would. It doesn't matter if it was a nuclear bomb or a piece of toast popping up—we are all guilty.*

Having finished the sandwich, the dog is choking itself, trying to escape, so Mykelti unties it. It jumps up and down happily, apparently having already forgotten its previous owner, who must be one of the customers nearby. Is it the woman in the fancy hat? Or the hipster couple? Or the jogger? Or is it the old smoker? He takes her pack of cigarettes. "Thanks, lady."

Mykelti can guesstimate how much oxygen remains in the atmosphere by lighting a cigarette. The cigarettes are a corporately enhanced variety with hundreds of chemical additives. Still, there's a reason bad habits are so good: if he's lucky, there's enough oxygen for him to forget about the next ten minutes of his life. He places the cigarette in his mouth with the cavalier attitude of a movie star and flicks the lighter. Nothing happens. He flicks the lighter again and gets a few sparks and sputters. A third and fourth try, fiddling with the knobs. "Damnit!" He hurls the lighter into the street. It bounces off the hood of a car, and part of him expects the backlash of an angry driver. The car gives him an idea. He opens a nearby vintage model, and after a brief confirmation that the driver is as dead as he looks, Mykelti charges the electric cigarette lighter. When hot, he touches the cherry-red lighter to his cigarette. The tobacco doesn't catch fire; instead, it fumes vapors. Mykelti chokes and looks at the tip of his cigarette. It has turned into charcoal. "Damn! How am I even alive?"

He returns to the patio to finish his meal. Nothing has moved since Fitzpatrick rescued him, since the ghosts left their machines. It's an eerie feeling, like everything has been preserved in time. In the distance, a broken fire hydrant acts like a fountain; its endless stream of water seemingly frozen. It feels like he's living in the Twilight Zone. He loved that show: all those picture-perfect American families with lives that every Cameroon aspired to, except for the horrors lurking beneath the surface. In his favorite episode, there was nothing in the world that Burgess Meredith loved more than reading books, but his nagging boss and mocking wife never allowed him the simple pleasure of sitting down and peacefully reading his books. One day, as he was hiding in the bank vault during lunch to read a book, the world was destroyed by a nuclear attack. Burgess emerged from the vault to a new world, a personal paradise with all the books in the world and all the time anyone could ask for. But, careful what you wish for: the episode ends seconds after he drops his glasses on the ground, shattering them beyond repair and becoming, effectively, blind.

That was a tragic irony. Presumably he died of boredom, but the real question was: if Burgess found a new pair of glasses—would he be happy with books as his only friends?

Mykelti wonders if he is trapped in an ironic version of his own personal paradise? Indeed, it seems like a self-fulfilling prophecy that the very thing he tried to prevent has happened. Is it some kind of divine poetic justice that everyone's version of paradise is really a personal hell?

After he finishes his coffee and muffin—what might be his last hot coffee and fresh banana muffin—he sighs at what must come next. He needs to find Brandon. Brandon had just arrived back in Chicago, so he must still be acclimated to the high altitudes of the Andes Mountains, where he was doing research. Brandon has been with him since graduate school. He believed in Mykelti when no one else would. It's hard to imagine losing his only true friend. If anyone can survive, it is Brandon; Sherbert, however... After all the needless death he's seen so far, he's surprised how much these thoughts sadden him.

No matter how much he is dreading the outcome, Mykelti needs to stop procrastinating. He picks up Schrödinger's box again and calls Brandon. No answer. Like Sherbert, the chances of Brandon being alive just went way down. Dead or alive, Brandon is probably in the lab or their apartment. Either way, he should be there already. He owes it to his friend.

The dog follows Mykelti home. He tries to shoo it away, but the dog thinks of it as a game. So he returns to the shop and throws a pile of sandwiches on the ground to preoccupy the dog while he sneaks away. He feels guilty, but he's scared of dogs. In his village, there was nothing but mangey mongrels. Most lurked in the shadows waiting for scraps, risking being beaten by sticks. But some had gone feral. As a small child, you learned quickly to avoid being surrounded by a hungry pack of dogs.

The return home
36 hours

Dejected, having not found Brandon at the lab, and having seen nothing alive but a drunk, a dog and fleeting shadows, Mykelti stumbles home, light-headed and heavy-footed. His body burns from the aftermath of thousands of cells having exploded from hypoxia, compounded by a splitting headache. *How many brain cells have I lost in the process?* He reaches his apartment without further incident, avoiding the morbid scenes by keeping his eyes glued to the ground. After four more flights of stairs, he feels like he's summited another mountain. He wishes he could open the door to a night on the couch eating popcorn and watching movies—things that have no value except to dull the senses. But now, he must face the final answer: *Is Brandon alive?*

Mykelti breathes deep to steady his nerves, but to no avail and slowly opens the door. He expects the door to creak open like a horror house, but it is silent in the thin, dead air. Everything appears normal: the television is chattering, and Brandon sits in a chair: "Cities across the world are reporting what appears to be—" Upon closer inspection, Brandon is slumped in the chair with the Chicago Times neatly folded in his lap and coffee on the table beside him. He appears as if he just fell asleep.

"Brandon? Buddy? Are you okay?" Mykelti shakes Brandon's limp body until his head rolls to the side, and his tongue lolls. He presses his forefingers against the carotid artery and feels no pulse. "Brandon…?" It is difficult for him to comprehend that the lifeless figure is actually lifeless. The thousands of nameless corpses he had passed were like rag dolls, but this was his friend. Brandon probably fell asleep as the oxygen was slowly drained from the room. *If only he had left a window open, maybe he would have woken, been able to do something… Like what? Suck the air out of the yoga ball for an extra fifteen minutes of life?*

Mykelti's emotions boil with sadness, loneliness, and most of all, guilt. Brandon wouldn't be here if it weren't for Mykelti's "wild goose chases." He was Mykelti's biggest supporter. Even when Mykelti retired, Brandon continued his research. Brandon said those in power didn't understand science. He tried to answer all their questions; however, no amount of logic ever overrode their yes-buts: Yes, but the economy… Yes, but foreign relations… Yes, but the pandemic… Yes, but the drugs and human trafficking… What would Brandon say now? "Yes, but you are all dead."

Mykelti snorts with contempt. "We've cured it all now, haven't we? We've solved all the world's problems. War. Hunger. Overpopulation. The energy crisis..." Did anyone ever care about the world? When people used to preach about saving the world, did they mean saving humanity's convenient way of life?

He splashes some water on his face to reset his mood. It feels good. It's been days since he's washed. Mykelti is mesmerized by the cool, sweet Lake Michigan water flowing out of the faucet. He had feared the faucets would run dry, but deep underground, mankind's robotic servants still perform their job dutifully.

Mykelti used to tell his audiences. "Water is commonly thought of as the most important ingredient of life. Water is so important that it is considered a human right to be given a free glass of clean, clear water. However, how often have people thought of fresh air as an essential right? There are five macronutrients considered essential to life, and oxygen isn't one of them. We can exist for months without carbohydrates, fats, proteins, fiber. Days without water. But the average person can hold their breath for only thirty seconds. If deprived of oxygen for more than a couple minutes, permanent brain damage can occur."

He tried hard to emphasize the importance of oxygen from every conceivable angle. "The invention of the Roman aqueducts was at the forefront of human civilization. And, without modern-day aqueducts and sewers to distribute and recycle water, most urban cities would become a desert. But we have no such systems in place to recycle oxygen. It is said that we are still breathing molecules of air from Caesar's last breath. But not even Mother Nature can easily recycle oxygen molecules into breathable air. Some are converted into water vapor, some carbon dioxide and some are used as building blocks in the body. About 65% of the human body is composed of oxygen—more than any other element—so all the oxygen Caesar filtered out of the air with his lungs lies in his grave or has disappeared into the ancient sewers in his waste material."

Mykelti cups his hands and drinks the water, gasping for breath between gulps. He watches the water disappear down the drain, back into the sewers. In his village, girls would spend their days gathering buckets of muddy water. Here, it pours free and clear down the drain. It's wasteful. And it wastes the oxygen needed to power the filters and pumps. But, there's no one left to care. He could plug the sink and let his apartment turn into a swimming pool, and no one would care. Mykelti walks away, allowing the faucet to run. It makes noise like a soothing waterfall, but to Mykelti, it is a reminder that nothing matters anymore—he will have to get used to it.

He grabs a couple beers from the refrigerator. Alcohol is the sixth macronutrient, but it is not essential to life. Or is it...? Since Mykelti has been in the United

States, he's lived a privileged life. The only death he experienced was his adoptive grandfather passing away from natural causes. Such a pleasant phrase: *passed away from natural causes.* Mykelti's entire village died of natural causes. Brandon died of natural causes. They were the victims of Mother Nature. However, his grandfather was the victim of himself: the natural causes were a lifetime of numbing his anxiety with cheap booze and junk food. It was a slow-motion suicide, killing hours every day. It saddened him that a man who had everything, unlike the red-eyed drunks in his old village, lived his life as if a bottle was the most important thing. But now a bottle was one of the few things left to Mykelti. He takes a healthy swig to make life—what's left of it—more bearable.

Mykelti sits down beside Brandon. "Here you go, buddy." He places a beer in the armchair's cup holder. Together they watch the city lights. The haze and smoke are dissipating, and it's as beautiful as ever—more so in the eerie orange glow of sunset. Though the city appears alive—building windows flickering with the light of televisions—there are no silhouettes in the windows, no people going about their routines of turning lights on and off, no voyeurism to be had. Certainly, somewhere a candle must have tipped over, or food left on a burning stovetop, or a cigarette dropped, but there are no fires because there isn't enough oxygen in the air. And, certainly, someone requires help, but no ambulances come to the rescue. Mykelti scans the city streets nine stories below, looking for any signs of life: humans, dogs, birds. Nothing. *What happened to Fitzpatrick?* he wonders. And, Sherbert, she's out there, too. He should go to her, but he can't bear to find her in disrespectful repose. *I'd rather remember her as she was,* he thinks.

It's only the end of the second day, and the questions are banging around inside his head, but Brandon can no longer offer solutions. They weren't always friends; that came later. It helped that they were both strangers in a strange land. They met when Mykelti advertised for a research assistant. Mykelti admired Brandon because he disagreed with his theories. It helped Mykelti fill in the holes. Brandon also made light of almost every situation, which counterbalanced Mykelti, who is predisposed to depression. If he were here, what would he say now? Mykelti struggles to find something—anything—funny about the current situation. "Not thirsty? That's a first," and takes Brandon's beer. Mykelti can almost hear Brandon replying, "Well, we always have each other," followed by a lascivious wink and thump on the shoulder.

If only he were really here, then Mykelti wouldn't have to bear the burden of these thoughts alone. He could deposit them in someone else's care. *That's rude,* he thinks. *Have I always dumped my trash on other people?* It's a minor epiphany, one that won't matter if he never sees another person again.

After one more beer in lieu of supper, Mykelti gives up for the evening. He should analyze his options and make a plan, but he's too tired. It seems like a good idea to forget his troubles until tomorrow. Mykelti throws a blanket over Brandon and wheels the chair into the hallway. "I'm sorry," he says to the unceremonious dumping of his friend and closes the door on his new morgue.

The smell of death fades fast. He marvels that his sense of smell still functions. He makes himself ready for bed, then plugs in the oxygen concentrator so that it will continue running all night, but he realizes that if the power goes out, he may never wake.

He's not sure he cares.

The third wave of deaths: The erosion of the infrastructure
Ongoing

While humanity was preoccupied with their survival, machines were left to run the world on autopilot. Perhaps if man and machine had evolved a little further, the machines would not have missed their creators, but as they stood now, they were thoughtless automatons. Any action they took had to be predicted, planned, coded and hardwired into the infrastructure. Mankind had done a thorough job of making plans and installing fail-safes; however, the last step in the backup plan was that humans, themselves, would intervene. Humans would repair the damage and restart the machines, but there were few humans left capable of repairing the machines, and fewer that even tried.

Initially, everything operated within normal parameters. Water flowed. Communication lines remained open. The streetlights went on at dusk and off at dawn, heaters and air conditioners hummed, neon signs advertised a better life, radio stations played music, and some survivors even surfed the web for pornography and gossip—two of humanity's favorite pastimes. But the infrastructure was already in disrepair before doomsday. It had become increasingly difficult to repair the damage caused by climate change, which ironically caused more damage to the climate—a downward spiral. Humanity needed to rebuild itself in a more environmentally sustainable manner, but it had squandered the free energy that oil and oxygen provided and wasted its rare, non-renewable resources on things like disposable cell phones and video game consoles. When the storm hit, most power plants were destroyed: windmills and solar arrays were ripped to shreds; trees toppled, jamming hydroelectric dams; the coal and diesel power plants could no longer burn their fuel; and even if the power plants did not fail, the safety protocols triggered a shutdown. The capacitors and batteries slowly lost their charge, and one by one, the machines powered down.

Many vital systems rely on the day-to-day maintenance of humans, like the hundreds of nuclear power plants or the millions of giant chemical vats that must be maintained at a constant temperature. Without their climate control systems to expel heat and humidity, buildings that housed humanity's most treasured belongings rotted away.

With civilization's caretakers gone to the grave, and no one left to paint exposed wood, sand rust or fill cracks, the elements quickly encroached. Fine particles of dust caught in the winds of the superstorms shattered windows and sandblasted structures. The excessive amount of carbon dioxide in the atmosphere produced carbonic acid, also known as soda water, that slowly rained down and is powerful enough to dissolve teeth, concrete and steel. The perpetual rains caused rot and mold. But, it was winter that did most of the work. The repeated freezing and thawing caused roads and buildings to swell and contract as they breathed with the seasons. Cracks appeared, and ice wedged them open even further. Nails were loosened and wiggled out. Pipes, designed to withstand thousands of pounds of pressure, burst. The buildings were soon flooded with water, corrosive dust and noxious air. There was one saving grace: due to the lack of oxygen, there was little rust, and few plants or animals left to dig their roots and claws into mankind's monuments. But mold does not need much oxygen to thrive, and it began to creep over cities like day-old bread.

So, much the same way that mankind had toppled forests to build houses, leveled hills to build roads, and dug trenches to water the thirsty, Mother Nature undid their work. It was the devolution of mankind, starting with his latest and most fragile works of magnetic storage devices and airborne messages. When the internet turned itself off, it erased 150 years of mankind's intellectual property. Even if humans magically reappeared, most of their progress would be lost: their magical boxes would be blank; they would be able to communicate no faster than a pigeon could fly, and they would have no more collective wisdom than the rotting books and artifacts left in libraries and museums—both having been long neglected in favor of the ethereal digital mediums.

Few humans left behind had the basic skills to survive like water purification, waste removal, gardening, et cetera...

Making a survival manual
Day 2-3

As sleep drags Mykelti under, he is still kicking himself. If he knew so much, why didn't he prepare for the worst-case scenario? He could have bought supplies. Prepared a bug-out bag. Identified safe places to go. The thought, "If the power fails...," grows larger and larger until he is wide awake. How could he be so stupid? Power is his only connection to the world. It's his only source of information. There are no bookstores anymore, and libraries have few modern books, nothing compared to the amount of information that is constantly being updated online.

He looks out the window. The city lights are still on. He splashes more water on his face to wake up and leaves the faucet running again. Now, it is the canary in the coal mine. Will the power fail and shut off the water pumps? As a precaution, he fills the bathtub with water. Next, he makes sure all his devices are plugged in and charging: laptop, phone, batteries and, most importantly, the oxygen concentrators. They're not working efficiently because there isn't as much oxygen in the atmosphere to extract, so he uses both simultaneously. He must not have been thinking straight for days. He'll need all his brainpower now.

He turns on the television and flips through the channels. They're all broadcasting emergency signals or reruns. Even CNN and Fox News do nothing but repeat warnings. That means the East Coast must have been hit by the same storm. He checks BBC. Nothing. He switches to his computer and checks their website. They are full of stories of the unfolding disaster, but it's been 25 hours since the BBC has posted an update. Does that mean the United Kingdom and all of Europe are down? He checks his social media feeds to see if there is any chatter. None of his friends are online. Surprisingly some topics are trending. He skims a few posts:

I was made for the zombie #Apocalypse. #BringItOn!

How many people are left alive? Let's start a count. #Survivor #001

At long last, the #Rapture. Glory be to God.

Need #HELP. Won't last long. PM me. #Milwaukee #Eastside

It's been fun. FWIW. #Doomsday

...

The feed scrolls endlessly with panicked statements. If there is anything useful, there is no time to find it, but it's reassuring to know that he is not the only one left alive.

He begins his internet search with: "What powers Chicago?" His first hit results in the answer: "Chicago is powered primarily by coal and nuclear energy." To his luck, Wikipedia has a list of power stations in Illinois. Two more clicks, and he has a map of all the power stations. The nuclear power plants are nearby, but further away, to the southwest, are windmill farms. He prints out the map. It may come in handy.

Next, he searches: "How long will the power last without maintenance?" And then revises his search to "...last without humans." The news is not encouraging. A large coal power plant requires a trainload of coal every day. That's about 130 rail cars, each carrying 100 tons of coal. The power plants require human-operated machinery to transport the fuel from the train to the furnaces. So, the power would last less than a day, maybe even less than an hour, depending how much coal was in the chutes. *Wait. What am I thinking? Coal won't burn. We must be running on nuclear power.*

Next, he looks up: "How long can a nuclear reactor last without humans?" Again, the news is not encouraging. About 48 hours after computers detect a reduced load, they will initiate safety protocols and automatically shut down. Mykelti doesn't fully understand—nor have time to understand what he is reading—but it seems that if there is nowhere to send the power, the reactors will overheat.

So far, it appears Chicago is still consuming energy: the streetlights and televisions are glowing, so it must mean the heating, air conditioning, stoves, water heaters and thousands of other electrical devices are also operating, helping to drain the power. But how long before a cascade of failures triggers the safety protocols? He remembers the power glitch in the elevator. "Shit. Shit. Shit. How long ago was that? That was this morning. Um! So, I have about three days? But it's been—" he checks his watch— "forty-one hours since the storm. Does that mean I only have seven hours left? Shit! Okay. Okay. Get it together. Use your time wisely."

Mykelti sends the information to the printer to read later and pauses long enough to make a pot of coffee and use the toilet. How long will the flusher last? "Shit! Literally, Shit!"

Mykelti digs deep into the internet for anything that may help him survive while periodically checking his phone and television—nothing. At first, he is so worried about the so-called four basic necessities of life—water, food, shelter, clothing—that he almost forgets the most important one. He searches for: "How to make oxygen…" and sees an option for "…at home." He finds multiple solutions. *Damn, the internet is a miracle,* he thinks. One of the first solutions is photosynthesis—house plants. But that won't produce nearly enough. It would take about one mature pine tree to produce enough oxygen just for him. He smirks at the thought of carrying around a tree on his back like a scuba tank. This gives him an idea, and he prints those pages. Next, he finds a few solutions to making oxygen that might work, most importantly, the electrolysis of water. He prints them all out.

His typing becomes more frantic as time goes on. By the end of the next day, he has drunk coffee nonstop and printed out a ream of paper, front and back. It contains maps of all kinds; instructions on how to navigate using a compass; a guide to predicting the weather and a chart of prevailing weather patterns; a first aid handbook; instructions about how to start a fire without matches (wishful thinking at this point); how to filter water; hunt and forage for food; build a shelter; tie knots; create a bug-out kit, and much more. He didn't have time to sort through all the internet garbage; instead, he printed anything that looked halfway useful. He'll have plenty of time to read it later.

There is no shortage of prepper websites—that made his job easy. Unfortunately, it is too late to follow the number one piece of advice: "Be prepared or be dead." Though disaster has already struck, he will begin preparing by hoarding supplies tomorrow.

He can barely keep his eyes open, but as an afterthought, he grabs the empty bottle of medicine that he found in his father's hotel and searches for the name online. It's an anabolic steroid with many potential uses, but what catches his eye is that the steroids promote better metabolization of oxygen. Mykelti retires to bed with a head full of new information and spinning with questions, like: "What next?" and, not least of all, "Why would my father need steroids?"

Scavenger hunt
Day 4

The following day Mykelti awakes with another splitting headache. He's afraid the power is out and his oxygen concentrator failed, but the green light is on and the battery fully charged. He still has time. But how long? He opens the curtains that overlook the balcony and city. Everything appears normal. It even seems to be a nice day. Most importantly, all the streetlights are working. There appears to be no imminent danger that would trigger the nuclear power plant's safety protocol and an emergency shutdown.

Mykelti's plan is so simple he doesn't know if it qualifies as a plan. He only has two choices: stay in one place and wait for help, or leave and find help. "If I can smoke a cigarette, I can go. If not, I stay." He puts a cigarette in his mouth, thinks positive thoughts and strikes the lighter. It sparks, but the gas doesn't ignite. "Damn." He tries again and again. "Damn. Damn. Damn."

If there was any fresh air, it should have rushed to fill the gap, like ocean water filling up a bucket hole. But the atmosphere has not returned to breathable levels, which means that not only has Chicago been destroyed, but there is nowhere left untouched in North America, probably nowhere left in the Northern Hemisphere. For now, he is safer here, simply because he knows where everything is located; but soon, the city will become uninhabitable as the rotting bodies start to spread pestilence and disease into the air and water supplies. And, when he leaves, he won't be able to carry all the supplies needed, so he'll need to find survivors. He just needs to survive long enough to adapt. It's not a brilliant plan, but it gives him comfort to be moving forward.

The obvious next step is to gather supplies. After yesterday's research, he has an odd list of supplies, but he might not need to go far to obtain them. His neighbors should have most everything he needs. He'll need to start immediately while the lights are working. Judging by his headache, he'll need both oxygen concentrators. He puts them in a backpack to keep his hands free, jams both cannulas into his nasal cavity and pulls the straps tight, so they won't fall out. He should be good for four hours.

He opens the door and is shocked to see Brandon's dead stare, with his head rolled up and to one side, his posture one of disdain at being dumped in the hallway. Mykelti forgot about Brandon and is still unsure what to do with him. It would take too much effort—too much oxygen—to bury him. "You deserve better," he says. It's too late to save Brandon, but maybe there is someone else in his apartment building that needs help. There's almost no chance anyone is alive, but as he scavenges for supplies, he performs a search and rescue for his neighbors.

He starts on his floor and goes from door to door. No one responds to the increased fervor of his pounding and shouting. He retraces his steps, now rattling the door handles. He finds one unlocked and cracks open the door. There is no smell of death, but it is musty. "Hello?" he shouts. "Hello? Missus

Jakowski? Are you okay? It's me Mykelti, from four fifty-one. I'm here to help." He creeps inside, half expecting to be walloped with a frying pan, but nothing moves. A large woman is apparently asleep on her couch. "Hello, Missus Jakowski. Are you okay?" She's covered in an afghan and four cats that also appear fast asleep. He's never been fond of Missus Jakowski. She always tried to trap him into a conversation about something going wrong: a leaky faucet, a new tax, her petunias not getting enough light, how people have changed, "In my day…" Any show of sympathy would inevitably lead back to a story of her husband. Despite Mykelti's helpful suggestions and platitudes, and even running errands on her behalf, nothing ever improved, not from her point of view, anyway. Her unhappiness drained him.

He shakes her arm gently. "Missus J?" The cats don't move a whisker. He rattles her arm more forcefully and even tugs on a cat tail. Nothing happens. They are all dead.

Her shelf is full of photos in gilded frames. In one, a young, lithe and beautiful woman is smiling, heel kicked up, hand on the shoulder of a handsome young man. It's a black-and-white photo, but the smiles and the emotions are in full bloom. More pictures of the couple fill the shelves and walls. As Mykelti walks down the hallway, the photos progress through time: the couple ages, the years adding weight and wrinkles, but the smiles still bloom. Children are born, grow old, graduate and leave to form their own families. Gaps in time indicate seldom-seen grandchildren. The last photo is a portrait of her husband, a young man again, looking dapper and ready to conquer the world. He's the man she met and the man she will always remember. Perhaps they are together now.

Mykelti feels guilty for having avoided her. She was a sad and lonely woman that would never stop talking, but she hadn't always been sad and lonely—she had been as full of life as anyone, and she still tried to connect and make the world a better place. Five more minutes of his life to comfort an old woman would have done more good than harm.

He doesn't have the heart to ransack her apartment. Instead, he rolls Brandon down into the room. His body gets jostled and almost falls out of the chair when it hits the threshold. He positions Brandon so he can look out the window. "I hope you two enjoy each other's company," he says as a way of paying his last respects to Brandon, though it doesn't seem respectful to abandon him. Mykelti wonders how long it will be before the rats find them. Even if there aren't any rats left, the bodies will begin to rot and leak disease. Maybe he needs to remove all the bodies from the apartment building?

Mykelti searches the building until he finds the keys on the superintendent and a shopping cart left in the parking garage. Then he continues his search and rescue. It is more of a search for supplies than a rescue. He begins on the first floor and fills his shopping cart. Then he puts the shopping cart in the elevator, sending it to the next floor while he takes the stairs. When the cart is full, he unloads it in his apartment and begins again.

By the time Mykelti gets to the penthouse floor, all he has found alive is a pet turtle and a few fish, bottom feeders. The rest were floating belly up. Even though the pumps still bubbled air through the tanks, there is not enough oxygen left in the atmosphere to saturate the water.

He's excited by what treasures he might find in the affluent penthouse of Mister Nicholas Jacobs. All the tenants knew his name, but no one knew the man. After a few perfunctory knocks on the door, Mykelti turns the key.

The door bangs open as Mykelti pushes his cart through, and a whoosh of air ruffles his clothes.

"Stay back!" A man with a salt-and-pepper beard, neatly trimmed, is pointing a gun at Mykelti. His hands are shaking. "I don't want to hurt anyone. There's plenty for you elsewhere. Leave me to mine."

"I'm here to help," Mykelti says, surprised but grateful to see anyone alive.

"One more step, and I'll shoot. I'd shoot you right now, except I don't want your diseased mess all over my floor."

It's been a long time since Mykelti has had a gun pointed at him. When he was a child, his brother's friends—rough, young poachers—pointed their rifles at him, "Are you scared?" they would tease. They were terrible poachers and could barely put food on the table; the rifles were the only power they knew. "No," he'd say. "Why not?" they'd ask. "Because you don't have enough money to waste bullets on me." They'd laugh it off, but it was true, so they gave him a push into the dirt instead.

For a similar reason, Mykelti knows that this person wouldn't be talking if they were going to pull the trigger; nonetheless, he holds his hands up. "I've been looking for survivors."

"This is your last warning. Take your disease elsewhere."

"Disease? What are you talking about?"

"The disease that killed everybody out there," he nods in the direction of his windows.

"It wasn't a disease." Mykelti says, "It's the air."

"Exactly. It's a sick world. You can't breathe even on a good day."

"No, I mean there's hardly any oxygen left to breathe. How did you survive?"

"I have money if that's what you want. You're welcome to it. Take it and leave."

"Money is not worth anything anymore."

The man shakes his head, not wanting this to be true. "What do you want? Food? Booze? There's plenty of that in the other apartments. And, this art—" he gestures to what appears to be a Rothko. "Take it. Use it as firewood for all I care."

"We can help each other."

"What makes you think that?"

"You survived."

"It's not me. I've got this place bottled up—hermetically sealed. Nothing bigger than a nanometer gets in here… Until you."

"Look, it's about to get real tough when the power goes out. If we band together, combine skill sets, we may have a chance to—"

"Sorry to disappoint you, but my job is to tell people what to do, not to take orders. I'm the guy with the big ideas. Now here's my big idea: Get Oouuut!"

"It's not hard. We just need to gather supplies as soon as possible—before the power goes out."

"Like I said, I have everything I need, including a backup generator with months of fuel. Help will be on its way soon."

"We need to help each other."

"How do I know you're not lying? Get your sick ass out of my home."

"Okay, okay," Mykelti says. "Think about it. I'll come back tomorrow. We'll—"

"Why am I telling you anything? Get out. And don't think about coming back with any friends."

"What friends?"

"Have you even seen what's going out there!?" He gestures to a telescope in front of the floor-to-ceiling windows. "You're either sick, lying or a moron. GET OUT!" he yells at the top of his lungs.

Mykelti retreats into the hallway. The door slams in his face before he can mention that a backup generator also needs oxygen.

"And don't come back. I have a gun!" Jacobs yells through the door.

§ § §

Aside from Jacobs, Mykelti's scavenger hunt was successful. Sitting back and surveying his plunder, he feels satisfied and safe—almost. This must be the feeling the preppers seek. His apartment looks like a jungle. The turtle has a new home in the corner, and he has collected every plant he could find. They should produce enough oxygen to take the edge off, but it won't be enough. He also gathered all the batteries he could find, as well as bleach and hydrogen peroxide. He even found another oxygen concentrator and two bottles of oxygen in the apartment of a shut-in he had never seen. He was lucky to find some travel gear in the possession of a young couple preparing for a backpacking honeymoon in Europe: cookware, a pocket knife, solar panels and a durable backpack. He also gathered a set of tools, a first aid kit, and anything that looked useful. Counterintuitively, he left behind the water purification tablets and non-perishable food because he lives in a world filled with millions of bottles of water and cans of food. But he did collect a smorgasbord of perishable food—most of it won't last a week even with refrigeration—and a full bar of liquor. The vodka will make a good disinfectant. He imagines what his family would have done with this fortune in Cameroon. There, it would have bought a feast and friends; here, his fortune will only buy another week.

His search was a success, but he made many grisly discoveries of friends and acquaintances in their final repose—so many painful memories he must now live with. Even seeing the strangers was heartbreaking. Some, like Missus Jakowski, were accompanied by photographs of their loved ones; while others, more fortunate, embraced their lovers. After a lifetime of climaxing in each other's arms, what more intimate thing remains but to die in each other's arms? Presumably, transcending hand-in-hand into life hereafter.

It is remarkable how similar people are with the giant TV in the corner, tables and chairs ringing this artificial window like an amphitheater. Everyone was surrounded by the accoutrements of their life. Vacation knickknacks decorated bookshelves with books that were meant more to impress than to be read. Awards displayed how much worth an individual person had earned. And most had a tendency to collect something. In one apartment, it was owls; in another, cat paraphernalia... All of it designed to strike a balance between being an individual and fitting into society.

He had always wondered why when he met people face-to-face, everyone seemed to understand his explanations of oxygen depletion, everyone seemed to be of an enlightened mind and wanted to change, yet did next to nothing. He used to blame ignorance, but all his neighbors heard his complaints, saw his flyers, maybe even listened to his podcast... now, he realized that everyone was just living a life populated by desires and plagued with struggles, just like his. Perhaps some were fighting to cure cancer, thinking that would save the world. Maybe others were fighting a cancerous thought: "What kind of god would take my loving husband?" It seemed most only had the goal of making it to the end of the day.

Though Mykelti had hoped people would be actors on his stage, he was nothing more than an extra in theirs, appearing for a brief time, perhaps uttering a life-changing statement, but probably being nothing more than a blur in the background: the conspiracy theorist; the server that filled their cup with the smoothie of the day; the person who owed them a smile or reassuring words… the person soon forgotten.

A chemistry experiment
Day 5

When Mykelti awakes, he checks his messages. Nothing. He tries calling Sherbert and his father again. Still nothing. Maybe too many cell towers were damaged in the storm? He turns on the television. The Emergency Alert System is broadcasting on all channels, repeating another generic warning and advising listeners to please stand by. Mykelti does just that, waiting for either news or the power to fail. If he's lucky, they'll announce a pop-up refuge. He laughs at the thought of *they*. Who are *they* now? The Red Cross? The National Guard? The militia?

It's unfortunate Jacobs has isolated himself in his hermetically sealed penthouse, but it doesn't change Mykelti's plan; even if he were invited, the power and bottled air wouldn't last. Mykelti needs to learn how to survive. According to his research, it will take his body weeks to acclimate to this new low-oxygen environment. However, there is so little atmospheric oxygen, his body may never adjust. So, the next item on the agenda is to test various ways to make oxygen, especially while he can still consult the internet.

He erects a pop-up table as a chemistry lab and unpacks the resources he scavenged: hydrogen peroxide, bleach, baker's yeast, batteries, salt and water filters. According to the internet, the "simplest" way to make oxygen is by "disassociating the bond" in hydrogen peroxide, which means splitting the hydrogen from the oxygen. All Mykelti has to do is add a catalyst to the hydrogen peroxide and let chemistry do the magic.

He even found a gallon of hairdresser's hydrogen peroxide, which is thirty times stronger than the drugstore variety. It's V40 strength, which is a convenient measure for Mykelti. The V stands for volume, and the 40 means that it will release 40 times its volume in oxygen. So, he can get 40 gallons of oxygen. *That seems like a lot,* he thinks.

To begin his experiment, he pours a small amount of hydrogen peroxide into a glass and adds some baker's yeast. It's a catalyst. Even saliva or blood acts as a catalyst. When using hydrogen peroxide as an antiseptic, the bubbles that help cleanse your wound are bubbles of oxygen and hydrogen gas. Mykelti expects the glass to foam over, but hardly anything happens. Next, he saws open a water filter to get the activated carbon. It works a little better as a catalyst. Then, he tries sawing open a battery to get the carbon-zinc paste, but it's too labor-intensive, consuming more oxygen than it is worth. Finally, he tries bleach. The glass foams vigorously. Bubbles pop, sending a spray of droplets that sting his face. He wafts the fumes towards his nose and inhales tentatively. Immediately his eyes and sinuses burn, and he starts coughing. There may be oxygen, but it's unbreathable.

The only other simple, homemade solution is the electrolysis of water. Electricity will split the water into hydrogen and oxygen. Mykelti starts small with a 9-volt battery. His instructions say to use Epsom salt to help conduct the electricity. It warns: "Table salt, which is composed of sodium and chloride, can break down and produce chlorine gas, which is toxic and was used as a chemical weapon in World War I."

"Shit! I should have read this before I dumped all that bleach into the hydrogen peroxide. Damn! I'm going to end up dead one way or another."

As if his fearful thought has become reality, he hears an unusual popping noise outside. It can't be a car backfiring. Fear reaches out and grabs him. Gunshots? Cautiously, he peers out the side of the window. Nothing moves. Not even the televisions filled with the unwavering red glow from the emergency signal flicker anymore. *Maybe I'm imagining things?* he thinks. *I hope I'm imagining things. If there is anyone out there, certainly they saw me pull the curtain aside. If there are survivors, they'll start to panic soon. Start looting.* Then he laughs, "I've already looted my entire building." After a few more minutes staring out the window, trying to be as inconspicuous as possible, he concludes that the source of the noise must be gone, and not willing to risk himself even if it isn't, he returns to his experiments.

He mixes a small glass of water and Epsom salt, then submerges the battery into the solution. Immediately, bubbles start flowing off the terminals on the top of the battery. One side bubbles twice as much as the other, which means that's the hydrogen gas, and the other side is the oxygen. It's encouraging. He'll have to amp up the experiment to create enough oxygen to breathe. He dons a pair of rubber gloves and safety goggles and moves a car battery and jumper cables to the bathroom that he got from a vehicle in the parking garage. He adds two cups of Epsom salt to the bathtub—it is still full of water from yesterday—and stirs until the crystals dissolve. He submerges the battery and attaches the black cable first, as if jumping a car. Nothing happens. Next, while shielding his face with his arm, he gingerly dips the red cable in ever so slightly. It begins to bubble before he even touches the battery. As his confidence grows, he submerges it deeper. It bubbles vigorously. He guesstimates how many bubbles it would take to fill his lungs. It looks like enough, but most of the bubbles are hydrogen.

It occurs to Mykelti that he forgot to research one vital piece of information: he doesn't know how much oxygen he will need to live. Luckily the power and internet are still working. He types into his browser: "How much oxygen does a human consume per day?" He cross-references a few websites. The only reliable number comes from NASA's website. *That's ironic,* he thinks, *that they calculated these numbers for astronauts, but I can't find a reference to people on the ground.* Rounding off the numbers because it depends on a lot of factors—he assumes he will be very active and very stressed—he will need two kilograms of oxygen per day. "Is that right? Kilograms!" he exclaims. "I don't even drink two kilograms of water a day." In terms of volume, that's 1400 liters of pure oxygen per day!

"Where am I going to get that much? And—Shit!—half is probably going out the window." On second thought, he only needs enough oxygen to bring the percentage in the atmosphere back up to normal—just a few percent. "That's doable."

He decides to perform one more experiment. It should yield even better results if he doesn't blow a fuse or electrocute himself. He gets an extension cord and clips off the female plug. He slices the wires apart, being careful to leave the insulated casing around each wire except for the tips. He places the wires in the bathtub, ensuring they are far apart so they can't touch, then retreats to the kitchen. He plugs the male end into his power strip, braces himself, and hits the on button. In a few heartbeats, he can hear bubbles and see steam emanating from the bathroom doorway. He creeps closer, careful to go nowhere near the cord, and peers around the corner. The bathtub is a boiling cauldron. He couldn't have hoped for better results. He removes his breathing tube and is rewarded with a refreshing breath of air. He pauses to just breathe. "I might live, after all," he sighs.

The bubbling tub causes the cord to slither back and forth like an angry snake. The cords take a big bounce, and the wire tips touch. Even underwater, they spark. The hydrogen and oxygen gas, common ingredients for rocket fuel, ignite. BOOM! The explosion sends Mykelti flying backwards into the wall opposite the bathroom. The ball of fire reunites the hydrogen and oxygen and turns into a light rain. The circuit breaker flips, killing the snake. And, Mykelti slumps to the ground with his hair singed and the wind knocked out of him.

But now, the shower curtain and towels are on fire. Knocked dizzy, he struggles to rise and extinguish the flames. But he's too weak. He slumps to the floor, resigned to die, but the flaming curtains soon burn the remaining oxygen out of the air, and the fire extinguishes itself. Any other day and Mykelti would have burned himself, and the apartment, to the ground.

The last supper
Later that night

His phone hasn't worked in days, and the television still broadcasts the Emergency Alert System advising him to stand by. The only way to communicate is to post notices online to any survivors that may be nearby. However, most social media platforms cater to a global audience, so the chatter is overwhelming. But it is fading. People seem to be dying fast. The few survivors that he located in the Chicago metro no longer post updates. They begged Mykelti for help—it was gut-wrenching—but they were too far away. All he could do was give them the same advice he gave himself. Apps and websites, one by one, have been going offline, which means the cities where their servers are housed must be dying as well.

The electrolysis unit is supplying a breathable amount of oxygen. Mykelti labored hard all day to switch the power source from alternating current to direct current. He also used his dryer's exhaust hose, a flexible aluminum tubing, to vent the hydrogen gas out the bathroom window. As long as the power works, he'll be able to breathe easy.

It's late, and with nothing urgent left to do, it's time for Mykelti to enjoy himself—if that's possible—and let his body acclimate. He has gathered ingredients for a gourmet feast: giant king crab legs, filet mignon, thick-cut bacon, a spring salad and garlic bread. He looks up cooking instructions on the internet and laughs, "All of mankind's wisdom at my fingertips and this may be the last thing I ever do on the internet."

Not wanting to risk another explosion, he dons his oxygen concentrator and carries his ingredients to an empty apartment with a gas stove. Like the faucet, how many thousands or millions of stoves and gas furnaces were left on, all pumping more methane into the atmosphere? He turns the knob and gas whooshes out. Sparks fly from the ignitor, but the gas refuses to burst into flames. He's both surprised and not surprised. He packs up his groceries and heads to the next empty apartment with an electric stove.

He's not an experienced cook. In his village, there was little food to eat, and his job was to find it, not to cook it. These habits rolled over into his new life; as an American citizen, he no longer had to find food—it was everywhere. And working long hours in the field or the lab, he never had time or need for more than the most basic foods for nutrition and energy. To him, a fancy meal meant a wood-fired pizza and craft beer from the local brewery. Now, he is preparing the most decadent meal of his life. Not even his meal, a year ago, in the French restaurant was this lavish, mainly because it was an unsatisfying vegetarian meal. His body has craved meat for years, but he denied himself because factory farms were one of the biggest contributors of greenhouse gases. Bovine flatulence sounds like a joke; however, the amount of methane a billion cows produced was significant and the subject of many podcasts. But none of that matters anymore…

Mykelti follows the recipe as if duplicating an experiment in the lab and prepares enough food to feed a family. He uses a cookie sheet as a platter and delivers heaping portions to Mister Jacobs' penthouse. Even if civilization is dying, Mykelti intends to keep being the Good Samaritan. He knocks politely. No answer. He knocks again. "Mister Jacobs? It's Mykelti from apartment four fifty-one. I've cooked a really nice dinner. Surf and turf. I'm leaving you a plate. Get it while it's hot. Don't worry. I'm leaving. You're safe to open the door. Enjoy."

Back in his apartment Mykelti is lightheaded; he miscalculated the effort to deliver Jacobs' dinner. He opens his window a crack. The air outside is stale, but the slight wind circulates the oxygen from the electrolysis unit—his artificial tree. He feeds his turtle some spring salad and opens a bottle of Argentinian Malbec. His landlord had gone to Argentina a year ago. It must be an expensive bottle of wine that he had been saving for a special occasion. *Well,* Mykelti thinks, *it's not going to get any more special than this.*

He sets up his dinner in front of the plate-glass windows. His dinner companion, the city. The emergency-red glow of the televisions makes the faraway windows look like burning embers, and the buildings, backlit by the sunset, are like logs on a dying fire. The silence is disconcerting. He never realized how the hubbub of traffic was so soothing, a white noise to drown out his neighbors. The sirens of emergency vehicles were a comforting reminder that help was only a phone call away. His ears are pained by the silence, especially in the absence of a potential friend and alliance with Jacobs.

His first forkful of buttered lobster—Brandon loved lobster—makes his saliva glands explode. To think of how proud he used to be to catch a skinny fish. Even with his mouth full, he can't believe he's indulging in the most wasteful meal of his life. Most of it will end up in the trash because tomorrow, he will have lamb chops, truffles, lion's mane mushrooms and a dozen other things he's never tried. And the day after, ice cream—every flavor of ice cream. He will eat like a king until the power goes out. It used to anger him—people knowingly sacrificing the world's resources for their own pleasures, whether it was meat, or cars, or a new pair of shoes, or even a half-eaten donut. At least, that's how he blamed the random passersby—ignorant at best, greedy and selfish at worst.

But looking around his apartment, he feels comforted. His hoarding will keep him safe. And, after visiting his neighbors during his scavenger hunt and realizing people were just living their lives, maybe their actions weren't a conscious thought; people were just operating on automatic pilot, following an instinct or a timeless rule like Aesop's fable of the ant and the grasshopper. And somehow the greedy, like Mister Jacobs, rose above the altruistic. Maybe it was survival of the fittest? Were humans evolving into giants stomping out all the Jacks and the beanstalks? Even though mankind had reached the so-called Age of Enlightenment, it's unrealistic to think that an instinct like greed would disappear. Greed doesn't lay dormant; it writhes below the surface seeking to fulfill its purpose. Mykelti sighs. *The human race was doomed from the beginning.*

As he enjoys dessert—gourmet chocolate and more wine—a building goes dark. There is one less log on the fire. The power grid is overloaded. Mykelti checks his watch. It's 10 o'clock on day five. He has no more than 48 hours before the nuclear reactors shut down. "Here's to Chicago," he says, toasting the dying city outside the window with a glass of wine, courtesy of his landlord's hard work. On second thought, did his landlord work any more hours than he? Did his landlord make smarter decisions? Or have more passion? Or more greed? Maybe, but there is another factor at play, one that may save Mykelti. He makes another toast, "To luck."

Every man for himself
Day 6

The emergency alert system is now broadcasting a countdown until an important announcement. It's the most exciting thing to happen in days. Until then, Mykelti must go about his chores. He didn't think pestilence would be a problem so soon in these hypoxic conditions, but he's seen a few rats, and yesterday a cockroach scurried under Missus Jakowski's door. A quick internet search revealed that cockroaches "have been observed to consume human flesh of both the living and the dead." What's worse is that they will soon be spreading disease. If he's going to stay here, he'll need to move the bodies. And if he moves the bodies, he'll need to do it while the elevators are still working.

He starts in Missus Jakowski's apartment. It's easy enough to roll Brandon's chair to the elevator. He deserves a proper burial, like his mother, but doesn't everyone—familial or not? He dumps Brandon's body. "Sorry again. I truly hope you are in a better place." After a moment's silence, he goes back for Missus Jakowski.

He positions the chair in front of Missus Jakowski's couch and pulls her arm, attempting to roll her into the chair, but her bottom half is so big it refuses to move. He tries pulling her clothes near her belt line, her center of gravity. The fabric stretches uselessly. He has no choice but to wrap his arms around her midriff and pull with all his might to lift her out of the sagging middle of the couch and into the chair. But she rolls off the couch and hits the floor with an intestinal *splat*—as if it wasn't hard enough to breathe. He changes plans and rolls her onto a blanket and slides her towards the door. He pulls with all his might to overcome friction and rushes out of the apartment as quickly as possible to avoid further contamination. When the blanket hits the carpet in the hallway, he must exert even more force. Mykelti gets lightheaded, his vision sparkles, and he collapses to the floor in a painful *bang* of knees, elbow and head.

Who knows how long he lay there, spooning Missus Jakowski before his vision begins to clear and consciousness slowly returns. He sits up, rubbing his burning sinuses and aching eyeballs. He dumps her in the elevator alongside Brandon and says another prayer. He repeats the process a third and fourth time, huffing and puffing painfully. It becomes obvious he won't be able to clear his apartment complex. He thinks it might be easier to throw everyone out the windows, but that proves even more difficult.

By the sixth person, he can barely breathe, much less utter more prayers. *What am I doing? I don't know these people. I don't have enough words for the millions of people that have checked out of this life.* Mykelti's not sure if his intentions are based on some universal human instinct to pay respects to the dead, or an attempt to alleviate his grief. Probably the latter; he feels he must apologize to everyone as penance for his sins. Survivor's guilt, isn't that what it's called? He weeps as he continues his work.

After a day's work, Mykelti has a piercing headache similar to a migraine, but more real, more biting, like a part of him had died in the process. And, all he managed was clearing the bodies from his floor, and the floor above him—like his father said, shit flows downhill. He's piled dozens of bodies in the parking garage. Hopefully, the vermin, with this mountain of food, won't have any reason to come up to the ninth floor, but whether the vermin make it to his floor or not, the bodies, not just here but all over the city, could be leaking all kinds of diseases into the water supply, which he won't have the power to boil or disinfect for the foreseeable future. *Note to self,* he thinks, *drink bottled water.*

He has a few hours to relax before the emergency broadcast. With a concerted effort, he tries to shut the experience out of his brain—block himself from further thoughts of what just happened. Denial is more difficult than people think—that old pink-elephant-in-the-room phenomenon. He is almost successful until he realizes that he will have to return to the parking garage to harvest all the batteries out of the cars.

§ § §

The text scrolls across the bottom of the screen: "Public announcement from the acting President of the United States." Mykelti doesn't recognize her, so she must be far down the presidential line of succession.

> *Dear citizens,*
>
> *By now, you are aware that our country—in fact, the entire world—has suffered a natural disaster of an unprecedented and unmitigated level. And you're aware that we have failed our most basic duty to provide for the common defense and general welfare of our people. For that, I apologize. I am truly sorry. Even if the infrastructure of our once great nation still existed, there simply is not enough manpower or resources to render emergency assistance. Nor can we rely on international aid because it is a global crisis.*
>
> *Not even the world's leading scientists predicted that global warming could cause instant and cataclysmic climate changes. Until we know more, suffice to say that a rapid destabilization of the arctic ice has released untold amounts of methane gas that have been locked in the permafrost since before the ice age. The methane has destabilized the Earth's atmosphere, causing global superstorms capable of destroying cities.*
>
> *I must be forthright; there is no time for pretense.* [She hesitates as unrehearsed emotions wash over her face.] *I'm telling you—as one citizen to another—the situation is dire. We are like the proverbial frog that has jumped from the pot of boiling water into the fire. Rest assured, we have done and continue to do everything we can to remedy the situation and alleviate the hardship; however, it is with a heavy heart that I inform you—effective immediately—I am declaring martial law. Citizens must take responsibility for the safety and security of themselves and their communities. Do not expect*

rescue. I repeat. Do not expect rescue.

When I took this office, I never imagined— What I am saying, my friends and compatriots, is that effectively, The United States of America exists only in spirit now. All I can offer is hope in these words from our beloved leader, Abraham Lincoln, during another time of national crisis; I paraphrase slightly, time is short:

"Many years ago, our forefathers brought forth a new nation, conceived in liberty, and dedicated to the proposition that all people are created equal. Now we are engaged in a great civil war, testing whether this nation, or any nation, so conceived and so dedicated, can long endure... It is for us, the living, to be dedicated to their unfinished work, which they, who fought here, have so nobly advanced—That we here highly resolve that these dead shall not have died in vain—that this nation, under God, shall have a new birth of freedom—and that government of the people, by the people, for the people, shall not perish from the Earth."

*On that note, the final decree of the Office of the President of the United States is this: The dangers we face are real; they are serious; and, they are many. We must unite and stand strong against them, for it will not be an easy or short battle. Officers and employees of the government, and citizens alike, are requested to defer all authority to their local governing district. If no local government exists, you are reminded that **we, the people,** have not only the right but the duty to institute a new governing body based on principles that best effect the safety, liberty and happiness of not only the citizens of the United States but of the world.*

I still believe that together we can solve this climate crisis. Together we can raise our country out of the ashes and once again reach for the stars.

You have my heartfelt apologies and sympathies. May God be—

"—damned," Mykelti finishes. "God damn us all to hell." The screen reverts to the Emergency Alert System with a countdown until the next update and warnings scrolling along the bottom. There are no talking heads to analyze the broadcast and discuss possibilities ad nauseam.

"Damn them all! They are still blaming global warming. Well, there is no reason to go off script now. Let them think what they want to think. One way or another, it is their fault. If there is anyone alive, let them fix it." He curses vehemently.

Mykelti doesn't have the breath to keep shouting, so he sinks back into his chair and broods: *mankind* is an ironic word. Most men are not kind; they aren't necessarily unkind, but when it comes to kindness, they start with themselves. The word *mankind* has fallen out of favor. It used to be an abbreviated version of *humankind,* like *man* is an abbreviation of *human.* In the modern era, *womankind* think these labels neither representative nor flattering. As time progressed, *man* took on the connotations of *the man,* meaning the white establishment. Mykelti could relate: America still reeked of the same colonialism that divided Africa into pieces. *The man* and their self-righteous drive to take what he could get—May the best man win! To the victor go the spoils! It wasn't just the white man, though. It was any man. Since biblical times, the patriarchy has ruled the world. It was man who hunted, conquered and tamed the land. It was man who first discovered the laws of nature and bent them to his will. It was man who subjugated the beast and the woman. For millennia, man poured his energy outward like the fires that turned forests into prairies and prairies into farms. But without the woman to tame the fire in her kiln, to temper man and forge new creations, man's fire burned the land until nothing could grow. It was even thought that God created man in his own image, but what man forgot—purposely erased from their history—was that they, mankind, created God in their own image. That's why Mykelti still uses this word. "Mankind—" he spat it out of his mouth— "what have you done?"

§ § §

Overwhelmed with emotions, Mykelti retires to bed, wrapping himself in blankets like a protective womb. Even though he's not in immediate danger, his mind and body don't recognize that fact. His temples throb with the blood pressure spike; his hands tremble; and, his breath is shallow, even with the electrolysis unit still operating in the bathroom. He forces his chest cavity to swell, intake more air and force it out again, but to little effect.

He hasn't had time for feelings. They are stuck in his throat like hair in a clogged drain. His anger has mutated into sadness. His eyes burn and well with tears. He tries to fight the embarrassment of such weakness, but part of himself thinks, *Just let yourself cry. Everyone cries. Your brothers are no longer here to torment you. It doesn't mean you are weak. It means you're human. It means you have feelings. It means you are caring and compassionate. It takes strength and courage for a man to show his true emotions.* Despite the logic, Mykelti is losing the inner battle until he realizes that no one is left to care. His eyes spurt tears and splatter his face like hot rain. The drain has been unclogged, and he swirls into despair.

He's tempted to turn off his air supply. It would be easier if he didn't wake. He imagines being thrown into a hole and covered with six feet of crushing dirt—a comforting blanket of death. But it is no longer possible to hide in death. There are no tombstones that make life meaningful. If he gives up now, he will lay here forever: his grave, an apartment building; his tombstone, a stack of irrelevant research papers turning to dust; his legacy—failure. Worse, he fears his failures will echo into his next life—if there is a next life.

When his grief has reached its limit, and his tears have exhausted themselves, a wave of relaxation washes over him. *I have to pay the price of guilt. Even more so than the dumb and ignorant and the willfully corrupt, it is my burden because I was the only one who could have prevented it, and I failed. Maybe I am the only one who can save what is left.*

He's not sure how long he will be able to survive; more importantly, he's not sure how long he will have the will to live. *My future will be nothing but pain,* he thinks as he drifts to sleep.

Rest in pieces
Day 7

The power only lasted for 36 hours. During that time, Mykelti searched for survivors online without any luck: the communities were in a frenzied panic. He gathered last bits of information in between cooking food. He had every electric oven on his floor drying meat. The mouth-watering odors of beef jerky commingling with the rotting flesh of the dead. And he waited… The second emergency broadcast by the acting president never happened. Finally, his computer screen winked out—most websites were dead already—and then the city lights winked out one by one, like an apocalyptic version of Goodnight Moon. It didn't take long. The diesel backup generators couldn't burn their fuel, and the backup batteries at the distant businesses and hospitals lasted less than an hour.

§ § §

Besides a few restless hours, Mykelti has been awake for two days; regardless, he decides to check on Jacobs—his air supply won't last long without power. The meal Mykelti left in front of the door is missing. He knocks repeatedly, but no one answers. "Mister Jacobs?" he shouts louder and louder. He tries the knob. It's unlocked!? He opens the door slowly. Another whoosh of air flows past. He ducks in quick to keep the oxygen from rushing into the vacuum outside created by the pressurized room. "Don't shoot. It's Mykelti." The lights glow dimly in power-saving mode. Jacobs must have a battery backup, but does it have a power supply? If there are solar panels or wind turbines on the roof, that would make Mykelti's life a lot easier.

He tests the air and decides it's safe to remove his oxygen tubes. He drops his backpack so he can move unencumbered, ready to duck and run. "Mister Jacobs? It's Mykelti." Still no answer. He moves slowly, calling out each step, not wanting to be shot. The hallway opens to a fishbowl room with a breathtaking view of the city below. It has a minimalist interior design meant to showcase the expensive furnishings and artwork. Mykelti sneaks through the penthouse until he sees Jacobs' slippered feet on the floor behind the bed. Thinking he passed out, Mykelti rushes to his side to find what's left of Jacobs' head lying in a pool of blood and his hand holding a pistol. The door on the safe in the closet is wide open. Money, jewelry, stocks, deeds, and other valuables are strewn about—most of it meaningless to Mykelti and all useless now. One bottle of bourbon is left standing, and another bottle spilled its guts next to Jacobs. There is a handwritten note on the bed.

Friend,

I apologize for getting off to a shaky start. As you can see, I'm not made for this world.

Thank you for dinner. It's the only hot meal—if you don't count a can of soup—I've had since this all began. Truth be told, I haven't cooked a meal in twenty years. You see, between my assistants and my dear wife—God rest her soul wherever she may be—I was guarded from the mundane chores. My job was to grow the business. It's the only thing I knew. But I was good at it. Very good. But, to be honest, I only had one good idea my whole life. Ever since then, all I've done is push papers. That's a leftover expression—shows how dated I am. But I mean that literally—pushing papers, pressing buttons and sweet talking, that's all I'm good for.

Please do forgive me for leaving you alone in this strange new world. I would be nothing but a burden. Again, truly sorry, but no hard feelings. Life smiled on me with favor until now. I do wish you the best.

~ Nick. (Only my friends call me that.)

P.S. I saved you a bottle of my favorite bourbon. It's rare, and it's expensive. You'll never see another. I suppose you could say that about most everything now. I suggest you sip it slowly. One cube of ice brings out just the right amount of flavor. And help yourself to the cigars.

Mykelti doesn't have room left for grief. He's seen a lot of death now. No matter what Mykelti thinks, Jacobs thought it was the right thing to do. Hell, just last night, Mykelti had the same thoughts. How many others who heard the acting president's broadcast didn't have the heart to continue? Jacobs couldn't handle the truth: it's a tired cliché, but it reminded him of what his father had said: "People don't need to know the truth. They can't be trusted to make decisions." He grabs the bottle of bourbon and closes the door on Jacobs.

The Sun has set, and the buildings are pitch-black monoliths, tombstones backlit by the moonlight. From up here, Mykelti can see four or five blocks in every direction. He surveys the city. Except for broken windows and a distant skyscraper torn apart by a jetliner, the city is intact. *What to do now? Where to go? Wait! What's that?* Mykelti sees movement. *A group of people. Maybe?* By the time he swings the telescope into view, whatever it was, is gone.

Suddenly paranoid, Mykelti flips off the penthouse lights—the only lights visible in the city—and retires to the couch to think about what to do next. Jacobs' hermetically sealed penthouse is now acting as a hyperbaric chamber. Even if there is no solar power supply on the roof—he'll have to check that tomorrow—he should move his plants and supplies up here. It won't be easy, but his apartment is drafty and losing oxygen. That seems like as good a plan as any. There's nothing else to be done until the Sun rises. He gives himself permission to relax.

Mykelti looks at his gift: Old Rip Van Winkle. It's Kentucky bourbon that's so fancy the bottle comes inside a wooden box. "Asleep 25 years in the wood," reads the placard. He uncorks it and wafts the bottle under his nose. It smells faintly of vanilla and caramel. He always joked that he'd take up drinking and smoking shortly before he died because it wouldn't make any difference. He wasn't sure of the attraction, but it seemed that people must grow bored with old age or that their senses go numb. There's a bar in the corner of the room. He prepares a drink in a crystal glass with one ice cube, as suggested. In a few days, there will be no more ice anywhere in the city… until winter. *Damn! How am I going to survive winter?* Mykelti shoves that thought back into his subconscious, raises his glass to Jacobs, "May you rest in peace," and takes his first taste of bourbon. It burns his tongue and sinuses. After the initial shock, the second sip is bearable, like a liquid-fire caramel that tickles the nose and waters the eyes.

Mykelti is almost jealous of Jacobs; he won't be resting any time soon. Or will he? He has an idea—a macabre idea considering Jacobs is lying dead in the next room—one final decadent thing: a hot bath, probably the last opportunity for a hot bath in his life. Jacobs' master suite has a gigantic bathtub. The hot water is still hot… but not for long.

Suffering from decision fatigue, Mykelti commits to the bath without further ado. Searching through the cabinets, he finds some bath salts and candles, but instead of a candle, he sets a flashlight on the bathtub's edge. To double and triple his decadence, he prepares a tray filled with bourbon and delicacies from the refrigerator, like strawberries, grapes and gourmet cheese. It is the most romantic setting of his perpetually single life.

He gets into the tub and lets the hot water flow over his aching body. Though there is no power, there is a lot of pressure in the pipes, and there are thousands of gallons of hot water left, enough for the entire building. The tub fills to the brim and begins to overflow. "What does it matter anymore?" The sound is soothing and washes away his troubles, and the running water keeps the tub steaming hot. Part of him wants to use every drop of hot water—it's the last vestige of civilization. Who else is left to enjoy it?

He has also set aside a cigar and lighter, partially as an indulgence and partially as a test to see the availability of oxygen in the room. The lighter sparks and catches fire. He touches the flame to the tip of his cigar and puffs repeatedly. It comes to life. It feels good. Creating fire and being a man—go together. He smokes until he gets dizzy and then drowns his cigar in the tub.

The cigar and bourbon make the strawberries taste terrible. On a whim, he dumps them into the tub and watches them bob around like rubber duckies. They may be the last strawberries he ever sees. He raises his glass, "To strawberries," and takes a sip. It makes him grimace. On another whim, he toasts, "To civilization," empties his glass and throws it against the wall, like an angry child knocking over his blocks. The glass shatters and tinkles down on the ground. He has diffused some anger, but now he feels guilty. *Such a waste.* How many minutes of a person's life were spent learning how to forge the crystal? How many of the Earth's resources—lead, silica, oil, oxygen—were used to make and transport the glass? He imagines each of mankind's creations hastening the onset of the apocalypse by a minute.

Surely, it can't matter anymore if he destroys one glass or a thousand. There is no one to hold him accountable. There is no one left to miss these glasses. But these logical thoughts don't overrule his emotions. He hops out of the tub to fetch more glasses. No doubt, expensive crystal glasses. He pours another serving, "May humanity rest in peace," he toasts and tests his guilt by shattering another glass against the wall. Each toast becomes a way of saying goodbye. *Acceptance,* isn't that what psychologists call it? When he comes to the final glass, he toasts, "May the world rest in peace. *Haha.* Or, should I say pieces?" and shatters it.

"Damn. I forgot the most important toast of all," he says drunkenly. In lieu of a glass, he raises the bottle of bourbon and toasts himself. "It's not the rest of the world that needs peace—it's me. May I rest in peace." He heaves the bottle at the wall; it bounces off, hits the floor and shatters. Despite lingering guilt, he does feel better. Is it his recklessness empowering him, or just the bourbon?

Ironically, it's not until the end of the world that he becomes wasteful and uncaring. Nor has Mykelti ever resorted to drinking or drugs as a method to avoid reality, but he can't stop envisioning Jacobs' suicide. Maybe that's why people drink—to try and erase what they've seen? For one night, Mykelti manages to forget the horrors of the last few days, but he doesn't succeed to erase the memories; they will return with extra vigor the next morning. In the meantime, relaxation sets in, and he falls asleep, sliding deeper into the bubbles. The bathtub faucet continues to run. The water fills the bathroom and runs into the living room. When the carpet has sponged up its share of water, it flows underneath the door, down the hallway, into the stairwell, over the stairs like a waterfall, and down the elevator shafts, raining on the corpses below.

The search for survivors
Day 9

Unfortunately, Jacobs' penthouse isn't powered by renewable energy, so by the next morning, Mykelti's breathing has already drained the rooms of oxygen.

Even if he hadn't ruined the carpets, Mykelti realizes the hermetically sealed penthouse, which must have cost millions, won't work. He needs to be able to vent the hydrogen and chlorine gas, especially now that he must use car batteries as his power source. So he returns to his plant-filled apartment and uses duct tape to seal the windows and doors, leaving a gap at the bottom of the doors, so the heavy chlorine gas can escape.

While checking for leaks, Mykelti admires the city. It doesn't look much different in the day. As usual, he scans the streets for survivors. He has been performing daily reconnaissance missions. So far, he hasn't seen more than one human at a time, and they've all scurried away like feral animals. And no one has used the message drop he created outside his apartment. It's advertised with a big sign and three red balloons filled with helium he'd found during his search for oxygen.

Mykelti had one last good idea before the power went out. He gathered the ice cubes from all the apartments and created an ice chest out of a refrigerator. He flipped the fridge on its back so the doors faced up and the cold air couldn't run out. He'll have fresh vegetables, meat and dairy for another two weeks. For breakfast, Mykelti has cold, instant coffee with lots of cream, raw salmon (he tells himself he's eating sushi), and a giant leafy green salad. Besides needing to eat the fresh food before his ice melts, this meal, high in vitamin B and iron, will help increase his platelets, which transport oxygen in his bloodstream.

He'll search for more survivors today while he attempts to solve his newest problem: the solar panels he scavenged have failed to recharge the oxygen con-centrators. There hasn't been any sunlight in days—it won't stop drizzling. And the car batteries don't work either. He needs to find a way to convert the voltage. He failed to look up *adaptors* online before the internet failed—an oversight that might kill him. Now, he'll have to learn by trial and error. "Fuck! All hu-manity's knowledge just fucking gone."

His outburst causes a spate of dizziness. He reminds himself to stay calm and breathe deep. "In one, two, three, four. Hold one, two, three, four. Out one, two, three, four. Hold…" He had added meditation and breathing practices to his survival manual to train his body to become more efficient at using oxygen. The meditation calms the body, which uses less oxygen, and the deep breath-ing hyperoxygenates the body. Another trick he learned was to drink as much water as he can stomach. Water contains saturated oxygen, which the body can absorb, like the gills of a fish. Though tap water has less oxygen than a babbling brook, he's just glad the faucets are still working. There must be a lot of pressure in the system.

He continues what has become a daily routine. He temporarily disconnects the electrolysis unit and tops off the water in the tub. *I should look for some buckets today,* he thinks. He dons his backpack filled with supplies. Instead of the oxygen concentrators, which are slow to charge, he has to bring the iron lung. He replaces the canister and checks his oximeter. Good. Still within normal ranges. Outside, he sparks his lighter. Nothing. The atmosphere doesn't appear to be regenerating. He checks his mailbox, the post-apocalyptic inter-net. No messages yet.

Instead of the library, he heads towards the hardware store. He'll take every adaptor on the shelf. If he's lucky, they will have better solar panels, maybe even a wind turbine. Every block, he stops to blow his whistle, hoping to attract survivors. The whistle echoes off the walls of the artificial canyon. When the echoes dissipate, he listens. With no cars, lawnmowers or laughter filling the streets, Mykelti can hear someone pushing a shopping cart a block away. The cart is making a tremendous noise on the rough pavement. Mykelti blows his whistle until the man looks up. Mykelti waves and smiles. He pulls down his face mask and shouts, "Hello!" The man doesn't return his greeting but stops and considers the situation. His brown and gray garb is like camouflage.

Mykelti rushes forward, waving his arm. "Hello. Hello. Hello." By the time he narrows the distance, he can barely speak, "I… I'm… glad… to finally… see someone… Nice to meet…"

"I have nothing for you," the man says.

"We can… help… each other." The man seems wary but not menacing. Mykelti approaches cautiously until they are face to face, unshaven face to un-trimmed beard, baby buggy to shopping cart.

"I'm a one-man show. Almost always have been."

"But… there's safety… in numbers." Mykelti inhales deeply.

"Depends whose numbers they are."

"Have you… seen anybody else?"

"Yes," he doesn't elaborate.

"Are you with them?"

"They have no use for me."

"Where are they? Are they okay?"

"I wouldn't go looking for trouble if I were you."

"I'm not looking for trouble. I'm trying to survive." Mykelti changes topics, seeking a better report. "Say, how'd you survive?"

"God frowns on me." The man's wrinkles tell a story of a hard life. His be-draggled clothes make him seem like he's been battling the apocalypse for years.

"Are you homeless?" Mykelti asks, wondering if he was accustomed to living in a low-oxygen environment, like sleeping under highways and piles of blankets in the middle of winter.

"Aren't we all, now?"

"Look, you sure you don't want to try to help each other out?"

"Why don't you give me some of that fresh air you're breathing?"

"It's the only bottle I got. But I know where we can find some more."

"Got anything good to eat or drink in there," he refers to the baby buggy.

"Just some water and fruit. Just enough to get me through the day." The man frowns, so Mykelti amends, "Take it. I'll get some more at the corner store."

"Funny, now, the end of the world, and you pretending to want to help me.

Seems you're the one needing help. Well, I'm not feeling so generous. Just like me, my whole life, you're gonna have to learn the hard way. I made it this long without help."

"Where are the others? Maybe they'll want to team up."

"Trust me, you're better off without them—without anyone."

He leans into his cart and trundles forward, signifying the conversation is over.

Mykelti steps into his path to slow him down. "What's your plan?"

"Same as it's always been. Read me a good book. Maybe drink a drink… now that it's free for the taking and life is short."

"What about winter?"

"Plenty of fancy homes available. Great time to buy," he laughs. Rather than go around Mykelti, he turns right and continues off in a new direction. Without a purpose, one direction is as good as another. After a few steps, the man turns and says, "You want my help? A word of advice then: Not everyone is as friendly as me. There are guns everywhere. Free for the taking. Find a squad car, and you'll have your choice."

"What are you saying?"

"You haven't seen what I've seen."

"And what's that?"

"Human nature." He trundles away, not heeding any more questions.

Mykelti notices that the man wears a new pair of shoes, and his cart is full of food and books. He might be the only man better off for the apocalypse. Mykelti had been blaming the storm for destroying civilization, but, in fact, society had failed long ago.

A surprise encounter
Day 11

It is dark in the pharmacy, and Mykelti is combing shelf after shelf, his flashlight swinging back and forth like a lighthouse beacon. He has gathered enough oxygen, water, and food to last the foreseeable future—about a week, though much less if his equipment fails—so the next item on his supply list is medicine. Specifically, he wants to find the steroids his father had been using to boost oxygen metabolism and any other performance-enhancing drugs he had noted in his survival manual. His body needs all the help it can get. "Aha! Here it is."

Without warning, the pharmacy door bangs open, and a man barks, "Who do we have here?"

"Whoa!" Mykelti exclaims, backing into a shelf and knocking a stack of bottles onto the floor, including the one he just found. "You scared me."

Three more people walk through the door. All Mykelti can see are their silhouettes against the glare of the plate-glass windows.

"What are you doing?" says the apparent leader. The green top of his supplemental oxygen tank protrudes from his backpack.

"Looking for supplies."

"Is that right? Matter of fact, so are we." While he speaks he pulls his plastic face mask off his mouth and, when finished, lets the elastic bands snap the mask back into place.

"And survivors," Mykelti says, implying that he is a potential friend.

"We have so much in common."

A short and stout man steps forward and instructs, "Come out from behind that counter and keep your hands where we can see them," his voice echoes inside his apocalyptic-looking gas mask hooked to an oxygen tank.

"Okay. Sure. I'm just going to get my air supply first. I don't have any weapons. I'm anti-gun, actually," Mykelti uses the distraction to slip a bottle into his pocket as if he were sneaking a sweet under Tanginika's watch.

"Dr Mykelti Mouse, is that you?" a woman's voice calls out.

Mykelti shades his eyes against the light. "Sherbert?" She's wearing so much gear that he didn't recognize her silhouette. "Sherbert! I can't believe you're alive."

"I like what you've done with your hair," she calls back.

Mykelti strokes his hair, not knowing the acidic rain from the storm has turned it a peroxide blond.

She rushes forward to greet Mykelti, but the leader blocks her path. "That's cute. You have nicknames for each other."

"Henrick, stop. I know him," she protests.

"First, I'd like to have the pleasure to meet. Can't be too sure about anyone these days." Even with the mask, Henrick has charismatic enunciation.

"Sherbert, are you okay? Are these your friends?" counters Mykelti.

"I'm fine. They're just assholes. If you haven't noticed. It's the end of the world. There aren't a lot of options."

"Misery acquaints a man with strange bedfellows," Henrick says. "But our goal is all the same—to survive. Maybe you'll want to join us."

"We got too many nut jobs already," says the stout man.

"Give him the test," says the other man. He's a head taller than everyone and has no mask or oxygen gear.

"What test?" asks Sherbert. "I thought this was supposed to be a supply run."

"It's her first time," giggles the stout man.

"This is how we find new recruits," clarifies Henrick. "People we can trust."

"I'll vouch for him, Henrick," says Sherbert.

"Humor me, Dr Mouse. Can you say the alphabet backwards?"

"Mykelti. My name is Mykelti."

"Let them go through their he-man routine," Sherbert says indignantly. "Then we can all be friends."

"Backwards alphabet the," says Mykelti facetiously.

"*Haha*. Okay, you still have your wits. Some people, they didn't get enough air to breathe. Gone a bit crazy," says Henrick. "Others seem to be—how should I say?—*enjoying* the mayhem. A few, like myself and my friends here, try to keep the peace. The question is: which are you? The law-and-order type or…?"

"I'm all for keeping order," Mykelti says.

"Do you have a weapon?"

"Do I need one?"

"How do you protect yourself?"

"Like you said, we're all in this together."

"I said, we're all trying to survive," says Henrick. "Okay, final jeopardy time. Tell me, what did you do in the Old World?"

"I was a political activist. Before that, a research scientist."

"Hmm. We don't need opinion makers."

"He's not on our list," says the tall man. "Let's just take his air. Be rid of him."

"You heard him," says the stout man, "He ain't no good anymore."

"I'm afraid Eddie and Gregory may be right. That is the rule."

"What list? What rules?" Sherbet asks, "What the fuck is going on?"

"We're looking for VIPs. I'm sorry to say, political activists and people who ask too many questions don't make the A-Team."

"Tell me," says Mykelti, "what did you do?"

"I was a broker at the Chicago Stock Exchange."

"Doesn't sound like much use to me. Even in the Old World, all you did was take a piece of other people's pie. You never made a pie in your whole life, I bet."

"Au contraire. I am an expert in buying and selling—that's my pie. As long as people want something—and they always will—they'll need someone to get it for them—and that's me. I smooth the roads to prosperity. That's what we are doing right now, negotiating a trade."

"The only thing I need are friends," says Mykelti.

"And I need goodies. Tell me, Mykelti, what makes you think that you can take all the goodies?"

Mykelti's losing control of the situation, so he attempts levity. "First come, first serve. Just like the sign says."

"I gotta number here—" Gregory displays a gun, rotating it back and forth—"that says *I* come first."

"I thought we were all in this together?" Henrick mocks Mykelti. "And, here you are, holding out on us."

"There's plenty to go around, Henrick," Sherbert says.

"She's right. There's hundreds of pharmacies," says Mykelti, "And if you want oxygen, there's plenty of tanks in the hospital."

"Seems like we got what we need right here," says Eddie.

"I'll tell you what," says Henrick. "you give us everything you have, and you're free to go. I'm not supposed to leave loose ends, but you're friends with Sherbert, and I have a soft heart."

"What makes you think I'm sticking around?" says Sherbert.

"Let's disappear him," says Gregory. Mykelti notices that, despite his intimidating stature, there is fear in his eyes.

"Yeah. Better safe than sorry."

Mykelti's more cautious than scared. He's seen guns before, brandished like advertisements of power. He didn't believe people ever wanted to take a life; nonetheless, it was easier to give the village marauders what they wanted. "Here." Mykelti throws his duffle bag on the ground full of medicine bottles. "You'll need a prescription for that," he laughs.

"His sense of humor has always been terrible," Sherbert says, trying to defuse the tension.

"Shut up," says Eddie. "Henrick is negotiating."

"I don't need this shit. I'm outta here. C'mon, Mykelti."

"No one's going nowhere," says Gregory.

Henrick kneels down and searches the bag. "How generous. Bananas—"

"They might be the last bananas you ever see."

"I got a banana right here for you," Eddie grabs his groin.

"... Antibiotics. Steroids. Medical grade cannabis. Aspirin. Of course, nothing worse than a nasty headache. Breezy—"

"I'm gonna puke if I have to breathe more of that Breezy strawberry shit."

"This will make a nice addition to my investment portfolio." Henrick rises and pauses in thought. "You must be well-supplied to give this up so easily. Maybe we should visit your secret stash?"

Mykelti is becoming scared. If they raid his apartment, he won't be able to recover. He tries to deflect them with an obvious statement. "There are supplies everywhere. I'll just get more."

"Is that so? We might be needing those, too. Oxygen canisters are—what do you liberals call it?—a non-renewable resource."

"He's got more stuff on his back."

"We'll be taking that, too." Henrick motions for Mykelti to toss his backpack at his feet.

"Taking my air is the same as killing me," Mykelti says, but he is more worried about his survival manual.

"You'll be fine, I'm sure. You made it this far. I don't want any harm to come to you, but I'm sure you understand, I also have an obligation to ensure the safety of our small group of friends."

"Look, I can tell you where to get more. Let me and Sherbert go."

"The woman stays."

"If there's one thing the apocalypse ain't got, it's women," Eddie says.

"I'm not a fucking object. Mykelti. Let's go."

"Keep her quiet," Henrick says with a dismissive flick of the hand.

Gregory puts one hand over her mouth and levers her arm into a vulnerable position behind her back.

"Mmmph."

"My companion is not very creative with his word choices. What he means to say is that Sherbert has a valuable skill set. Look, I'd be happy to let you both go. But I just can't do that. I don't make the rules, and I don't want to pay the price of letting her go. But, I can guarantee no harm will come to her. Consider this a friendly acquisition and merger."

"Sounds more like a hostile corporate takeover."

Henrick laughs, "My friend, we speak the same language. I miss that already. Look, I'm not saying I don't sympathize, but I have my own problems, just like you. Now hand over your backpack before we take it. Then you're free to go."

Mykelti tries to appeal to the money-man inside Henrick, "You have no supply of oxygen. You need workers to manufacture the goods. I can help."

"Now! Give!" shouts Gregory.

"That job, unfortunately for you, has been taken."

"I know how to make oxygen," Mykelti pleads.

Gregory chambers a bullet in his gun.

"Okay, okay." Mykelti knows where to get more air, but his survival manual is irreplaceable. As he removes his backpack, he reaches into the bag, disconnects the hose from the oxygen canister and cranks the valve open. He places it at his feet. The canister whooshes loudly. "That's pure oxygen," says Mykelti. "If you shoot, you'll blow us all up." He takes his lighter out of his pocket, the one he has been using to test the ambient air. "And if you make any sudden moves, I'll do it for you."

"He wouldn't kill himself," Eddie says.

"Look around. What's to live for?"

Henrick is laughing so much that he has trouble speaking. "That... *Haha...* That... is a good one. Eddie, take the backpack."

"But..."

"Take it, or you won't be enjoying your drink tonight."

"Stay back. I'm warning you." Mykelti extends his arm and holds his thumb over his lighter like a detonator.

"Don't do it!" shouts Eddie.

Gregory freezes.

"You may have fooled my friends here. As for myself—" Henrick aims his gun at the oxygen container and pulls the trigger. The bullet explodes at Mykelti's feet. Shrapnel ricochets off the pavement and tears at his pant legs. But the oxygen doesn't ignite. "I happen to know that oxygen is not flammable. Sounds like a contradiction, I know."

Mykelti is disheartened that his bluff didn't work. Henrick is right. The Old World was filled with oxygen. Combustion, including explosions, is a chemical process that needs both a flammable fuel and oxygen.

"Now! Give me your backpack! I'm losing my patience."

Sherbert struggles futilely against Gregory's grip.

Eddie moves forward threateningly under the guard of Henrick's pistol, his horseshoe mustache a prominent feature even inside his gas mask.

Mykelti has to decide what to do immediately. One can't bargain with people whose blood runs hot, and he's not a fighter. He has two choices: give them what they want and asphyxiate, or run and risk being shot in the back. He takes a deep breath, gives an apologetic look to Sherbet, rips Eddie's face mask off and heads for the door, but not before Eddie gets a hand on his backpack. Mykelti can't break free of his powerful grip. He's forced to drop the backpack—and the survival manual.

The backpack trips Eddie, giving Mykelti a few extra steps.

Sherbert bites down on Gregory's hand. When he releases his grip, she calls out, "Mykelti, your fa—" Gregory clubs her before she can finish.

Gunshots splatter the ground and shatter the windows. It makes Mykelti's escape easier as he races out the broken glass wall instead of stopping to open the door. The two henchmen give chase. Henrick waves them back. "Let him go. He'll be dead soon enough." But they don't listen.

The fourth wave of deaths: Survival of the fittest
Ongoing

When the Great Grandmother of Superstorms finished her circumnavigations, almost every air-breathing animal bigger than a cat had died because the bigger the animal, the more oxygen it required. Most water-breathing animals survived the storm; they breathe the oxygen dissolved in the water, but as the ocean and the atmosphere exchanged gases, establishing a new balance, the oceans quickly lost their supply. The remaining phytoplankton would require hundreds of thousands of years to replenish the oxygen; meanwhile, the remaining marine animals would drown in the hypoxic seawater. There were exceptions: some cold-blooded animals survived, like sharks and crocodiles; they have survived many mass extinctions. Scavengers survived; they are accustomed to consuming rotting scraps in hypoxic environments, like stagnant water, trash heaps and sewers. And many individuals with natural immunity survived, but their species were functionally extinct. For example, even *if* one elephant survived to find a mate, and even *if* their children survived, they would not be a genetically viable population. The largest species of land animals to survive, ironically, were the clever humans, which owed their initial success to being scavengers themselves. The largest air-breathing marine mammal to survive were the dolphins. They are also clever and accustomed to holding their breath, with lungs better adapted to utilize oxygen and expel waste gases. So, for a long time, dolphins held the record for the most civilized species on Earth. But the record for the most successful species now belonged to the microorganisms that made a home in the trillions of rotting bodies; in particular, anaerobic bacteria would find a new foothold.

As adaptable as humans were, most that had survived would not last long. First, the vulnerable died: the weak, old and sick—like the bedridden, people with cardiac and respiratory conditions. Pregnant women rarely survived, their offspring even less so. Almost all orphaned children, even with a natural tolerance for hypoxia, died. As time progressed, medicines would run out or expire. Minor ailments claimed many of the remaining survivors: the common cold, allergies, malnourishment, exposure… Some were injured: scratches became septic with anaerobic disease, broken bones would heal at odd angles or not at all.

Few humans possessed the skills necessary to survive, so the next to die were those lacking the wit or wherewithal, which included members of the so-called upper echelon of society and the intellectual elites lacking the ability to adapt or climb down their ivory towers. They mostly died of chronic asphyxiation or victimization as the world grew more ruthless.

Even if people had their health and their wits, it did not matter if they lacked the willpower to live. For everyone left alive, their lives no longer had a purpose. It seemed hope had finally escaped Pandora's box. In the Old World, everyone had been listening to their fears for so long, expecting to lose everything they loved, that the apocalypse was just an excuse to leave. Either they turned the knives of self-pity upon themselves, or if they did not have the courage, they simply curled up and waited to die. They were not to be mourned; they preferred dying to living. Nor were they to be blamed; the now-dead culture of mankind had made the choice for them.

Eventually, more skilled and willful humans, like government specialists, including the military, and doomsday preppers, were forced out of their underground bunkers to prep for a different kind of long-term survival. Long-term, in this sense, meant one harvest season. Most of those who emerged, regardless of intelligence or skill, had no latent ability to survive the low levels of oxygen and no time to acclimate to the new atmosphere; so, like most of the population, who had no refuge, they died shortly after exposure. Ironically, it was those accustomed to living in poverty without clean food and water, medication and props like glasses, those that manifested hope out of thin air, that would have the highest survival rate.

Those who survived the third wave of deaths would once again meet face-to-face and compete for resources. There were two types of people: those who subscribed to a higher order and those who succumbed to their animal nature. Darwin's law, which science had circumvented, once again came into play. Mother Earth had reset humanity back to its default mode: a mode where no one is born with any guarantees except the simple genetic need to claw and scratch their way out of the primordial ooze and spawn. It was the human prime directive—as if the species itself had a collective consciousness and a will to live.

Humans, themselves, thought of it as a law of nature: the survival of the fittest. However, survival of the fittest is a misnomer. What Charles Darwin, the inventor of the concept, meant was that natural selection favored the survival of those most well-adapted to their environment—but that did not roll off the tongue as smoothly. Animals are not evolving to a higher order. Sometimes, species need to be taller to reach the leaves, and sometimes shorter to reach the grass. And a species neither needs to be strong nor smart to procreate; in fact, it can be quite the opposite. In the case of Homo sapiens, being intelligent and educated often led to lives of barren solitude.

In Darwin's opinion, the key to a species' success was not about individual competition—one individual besting another—but about the cooperation of the species as a whole. It was the ability of a species to create safe havens, share food and guard the weak. These factors guaranteed success more than anything else. However, mankind loved competition and grasped onto this idea of the survival of the fittest and embedded it into their culture as if it were a true law of nature. It was a convenient justification that one deserves something because they are better than another. And, it made comforting bedtime thoughts that others plagued by illness or war, or those poor and weak, somehow deserved their fate: it must have been God's will to select a few chosen ones.

So, born out of fear, the third wave of deaths—tribal warfare—began. It would last for generations until the Old World, and those born within it, were nothing but a myth to their descendants.

Fugitive
Seconds later

Mykelti runs out of the pharmacy to the nearest intersection and around the corner. He glances back. No one. Hopefully, they took a wrong turn. He slows to a walk. "Calm down, calm down," he tells himself. His oximeter has gone from green to yellow to orange. He only has about two minutes before the dissolved oxygen in his bloodstream runs out. He holds his breath, soaking every last molecule of oxygen out of his lungs. "Think. Think. I know it is around here somewhere." His extremities begin to tingle then burn. He runs a few steps further before his chest begins to spasm, and his throat gags to take a breath. When he can take the pain no longer, he exhales slowly and then breathes in deeply. Praying he has adapted. At first, he feels relieved, but gradually his breathing becomes more rapid, his head more faint. *I'm not going to make it.* His oximeter is blinking red and vibrating. He might live a few more minutes, but he only has seconds of useful consciousness.

He dashes to the nearest car and slides before the front tire in a bone-crunching kneel. His hands fumble to unscrew the cap and push down the pin. A whoosh of air escapes the tires. Mykelti breathes in too quickly and chokes on the dust of disintegrated rubber. His vision sparkles. His body is in a panic and wants to flee. It takes all his willpower to force himself not to cough and inhale more stinky, dusty air. *Inhale one, two, three, four. Hold one, two, three, four. Exhale one, two...* Tingles of relief wash over his body. A few more deep breaths—*like waves washing on the shore*—make his thoughts more coherent. *How is that for irony?* he thinks. *The only breathable air left is inside the tires of a car.*

As his senses return, he hears shouting. They are still searching for him. He pops a handful of steroids that he pocketed at the pharmacy. They are a type of performance-enhancing drug that boosts the oxygen uptake between the lungs, blood and cells. "How long does this stuff take to work?" He sputters and coughs, his lungs aching from the dusty air. "Too long."

After deflating one tire, he's still feeling discombobulated, but he must keep moving. Though he has the urge to dash, he walks as calmly as possible to the furthest possible car a block away.

"Hey, there he is!"

Mykelti turns to see Eddie and Gregory. They are jogging after him. Even with masks, they can't get enough oxygen to run. It's a slow-speed chase as Mykelti rounds another corner. He can't stop at another car without being caught. He looks around. Desperate. His oximeter is red, and his heart rate has maxed out. He sees a beauty salon and breaks into a run. The pain of anaerobic exercise nearly cripples him. His vision is narrowing. Tunnel vision. He's beginning to blackout. He breathes as deeply as possible to suck all the oxygen out of the air.

He stumbles into the beauty salon. His body is on fire. His head feels like it is going to split open. He can barely think. "Focus. Focus. Focus," he repeats, like a mantra, anchoring his brain to consciousness. He rummages through the cabinets until he finds the first ingredient—hydrogen peroxide. He pours gallon after gallon onto the floor. Running out of time, he takes the caps off a few more jugs and throws them across the room. As the henchmen's shadows loom in the doorway, he finds the final ingredient. Grabbing two gallons of bleach, he climbs the barber's chair like a ladder. "Pray to God this— Nevermind God. Pray to science this works." He pours the bleach onto the floor just as Eddie and Gregory burst through the doors. The chemical reaction turns the room into a bubbling cauldron. As the hydrogen peroxide disassociates, it forms oxygen and a poisonous, yellow-green cloud of chlorine gas.

The acid splatters Eddie's mask and Gregory's face, obscuring their vision, and the fumes cause them to gag. Their face masks supplement their oxygen, but they are not airtight.

"What the—" *Cough. Cough.*

"Mother f—" *Ack!*

Atop the chair, Mykelti can breathe the oxygen as it floats to the top, and since chlorine gas is two and half times heavier than air, it sinks to the bottom, drowning Eddie and Gregory in its toxic fumes. Feeling giddy, he laughs, "Ha! Beware the God of Science!"

Gregory doubles over and vomits before Eddie pushes him out the door. Mykelti is almost able to breathe freely, though the rising vapors of the chlorine gas are giving him a terrible headache.

When the coast is clear, Mykelti peeks out the back door to get his bearings, rushes back to the salon to fill his lungs like a whale before a deep dive, and then slowly, but with no wasted motions or thoughts, heads to the next car. He uses a piece of his shirt to filter the rubber dust out of the tire's air. With his back to the car and lungs full of air, he can almost relax and admire the view—the sparkling skyscrapers with puffy orange clouds reflecting in their windows. The Sun penetrates easier now through this thinner atmosphere. It can be blinding. *It's odd,* he thinks, *that civilization consists of arranging things in tidy lines and columns.* But on the ground, the corpses break the continuity. They are showing signs of decomposing, swollen like balloon animals. They are fermenting. It's an anaerobic process similar to what makes his legs ache. "I'm rotting alive!" he laughs out loud.

He sucks the air from eight more cars before he reaches his destination: Underwater Adventures. A scuba shop. While searching the internet for sources of oxygen, Mykelti discovered that diving in Lake Michigan is a popular hobby. There are over a dozen scuba shops. This store is on his list of places to visit.

Mykelti has to keep going outside to breathe and drains the air out of many more tires before he figures out how to use the scuba gear. He was hoping to find a tank of oxygen, but the store used a compressor to condense the ambient air into a tank. Fortunately, the store has some tanks full of air ready for customers, because now the compressor is useless. He puts on a tank, "Ah! Certified fresh Chicago air."

A scuba tank holds 80 cubic feet of air and will only last about an hour, depending on activity level. Mykelti estimates he will only need one tank to get home, but he takes two tanks just to be sure. Unfortunately, the tanks weigh him down, increasing the amount of oxygen he will consume. As an extra precaution, he uses a rebreather mask. The human body is remarkably inefficient: the lungs can only absorb about 25% of the oxygen in one breath; the rest gets exhaled. The rebreather is designed to absorb the carbon dioxide and recirculate the unused oxygen. He doesn't want to waste a drop.

Mykelti walks home on the bottom of an ocean of dead air. He feels like an astronaut visiting an alien world, searching for signs of intelligent life. This culture appears to have died. *Culture* is an interesting word used to describe a civilization's collective agreements—like for men to wear pants and women dresses. *Culture* is also the word used to describe a colony of yeast—a microscopic civilization. Yeast is used to brew beer, ferment cheese and many other things. In the case of making bread, the yeast eats carbohydrates and excretes carbon dioxide, which causes the bread to rise. A culture of yeast is like an alien invasion of body snatchers, slowly transforming its host into itself. It knows no restraint; yeast will eat until there is nothing left to eat. "Beam me up, Scotty. There's no intelligent life down here," Mykelti jokes halfheartedly.

After two hours of weaving in and out of the obstacles on the road and sidewalk—good thing he brought the extra tank—Mykelti returns to the safety of his bunker; that's what he thinks of his apartment after reading all the prepper survival blogs. He rips the sign and balloons off his message drop. As an afterthought, he checks the mailbox. There's a letter. Suddenly paranoid, he looks down the street in both directions and then dashes towards his apartment building, tipping over a garbage can to make it look less inviting, and locks the door behind him.

Home unsafe home
Day 12-13

Mykelti awakes with a terrible hangover. He stumbles to the kitchen for some Ibuprofen, then, on second thought, checks the electrolysis unit in the bathroom. The car battery is dead. Mykelti stumbles to get his oxygen concentrator. His hands fumble to attach the cannula and flip the power switch. It still has full power. It takes many breaths for the pounding in his head to ease.

Damn, if it weren't for taking half a jar of steroids, I'd be dead, he thinks. *Thank God I'm still alive.* After a second thought, he curses, "Fuck God. Obviously, God doesn't give a fuck. Thank me. Thank me I'm still alive. If it weren't for me, I'd be dead." Mykelti's startled by his own blasphemy. The words flow out so naturally that he realizes he has lost his religion.

Even after a hot cup of coffee—he had found a hotplate at a hardware store—his head spins from too little oxygen and too much drink. But, mostly, his head spins from overwhelm. He's been forsaken by both man and God? There is no one coming to his rescue. And Sherbert? Who's going to rescue her? He feels ashamed for leaving her, but she is in no immediate danger. If she escapes, she'll surely come looking for him here. That reminds him of the letter. He's reluctant to open it, but maybe it's a message from Sherbet?

> If you want to live, join us. We have supplies and a plan. Come to the Water Tower Place. Leave your weapons behind. Armed intruders will be shot without warning.

A few days ago, this would have been a godsend, he thinks. *Ha! There I go again. No, this is man's doing. And it could be a trap. Well, at least I know where to start looking for Sherbert.*

He gets Jacobs' gun out of his kitchen drawer. It's heavy. The metal grip is like a file on his soft hands. Would it have helped? Could he have saved Sherbert? Or would they have just killed each other? The gun will weigh him down and cost more calories and more oxygen to burn the calories. He's not sure it's worth the risk, but he chambers a bullet and places the gun within easy reach.

How fast civilization has collapsed, he thinks. *And how far and fast I've fallen.* Mykelti may have lost his religion—and his survival manual—but weren't religions just instruction manuals for civilizations, written by men in the guise of God? He has not forgotten the words of Hillel the Elder: "That which is hateful to you, do not do to your fellow." It is a variation of the Golden Rule. Hillel said the entire Torah was just an explanation of this one idea. But if the Torah and every other fake book of God had failed mankind, what hope had he?

Is civilization even worth saving? he wonders. *No. Not in any way resembling what it was… But can it be any different? Humans are like the proverbial lemmings, running themselves off the cliff with their bad ideas. The human race racing itself to extinction.*

Mykelti barely has the strength to replace the car battery in the bathtub. "Why do I even care?" he mumbles. "What good has civilization ever done me? The only solution is to keep going. To not think any more than necessary. I'll worry about tomorrow—" he clamps the electrodes to the battery, and the tub bubbles to life— "tomorrow. One day at a time, starting with a day of rest to heal my aching body. I declare today—whatever day it is—the new Holy Sabbath of the Apocalypse." He can almost hear Sherbert say, "Well, at least you still have a terrible sense of humor." He laughs. "At least I have that."

Mykelti sees the scuba tank from yesterday's adventure standing in the corner, the rebreather now useless. He should have grabbed extra CO_2 scrubbers. It reminds him that he had brought home a box of bottled air from the lab. He sets the box on the counter and grabs the bottle labeled "The Middle of

Nowhere" and gently depresses the valve. Cold air hisses out. He wafts it under his nose, breathing deeply. "Ahhh… fresh Hawaiian. Beaches, suntan oil, fish tacos…" Next, he tries the Andes Mountains. "Ah, I can practically smell Machu Picchu." He tries Antarctica and compares it to the Arctic. "Penguins and polar bears." And he keeps sampling air, doing a round-the-world tour.

Feeling high from the fresh air, Mykelti gets a bottle of bourbon and retires to the couch. He remembers some of Hillel's other words: "If not now, when? If not me, who?" For the remainder of the day, the words burrow deep into his mind, unraveling his self-pity and doubt as wise words do. Was he going to wither away, alone with nothing but an endless supply of bourbon, or was he going to survive and thrive? The latter he couldn't do alone.

By the time he falls asleep, he has the answer to Hillel's question: "I might fail, but I have to try."

An un/happy reunion
Day 14

As Mykelti approaches the entrance to the mall, which is now a refugee camp, he sees heads on pikes like medieval Europe and no trespassing signs. Two guards are posted at the ad hoc barbwire gate. A spray-painted sign says, "We don't take prisoners. We bury them." One guard raises his weapon. "No sudden moves."

"Yeah, no sudden moves, or—" the second guard fires his shotgun, and a rat feeding on a corpse explodes into pieces. Another dozen rats scurry away. "You'll get it just like that."

"Damn't, Lorenzo. Stop wasting ammunition. And you—"

"¡Malditas cosas! They'll be chewing on us next."

"What do you want?"

Mykelti shows him the letter in his upraised arms. "I have an invitation to join the party."

"You'll have to pass inspection first. Lorenzo, do something useful."

"I'll need to pat you down. Arms up. Legs spread," says Lorenzo. He treats Mykelti more like baggage than a person. "And let's see what's in that backpack."

"Full disclosure: I have a gun."

Lorenzo dumps Mykelti's backpack on the table and pulls the gun out. "No weapons allowed."

"I'll need that back. I won't be staying," Mykelti says, but his gun is a red herring. What the guards don't realize is that Mykelti is rolling a bomb into the compound disguised as a tank of oxygen. He's glad he stopped by the welding shop for his insurance policy.

"If you're lucky, you'll leave on your own two feet."

"Anything else in here I should know about? Anything hazardous, fragile or liquid?" Lorenzo laughs.

"Nothing dangerous but me and my big ideas," Mykelti returns an awkward laugh.

"What's your business?"

"I'm here to see Sherbert. She has pink hair. Can't miss it."

The guard doesn't take the bait. "What did you do before the world went to shit?"

"I was—uh—a nurse."

"Hmm."

"Have you seen the woman?"

"We're all looking for women here."

"You'll have to meet the boss before you do anything," says the first guard.

"Who's the boss?"

"The only one around here willing to make decisions."

"Why's that so hard?"

"Because a wrong decision means someone dies."

"We've seen plenty of dead people now," says Lorenzo. "I'm practically immune."

"Problem is, we're running short of useful people," the first guard says. "If you made it this far, maybe you're the useful variety. We'll see."

Mykelti follows Lorenzo into the atrium. It's filled with tents and supplies. A few men patrol the area and more are moving boxes. It appears they have emptied all the department stores of valuable objects. Value has a different meaning now: the electronic and jewelry stores appear untouched. "That—" Lorenzo points to a giant squid-shaped, steampunk assembly— "is what's keeping us alive. We call it the water cracker." The department store's fountain is rigged with a giant electrolysis unit with pipes, like long tentacles, supplying what must be the most important tents with air.

Sitting on the fountain ledge is an old woman with wild eyes and frazzled hair. She sees Mykelti and screams, "It was you! You left us to fucking die!" The words spark guilt within him: the years of wasted research and words that fell on deaf ears. The woman gets up and paces back and forth, hands clenching and unclenching her dirty rag of a dress. Curses and spit fly out of her mouth.

"You left us to die. It was you."

Mykelti barely recognizes her. "Mildred? Is that you?"

"Never mind her," says Lorenzo. "She lost her mind. Didn't get enough oxygen. She's harmless enough."

"Mildred. Where are the others?"

Her glazed-over eyes don't recognize his words, but her curses are the same as an answer, "You fucking left us to rot in hell."

"We banished her for not contributing, but she keeps showing up like a friggin' brain-dead boomerang. No one has the heart to do anything about it. C'mon. She's a broken record."

Mykelti is still wondering if he has found Sherbert's group of people. As they approach a large tent near the center of the atrium, what appears to be the leader's tent, he fishes for information, "Is Henrick the boss?"

"No—" Lorenzo opens the flap. Henrick sits at a table full of paper maps. Gregory and Eddie stand by his side like officers of the army "—he's in charge of new recruits."

"Well, well, well. Lookie who we have here," says Henrick. "Ha! I've always wanted to say that."

"We've already rejected this one," gloats Eddie.

"His tenacity is remarkable. It seems he may have something to contribute after all. Maybe he deserves a second chance. What do you say? Care to join our little party?" he asks Mykelti.

"That depends on Sherbert, but I'm leaning against the idea."

"How so?"

"You realize it will take more than thieves and gunslingers to survive!?"

"Gunslingers—I like that. It is the Wild West again, isn't it?" Henrick says. "I think we're doing a pretty good job surviving. How about you boys?"

"As long as there's a drink in one hand and a woman in the other," says Eddie.

"No complaints as long as my belly is full," says Gregory.

"People have much lower expectations in the New World," says Henrick. "It makes management's job a lot easier... Except you. One question remains: Can you follow orders?"

"You only have one question!?" Mykelti replies sarcastically.

Henrick laughs, "I can't help but like you. Still, I need to know: Are you a team player?"

Back in Cameroon, Mykelti wasn't the most popular of his brothers. It's not that people disliked him or that he was cruel or aloof, but he kept to himself, exploring the world. When it came to chores, he preferred to help Tanginka with her shop rather than hunt or fish with the men. And he'd rather mend a bird's wing than eat its flesh. His birth mother told him, "Mykelti, you're different. You have empathy for all of God's creatures. You stand by your convictions. People won't understand you, but when they do, you'll have friends for life." He didn't understand his mother. He didn't feel different. But his American mother saw the same thing. "Mykelti, you're a boy of ideas and strong opinions. People are not your stepping stones but doors of opportunity." Now, he knows that life is full of turning points—doors—and he has reached another one. Though he doesn't understand why, he believes Sherbert is the key to the future, and his beliefs are the only reality he can trust in this strange New World. "My decision is contingent on Sherbert's well-being. I'd like to speak with her now."

"A reasonable request. Lorenzo, would you please fetch our beloved rapscallion?"

The minutes tick past and Mykelti grows weary of Eddie and Gregory's banter, but his ears perk up when a commotion grows closer. "Let me through. Get your hands off me." And suddenly, Sherbert enters the tent. She sees Mykelti, runs up to him, and throws her arms around his neck. "You're here? I didn't believe it was you."

"I can't believe I found you. Are you okay? I'm here now. Don't worry," Mykelti rattles.

"I'm not a damsel in distress. I was doing just fine until you came along and made everyone go all he-man ape-shit."

"Look at the happy reunion," says Henrick. "It warms my heart."

"Let's get outta here," Mykelti says. "But first, do you remember a quirky old man—" before he finishes his question, Sherbert averts her eyes in shame— "from the smoothie shop? I'm looking for him and a baby."

"Don't worry," Eddie chimes in, "We'll make more. Isn't that right, sweetheart?" He ribs the taller man. "It's our duty to repopulate the planet, ain't it?"

"You're both pigs."

"The way I see it, I'm the most handsome man left alive." Eddie's eyes flick from person to person, waiting for laughter.

"I'd rather let the human race die out than even look at that porn stash of yours, Eddie."

"And I'm the most charming." The tall man laughs.

"Said no one ever."

Mykelti, feeling protective, asks, "Sherbert, you do want to go, don't you?"

"Yeah. Let's get out of here."

"It will be harder alone."

"We'll find others. I'm not spending the rest of my life shacked up with these bozos," she says, giving the henchmen side-eye.

Eddie laughs.

"Look," Henrick apologizes, "like I said, we need her. We could use your help, too."

"She doesn't owe you anything," says Mykelti. "We're leaving."

Gregory and Eddie raise their weapons.

"As you can see, my friends can be persuasive negotiators themselves."

The moments seem to slow as Mykelti braces himself to make a decision. Like Lorenzo said, it's hard. It could mean life or death. Should he abandon himself to their whims or try to save Sherbert?

Henrick sits at the desk, arms crossed. Eddie with his sneer. Gregory big and dull but standing ready. The tent ruffles from a slight wind. Noise grows outside. Fear rises within Mykelti, then fades away into a quiet resolve. He realizes that it is moments like these that make him different. Despite the consequences, he must follow his beliefs. He takes a deep breath to calm his nerves and walks out as threats are hurled at his back.

In the atrium, he is surprised to find a crowd has gathered. Gregory and Eddie use the opportunity to barricade his way with guns.

"You might not want to kill me just yet. I have a lot more information you'll find useful." Mykelti surreptitiously detaches the tubes from the tanks he pulls behind him and cranks open the valve. The gas hisses out, but no one notices because of the gas whooshing in and out of their face masks.

"Why do you think you are not dead already?"

"We're free people. Even if we stay, it's because we choose to stay. If you force us to stay, that makes us slaves." Mykelti turns to the crowd and shouts at the top of his lungs. "Are you all slaves?"

The crowd watches the scene like they would a movie, but they barely react.

"No one here is a slave," Henrick says as he emerges from the tent, but the fear in the eyes of the crowd tells a different story.

"What does that make Sherbert?"

"Sherbert is a valued member of our community. If she leaves, it jeopardizes us all."

Mykelti addresses Sherbert, "She's a valuable part of my community," and to the crowd, he shouts, "You can all come with us! We'll rebuild together!"

"No one is going anywhere," says Henrick.

How much is one person worth? Is it a one-to-one ratio? Are any two people worth more than any one person? What if that one person is the person who cures cancer? What if that one person represents hope? How much is that worth? Mykelti has already made this decision. It's a flawed decision—or rather, another flawed instinct—but that's what it means to be human. Right or wrong, you do anything to protect your loved ones. He gives Sherbert another apologetic look, like he did in the pharmacy, before telling Henrick, "We're leaving, dead or alive. And, before you get any ideas of shooting me, if you haven't noticed, this isn't just a couple tanks of oxygen I'm pulling behind me. It's a bomb. One spark, and you'll kill us all."

Henrick laughs. "We're not falling for that one again. In fact, we didn't fall for it the first time, did we, boys?" Henrick has a natural way of enlisting help.

"Unlike you, I've learned from my mistakes. This—" Mykelti points to the green and red tanks he's rolling behind him— "is an acetylene torch. It has both the fuel and the oxygen. It works even underwater. I've disconnected the hoses. The gases have been filling this room for the last few minutes."

"Just when you think all the stupidity in the world died out, we've got ourselves a suicide bomber here." Mykelti can't help but admire Henrick's pragmatic assessment of reality along with the undertone of regret that things could be better. "Are you going to kill us all, including your girlfriend?"

"Do it, Mykelti. I'm not their baby machine."

"A person has to live or die with their convictions," Mykelti says. "Most have died on the inside a long time ago."

"And..." says Henrick.

"I mean to say that I have nothing left to lose." He holds his lighter high for all to see. "Stay back."

"How do you know we're not the only humans left on the planet? Are you willing to destroy what's left of civilization?" Henrick has appraised Mykelti's weakness and sticks a knife of words in his weak spot.

"It doesn't look like there is much here worth saving," Mykelti stabs back. He moves forward, trying to part the men, but they don't move.

"He's already tried to kill us," says Gregory.

"Looks like we've got ourselves a good ol' fashioned Mexican standoff. Is that a racist thing to say?" Eddie asks. "I hope not because I love Mexicans. Ain't that right, Lorenzo?"

"Actually, Mykelti, I admire you," says Henrick. "How can anyone not admire someone who stands up for their values? I don't want to kill you. I'd regret not having someone to talk to, especially someone like yourself, that understands the Old World and doesn't have a monosyllabic vocabulary, like my companions here. But I can't let you go. It is up to you now. What are you going to do? Will you be able to live with the consequences of your decision? Most of these people are innocent. Lookie-loos that lost their television sets."

"I'm walking out of here, or I'm going to die trying."

"As you wish."

Mykelti was hoping they would fall for his bluff. He tries walking forward, but the crowd won't budge. He contemplates rolling the torch into the crowd and sparking the lighter. The explosion would probably be nothing more than a big harmless fireball like his bathroom; then again, if the tank rockets off and cracks open on the wall or gets pierced by a bullet, it would kill them all. Is he willing to take a chance? Part of him, the righteous part, thinks fate will protect him. He drops the torch backwards onto its third wheel and puts his foot on it, ready to roll it forward. "Last chance," he says.

"Henrick!" shouts a man entering the atrium. The crowd parts to let him through. Despite the mask, Mykelti recognizes the swarthy figure and his swagger. "You're supposed to be gathering survivors, not killing them."

"You said to get rid of the troublemakers. He failed the test."

"And yet, here he is. How many other aggrieved souls have you left behind? This is your first warning. Three strikes, and you're out. Now, see to it that we have armed guards standing watch day and night." Then the man approaches Mykelti without fear and holds his hand out.

Mykelti sighs, and his posture wilts. He hands over the lighter and resigns command of the situation.

The man's fist closes around the lighter as if it is a peace offering. "Come. We have much bigger problems to discuss," he says perfunctorily.

"Father," Mykelti honors him with the title and to explain his concession to those around him, "I'm not surprised to see you."

Jonathan turns to the stunned crowd and laughs, "What? Can't you see the family resemblance?"

"Wait, I thought you don't play favorites," Henrick says, trying to regain some power.

"I don't," says Jonathan. "Mykelti will vouch for me. He knows better than anyone."

The fifth wave of deaths: The pollution aftereffect
Ongoing

The world resembled a teenager popping pimples in the mirror. Without power, the coolants ceased to flow. The volatile chemicals and radioactive elements reached critical temperatures, expanding and exploding out of their containment vessels. Even the containment vessels that did not immediately fail eventually eroded in the wind and rain, or developed micro-cracks from the Earth's relentless quaking.

Raw chemicals from broken shipping vessels and factories spilled and flowed into the rivers and oceans, and gaseous chemicals rose into the air like clouds. If there had been enough oxygen in the atmosphere for combustion, fires would have ravaged the world. No city would have been left standing. If the world had burned, many of the chemicals would have been converted into less harmful compounds, like carbon dioxide and water. Instead, the chemicals diffused into the atmosphere and oceans, combining with other chemicals and the remaining oxygen like a free radical in a process similar to combustion but more insidious, creating lethal chemicals that never-before existed.

Less volatile materials like asbestos, styrofoam and plastic would be exposed to the weather and ground into a fine dust. The turbulent weather swept the chemical dust and radioactive dust into the upper atmosphere and seeded the clouds. The resulting storms spread poison around the planet. The particulates blocked the Sun, coated the shriveled plants, and clogged already troubled lungs. The dust decimated the Earth's remaining ability to renew itself and replenish the oxygen needed to stabilize the atmosphere and nourish life.

Pollution was mankind's most enduring legacy. Similar to how the Chicxulub meteor left a layer of ash worldwide that delineated the end of the dinosaurs, the debris of mankind would deposit a layer of sediment around the globe that would become a marker to future archaeologists that defined the end of a geological era.

Meltdown
Later that day

Like ducks in a row, Mykelti follows his father, followed by Sherbert, Henrick and his two favorite henchmen. "The atrium is just a buffer," Jonathan says. "It helps pressurize what I like to call our inner sanctuary. We'll talk there."

They pass camps of refugees. A group of adolescents prepare fresh food while watching over children playing with toys. Some children don't wear face masks. They must have some natural ability to live in low-oxygen environments.

"How did you survive, Sherbert?" asks Mykelti.

"I guess all your nagging to quit cigarettes paid off. Besides, I'm scrappy." Her chest heaves with laughter. Mykelti missed that.

"You could have mentioned my father was alive."

"Sorry. You were too busy running out the door."

"I looked for you. Tried calling. I'm sorry. I should have come for you sooner…"

"Don't worry, you're here now." Mykelti's heart floods with relief until she adds, "Whether I like it or not."

"What would I do without your backhanded compliments?" He laughs.

They approach the sporting goods store. Plywood seals off the department store from the main hallway. Jonathan pulls back a heavy curtain to reveal a small door. "Welcome to the inner sanctuary. You can take off your masks now, but leave them here, just in case." He points to a rack of face masks, oxygen canisters and condensers. Nearby stands a guard armed with an automatic rifle. Inside are smaller electrolysis units—water crackers. Mykelti wonders where they found the gun and how they vent the hydrogen.

Jonathan pauses at a small tent. Inside is a table full of electronic gear, microphones, and a shortwave ham radio plugged into an array of car batteries. Mykelti is impressed. The world had grown too dependent on technology, a system of communication with too many moving pieces. Finding or building an old-fashioned radio was the next thing on his list. "Any news, Benjamin?" asks Jonathan.

"You know I prefer Benji. Benjamin was my grandfather. Ben was my dad." He is a lanky teenager, proud to be nerdy. He sees that he has an audience and switches to his announcer's voice. "Welcome to Apocalypse Radio. You can't say we didn't see it coming." Then in a serious tone, "Good news is, more people are broadcasting. But still the usual chatter. No one knows what to do. There are still interesting rumors about boats being floated. Ha! Get it? Floated."

As his father gets news from Benji, Mykelti gathers information from Sherbert. "What happened to Fitzpatrick and the baby? I promised I'd return."

"Your father sent them away. He said—"

"I said—" Jonathan interrupts, overhearing the conversation— "we don't need any dead weight sucking the oxygen out of the room. That goes for you both. Everyone has to contribute. That old man wasn't—how should I say?— cooperating with the plan."

"And the baby?" Mykelti asks.

They arrive before Jonathan's desk full of books and papers. A map of Illinois hangs on a bulletin board. It's marked with many colored pins and strings. His father is no longer playing the role of diplomat. Gregory, Eddie and Lorenzo file into position, a ragamuffin version of the military. And Henrick, the taxman, standing nearby.

"They're alive. You can go look for them if you want. Seems you like to play savior. If you find them, you can babysit them until the end of days."

"So, your idea of survival is abandoning the weak?"

"And what have you done, Mykelti? Cower in your hidey-hole? As you can see, I have gathered survivors. I have put down the troublemakers. Secured the perimeter. Created a safe haven. Most importantly, I have a plan."

"Yes, I've heard your theories on repopulating the planet."

"Please, those are heathens talking. Look around, Mykelti. What do you see?"

"A bunch of dirty, unhappy men needing a mother."

"Your sarcasm disappoints me, but you're not far off. Isn't it obvious what Sherbert contributes?"

"Hey, I'm right here," says Sherbert. "I'll tell you what I contribute—a black eye to the first man who touches me. And y'all better find some other wench to cook your meals."

"Sherbert, you're not helping," Mykelti says, fearing for her safety.

Jonathan laughs. "Actually, she proves my point. Mykelti, think of your mother. What role did she have in our family? Who was she in business? I'll tell you. Women are the peacemakers. The planners. Leave it to the men, and they'd tear this place up with their squabbling."

"But against her will?"

"Before you leave, ask yourself what better options you have? And, second, are you willing to leave the rest of us to die?"

"How melodramatic."

"Is it? You may not agree with my methods, but here we are—safe."

"We would be safe had you listened to me years ago."

"That's a discussion for another time. Despite what you think, I'm proud of you. You follow your heart, and somehow you survive. You've always been a survivor. Let's not waste any more air arguing. We have a problem—" Jonathan throws a book down on the table. It lands with a thud. "Have you read your own survival manual?"

Mykelti's relieved to see it. "Only what I needed to know to survive one more day… Then your henchman stole it."

"We're all just trying to make a living," says Henrick.

"You almost killed me."

"Henrick has read your manual, and if it weren't for him, we would have all died of ignorance. Listen. We're surrounded by nuclear reactors. The safety protocols shut them down, but that does *not* mean we are safe. The uranium power rods are still thousands of degrees. Under normal conditions, they would take months to cool. Fortunately, the rods are still hot enough to generate energy to power the cooling pumps. However, here is the big *but*—"

Eddie laughs.

"There is no way to refill the cooling pond. Once the pond evaporates, the core will overheat—meltdown—and explode. You remember Fukushima. We're not talking a nuclear explosion, but a series of small gas explosions filled with radioactive waste. And—" Jonathan points to the map of Illinois— "you can see Chicago is surrounded by a semi-circle of nuclear power plants on one side and a Great Lake on the other."

"We have to evacuate," Henrick says. "And the only way out is through."

"The good news is that on the other side of the nuclear reactors—upwind, so we'd be safe from fallout—is a windmill farm. This information is thanks to Mykelti's foresight to print a map—even if he didn't read it."

"I was getting there," says Mykelti.

"We plan to leave in three days. Even by then, it might be too late. Henrick, now is as good a time as any to break the news. Call a general assembly."

§ § §

After the group hears the news, the talking turns to shouting as each person tries to make their point heard, their shouts blending into one anonymous voice.

"Move!? We can hardly breathe just sitting here, much less move?"

"What about the gangs? If we step one foot outta here, they'll steal everything we have and leave us for dead."

"They're still good people. They're just trying to survive. Like we all are. They don't want blood on their hands. Let's warn them of the danger."

"We don't know what they want. Desperate times breed desperate people."

"We're all desperadoes now, amigo."

"We won't have enough oxygen to make one day on foot. I vote we stay. We have everything we need here."

"You all don't know nothing about where your food comes from or where your shit goes. We're screwed whether we stay or go."

"We can't stay here. There are a million rotting bodies. I can smell it through my face mask."

"Soon, we'll be swimming in cockroaches."

"Stop!" shouts Jonathan. "This is *not* a negotiation. We have to leave. The plan is to load everything in electric trucks—"

"Electric trucks? It's hundreds of miles away. How are we going to recharge them?"

"The roads are clogged."

After listening to the hubbub, Mykelti feels he needs to help the group reach a consensus. "There must be other options. We could go north. It would be safer in a less densely populated location."

"Have you been to Wisconsin in the winter?"

"What does he know? He's not one of us."

"We can't even build a fire to stay warm."

"We need to go south."

"Who cares about staying warm when we can't even breathe?"

The shouting grows into an incoherent uproar.

Jonathan bangs the butt of his handgun on the table like a gavel until the crowd quiets. "The decision has been made," he speaks softly so that the crowd must stop to listen—and he speaks with finality. "Stick to the plan. We go to the windmill farm. Then we decide what to do next."

"Who has made that decision? We should put it to a vote."

"I make the decisions," says Jonathan.

Mykelti marvels at how his father's charisma has gained so much authority over this ragtag group but, as always, without regard. "Is that your contribution?" Mykelti asks. "To reign judge? Criticize our mistakes? Let me guess: somebody has to, right!?"

The crowd melts down into a chaos of shouting.

Jonathan bangs his gun on the table. "Enough!" He shouts.

Henrick and his henchmen step forward menacingly.

"That's right! Somebody has to! It's going to take all of us if we're going to survive. Somebody has to oil this squeaky machine. Somebody has to replace the broken parts. Somebody has to clean up the mess. And somebody has to pull the trigger for you bunch of cowards."

Jonathan turns to the crowd. "Let me remind you of the rules…" He pauses for dramatic effect.

"Rule number one: Play, follow the leader. You all learned that one in the schoolyard, so it should be easy. If you are unwilling to get the job done, you get a strike. Dissenters that undermine our well-oiled machine get a strike. We can't afford to waste air questioning every god-damned decision. Mykelti, I'm putting you down for one strike for dissenting."

"You're punishing me *after* you tell me the rules?"

"Rule number two: Contribute more than you take. We don't have resources for handouts. If you are unable to contribute, you get left behind. That means the old, the weak, the sick—of mind or body. The only exceptions are children. People that make mistakes—that jeopardize our safety, knowingly or unknowingly—get a strike. And—"

"This is bullshit!" an anonymous voice cries.

"Rule number three: Stragglers will be left behind. Our group isn't strong enough to guarantee its own survival, much less run charities and rescue missions—"

"He's just going to leave us to die... after everything we've done!?"

Murmurs of consensus.

"There you have it: three simple rules. Three strikes, and you're out."

"I want out already," whispers Sherbert to Benji.

"When he says *out,* he means *out there.* You won't survive alone."

"I'm the one that has gathered you here. I'm the one who gets to run the machine. The rule of law is the only thing binding us together. Or would you all prefer to run amok like the savages outside?"

"Maybe I'll just leave myself behind," says a man wearing a red baseball cap.

"Tell me, Raymond, what did you do in the Before Time?"

"A farmer."

"Is anyone else here a farmer?" No one raises their hand.

"I'm not a good farmer," justifies Raymond. "All I can grow is genetically modified corn. And, believe me, I dump a literal shitload of fertilizer and spray the living hell out of the bugs."

"Like it or not, you are the best we got."

"You can't make me stay."

"Are you going to leave us to starve? Does anyone here want Raymond— our one and only farmer—to leave?" Jonathan asks the crowd. "For that matter, does anyone want Elizabeth, the doctor, to leave? Or Tiffany, the teacher? Or me, the one and the only one with a plan. Does anyone want me to leave...?"

No one dares to speak. A few shake their heads *no.*

"Good." He turns to Mykelti. "You see? Democracy in action. It's been decided. No one leaves." Jonathan pauses, daring the crowd to speak, every tick of silence becomes a vote in his favor. "Henrick will be giving you your assignments. Mykelti, follow me."

The group disbands slowly, mumbling under their breath: "What choice do we have?... I don't have any better ideas... He's right. We don't need any freeloaders... Let him take the responsibility. I don't want blood on my hands... You have blood on your hands just standing by and doing nothing... I don't even care anymore…"

The people and the comments fade away like the air.

§ § §

"Mykelti," Jonathan gives his name extra weight as if admonishing a child, "If you spread doubt, you will ruin everything we have built. I need to know we are on the same team."

"If not, is my head going to end up on a pike?"

"Those people were dead already. It's an effective advertisement. People run amok now, released from any moral obligation they previously had. The troublemakers are joining ranks. They don't stop to ask questions. We can help each other, but I need to know that when I say go, you go. There is no debate. Again, I ask: Are we on the same side?"

"I'd like to know the same thing." Mykelti removes the bottle of steroids from his backpack—the performance-enhancing drugs his father had been using to help oxygen metabolism—and slams it on the table in front of his father. The cap pops open, and the pills skitter across the table. "You knew all along."

His father leans back in his chair and scratches his gray, grizzly beard. It's like a nervous tick that redirects his anger. "Of course, I knew. The IPCC knew. Most of the world's governments knew. We've known for decades. Who do you think persuaded the public to reduce, reuse, recycle? And when that didn't work, who do you think spun the issue into carbon dioxide and global warming? And when that didn't work, who do you think created the pandemic lockdowns and fuel shortages? Shall I continue?"

"So you admit this was all part of an international conspiracy?"

"There were a lot of events more likely to happen before we burned all our oxygen. We were constantly measuring bellwethers. We were supposed to run out of oil *long before we ran out of oxygen…* We were supposed to die of air pollution *long before we ran out of oxygen…* We were supposed to run out of food *long before we ran out of oxygen…* The Midwestern aquifers—fresh water everywhere—were supposed to dry up. The polar ice caps were supposed to melt. The oceans were supposed to die. All our models predicted these things would happen, but happen very slowly. It was a crap shoot which would happen first, but by solving any one of these problems, we would have naturally solved the oxygen problem."

"Instead, your solution was to build carbon reclaimers and charge people carbon tax in the guise of environmental justice. You sound like a corporate pig feeding in the trough of everyone else's hard work."

"Mykelti, *we* could have capped carbon emissions. As a side effect, *we* could have earned billions. And—"

"And kick the can down the road to the next generation."

"It was easier that than getting people to change their bad habits. You could have done anything you wanted with your money. You could have created technology to make oxygen. Imagine fusion reactors floating in the ocean—giant electrolysis factories pumping gigatonnes of oxygen into the atmosphere."

"But you saved nothing."

"We reached an unforeseen tipping point."

"Unforeseen? Except that I told you years in advance."

"So you were right. Is that what you want me to say? Do you want a participation trophy? Shall we reconvene the group and ask them to thank Mykelti for *almost* saving the world?"

"Likewise, let's tell everyone you knew all along and did nothing."

"What I did do was clean up your mess for years. Have you ever thought that maybe you were the unforeseen tipping point? We might have had another fifty years if you hadn't panicked the world. You even convinced your own mother to panic. If it wasn't for you insisting on living in Chicago, we'd have been safe in Geneva. She'd be alive now."

"You haven't changed." Mykelti stands in anger. His fight-or-flight response looking for an outlet. "I didn't see you at the hospital watching her take her dying breath."

"We said our goodbyes every day, knowing it might be the last. Please—" he gestures to the chair.

Mykelti reluctantly sits back down, breathing deeply to regain his composure.

"We had a backup plan. It wasn't a very good one, but it was foolproof. The disease of mankind is a self-correcting problem: the less oxygen, the fewer the humans; the fewer the humans, the less the problem. I suppose you could say the backup plan is in action now, though it was never expected to reach an extinction level."

"The disease of mankind!? A self-correcting problem!?" Mykelti laughs disparagingly. "That was your brilliant solution? Letting humanity die?"

"C'mon, Mykelti," Jonathan scratches his beard. "All that research you've done, and you haven't figured out that the root of all problems is humanity. Not our machines. Not climate change. It's us. It's human nature. We got that fuck-you gene."

"Greed, I'll agree with you on that."

"Greed lies deep in our hearts. A little bit is fine. A rotten apple here or there, no problem, but there were too many people. We were destined to run off the cliff. I was trying to do it in an orderly fashion. Well... here we are—same end result. Oxygen depletion is no longer a problem. Now, all that matters is our survival. And trust me, *if* we survive, and *if* we are not careful, humans will cause a whole new batch of problems. Mankind is the problem."

As his father unknowingly reiterates Mykelti's thoughts of the last few days, he feels a growing sense of resignation. "Nothing I said ever helped."

"Most people don't know how to listen."

"So you've told me before," he frowns.

"Mykelti, not everything I say is criticism. You are still my son, and I still have things I can teach you. What I am trying to say is, we are hardwired to defend our beliefs, despite logic. It's tens of thousands of years of evolution. A new idea means you are wrong—vulnerable. A new idea means you will be viewed as different—a threat to your community's status quo. And, if you are a threat, you will be removed—excommunicated—one way or another. Being ostracized—whether it be death, banishment or just having your words fall on deaf ears—is the worst punishment our species can assign. Listening—thinking—is hard. Few people can be honest with themselves."

Mykelti finds his father's words ironic. "What about you? You say you heard me."

"Even I catch myself dismissing an idea too quickly because it doesn't fit my current thinking. It's hard to discover you're wrong and have to back up a few steps—but learning is a process."

"Hmm," Mykelti scoffs.

"I was wrong. Is that what you want me to say?" Jonathan concedes. "I believed we could fix the problem behind the scenes. You tried to tackle the problem head-on. We both failed. This time, we should work together, wouldn't you agree?"

"Haven't I been saying that?"

"I finally hear you. Loud and clear."

Mykelti is hesitant to reply. He believes his father is trying to buy his loyalty with flattery, but he also agrees they need to work together.

"Mykelti, you are still a trusted ally to me. I want you to know the big picture. There is hope of rescue—a boat. The United States Navy hospital ship. It doesn't appear the Navy exists anymore, but somehow a skeleton crew survived. They are picking up survivors. Benjamin is tracking any rescue efforts. If it exists, it may be our only hope."

"And why didn't you give this hope to everyone?"

"I gave them the windmill farm. Most can't imagine that, much less a boat.

These are carrots. Our priority is to escape Chicago. Wouldn't you agree?"

"Of course," Mykelti says, feeling baited into submission.

"Good. Then report to Henrick. We'll need all the oxygen we can find to survive the trip, a renewable source if possible. And figure out a way to charge the trucks," his father says as if handing out household chores. Mykelti is anxious to leave the room—he refuses to believe his father's flattery—but he doesn't escape fast enough to avoid more guilt. "Mykelti, I was a good father in the Old World. That has to count for something."

The sixth wave of deaths: Plague and pestilence
Ongoing

Most humans that chose to stay in the cities did not survive long. It was not the lack of oxygen. Nor was it the roving bandits. Nor was it the radiation. And neither was it the rotting corpses. Contrary to common belief, corpses are less likely to spread disease than a living person. The most common cause of death was fecal matter. Poor hygiene and sanitation led to the spread of gastroenteritis and worse diseases like dysentery, cholera and typhoid fever. The remaining humans had a countless stockpile of bottled water and packaged food; however, it only took one infected person and one cockroach walking through a stream of waste to transmit the disease to an unsuspecting survivor's dinner plate. And that one contaminated survivor could lead to the demise of an entire group.

The relatively infinite supply of food caused the cockroach population to explode. Likewise, rats, having made their homes in the sewers of humanity, could easily tolerate low-oxygen environments and now had a feast like never before. Like the Rat Flood in India, their numbers multiplied by 12 every two months. The rat population swelled from half a million to nearly one billion in just six months. Chicago had already won the award for "Rattiest City" many years running. Now, it was a rat tsunami.

The diseases piggybacking the rats multiplied even faster.

And dogs, living underfoot mankind for so long, had also become accustomed to hypoxic conditions. Millions survived, but most were trapped and died of starvation. Most that broke their bonds were not able to adapt. They were breeds designed for companionship and cuteness. Others, the hunters and workers that had served mankind for millennia, overcame their domestic training to scavenge upon the dead. In the hypoxic environment, bodies did not rot as much as they fermented, which created a food source that lasted for months, and when that ran low, they hunted the rats and humans. After several generations, the dogs would recombine into a mongrel, not unlike their distant, extinct relative, the wolf.

If the remaining humans survived the pestilence, they were swarmed by plagues of rats and dogs. Soon, they could no longer leave their safe havens to scavenge food. Finally, many died because humans were, as they always have been, a plague upon themselves, feeding off each other indirectly and, sometimes, directly.

Exodus
Day 17

A large group of survivors, along with the night guards, had snuck away in the night. Some had valuable skills that would be needed, and they took all the children—their future—but one. Despite himself, Mykelti thinks his father is right again. They couldn't afford to let anyone leave, but how could they force them to stay and cooperate? The remaining survivors have spent days preparing; now they are spread out next to their trucks, waiting for the order to leave. Thirteen trucks with four passengers each. *We're gonna need to find more survivors,* he thinks. *Fifty-two people is not enough to rebuild civilization.*

Mykelti fills every last nook and cranny with his house plants. It's surprising how many things he no longer needs: years of research, credit cards, insurance, entertainment. Leaving behind his sentimentals is what hurt most, but almost nothing matters except air, water and food, in that order. He did bring his passport in case some vestiges of civilization remained. If not, it will serve as a record of his existence, like removing the dog tags of a dead soldier after battle. Looking at his passport picture—the clean-cut, smiling, Mykelti—he feels that person has already died. Inside his passport is one picture of himself with his mother. She was the only reason he ever had to feel like he belonged in the lonely, overcrowded Old World.

Sherbert strikes an artful pose next to his truck. "Seriously, you're bringing your pet turtle?"

"Think of it like the canary in the coal mine. It's one of the few species to have survived, and if the atmosphere continues to deteriorate…"

"Does it have a name?" Sherbert puffs an e-cigarette.

"How are you smoking?"

"It's called vaping, Dr Science. And these don't burn oxygen. They just boil some chemical shit."

"I thought you quit."

"Life is short. Enjoy it while you can. Haven't you heard? It's our new motto."

Mykelti frowns. "Ever hear of lung cancer?"

"Ever hear of mind-your-own-fucking-business?"

"Sorry, I just—"

"Is that all ya got to smoke?" Eddie asks as he walks past with an armful of supplies.

Sherbert shrugs. "I used to grow my own stuff. Looks like the corporations won again."

"C'mon, Hamburger," Eddie whistles to his dog, which wears a backpack filled with dog food. "You too, Gregory," he laughs at the expense of the slow man.

"Hey, Eddie," Benji asks, "Why do you call your dog Hamburger?"

"Cuz if I ever run out of food, that's what he'll be—hamburger. He's my four-legged refrigerator." Eddie coos and rubs the dog's ears. "Isn't that right, boy?" The dog's tail wags from the extra attention.

"When we run out of dogs, we'll start with the soft ones that don't need no tenderizing, like you," Gregory taunts Mykelti, then looks to Eddie, waiting for praise.

"Not me. I'm starting with Sherbert. Do you think she tastes as sweet as her name?"

"One more word, and you won't have enough teeth left for anything but baby food," she says.

Sherbert's threat doesn't even register as Eddie keeps walking and laughing. "Can't believe my life depends on friggin' eco-friendly trucks. They're ugly as sin," he tells Gregory.

"Not as ugly as dying here," he replies as their voices fade into the distance.

At the head of the line, Jonathan removes his face mask long enough to bellow, "Okay, people! Load up!"

"Here we go," says Mykelti. As soon as he shuts the door, Henrick is at the window. "Move over. I'm driving. We've been nominated to lead this shit show." He has to part the houseplants to get into the driver's seat. "Damn, it's a jungle in here."

"Sherbert. Get in the back seat and put that damn thing out before you kill us all."

"You are the only one I'm planning on killing."

Once inside, they seal the doors and submerge a car battery in a fish tank, using the truck as a hermetic chamber. The two poles of the battery bubble vigorously. They attach a tube to the cathode to vent the hydrogen out the rear window. "It's not perfect," says Mykelti, but we should survive. Once the cabin fills, they turn off their oxygen canisters. They are irreplaceable and will be saved for emergencies.

The citizen band radio clipped to Henrick's belt crackles, "Hold on," Jonathan commands. "We got a dead battery already."

"Well, looks like we've got some extra time to get acquainted."

"You have courage," Henrick tells Mykelti. "I'll give you that. Brains? I'm not so sure. Tell me, would you have done it?" He refers to using the acetylene torch as a bomb.

"Would you have made me?" Mykelti counters.

"I was hedging my bets. Let you leave and lose respect? Or, let you stay and lose lives? The price of life is not very high right now."

Mykelti is reminded of Jacobs. Henrick and Jacobs were both paper pushers, but one felt useless and lost the will to live. "I'm curious how an accountant fared so well in the post-apocalypse? I thought the only skills you had were smudging numbers."

"I thought of myself more as a fixer than an accountant. When a company got in trouble, I was the hired gun. It was a dog-eat-dog, people-eat-people world. Not much different than now, really. You have to be ruthless to fleece the sheep—get a piece of everyone else's pie. I'm mixing my metaphors, but you know what I mean. *Ruthlessness* is a commodity more valuable than ever. It makes me very talented at allocating resources. Do you know what made me good at my job?"

"Prioritizing?"

"I'm surprised you don't know. Your father knows."

"Enlighten me."

"People. You have to eliminate people from your equation. You can't think: Those people earned it. Or, those people deserve it. Or, those people are underprivileged and need a leg up. You have to think in terms of what will benefit the company."

"Ah, you are a…" Mykelti searches for the right words, "a beneficent sociopath. One that doesn't regard the happiness of the individual, but the welfare of the group."

"Ha! A philosopher. I stand corrected. You do have brains. Yes, and theoretically a better company, makes a better world. That's all you—"

"The-ro-fucking-retically," says Sherbert. "I just can't...."

"—can focus on—the big picture," says Henrick. "I hear you tried to save the world. If saving the world was my business, the first thing I would have done was turn off the lights. I speak literally and figuratively. Price people out of causing problems. Anyway, enough talking shop. It's gonna be a long day." Henrick digs into his backpack. "I've been saving this, but—Hey!—what am I waiting for? The end of the world?" He laughs and pulls a bottle of bourbon from his backpack. "Even if you could find it, you couldn't afford it."

Mykelti laughs, "Old Rip Van Winkle. That's my favorite."

"Color me impressed. What are the chances of that!?" Henrick laughs.

"One hundred percent," says Mykelti.

As a way of making amends, Henrick pours the drinks and offers a compliment, "I suspect you might have had the courage to do it. But, tell me... How many people were you willing to sacrifice?"

"How many would it take?" Mykelti jokes, caught in the bravado. "To the New World," he toasts.

"To drinking and driving and not giving a shit," says Henrick.

They *clink* glasses and take a big swig.

"You know it's really a sipping drink best served on ice," says Mykelti. "When do you think we'll see another ice cube?"

"Hopefully never if we can get out of here," says Sherbert.

"You know, Sherbert," says Henrick. "Mykelti and his father are an awful lot alike."

"I'm nothing like my father," Mykelti says too quickly. Even as the words fall out of his mouth, he realizes he has followed in his father's footsteps, trying to be the model son.

"You have to admit they have our best interests in mind. Well, not me per se, but the group as a whole. They're our beneficent dictators."

"And?"

"And... I'm waiting to see who has the better policies."

§ § §

When the caravan rumbles forward, the noise scatters the stray dogs. They have begun to gather into packs as their hunger rekindles feral instincts. The corpses that line the streets no longer make an ideal food source.

The caravan rolls past the mall. Spray-painted across the front is Mykelti's message. "Danger! Radiation fallout! Go to the windmill farm." He figured any survivors savvy enough to make it to the windmill farm wouldn't be intending trouble. His father disagreed, but decided to sort them out later. Underneath the sign sits Mildred. "You're leaving us all to fucking die!" she screams. His father refused to save Mildred on account of her being a burden to the group. Mykelti disagreed, but it didn't matter; Mildred refused to be helped.

Not long after Mildred, another survivor sees the caravan and runs alongside. It doesn't seem possible to run, but she runs, mouthing, "Help me, please."

"Leave them. We can't risk picking up strangers," Jonathan's voice crackles on the radio.

Mykelti slows. "We have to help."

"We can't," says Henrick. "Remember, stay focused on the big picture."

He's right. We don't know who she is. We don't have enough oxygen. He tries to convince himself as they accelerate past her. She falls to her knees, sobbing. It's a sight Mykelti won't forget. But it gets a little easier every time.

As they proceed, the lead truck pushes a stalled car off the road, then it falls to the back of the caravan, and the next truck pushes the next car off the road. It's slow work, and when the roads are too cluttered, the caravan uses the sidewalks, parking lots and parks as roads.

"Using the trucks like battering rams is draining our battery. We're not going to make it at this rate," Henrick says.

"We should be fine once we get out of the city," says Mykelti.

"Should be? You are full of optimism today," Sherbert retorts.

"And you are your usual sarcastic self," Mykelti jokes.

"We don't have a choice. We have to make it," says Henrick.

"Quitting is always an option," says Mykelti.

"Quitting is the same as dying."

"It's a choice many have made."

Mykelti's vehicle happens to be in the lead when the caravan reaches the interstate. He gets out of the truck, the oxygen runs out of the car like cold air from a refrigerator, and climbs onto the roof of a nearby car for a better view. Looking down from the overpass, the highway appears like a child's playpen scattered with toys. Cars have drifted into the emergency lane. A semi-truck has spun sideways, blocking northbound traffic. And a tanker appears to be on fire. *But it can't be smoke,* Mykelti thinks. He removes his mask to sniff the acrid air. It burns his sinuses. Toxic fumes. In the distance, Mykelti can see more plumes emanating from sources hidden behind buildings. And, ironically, he sees a billboard advertising: "New! Lemon Squeezy Breezy."

"Mykelti?" Jonathan's voice crackles again.

"It's permanent gridlock down there."

"What about the emergency lanes?"

"Blocked in both directions. We'll have to use plan B."

"Okay. Keep it moving up there. The windmill farm is barely in range during good conditions. Over." Moments later, he addresses the group. "We're going to be taking the backroads until we can find a country highway that's clear. It's going to be close. Everyone, kill your radios, air conditioner, lights, monitors— save all your power for the engine. We can't recharge these batteries until the windmill farm, and we can't get to the windmill farm without fully charged batteries."

When his father finishes, Mykelti announces to the group, "Everyone, stay in your cars. Keep your masks on. Smells like we have a chemical spill nearby."

"Mykelti?" Jonathan says on the private band. "Next time you want to give orders, talk to me first," says Jonathan.

"Sorry. I was just—"

"I don't want to hear explanations. Over."

"—trying to help..." Mykelti isn't trying to assume leadership, but his instincts to protect people took over. "Do as father says, not as father does," he laughs awkwardly.

"You should tell him to stop breathing down your neck," says Sherbert.

"Let's get out of here." Mykelti folds his paper map—it was hard to find in this digital era—and turns on their GPS. Over 12,000 miles above, the solar-powered satellites still broadcast their signals.

"Hey, I thought we were supposed to kill the devices?"

"My job is to navigate. I'm navigating. What's your job, by the way?"

"I'm the sex object. Can't you tell?" Sherbert says sarcastically. "I keep the boys in line with innuendo and promises I'll never keep."

"Not everyone sees you as a sex object," he says, trying to be chivalrous.

"Like you? I'm sure you see me as a real person. Fucking feminist, you are. Platonic friends for life. Hey! Can we get some music while you're busy *navigating?*" Sherbert uses air quotes. "Henrick might not make it if I have to listen to him the whole way." She uses any opportunity to vent her distaste.

"Sure. What would you like me to sing?" says Mykelti. He's passing the time reading.

Sherbert sees the cover. "You titled your survival manual *To be or not to be?*"

"I was feeling morose at the time."

"How is that different from any other time?"

"You both better stop wasting air flapping your lips. I need a nap. Sherbert, you take over."

When Henrick falls asleep in the backseat, Sherbert confesses, "I'm sorry,

Mykelti. You make the apocalypse bearable. Really, I don't know what I would do without you."

"Aww. You make it giraffe-able. Get it bear-able? Giraffe-able?"

"I take it back."

§ § §

Midafternoon, the caravan enters a quaint midwestern city. The business district is a couple blocks long, a fraction the size of Chicago, but the cars and corpses are in the same haphazard pattern. Mykelti stops in front of the general store and calls his father, "We need to talk."

"Speak to me."

"We should pull over."

"Fu... uh... uck."

Jonathan's truck comes to a screeching halt, and Mykelti pulls alongside. Before he can get out, Jonathan is banging on his window. "C'mon on."

"We're not going to make it," Mykelti says, getting out of the truck.

"Are you trying to panic everybody again?"

"We got unlucky. D-day happened during rush hour; there are too many cars on the road. Clearing the wreckage was a big drain. And, we've done twice as many miles as expected, zigzagging."

"I assume you have a new plan."

Henrick gets out of the car. "More brains are better than one."

Followed by Sherbert. "Did I hear you need more brains?"

Jonathan ignores them.

"We need to recharge. The weather patterns—" Mykelti points to the gray sky and roiling clouds— "may be permanently altered. Solar is not an option. But I found a hydroelectric dam nearby, the Dayton Dam on the Fox River. It's small. It probably hasn't overloaded and automatically shut down. It's almost the perfect location for a new home base," says Mykelti.

"You could have told me this over the radio. Let's get going."

"There's... Uh... A small problem." Mykelti stumbles over finding words that will make his solution palatable to his father.

Jonathan's brows knot with frustration as he waits for clarification.

"It's only twelve miles from the LaSalle nuclear power plant."

"And... Do I have to drag everything out of you?"

"If the reactor isn't showing any signs of overheating—"

"Which would be what!?" Sherbert asks.

"—and if we can find some charging stations—"

"Which would be where?"

"Hopefully, we should be able to leave by morning."

"*If, maybe, hopefully,* and *should?* This is your plan?"

A small figure, looking even smaller underneath his oxygen canister, approaches. "What's the news?" asks Benji.

"This isn't a press conference," Jonathan reprimands.

"I'm the communications officer. It's my duty to communicate."

"Tell the others. We've got a new plan."

Benji looks excited.

"The plan is to sit back, suck their thumbs, and not cause any trouble."

§ § §

As they near their destination, visible on the horizon, toward the nuclear power plant, a giant white plume rises into the sky. "That can't be good," Henrick says.

"Is that smoke?" Sherbert asks.

"It can't be smoke. It must be steam," Mykelti says.

"Mykelti?" the radio crackles.

"It's not bad, but it's not good," he responds to his father's unasked question. "If we can see steam, there must still be water in the cooling ponds; however, if we can see steam, then the cooling systems have broken down. The power plant is venting the steam directly into the atmosphere instead of recycling it."

"Is it safe?"

"What choice do we have?"

"Okay, everybody," Jonathan announces on the group bandwidth, "No rest for the weary. We're going to overnight here. We will be working in shifts. Two-thirds of you will sleep in the vehicles to preserve oxygen. The other one-third will be gathering supplies. You know the drill: oxygen tanks, oxygen condensers, batteries, water, food—in that order. We also need a team to find a charging station for our vehicles. When you find it, move the fleet there."

Rule #3: Stragglers will be left behind
Day 18

The next morning, there is a break in the perpetual drizzle long enough to see three columns of steam rising from the nearby nuclear reactors. The steam being emitted from the closest reactor is an intermittent wisp. "We're running out of time," says Jonathan.

"Obviously," Sherbert rolls her eyes.

"What happens when the steam is gone?" asks Benji.

Jonathan looks at Mykelti, silently commanding him to answer, making him the bearer of bad news. "The core can't overheat as long as it is submerged in water. If the water boils off—if the steam stops—the core will melt down. If we're lucky, the containment vessel will hold."

"If we're not lucky?"

"The core could melt through the containment vessel, or the heat will generate hot gases—particularly hydrogen—and explode. It will irradiate everything within ten-to-twenty miles and everything downwind for hundreds of miles."

"How far away is that one?" Sherbert asks.

"About seventeen miles."

"That's comforting," she says sarcastically.

"Don't worry." Instinctively, Mykelti puts his hand on Sherbert's back to comfort her. "We should have enough warning to evacuate," but takes his hand off as soon as his conscious mind catches up, though she didn't object.

Jonathan radios the group, "We don't have any time to waste. We'll be moving out truck by truck as soon as they're charged." They had found a small charging station that could accommodate four vehicles. It is taking eight hours to charge a vehicle. Four trucks are ready to go, which leaves eleven trucks to be charged. Nobody is talking about the two missing trucks. Perhaps they are hopeful the others will rejoin the caravan; more likely, they don't want to face the reality that the trucks are lost to breakdowns or marauders.

"Okay," Henrick says to the first group. "Let's move out. You have the destination in your GPS. Hello?" He thumps on the hood of the lead car. "No lollygagging." He knocks on the window. "Hello?" The silhouette inside doesn't move, so Henrick opens the door. "C'mon, time to move—" Without the door to support the driver's body, it slides out and thumps on the ground. "Gregory.

Eddie. Help me out here."

They pop open the doors—all four passengers are blue-in-the-face dead.

Jonathan pushes through the growing crowd. "What the hell happened?"

Mykelti, seemingly the one to have to answer more questions, leans inside to inspect. "Strange. The water cracker is still functioning. Hmm. Best guess. The hydrogen wasn't being vented properly and displaced the oxygen—asphyxiation. They probably fell asleep before realizing what was happening."

"Shit. Those were good people. Useful people," Jonathan says.

"Jonathan, sir," a frazzled woman rushes up to the crowd, gasping for air behind her mask, "My hus... band. He's miss... miss... missing. He went out for supplies. La... late last night."

"Can't you see we have bigger problems?"

"He should... be here... would be here... if he could. We need to find... Help him!"

"We aren't risking any more people dying."

The woman decompensates into sobs, pleading between breaths.

"Rule number three," Jonathan says. "Stragglers will be left behind."

"He's not... a straggler. Something's... wrong."

"It doesn't matter if he *won't* or *can't* keep up. We're not risking any more lives."

"Please." She turns to everyone, "Please? Someone."

Mykelti's heart is breaking. "We have time. It will take all day to charge the vehicles. Who's with me?"

"We are *not* risking anymore lives," says Jonathan just as a low boom echoes in the air. In the distance, a mushroom cloud of steam expands high into the sky. The group stares dumbfounded at the nuclear reactor. "Times up," Jonathan says, snapping their gazes back to him. He pulls the body out of the passenger's seat and dumps it at the woman's feet.

She shrieks and jumps back. "You are an asshole!"

"That's one strike for you."

"You can't just leave him!" says the woman in a shrill voice of desperation.

"You agreed to the rules when you signed up. It's time to live up to your end of the bargain. Individuals are expendable, especially the unfit. The only thing that matters is the survival of the group."

"He's useful," pleads Abigail. "He's our best scavenger."

"Past performance is no guarantee of future results," says Henrick.

While they argue, Eddie and Gregory drag the bodies away, leaving them to rot like millions of others.

"Are you all dead on the inside!?" accuses Sherbert.

"I'll stay. Help," Mykelti says, thinking someone should lay the dead to rest and console the living.

"Focus on the big picture, Mykelti." Jonathan gestures to the mushroom cloud. "We need to evacuate and secure the windmill farm."

"Take Benji or Travis."

"If the windmill farm isn't safe or isn't producing power, we'll need to double back. It will give us time to form a new plan."

Mykelti would rather stay and help. He looks to the group for a consensus and finds none.

Jonathan offers a reprieve, "Abigail, you have until the last truck leaves for your husband to show up. Henrick, see that no one does anything stupid. Mykelti, don't make me ask again. Get in. And let's go."

"I'll go ahead. Make sure it's safe," Mykelti tells the group as he reluctantly gets in the car, but his eyes are focused on Sherbert.

She refuses to acknowledge him, but her frown is telling.

"Oh. Wait. My bug-out bag is in the other car."

"If the other trucks don't make it to camp, you'll have bigger problems than whether you remembered to pack your toothbrush."

"We need the survival manual."

"Make it quick."

Mykelti grabs his belongings and apologizes to Sherbert, "You'll be fine."

"I'm not worried. It's not like you are leaving me to die."

"There's room for you. C'mon."

"I'm good. I don't need daddy to protect me." She walks away before he can appease her.

Her comments sting as he unloads his essentials into the new truck.

"You brought your pet turtle?" says Jonathan.

"His name is Canary—like the canary in the coal mine."

"Just get in." Jonathan starts the truck and follows the GPS as if it's the yellow brick road.

"That woman—she couldn't hear anything except that you were leaving her husband to die," Mykelti says.

"I wasn't teaching her a lesson. I was teaching everyone that was watching a lesson."

"What? That people are expendable?" His tone takes on the sarcasm of Sherbert.

"If you had the courage, you would have done it yourself."

"I thought we were supposed to be saving the human race, not treating them like animals."

"Mykelti, you may not be American, but you've spent years being indoctrinated into the rules of this society. I'm sorry to burst your bubble of patriotism, but there is no such thing as self-evident truths and inalienable rights. Life, liberty and the pursuit of happiness are ideas—human inventions."

"Without our ideals, we are no better than animals."

"Don't pretend to give me a moral lecture. Morals are a product of a bygone civilization. Morals only exist if I say they do."

"And what makes you god of our universe?"

"Have you met God? Did He make you any promises?"

"What do you think?"

"Were you born with a silver spoon?"

"You know very well."

"Were you born with an instruction manual? Did you even ask to be born?"

Mykelti is fuming inside, knowing he's being led down a path he doesn't want to travel. He had never even met his biological father. He had left to earn money in the big city, Yaoundé, Cameroon's capital, but never came back.

"When you were born, did you sign a contract with your parents? No, of course, you didn't. It is one of the ironies of life that anyone can get pregnant and raise a heathen, or worse, a barbarian that tears down civilization for the joy of it. But, to adopt, I had to do months of paperwork, be vetted and make promises. I promised to care for you. To educate you. Feed you. Protect you. And I promised to clean up all your messes. My contract expired the day you turned eighteen. But, look at me, the good father, thirty-some years later, and I'm still teaching you and cleaning up your messes." Jonathan pauses for a deep breath. Even in the sealed truck, there is not enough air. "The truth… You want the only inalienable truth there is?"

"My ears are open."

"The truth is: the world doesn't owe us anything, and we don't owe the world a god-damned thing. The only guarantee is to be born and to die. In between, we are granted to be as selfish and miserable as we can afford to be."

"I'm afraid I'm missing the point."

"Read between the lines, Mykelti. The point is that we need new rules if we are going to survive. Why me, you ask? Because someone has to. Because I choose to. Like I chose to adopt you, I adopted this ragtag group. I promised to care for them, and they accepted my promise. *That* makes me the god of their universe. Not only do I get to make the laws, I also get to be judge, jury and executioner. My methods may seem harsh, but half these people would die of depression, and the other half would suck the juice out of the living."

"You can't force people to cooperate."

"Optimistic thinking isn't going to put food on the table."

"You have to give them a choice."

"The choice is: do something and live, or do nothing and die. Five people died this morning because they couldn't follow directions. Simple step-by-step directions. We did the thinking for them, and they're still dead. How much more evidence do you need that people can't be trusted to make the right choice?"

"Slavery is not in fashion anymore, if you haven't noticed."

"I was on my way to becoming Secretary-General of the United Nations, and I would have become one of the richest men in the world. Do you know how I rose to power? Simple. Punishment and reward. The carrot and the stick. I punished anyone who crossed me and rewarded anyone that supported me. That's it. I started in the schoolyard with a bag of marbles, a box of candy and a big mouth. I made friends and taught my enemies to respect me or get a bloody nose. I worked myself up the ladder from there. It's human nature. The survival of the fittest. Capitalism in its essence. And, you know what? It's not a secret. Everyone knew what I was doing because most were trying to do the same thing. I just did it better. It doesn't matter how much you intellectualize fear and pain—animals will go a long way to avoid it. Suffering and struggle are unavoidable. Everybody needs to eat, shit and die."

"Eat shit and die. Nice life motto."

"At least you listen. Now try to understand," Jonathan scolds. "You want our people to line up like good little soldiers and build a shelter and plant their gardens. Do you think they are just going to do it from the goodness of their own heart? No. Fear and pleasure are the secrets to running the New World. We need to incentivize them. If one of them doesn't want to contribute, throw them outside. Make a lesson of them. See how long they last before they come crawling back. If they cooperate, reward them, but not too much. People that are too fat and happy won't go to work. Give them a little something, enough money to last the day, or a little privilege that doesn't cost you anything. You don't even need to look deep into their hearts. Napoleon said a man would do anything for a piece of ribbon. Truer words were never spoken. Respect is what a man wants most. More notches on that bedpost."

"I disagree."

"Is that so? You still carry the pain of your childhood. The death of your village. Your brothers. Your birth mother. You've been working your whole life to put a bandaid on that memory, trying to earn back the respect you lost for yourself. You donate your life to charity and science, trying to fix the world's problems. Waiting for someone to come along and tell you, 'You're a good person, Mykelti.'"

His father's words burn.

"Am I close to the truth? Give me some insight into how Mykelti thinks. This can be a father-son bonding moment for us. Maybe I can find just the right thing to say to make it all better. We can hug it out."

"I missed all this father-son time when I was a kid."

"Look," Jonathan softens his voice, as if confiding in a close friend. "For what it's worth, I do respect you. I'm not trying to be an asshole. I'm making a point: Do you want a hug or food on the table? We hold the power now, Mykelti. And once I'm gone, you will hold all the power. And you need to be ready. Don't let your soft heart get in the way."

Mykelti finds his father's charisma hypnotic, and his arguments sound. He wants to agree, to be on the same team. And as much as he hates to admit, he does want his father's respect. "But... I'm not like you. I don't want to be a leader. I don't want any power. I'm happy to plant my garden. Write my books. Contribute something to society."

"Without a leader—without me—there will be no society. Does power make me a bad person? Power, money, fame: these are not goals; these are tools to get the job done. My ultimate goal is the same as yours, Mykelti—to save the world, to raise civilization to the next level."

"There must be a better way."

"When you find one, let me know."

Mykelti contemplates his father's words until they arrive at the Windmill Farm. It sits on rolling hills underneath a blue sky dappled in clouds. The windmills turn slowly in the light breeze. And a herd of cattle appears to be resting in the tall grass. It's an idyllic scene, as if D-day had never happened, but soon after they arrive, the clouds knit themselves together, the drizzle begins again, and the cows never move.

The big freeze
Day 22

It took three days to set up camp in the rain. There was only one choice: Bishop Hill, a historic tourist destination a mile away from the windmill farm. The brick buildings with relatively tiny windows were easy to seal with plastic and duct tape. Jonathan and his cohorts took residence above the old-fashioned general store turned gift shop. It is filled with local handcrafted foods, like candy, cookies, coffees, and especially useful is the wall of preserved foods. The useless tourist knick-knacks were dumped on the street to make room for supplies. Mykelti, Sherbert and the rest of the group set up camp across the street in the museum. Magically—technology seemed like magic now—the windmills hadn't shut down in the storm. Mykelti spent a day going around town and turning on lights and televisions to preempt an overload. Bishop Hill was a town that attracted elderly people to memories of a bygone era; they left behind a small treasure of vitamins, medicine and breathing machines. On the fourth day, they gather around the ham radio to get the latest news and make a plan.

"Okay, cross your fingers," Benji says. "I think I got 'er fixed up." While unpacking the truck, Jonathan had stepped on the cord of the radio, yanking it out of Mykelti's arms. The weight of the radio crushed itself into the pavement.

"This better work. It's our only connection to the outside world. Our only hope of rescue," says Jonathan.

"Is there anyone left to rescue us?" asks Raymond, the perpetual doubter.

"The boat," Jonathan reminds him. "A rescue ship is being sent to all the major ports. We need to know when and where."

"Oh, yeah. Noah's ark."

"Why would they try to save us? Seems like they should be saving themselves—like we are."

"*Like us,* they need survivors with skills to rebuild society. I know some of you have spent your lives protesting corporations and government." Jonathan's eyes touch upon Mykelti and Sherbert. "Maybe now you have a different opinion. It takes more than one person to build the luxurious lives you had all been living."

"Okay, ready?" Benji flips the switch. All the circuits light up. He scrolls through the bandwidths. Nothing but static. He scrolls back slower. "Well, this is to be expected. There might not be anyone transmitting right now. Probably not many know how. It could be the weather. The signal needs to bounce off the atmosphere to be transmitted long distances." He fiddles with more knobs. "Shortwave is finicky. Sunspots, maybe."

"*Maybe* you didn't fix it right?" says Raymond.

"I fixed it right! I think..."

"Damn Mykelti and your clumsiness," says Jonathan. "The radio is our most valuable asset."

"You stepped on the cord. Not me."

"Let's just get another," says Benji. "Davenport is not far. The trucks could make it there and back on one charge."

"Tell them, Mykelti, why can't we go to Davenport?" says Jonathan.

"It's too close to a nuclear reactor."

The crowd breaks into murmurs of discontent. "Great! Now what?... Are we safe?... Do the winds blow in this direction?... The wind blows in every direction... Why did we ever leave Chicago?... Someone will rescue us... Don't hold your breath."

"Stay calm, everyone," says Jonathan. "This doesn't change the plan. Mykelti."

"The plan is to get the radio working and find help. For now, this is the safest location on our maps. We don't know of any other power sources, and we can't survive long on batteries. We need to send out scouts for more power sources and more charging stations. More books and maps. We have a secure location. We need to make the most of it before we move: create better solutions for making oxygen, acclimating, scavenge supplies." Mykelti pauses for a deep breath before giving them the ultimatum. "Unfortunately, we can't accomplish any of this before the first freeze."

"What's he saying?"

"I'm saying we need to survive the winter."

"You dragged us all the way over here on the *hope* of making it through the winter?" Raymond exasperates.

"Do you have a better plan, Raymond?" asks Jonathan. "Please feel free to share it with the group."

"I think we need... We... Err..." he hems and haws. "It better be good if you want us to cooperate."

"I look forward to your cooperation," Jonathan says forebodingly. "Now for the bad news. I've asked Henrick to lock up all the chocolate and liquor. We don't need a bunch of drunks day and night. Mykelti tells me that alcohol lowers blood oxygen levels. Blood sludging, he calls it. You're likely to kill yourself if you drink too much. More importantly, since money is now worthless, and most of you lack self-motivation—alcohol and chocolate are our new currencies. You will be rewarded at the end of a successful day. Those that do more, get more. Within reason."

"Blood sludging?" Benji whispers to Mykelti. "Is that a thing, really?"

The seventh wave of deaths: Dieback
Ongoing

The Ireviken Extinction Event was a relatively minor extinction. What makes it notable is that only 8% of the ocean died due to hypoxia, yet it caused a global extinction and disrupted the climate for 200,000 years. It extinguished most of the prehistoric eels, half the trilobites species, and many more unnamed species were lost forever, their bodies not strong enough to leave behind any fossil record of their daily lives. Trillions upon trillions of animals died. Their combined legacy would be nothing more than to become a favorite decoration on the shelves of humans.

Flash forward 430 million years to when Homo sapiens swim and scuttle across the surface of the Earth, and the oceans are dying again. The exception that makes this Anthropocene extinction event different—and worse—from all others is that humans have added their poisons to the mix. No spot on Earth was left untouched by human activity. Lifeforms were so contaminated—fish with bellies full of plastic, plants full of pesticides, animals full of hormones and herbicides—that humans were eating their own garbage, and plastic particulates filled their veins.

Before Doomsday, most ecosystems were teetering on the breaking point.

In the oceans, pollution runoff was creating hypoxic dead zones. The infrared cameras aboard the weather satellites showed the continents were ringed in red dead zones, which were formerly the ocean's most fertile fields. And an island of plastic garbage twice the size of Texas floated in the Pacific Ocean. Until the late 1990s, humans were using the coral reefs, the most biologically diverse regions in the oceans, as testing grounds for nuclear bombs; by the turn of the millennium, phytoplankton populations were cut in half. As the ocean waters grew hotter, more polluted and acidic, the remaining oxygen-producing coral reefs and phytoplankton started to die.

On land, it was even worse. More than half the trees fell to chainsaws before the phrase *climate change* entered the nomenclature. As mankind cleared the way for farms and roads and golf courses, trees were cut off from their neighbors and vulnerable to wind, bugs and pesticides, like the ponderosa pine, which was rendered functionally extinct by the voracious mountain pine beetle. In the Arctic Circle, the permafrost was sublimating so fast that giant sinkholes, hundreds of meters wide, sucked down trees and wildlife. As the oceans rose, they drowned lowland forests with deadly saltwater.

After Doomsday, the environment was in a death spiral.

In the North Atlantic Ocean, the annual springtime phytoplankton blooms were so large they could be seen from space—a giant living organism dying and blooming with the seasons, breathing in, breathing out. But the aftermath of Doomsday disrupted this delicate balance. In the oceans, glacial melt stabilized the temperature, and the conveyor belts stopped flowing, in particular, the Gulf Stream. It no longer warmed North America nor transported nutrients like iron. The annual phytoplankton bloom was no more. Giant hypoxic doldrums formed. Coral bleaching occurred on a global scale, and marine animals would migrate long distances to find nothing remained.

On land, not only were the trees asphyxiating, their excess oxygen being blown away in the storms, but they were also dying of sunburn. The ozone layer, which is made of oxygen, was no longer being replenished and slowly dissipated, leaving life on Earth to be irradiated.

Even under ideal circumstances, plants produce almost no excess of breathable oxygen. The reason is that, like an animal, plants also breathe oxygen. This is called the respiration cycle, and it is the exact opposite chemical reaction as photosynthesis. A plant spends half its day making fuel (sugar) and the other half of the day burning that fuel with oxygen to create energy, exactly like an animal and similar to a car. And when a plant dies, bacteria in the decomposition process consumes all the excess oxygen the plant produced during its lifetime. It is the same as if the tree was burned. Most of the breathable oxygen in the atmosphere comes from phytoplankton in the ocean, and only if the dead phytoplankton sinks to the bottom of the ocean and gets buried, escaping decomposition. However, it is such a small amount that it took billions of years for the phytoplankton to fill the atmosphere with oxygen.

As the trees breathed their last breath, they transpired their moisture into the atmosphere, adding to the turbulence and torrential rains. The forests no longer acted as filters, regulating humidity and removing carbon dioxide and toxins. Nor could they absorb the heat or shield other plants and animals from the elements, and their roots could not prevent the nutrients from being washed away.

The trees were not the first plants to die, but it was the trees that humans noticed first. For as long as humans can remember, they have worshipped trees.

Legends from pagan cultures of the world tell of gods and goddesses—with names like nymphs, dryads and divas—that live in the trees as the guardian spirits of the forest. One legend that permeates many cultures tells the story of the foolish and greedy woodsman. Heedless of all the warnings, he begins to chop down the most magnificent tree in the forest. Exhausted from his labor, he paused to rest and fell asleep beneath the tree. While he slept, the shy dryad snuck outside the safety of her tree to steal the woodsman's breath. Perhaps what actually happened is that at night, the trees sucked up all the oxygen for themselves.

Along with the death of the keystone species, like plankton, coral and trees, came the death of entire ecosystems. Earth's ability to liberate oxygen faster than it was consumed ceased. And giant hypoxic doldrums formed, killing whatever life wandered in too far like the hapless woodsman.

The last bloom of spring
Day 208

Since the group arrived at the windmills six months ago, life has been almost normal. The windmills powered heaters, stoves and all the modern conveniences. The biggest luxury besides fresh air and hot water was being able to do laundry. But by the end of winter, they had watched every movie and played every video game they could find. Despite their comfort, three people committed suicide. One couple disappeared, probably having run out of air before they could return. One person died of either an obstructed bowel or appendicitis. Maybe a hernia. It's impossible to know without tests. Another died for no apparent reason; their body simply failed. And three people died under suspicious circumstances. They found a stash of liquor and were trading it for food and sexual favors. One day, they were discovered dead in their house—their water cracker frozen solid and the liquor gone.

For six months, the rain or snow or sleet dripping off the sky had never paused. Mykelti and Sherbert, whose friendship grew stronger despite winter's darkness, survey the town for signs of spring. Bishop Hill looks temporarily beautiful. No sooner had the trees unfurled their leaves than the green chlorophyll began to die, revealing hints of the reds and oranges normally reserved for autumn, but no birds migrated north to roost in their limbs. Likewise, some tuberous flowers bloomed briefly, using what energy they had stored in their roots, but no bees arrived to pollinate would-be seeds and fruits, no sunlight nourished their leaves, and little oxygen was left to burn their sugars.

Mykelti removes his mask. He performed this experiment weekly. Acclimating the group to the new environment was one of Mykelti's winter assignments. Per his instruction manual, he taught them nutrition, exercises and breathing techniques to increase red blood cells, lung capacity and blood flow. The air is fragrant with dying flowers. The air pressure and humidity seem normal, but within a few minutes, Mykelti grows faint. It reminds him of being in the Himalayan Mountains, miles above sea level. His lungs, if flattened, would fill a tennis court. Hundreds of millions of tiny air sacs waiting to absorb oxygen, but it wasn't enough. Perhaps the ambient oxygen was being displaced by carbon monoxide or overwhelmed by pollution, maybe even the rain? He feels a slight burning in his nose and chest.

"What do you think?" Mykelti asks when they arrive at their dying garden. While they wintered, the group grew seedlings, both as an experiment to see if the plants could survive in their artificially created environment and to see if they produced a significant amount of oxygen. The seedlings seemed fine until they transferred them outdoors. Little more than grass and bramble appears to be thriving.

"We could try building a greenhouse?"

"We don't have the materials. We could get them... Maybe..." But they couldn't even get a shortwave radio. He thought he was doing everyone a favor by sending Finley to find the radio. Finley's pessimism was causing the group to question all its decisions. He took a fully charged truck and was to get in and out of Davenport as fast as possible because of the potential chemical and radiation leaks. That was months ago. Mykelti had misjudged Finley's abilities and now had to live with the guilt and the criticism.

"Mykelti, you need to act with more confidence," says Sherbert. "People rely on you."

"It's my father's doing. I'm tired of being the scapegoat."

"Then be the leader."

"If you don't remember, I failed miserably at being an activist. 'Mykelti, the man who almost saved the world.' If only people had listened."

"I'm not talking words. Leaders lead by example."

"I'm not in charge."

"Whose plan is this? Who wrote the survival manual?"

"Making a plan is easy; finding people motivated to make it happen is the challenge."

"Look at you, sad sack. Try motivating yourself first."

"Like I said. My father is in charge. I'm just the fall guy."

"News flash. Your father isn't a motivational speaker. Everyone's tired of being told to eat shit and enjoy it. *You* are the only one around here with a plan; *you* are the only one people really listen to; *you* are the only one who makes people feel worthwhile; *you* are the only one that can get everyone to agree. People think of you as their leader. It's time to step up."

"I never wanted this responsibility."

"The best leaders never do."

"Look who has become the life coach," Mykelti jokes. Sherbert's sarcasm, which had always shined a light on the truth, had grown into a voice of reason.

"Yes, I get more serious every day. Adulting. The apocalypse does that to you." She runs her fingers through her pink hair, exposing the platinum blonde roots. "We'll be twinsies soon." Her rose tattoo jiggles when she laughs. Mykelti's hair, once dyed blond by the acid rains, now turns white with stress. "Mister and Missus Seriousness."

"Why don't you be the leader?"

"Who says I'm not?"

Mykelti laughs. "Okay, then. What do you think we should do? If my father has his way, we'll be moving soon."

"What!? Am I your advisor now?"

"Co-leader?"

They laugh and give each other a playful shove.

"Okay, serious face. I don't know. We have everything we need for now, but within a year or two, all the surrounding towns will be out of food. Eventually, the power will fail."

"That's okay. We'll all be glowing in the dark soon."

"We may not survive another winter. I'm afraid your father is right."

"Yes, but—"

"I hate your yes-buts."

"Yes. And. Not everyone will survive going south. And. We need everyone if we are going to survive. Damned if we do—"

"Damned if we don't. Sucks being a leader. One thing is for sure—"

"Everyone will die if we do nothing." Mykelti has always admired Sherbert's spunk; now her ability to channel these emotions into her newfound wisdom… It elevates his feelings into unknown territory.

From the edge of the town, Benji flags their attention and hurries over. Even without a radio, he is still in charge of communication. "Jonathan…" he gasps. "Called a meeting. We… found… a survivor… Actually… he found… us… Hindenburg… In ten."

"We'll be right there," Sherbert says, not seeming impressed with the news.

"What… What are y'all… doing out here?"

"Looking at the trees."

"What about 'em?"

"They're dying."

"Aww. Man." Benji breathes deeply to gather his words. "I thought we were effed. Now, I know we're effed."

"Super effed."

A survivor seeks asylum
Moments later

When they enter the Hindenburg, the remaining survivors, less than half of what had made the trip from Chicago, are gathered. What was once a group of misfits now has the uniform appearance of country farmers as they have been slowly replacing worn-out clothes, and they are all a little blue in more ways than one.

The discussion is already underway. "I don't know. I've got some kind of natural immunity to whatever's in the air," says the stranger. He's unkempt, unshaven and his clothes no longer indicate his station in life.

"Boy, I can't tell you how nice it is to breathe fresh air. I haven't breathed this good since God rained hell and fury down upon us."

"We call it D-day. Short for Doomsday," Benji extends an invitation to the group's inner workings.

"That's kinda disrespectful of the vets in the room, don't ya think?"

"Or, maybe respectful," Benji offers with a shrug.

The stranger reaches into his coat and pulls out a joint. "Those first few days without my Mary Jane's were hell on Earth. I've been holding onto these for a long time like an addict with a cigarette behind their ear telling themselves: 'You know, I can smoke if I want to, just not here, not now.' Well, my newfound friends, someday is today." He nonchalantly sticks the joint to his lower lip. As he raises his lighter, Gregory, who has been standing guard with Eddie, smacks the joint out of his mouth.

"Relax, dude," says the stranger. "I think we have worse things to worry about than a second-hand high."

"*Dude*," says Eddie sarcastically. "One spark and the Hindenburg could go up in flames."

"That's what we call this place: the Hindenburg," explains Benji. "We're running on electrolysis. We can't be sure we're venting the excess hydrogen gas to the atmosphere."

"Jeez. The irony of that!? Going from being hardly able to breathe to swimming in so much oh-two that I'm liable to spontaneously combust."

Jonathan enters and makes his way toward the front of the crowd. He seats himself in one of the museum's antique chairs raised on a pedestal and begins his interrogation. "How did you find us?"

"A little bird told me."

"Did you see, Finley?" Mykelti asks.

"Yes, that was the bird's name."

"Mykelti, I'd like to let our guest speak for himself," his father scolds. Mykelti had unintentionally given the man an alibi. "Where is Finley?"

"Going the wrong way. Whew! Who needs a smoke, anyway? This oxygen is making me feel stoned. I haven't felt this good in months. You guys know how to liven up a party, after all."

"Which way is that?"

"Straight into the mouths of those cannibals." This statement causes murmurs of panic to flow. The stranger can't suppress his mischievous smirk. "*Haha*. Just pulling your leg. Seriously, I'm kidding."

"I see what you did there. Cannibals pulling your leg," Benji laughs.

"Tough crowd, right, kid? Giving me the cold shoulder."

Benji snorts laughter. "Nice one."

"Save your comedy routine," says Jonathan.

"My sense of humor is the only thing I have saved."

"What do you know about Finley?"

"My father means to ask: is he safe?" Mykelti rephrases with kinder words meant to befriend the stranger.

The stranger looks from Mykelti to Jonathan and back. "Aren't you two peas in a pod? Seriously—I can be serious. He was looking for supplies, so he said."

"A shortwave radio," Mykelti clarifies, and his father glares at him. "It's not a secret. Everyone alive needs a radio."

"Say, you folks aren't as friendly as I hoped. How about a little quid pro quo? I'm the closest thing to a postman you'll find around here. I give you information. You give—"

"This isn't a negotiation," says Jonathan.

"We all have to make a living. All I ask for is lunch."

"Lunch will not—"

"Lunch," Mykelti interrupts his father's rejection, "will be served right away." He has been thinking about Sherbert's words; if he doesn't set the example, who will? Being a leader—isn't that what his father wants, too? But his father glares at him again.

"While we wait, why don't you tell us your name? What did you do in the Old World?"

"Name, rank and serial number. Right? *Haha*. Hardly matters anymore, does it? Now that we're all born again."

"Let's call him shit for brains, then," grumbles Eddie. "Or we're going to be here all day."

"Grow up, Eddie," chastises Sherbert.

Giggles erupt among the remaining henchmen: Eddie, Gregory and Lorenzo.

"That means all of you. For fuck's sake, do I have to be everyone's babysitter!?"

"Henrick, add a bottle of wine," says Mykelti.

"Trying to loosen the ol' tongue, eh?" says the stranger.

It takes little effort to prepare lunch: a can of food with a spoon stuck in it, a few sprigs of baby romaine, a candy bar and a bottle of red wine. The stranger examines the can. "Lamb and barley stew gourmet dog food. Ah, the good ol' days when dogs ate like kings. Nothing but the best, I see."

"Be glad you didn't get the Purina Dog Chow," says Henrick.

"Food is becoming a problem," Mykelti says. "You have a fortune of salad greens on your plate."

"Why are we feeding this guy? Shouldn't we be worrying about ourselves?" Raymond's cynical voice stands out amongst the crowd.

In answer, the stranger pours himself an uncouth amount of wine. "Grant. Grant Mathews." He gulps a spoonful of the lamb and barley stew and rinses it down with the wine. "I was an electrician, among other things. Shocking, right? *Haha*."

"We could use an electrician," says Jonathan. "We've already lost two windmills."

"I see my price just went up. I wouldn't want you to take me for *grant*-ed."

Benji bursts out laughing.

"See, the kid gets me." Grant takes another spoonful. "This stuff smells better than it tastes. Actually, it hardly has any flavor. Surprising. As for your friend, he offered me a ride, but, as I said, he was going the wrong direction. There's a group of highly undesirable people in Davenport. If he's not back by now, he's not coming back."

Murmurs flow back and forth as the group digests the information.

"Finley told you how to find us?" Jonathan asks.

"Not intentionally, I suppose."

"If he knows—" says Jonathan.

"We have to assume they know," finishes Mykelti.

"And you have one thing they don't," says Grant. "Power."

"We're going to have to move out sooner than planned," concludes Jonathan. "Everybody, get your assignments from Mykelti and Henrick. We leave as soon as possible."

A frenzy of comments erupts from the crowd: "Who made this decision?... No one asked me... We're safe here. Aren't we safe?... I say we launch a preemptive strike... Where would we even go?... I'll tell you where. Straight into another nuclear reactor."

Trying to prevent a meltdown, Jonathan stands and announces, "The decision has been made! We've discussed our options ad nauseam for six months. There is nothing left to discuss. Stick to the plan."

"What plan?"

"He's talking about the imaginary boat."

"Quiet!" Jonathan yells. "Yes, the boat. It's what you've all been training for."

"Tell me more about this boat. Don't forget, I'm new here," says Grant through a mouthful of dog food.

"Tell him, Benjamin," says Jonathan. "He's coming with us. Besides, seems the group needs a reminder."

"Well, there was a lot of chatter, a lot of rumors. I can't confirm the noise. Everyone is talking about being rescued. But if you ask me—"

"Give us the bottom line, Benjamin," Jonathan interrupts.

"Jonathan says we have reason to believe a group of survivors has harnessed what is left of mankind's technology. They are building a safe haven in Geneva, Switzerland, and they are collecting survivors and resources from around the world using the last of the military's nuclear-powered fleet."

"How's that for irony? Being saved by the military-industrial complex," says Grant.

"How do we even know the boat exists?" a person from the back of the crowd shouts.

"Yeah. Who here besides Jonathan heard this radio broadcast?" asks Raymond.

"Finley was supposed to find a shortwave radio so we could confirm the latest news," Mykelti says.

"So, we're supposed to just trust our beloved leader?"

"Let's pretend the radio reports were fake news. Where would a search team go? They can't travel by air. The highways are impassable. That leaves an international port as the first place rescuers will search. I know because that is what I would do. That's what I did. I made plans and backup plans to rescue the world from itself." Jonathan tries to keep the group focused on the goal. "Benjamin, what are the rendezvous coordinates?"

"Our options would be any city with an international port: Manhattan, Baltimore, Norfolk, Pensacola, et cetera. As we discussed, New Orleans is our best bet."

"How the fuck are we supposed to get to New Orleans!?" says Raymond. "We barely made two-hundred miles in a truck."

"Interesting fact," says Benji, "We could sail a boat all the way from Chicago to Geneva."

"So, we're all supposed to run off two by two?"

"Grant, you're coming with us," says Jonathan.

"Aye, aye, captain."

"I vote we stay. It's as safe here as it is anywhere."

"We can defend ourselves," says Eddie. Gregory and Lorenzo voice assent.

"I don't plan on fighting anyone," says Hannah. "And Charlotte is just a child—an orphan. I'm all she has."

"Let the raiders run this place. It's the difference between one devil or another," says Raymond.

"We'll end up slaves!" shouts Travis.

"Or in someone's bed!" shouts Abigail.

"Or on their dinner table!" shouts Grant as part of his ongoing joke. "Damn, I haven't had this much entertainment since the power went out."

"This isn't a debate," says Jonathan. He tries to placate the group with open arms. "It's *not* safe. And the windmills won't last forever. Grant, you're the electrician, am I right?"

"When you're right, you're right. I can only make repairs until the parts wear out. And we can't make spare parts," says Grant.

"We can't even make toilet paper."

"Soon, we'll be no better off than Neanderthals."

"Damned if we stay. Damned if we go."

The group's discontent grows louder until no one can be understood. Despite what Mykelti thought was a farsighted plan, the group is sliding backwards through the evolution of society. They are already eating each other. Maybe Sherbert is right. Now is the time to lead by example. "Listen, everybody!" He bangs his hand on the table. "Listen up. Let's talk it out. We can find a solution that works for everybody."

"This isn't a debate, Mykelti," Jonathan reiterates as a warning not to undermine his authority.

"I agree. It's not safe, but it's not safe anywhere," says Mykelti.

"Mykelti, I'm warning you," Jonathan says with the gravity only a father can command over his own son.

Mykelti weighs the option of confronting his father directly, but Sherbert jumps to the rescue. "You can't force us to cooperate," says Sherbert. "Do you understand what the word cooperate means? Even if everyone does what you want, that doesn't mean they're cooperating."

Sherbert's words echo inside Mykelti's head like his own mother's. "What Sherbert means is that we don't want anyone sabotaging us the minute we have our backs turned. We all need to agree."

The shouts from the crowd come so fast that they mingle into one voice. "Yeah, if you want my cooperation, I want my opinion to be heard… Me, too. My opinion matters… We all matter… You need us. You said so yourself… There's no good solution. The least we can do is agree on the lesser of two evils… Let's call a vote… I'm voting with my feet… Fine. You're not doing any good around here… I'm with him. We'll start our own community… If you think you can survive, good luck."

Trying to restore order, Mykelti plays the diplomat. "Let's put our best ideas up for a vote. Does anyone else have any ideas they would like to put on the table before we vote?"

"If you don't know already," says Sherbert. "Our garden didn't survive the great outdoors. The trees are dying. Not to mention the threat of radiation. We need to move. The question is where."

"We should head south towards warm weather and food," says Eddie. "I want to die on the beach with a drink in one hand and a—"

"If everybody left in the world is migrating south, they'll suck up all the resources long before we get there. How long do you think it will take to eat every can of food or use every roll of toilet paper?" says Abigail. "Besides, you all forgot what happened to my husband. That could be you. I vote we stay."

"Toilet paper!" says Raymond, "You gotta be effing kidding me. I think toilet paper is the least of our worries."

"We're sucking up all the resources here," says Henrick.

"You know what they say about a Wisconsin winter? It keeps the riffraff out. I vote we go north and build a new life for ourselves."

The group continues shouting out ideas: some old, some new; some wanting to stay, some wanting to go; some wanting the decision to be made for them; some predetermined to be unhappy no matter what. Mykelti lets the group argue, hoping they will come to a consensus, but the pent-up angst and resentment grow into a cacophony. Everyone argues except Sonja, who refuses to speak; Benji, who is hyperventilating; and Jonathan, who watches with contempt, waiting for Mykelti to lose control.

Raymond's voice rises to the top, "I'm going to do what's best for me. If you want to let these—" he makes a sweeping gesture towards Jonathan— "buffoons decide your fate, you're welcome to it!"

Jonathan stands on his antique pedestal and raises his gun. "ENOUGH!" he shouts as he simultaneously pulls the trigger. *BANG!* The gunshot ignites the hydrogen hovering near the ceiling. The explosion is more flash than bang, and the hydrogen quickly burns itself out on the sparse amount of oxygen. A moment later, a mist of water rains down.

The crowd is left gasping for air.

"Democracy died on D-day!" shouts Jonathan. "The only vote around here that matters is mine. We can't stay here. It will take years, perhaps decades, to rebuild. That is, if we even have enough air to breathe, and the plants yield a harvest, and we don't freeze to death when the power fails. There are too many big what-ifs. We don't have time for an existential argument. We're heading to the boat and joining the other survivors. They are already rebuilding society. We just need to survive long enough to get there. It's easy to point out problems—" he turns to face Mykelti— "isn't it?"

"I was searching for a solution," says Mykelti.

"You found it. They can't agree. You saw it for yourself. Your idealism failed again. If you want to be able to lead this group, you will need to do better."

"We have to reach a majority agreement at least."

"Do you *really* want to put the average person in charge? Really!? I was like you. I used to have faith in humanity. Believed we were improving, learning from history. But I'm old enough now to see that the new generations keep making the same mistakes all over again—despite having humanity's collective wisdom at their *literal* fingertips. Worse, we no longer let nature weed out the misfits. The idiots and their idiotic ideas keep propagating into the future. By definition: half the people here are below-average intelligence. That gives your democracy a fifty-percent chance of being ruled by idiots—an idiocracy! Is that what you want?"

"Are we going to give everyone a test before they can vote?" says Mykelti.

While the crowd is distracted and the danger of an explosion has passed, Grant lights his joint, takes a puff and offers it to Benji. "Humanity is fucked. *Haha.*"

Benji takes a puff. "*Haha.* Yeah, we're fucked."

"Even if you are born with a genius brain, you need to be taught how to use your brain. People aren't hardwired to reason logically. One has to be trained to overrule their emotions. Very few people can do it. Reason me this, Mykelti. Who do you blame for the mess we are in?"

"Everybody... Nobody... I mean, we tried, but nobody would voluntarily switch off civilization."

"I see you are finally learning. It's easy to blame religions for fearmongering, or governments for starting wars, or corporations for profiteering, or the media for brainwashing, or... You name it. But one group of people has caused more damage than any other—Mister and Missus Average Citizen. Average people are the intrinsic weakness of democracy. Politicians are nothing but average citizens with no credentials needed. Corporations are overruled by greedy, anonymous stockholders that know nothing about business. Letting the marketplace determine what works... What kind of joke was that!? Mob rule—that's what's wrong with this world. That's the reason we are in this mess. You and every person, and every selfish, ignorant thing anyone has ever done. Mykelti, do you *really* want the average majority to vote you off the island!?"

"Does this happen often?" Grant whispers to Benji.

"Yeah, he loves to give speeches."

"And hand out life—" Sherbert makes air quotes— "advice."

Mykelti both admires his father and is horrified. On the one hand, he's right. He cares. On the other hand, his method of forcing people is everything wrong with society. It was the old way of doing things. *But there has to be a better way,* he thinks. *And I have to find it. This is what Sherbert meant by being the leader.* He explains more to the crowd than his father, "I'm trying to avoid the soap opera. Everyone in this room thinks they are right, and everyone else is wrong. I am looking for a solution that we can all live with. Call it a compromise, but it is the only way that will work. You can only control us for so long before someone rebels."

"Like you, for example," says Jonathan. "Society is like a child who has run into the road. Do you stop to rationalize with them? Do you want them to learn from their mistakes? No! You grab their hand and slap their ass, so they never forget the pain of running into the road without looking. Afterwards, they can go cry to their mother. But Mykelti, I'm tired of slapping your ass. It's time I kick you out of the nest. And if you can't fly, so be it. One less idiot."

Mykelti tries to frame his ideas in words his father will hear, "If you think we are a bunch of selfish idiots, use that to your advantage—find the reason that motivates us all."

"I have found it. It's called fear." Jonathan shifts his attention to the room. The crowd is waiting with bated breath. "Humans are animals. They need to be taught their place in the pecking order. We're never going to agree. Until we do, someone has to make the decisions. And that someone is me. Here is one more decision you force upon me: Anyone caught deserting the group will be shot on sight."

"So you admit we need each other!" Mykelti shouts, but his shout falls on deaf ears.

Jonathan holsters his weapon slowly and deliberately, turns and storms out of the Hindenburg. "Meeting adjourned. Mykelti," he calls over his shoulder as he leaves, "that's two strikes!"

"I guess we know how he really feels about us," says Benji, looking hurt.

"You're surprised?" says Sherbert.

On the road again
Day 212–215

It took days to prepare. Unknown to them, Bishop Hill was a bubble of the Old World. Outside, the world was dying and falling to pieces. Without windmills to heat and cool homes, water pipes burst, and mold grew. The tires, which had once saved Mykelti's life, were now flat. All the car batteries had discharged over winter, which meant that they couldn't rely on scavenging more batteries as they moved south. Nor could they rely on meeting civilized people or foraging food or hunting meat.

One team of people scavenged all the buildings within easy range of the trucks. Another team prepped the vehicles and charged a trailer full of batteries. A third team, led by Grant, rigged a compressor to bottle the oxygen from their primary water crackers. They made three of these machines, reserving one as a backup. The bottled air was essential for chores that required heavy lifting. They also crafted portable water crackers to carry in backpacks. Their most important invention was the hand cranks to recharge the batteries. The cranks were attached to their belts and needed almost constant cranking. Grant, the electrician, was a godsend.

Mykelti surveys the caravan. "And so our trek to salvation begins."

"Okay, who is going to say it?" asks Benji.

"It will be a miracle if we survive," says Henrick.

"Thanks for that depressing thought," says Sherbert.

"Where is Grant?"

"He's having one last smoke in the Hindenburg. Don't worry, he's coming."

"Too much of a coward to sneak off with the others, Raymond?" Eddie taunts while loading up his dogs. Over winter, he had rescued two more, Sausage and T-Bone, to go along with Hamburger.

"Who's missing?" asks Sherbert.

"The insurance salesman and the politician," says Mykelti. "I overheard one of them say, 'I'm done trying. I just want to live the rest of my days in peace… however long that is.'"

"They have names," says Sherbert.

"Their names don't matter anymore. I'm just glad we didn't lose anyone with valuable skills," says Mykelti.

"Like father, like son," says Henrick.

"He makes some good points, I'm afraid to admit," Mykelti says, shame-faced.

Nearby, Jonathan is supervising and overhears their conversation. "They have hands and feet. That's all we need right now."

"Don't forget sperm and ovaries," Eddie says. "On second thought, I have enough sperm to populate the entire planet. All we need are the ovaries, eh, Sherbert?"

"You come near me, and I'll cut your cock and balls off and feed them to your dogs."

"We're down to seventeen survivors," says Jonathan, approaching their group. "We can't afford to lose anyone else. Henrick, find them."

"And if they refuse?" interrupts Mykelti. "You can't argue with someone that doesn't have the will to live."

"Henrick knows what to do."

"Meaning, enslave them?"

"When I'm gone, you can do things your way and see how that works out," Jonathan says.

"What happened to rule number three?" asks Henrick. "Stragglers will be left behind? We don't have enough air or power to track them down. Not to mention, risk of injury."

"Actually, Henrick is right," says Jonathan. "You see, I am open to reason. Okay. Double-check the air, and let's roll out."

"We're triple, quadruple checked," says Benji.

When Jonathan is out of earshot, Benji asks Henrick, "You're okay letting them go? Since when are you on our side?"

"There's no easy decisions any more. But don't worry." Henrick puts a friendly hand on his shoulder. "I'm always on your side, Benji."

Under normal circumstances, the group could have driven to St Louis on one charge. And if they knew where all the power sources were, they could have driven all the way to New Orleans. However, there is no more normal. Instead of heading south along the highways, they aim east. Their goal is Burlington, the next biggest city south of Davenport along the Mississippi River, where they plan to find a boat. Even without energy, they should be able to drift on the current all the way to the Gulf of Mexico.

Burlington is only a fraction of the truck's estimated range, but many obstacles drain the batteries. There are fallen trees and mudslides to avoid. Pushing and towing the stalled cars off the road is a gruesome chore as their passengers get tossed around inside, sometimes banging against the windows and falling apart. And many road signs have been flattened by the wind, making it difficult to navigate.

To avoid getting stuck on clogged roads, the convoy bypasses Galesburg, a small city with tempting resources. Instead, halfway to their goal, they ransack a gas station for lunch. The perpetual rains have washed it clean of the dust and ash of humanity. From a distance, it appears busy with cars ready to fill their tanks with gas and customers ready to fill their bellies with coffee and donuts. It seems like a fun day on a road trip until closer inspection reveals the customers are slowly dissolving in the rains. Inside, the coolers are still full of drinks of a hundred flavors. And machines standby to make many more: hot or cold, solid or liquid, soft or crunchy. Many drinks had exploded during the winter freeze, and the last foods made by the machines are petrified lumps, but some still look edible. Ever since Mykelti came to the United States, he has been amazed by the opportunity, especially regarding food. Now, the gas station seems like a museum to decadence.

Mykelti selects some snacks and takes his lunch at a picnic table outside, upwind of the putrid smells. "May I join you?" Henrick asks.

"As if we don't get enough quality time together," Mykelti laughs.

"Just trying to preserve some vestige of civility. Who knows, we may be the last people on Earth with any semblance of civilization left, and when we're gone…"

Benji walks by with arms full of supplies. "Who knows how long we'll be on this boat."

"It's debatable whether humanity was ever civilized or if it was just a tenuous agreement: 'If you don't mess with me, I won't mess with you.'"

At another table, Grant throws his lunch wrappers on the ground.

"Pick that up!" says Sherbert.

"What?"

"Damn, do I have to be everyone's effing mother? Pick that up."

"Like it makes a difference anymore."

"So, we're just cavewomen, now!?"

The others at the table laugh. "Uh oh. You got Sherbert on your case."

Henrick and Mykelti take deep breaths from their face masks between bites of food and talking. "There's something about eating cold, processed food that is extremely unsatisfying, not only to my body, but my psyche as well," says Henrick.

Benji walks past with more supplies, "Never can have too many candy bars," followed by Eddie, "Beer doesn't go bad, it just tastes less good," and Gregory, "Get it while the gettin's good."

Their actions remind Mykelti of his father's words. "Average people are the problem." When moral restraints are loosened—when no one is looking, and there is no fear of repercussions—humans are like children in a candy store? "How did we get so greedy?" he asks Henrick.

"I don't know about you, but it's a requirement to get into business school."

"I don't mean us; I mean humans. Did we inherit this baggage from our parents, our culture? Or… Are we just born greedy? Like original sin."

"You could call it that. But I don't believe greed is bad. We all need to produce more than we use to guard against accidents and acts of God. Think of greed like a battery: we need to store up an extra charge. Without any reserves in the bank, you're stuck living hand to mouth. But if you can store up your energy and expend it all at once, that's power. Greed gives people the power to escape their drudgery."

"Power. Ha! That should have been the eighth deadly sin."

"People don't give the seven deadly sins any credit. They served us well for millennia. Take lust, for example, without it, humans would have gone extinct long ago. Sloth is just conservation of energy. Pride is motivation for a job well done. Wrath, the call for justice. Et cetera. Life is a balance sheet: in one column, you have work; in the next, you have rest. It's like one's capacity to love: with it comes an equal amount of heartbreak."

"Where did we go wrong?"

"That's easy! When we invented money. Money was invented to facilitate the exchange of goods and services. Greed is a given—money weaponized it. In the old days, you'd have to trade your eggs for salt or bricks or whatever. Imagine going to the store with thousands of eggs to trade for a television? Money made everything easier. It was hard to steal a man's chickens, but money—you can steal that without anyone noticing, especially those digital dollars. When we created money, we created an artificial world. Then came the industrial revolution and the idea that *bigger is better*. Surviving was no longer good enough; we had to thrive, and there had to be a return on investment. We monetized everything. Clean water. Fresh air. We even figured out how to monetize people's self-esteem with *likes*. We created an artificial need and made people pay for something that was free with a digital currency that didn't exist. How do you *like* that? *Ha!*"

Benji walks by with another armful of treats. "Get 'em while you can."

"Supply and demand. Right, Benji?" Henrick laughs. "Anyway, you get the idea. The balance sheet is in the red. If you want to blame something, don't blame greed, blame the artificial environment, blame unrealistic expectations, blame a culture of entitlement, blame ignorance. No one is encouraged to think anymore. Blame learned helplessness. I love that phrase, don't you!? Blame the rotten apples. But don't blame greed. Greed is our dream of having more, being more, doing more. Greed built the human empire. Greed launched the human race into space to spread our greed to other planets… albeit, not soon enough."

"That all being true, look where it got us."

"If you blame greed, you might as well blame yourself."

I do, thinks Mykelti, but rather than voice his insecurities, he asks, "What's your solution?"

"Somehow, we built a society full of businesses, not communities; consumers, not citizens. On an individual level, the world will always be full of crooks; it simply cannot be any different. Can you blame a starving man for stealing food? However, we—as a society—*can* be different. But will we change? That's the big question, methinks."

Mykelti files away Henrick's ideas for future consideration. "Henrick, we're friends, right?"

"Maybe you're not my favorite person left in the world, but I can trust you. Can't say that about most. And we do have some of the finer things in life in common. That reminds me, would you like a tipple of my contraband bourbon?"

Mykelti laughs, "Oh, you snuck some along, did you?"

"Seriously, I've grown fond of our discussions. I hope you do forgive me for the bumpy start to our relationship. It is the apocalypse and all."

"My father, what do you honestly think?"

Walking past, Raymond overhears and interjects, "He's a man that thinks, 'What a nice guy,' one moment, then, 'Fuck that asshole,' the next. Those thoughts are too close together for my comfort."

When Raymond and the other eavesdroppers are out of range, Henrick confides, "His reasons make sense, but his methods leave something to be desired."

"Yes, that's the problem."

"He's a paradox. On the one hand, he understands humanity's potential. Imagine what we could accomplish if governments and corporations cooperated for the greater good! Instead of all the war machines, do-nothing gizmos, and hundred competing brands of sugar water, we'd be living on Mars by now, ready to launch ourselves to the next star. On the other hand, he understands that we can't expect anything from anyone. No one owes you shit. Excuse my French. Most people simply can't be trusted. It's no more their fault than greed; like I said, it's the world we've been raised in. And he understands that if he doesn't do the job, no one will. It's an unparalleled level of commitment. It's admirable."

"There has to be a better way than forcing people, undermining their motivation."

"I used to just bribe people."

"Is that any different?"

"Let me know when you find a better way."

Resupplied for the first time in months, the group continues its tedious trek. Near evening they reach the Mississippi River. Muddy, roiling water drowns trees and buildings near the river's edge. Luckily, the bridge is still intact. Below, they can see the marina has been flooded. The piers are underwater, and the boats are overturned or sunk from banging into one another.

"Do we have a plan B?" asks Sherbert, looking out the window of their truck.

§ § §

After a quick search of the city—which shows signs of being looted, but no people—they find undamaged boats in a dry dock at a local boat dealer. It is a simple matter for the trucks to tow them to the river. The trucks will soon be abandoned, but in the meantime, their powerful lithium batteries supply a small buffer of air and time. Most of the batteries will be removed and transferred to the boat. Solar cells are nearly useless under the bleak and cloudy gray sky, so Grant and Raymond install wind turbines and jerry-rig a bicycle generator in the back of each boat. Meanwhile, Benji is fiddling with the radios in the harbor, and the others raid the nearby town. Everyone pitches in except Abigail. She gathers shoes; matching shoes is all she has left of her old life.

The night before the boats launch, Mykelti takes Sherbert to a restaurant. He had spent the previous day cleaning out the corpses and rotten food, or what was left after the rats got to them. It once was a cozy diner, but he pretends they are back at the fancy French restaurant in Chicago. "I've taken the liberty to order for us. Garçon," he calls to the kitchen.

Moments later, Benji rounds the corner wearing a waiter's uniform and carrying a large platter. "Here you are, Sir. The catch of the day. Just as you ordered." He presents them with a platter of fried catfish on a pile of steaming rice and surrounded by pickled vegetables.

"How did you...?" Sherbet says, stunned. It's the first fresh meat in half a year.

"Eddie, actually. He found a bait shop and has been trying every lure they have. It doesn't seem there are many fish left. I'm guessing the waters are running out of oxygen, too. But catfish are bottom feeders. Scavengers. So they don't need much. And since we have an excess of power at the moment, I used the trucks to power a hotplate."

"May I interest you in some wine?" says Benji, prematurely filling their glasses to the brim. "I hope the house red will do. These days, it is a matter of quantity, not quality."

"I can't believe you guys."

"If you have everything you need, may I take my leave?"

"Thank you, Benji. That will be all."

They don't waste air on words while the food is hot. As the meal comes to an end, Sherbert feels the need to fill the awkward silence of what comes next. "We're really going to do this? Float down the river Huckleberry-Finn style?"

"You can row the boat if you like."

"That was a rhetorical question."

"Oh, ah—"

"Despite circumstances, your sense of humor is improving," she laughs.

"Sorry, I wasn't trying to be funny, I was—" Mykelti's hand hovers near hers. "I am—"

Instead of focusing on Mykelti, Sherbert's looking at the restaurant. "This place is almost romantic. You know, if it weren't for the apocalypse..."

Mykelti moves his hand to the bottle of wine instead and refills their glasses.

§ § §

The boat launch was a solemn event. Eddie had spray-painted over their original names and rechristened them SNAFU, TOFU and FUBAR. Once the boats touched the water, the timer was set. They didn't know how long the batteries would last—years, maybe, depending how often they could be recharged—nor did they know how long it would take to arrive in New Orleans.

They underestimated how many locks and dams there would be on the river. Fortunately, the Mississippi had overflowed and they could float over or around them. Unfortunately, all the hydroelectric dams were clogged with trees and debris, so there were no additional power sources. No opportunities to, as Sherbert called it, "Take a breather." Benji was unable to find any useful broadcasts on the radio. And now, they couldn't afford to waste electricity. They floated in silence watching the apocalyptic scenery flow past. And so, the days blended together on the brown river under the gray skies.

Air supply
Day 236

Mykelti captains the TOFU. They take the lead to clear debris. The other two boats fall behind to scavenge supplies from other ships run ashore by the flooding waters. Benji is riding the stationary bike to power the water cracker. "There must be a dozen end-of-the-world scenarios better than this one," he says. This is a new topic that catches the group's interest; after weeks on the boat, drifting down the muddy river, watching the leaves on the riverbank prematurely turn from green to red to dead, the group is growing depressed and running out of things to talk about.

"Oh yeah. Like what?" says Eddie, catfishing off the back of the boat.

"How about an EMP blast? That would have just knocked us back to the Stone Age. I would still be able to breathe. The grass would be green. The skies would be blue. The birds would be singing in the trees. My life might have actually improved."

"Imagine all the people left. We would have run out of food in twenty-four hours. Chaos!" says Sherbert. "Damn, they got pissed if we were out of strawberries at the smoothie shop. What about," she suggests, "time travel? Those are my favorite. We could keep going back until we fix it."

"I'll be back," laughs Eddie.

"And get stuck in a loop for eternity!?" says Benji. "No, thanks."

"Well, what do you think?" asks Raymond. "Zombies? Nuclear winter?"

"I'd kick ass in a zombie apocalypse," says Eddie. "Or, an asteroid, like that movie, what was it? I'd party like there was no tomorrow. *Haha*. Get it?"

"Yeah, the dinosaurs had it so much easier. Just being wiped out in a single blow."

"Actually, most of the dinosaurs suffocated," says Mykelti. "Contrary to popular opinion, it wasn't the colossal amounts of debris blocking the Sun and causing the photosynthetic ceiling to crash. When the asteroid hit, it created a firestorm that circled the Earth at near supersonic speeds. The plants burst into flames and the animal's lungs were seared from the heat."

"Okay, Mr Science..."

"So, what you're saying is all of this has happened before...?"

"I'm happy to let machines rule the world," says Raymond. "They'd probably do a better job. How could they not?"

"How about a Martian invasion? War of the Worlds style."

"Yeah, aliens?" Benji says. "Maybe we could have negotiated for a deal. 'We'll trade one billion human beings for some air scrubbers,'" he laughs at the absurdity of it, but the grain of truth burns.

"How about another billion for clean energy?"

"Would we include a cookbook? Human pâté, chapter three of How to Serve Mankind."

"Even if we had solved climate change or clean energy, humans would have overrun the Earth," says Mykelti.

"It would have been standing room only and Soylent Green for supper," says Benji.

"Better than eating Eddie's catfish sushi every day," says Raymond.

"No supper for you!" says Eddie.

"Disease," says Sonja. Her comment is ominous since she rarely speaks, rarely does more than stare off into the distance. Mykelti often watched her, worried that others with the same look soon disappeared. "That's the only thing that would work. A slow disease. Then we could have said goodbye..." Her words land heavily.

"Depressing. But it'd be better than this," says Benji.

"A pandemic would have worked," says Mykelti. "We needed to get rid of the excess population but still leave the infrastructure in place."

"Look around. Seems like we did a pretty good job at that."

"A pandemic wouldn't have destroyed the world. Besides, it happened too fast and too big. There's not enough people to maintain the infrastructure. Probably not enough to prevent inbreeding," Mykelti voices a concern seldom discussed.

"So what you're saying is that even *if* we live, we're still fucked," says Raymond.

"What he's saying is: we'd better get started fucking," says Eddie.

"One more comment like that, and you're going overboard," says Sherbert.

"Damn!" says Benji, "Just think, if those government laboratory geeks had invented some supervirus—took half us out—they would have saved the world."

"Close your pie hole, Eddie. Can't you see Sonja's sharing?" says Sherbert.

"It's okay," says Sonja. "He's right."

"Well… It's apocalypse now," says Benji. "Maybe the question we should be asking is whether it's worth rebuilding? Is it our plight, us few remaining people, to eke out a living, produce a few viable offspring and hope they reinvent ice cream someday?"

"I don't plan on being post-apocalyptic Adam and Eve," says Sherbert.

"What's the point?" says Raymond, "We won't stop at ice cream. We'll reinvent the internet and restart a Doomsday countdown all over again. I say we leave the world to the bugs."

"Man can't survive on cockroaches alone," Eddie laughs. "Get it? I'm writing my apocalyptic bible. If we survive, that will be my legacy. Mykelti's always talking about leaving a legacy."

"Mykelti, what do you think?" asks Benji.

"Asking Mykelti what he thinks? We're gonna be here all day!" says Raymond.

"Seriously," asks Sonja, "What do you think?"

"If not us, who?"

"Hey. Hey, everybody! What's that?" Raymond shouts.

About a half-mile inland, an airplane is lying broken on the ground.

"Signal the other boats, we're going ashore," Mykelti decides.

§ § §

After the scouts report the airplane is mostly intact and full of supplies, Jonathan orders the group to anchor their boats and set up a temporary camp. They are only halfway to their goal, worn out and needing some rest on dry land.

Gregory, Eddie and Lorenzo clear the remaining corpses out of the plane so they can use it as a shelter. Grant and Benji track down the plane's emergency oxygen supply and turn it on. Conveniently, the face masks have already dropped from the ceiling. Elizabeth and Sonja huddle in the back of the airplane. The momentary physical relief has transformed into a waterfall of tears. Mykelti is worried about them, but Sherbert is helping them decompress. *What an odd word, 'decompress.' No one ever decompressed in Africa,* he thinks. Abigail searches suitcases, hoping to find a former passenger that matches her size. Travis and Tiffany, a soft spoken-couple that has been with Jonathan since day one, search the perimeter for anything of value. Raymond, as usual, is not contributing; instead, he is oohing and aahing at an airline magazine. "Imagine being transported to Fiji overnight. God! What I wouldn't give?" The teenager, Hannah, works double time to provide for two people while trying to keep the child entertained. And, as usual, Jonathan barks orders and Henrick tries to herd cats.

After Mykelti hands out some snacks and miniature bottles of alcohol, like Brandon years before, he excuses himself for "a breath of fresh air." Outside, the dogs frolic and stretch their legs, and Sherbert warms herself on a piece of the broken wing. "I'm going to scavenge the houses up on the bluff. Can I get you anything?"

"Oh, the usual. Milk, eggs, butter," she says.

"Consider it done," he laughs.

"Seriously," Sherbert says, "be careful."

"What could possibly go wrong? I think the universe owes me a couple favors at this point."

It's a tough trek through the weeds and mud. Mykelti is literally falling uphill. Atop the bluff, he chooses the most expensive-looking house. The door is un-locked, which means the owners—or what's left of them—are probably inside. First, he checks the garage for tools and oil for their bicycle generators. He's surprised to find an array of industrial-strength lithium batteries. The meter indicates the batteries have half a charge. The solar array on the roof must still be working, even under the haze of a dying world. It's a minor miracle, but they are useless; it would take a forklift to move them. Perhaps he could make a hot cup of tea or find a movie to watch, but he doesn't want Sherbert to worry about his absence.

In the kitchen pantry, he fills a backpack full of canned food. His priority is calorie-dense food, preferably dry to save weight, but the flour is moldy, and the cereal boxes have been hollowed out by mice. After a quick peek into the base-ment for preserved food—homemade preserves are the best—Mykelti moves onto the bathrooms. He wouldn't be surprised if Eddie were here raiding the medicine cabinets for drugs. Any kind of depression medication seems to be a good way to drift carelessly through the days.

After searching the obvious places for staple supplies, Mykelti checks the rest of the house. He has acquired the morbid habit of analyzing people's private lives. It's a sentimental curiosity for the Old World and the next closest thing to watching a soap opera or the news. In one bedroom, a teenager has died face down on his computer's keyboard, and in the master bedroom, he finds the owners. They apparently died in bed watching television. He utters many *I'm sorry's* and *thank you's* as a way of paying homage, especially when he finds a beautiful necklace. "Don't worry. I'll give this a happy home."

The master bathroom is tiled in marble with a whirlpool bath sunk into the floor. Except for some dust, it seems as good as new. Mykelti remembers a 500-gallon drum of water visible on the roof. On a whim, he opens the faucet. It hisses air. Mykelti bangs it twice with his hand and a third time for luck. It begins gurgling, then some sludge is pushed out by the pressure. The sludge turns to rusty water, and soon the water runs clear and fresh. The barrel must still be collecting rain. It is another minor miracle.

The batteries, which weren't much use previously, give him an idea. Invigorated, and despite the heavy breathing and burning pain of being low on oxygen, he cleans the house, starting by dragging the corpses into the garage. It's much easier now that they are mummified and a fraction of their weight. He doesn't have the calories or the breath to bury them, but he does arrange the owners into a loving embrace and places a framed photo of their honeymoon in their arms. Next to them, he lays out their dutiful and loving son—he imagines that's who he was. On second thought, it could be their daughter. It's hard to tell. He's run out of words for the dead but wishes them well as he covers them in a bedsheet. It seems the respectful thing to do. More importantly he doesn't want Sherbert to see them.

The end of the Space Age
Day 236

The Moon is one of the more inhospitable places in the Solar System. A lunar day is the equivalent of one month on Earth, so for about two weeks, the colonists must live in darkness, and for two weeks, they live in blinding brightness. Not even water can survive the sunshine long before dissociating into hydrogen and oxygen and floating away into space. However, the Moon's proximity to the Earth made it a good experiment for mankind's ambitions to colonize Mars.

The colonists were reasonably self-sufficient. They had greenhouses that were successful at producing root vegetables and some hardy, leafy greens, like kale. They could harvest water from the frozen dust at the bottom of craters that never saw the Sun. And they could even harvest oxygen from the regolith using electrolysis, but this process required a small nuclear reactor to generate enormous amounts of energy to melt the stone. They even had 3D printers for spare parts. However, once communications with Earth were severed, the humans began to lose hope.

The colonists survived a few lunar days, but then the prepackaged food and vitamins ran out. Moving parts wore out and broke. And when the supply ships did not arrive, the colonists lost all hope of rescue. It was just a matter of how long it was worth the struggle to survive. They were resilient, though, and enjoyed what time they had left. They did have the arguable advantage over the rest of humanity, knowing that they were going to die.

The situation deteriorated much faster on the aged International Space Station because they could not produce new air, water or food; they relied on regular supply runs from Earth. And rather than being cut off from civilization on the dark side of the Moon, they witnessed the global firestorm march across the planet like the Sun's penumbra. When the clouds occasionally parted, the astronauts watched the lights of the cities blink out one by one. Soon, the clouds and chemical haze blotted out the planet below them. The Russian, Korean, Chinese and American astronauts were left to debate what had happened and to, of course, blame each other.

The Doomsday Storm changed the composition and density of the atmosphere. It slowly expanded and reached up—over 400 kilometers—to drag the International Space Station back home. Decades ago, Skylab, NASA's first space station, also suffered a similar fate. Solar flares heated the outer layers of Earth's atmosphere, causing it to expand and drag down Skylab in an uncontrolled reentry. Humans wagered money on where it would land, and some wore shirts and hats with bullseyes. Skylab disintegrated during reentry and rained down in Western Australia. No one was injured, but the Shire of Esperance fined NASA 400 Australian dollars for littering on top of the millions of dollars lost. It was an expensive lesson that the atmosphere regularly expands and contracts as it circulates gases between the upper and lower atmospheres. Breathing in. Breathing out.

The space station was equipped with escape pods. Though the astronauts had little control over where they would land, no hope of a rescue team, and no guarantee of being able to survive the atmosphere when their spacesuits ran out of air, one group of astronauts risked going back to Earth because there was still an infinitesimally small chance they would survive. It was a testament to the human spirit. The rest of the astronauts opted to stay aboard and go out in a blaze of glory when the International Space Station fell to Earth like a shooting star.

Wish upon a star
Later that evening

Mykelti had given up on happiness. It was the price of his guilt. Paying penance gives him a reason to live. But to others, happiness is their only reason for living. *If I can buy Sherbert some happiness,* he thinks, *it is like buying her a life insurance policy for a few extra days.*

He opens the door and stands back to reveal his surprise. Unlike some buildings which cracked open during the rains—joints weakened and askew, ceilings caved in, plush couches melting into the floor, debris piling up in the eddies, wallpaper sloughing off like the bark of a eucalyptus tree—thanks to the electricity, this house is well preserved. It is dry and cool, and there is little oxygen to tarnish the fixtures or yellow the paper. The light filtering through the dusty windows gives the room a soft and romantic glow. It is modern and fashionable, but in their apocalyptic world, it is like visiting a museum. "It's hard to believe people ever lived like this," Sherbert says.

Mykelti removes his mask and tests the air. "It's safe. I've had a water cracker running for hours."

"This house has power?" She peels off her mask and rubs the creases out of her face. "Damn. That feels good."

He leads her into the kitchen. "Gas stove—useless—but a microwave and teapot. And look what I found." He guides her to the table full of packaged food that he collected.

"Hot chocolate!" Sherbert says excitedly. "And marshmallows!"

"I have another surprise for you." He leads her into the laundry room.

"And?"

"You're looking at it. A washer and a dryer. When is the last time—"

"It works!? Oh. Em. Gee. Yes!" Sherbert doesn't think twice before removing her jacket and stuffing it into the washing machine, followed by her shirt. When she reaches behind her back to undo her bra, Mykelti quickly becomes embarrassed.

"Whoa! I'll give you some privacy," he says as he turns his back, but the image of her voluptuous form dances in his mind.

"Oh, don't be so prudish! Hand me a towel." He grabs a towel and reaches back blindly to give it to Sherbert. "What are you waiting for?"

"I'm being respectful of my audience."

"Who said chivalry is dead?" Sherbert mocks. "Okay, Mister Prude. I'll be in the kitchen."

Alone, Mykelti removes his shirt, examining the damage from weeks on a boat, "Whew! I smell like a homeless man!"

"You are a homeless man," Sherbert calls back.

Mykelti dons a bath towel and enters the kitchen. Sherbert is preparing lunch. "I didn't realize you were so buff," she says, giving him a coy look, wearing an apron she found.

"I work out. And—"

Sherbert turns to stir the pot on the stove, exposing her naked caboose.

"You— Ah… Um… Obviously, do, too."

She laughs. "Make yourself at home."

Mykelti drops into a chair. He's exhausted from giving the group more consideration than his own welfare. "It feels selfish. Good, but selfish."

"This is normal, remember? Let's pretend the world still exists. Chicago exists. Tomorrow we're going out for a slab of pizza the size of Lincoln Park."

"Yes, it's good to forget."

"What do you want for lunch, dear? Look at me, Susie Homemaker. Have you ever imagined?"

With her two-toned hair, pink and blonde, and rose tattoos decorating her bare shoulders, she appears to be a rebellious member of the selfie generation. But she has matured. Her enemy is gone. In a way, she had succeeded in tearing down *the establishment,* as her generation called it. Now, she is building a new society—though she may not realize it. While the men fought, she stood by and observed, and with every sarcastic remark and chastisement, she was guiding the group towards a new set of morals. The men hated to be shamed. Did Sherbert even notice how the men would line up, waiting for one kind word? What he wouldn't do for one kind word!

Mykelti laughs as Sherbert strikes a pose, one arm on her hip and one holding a spoon high. "Well… What'll ya have? And, please don't say smoothie."

"As long as it is hot, I don't even care."

"Okay, boiled water. Coming right up."

§ § §

After lunch, Mykelti swings the door open to the master bathroom. Steam billows out. "Here's your *big* surprise." Inside, the whirlpool is glowing blue and bubbling. Sherbert is speechless, eyes wide. "And that's not all." He hands her a bottle.

"Bubble bath! Mykelti…" She begins to cry.

"You have an odd way of expressing gratitude," he says awkwardly.

She drops her apron and sinks into the tub. "It's the hottest thing I've felt in years." She swirls the water. "Come."

"I was going to give you your privacy."

"Drop the act, Mykelti." She beckons him with her hand.

He enters the tub, holding his towel in modesty until he is submerged. "Ow! It's actually hot. Really hot!"

"I can't believe it. I mean, it's just a bath—hot, soapy water—yet, I feel like I'm living in a fantasy. Let's close our eyes and imagine we're on vacation, relaxing in a spa. The world is just perfect. The birds are singing. Everything is such a lovely green—a world full of a million shades of green. When we're done here, let's get a hot dog. Chicago style. What do you want on yours? I'll have everything. Absolutely everything!"

Mykelti reaches for a bottle of wine that he had hidden next to the tub. His hands are shaking, and the bottle slips and hits the floor with a thud, spinning and spewing out a spiral of red. "Oops."

"Leave it," says Sherbert. "The maid will be in tomorrow."

Sherbert looks more beautiful than ever, with the swell of her breasts pushing aside the bubbles. And her hair once again looking flaxen and tinted with the juice of raspberries.

Sherbert sees him looking. "Mykelti, I know that I am almost literally the last woman on Earth, but—"

"There's a few more waiting for my return," he jokes.

"Abigail still thinks her husband is alive. Elizabeth is well past her prime. Sonja: she ran a little too low on oxygen, if you know what I mean? Hannah is a teenager, unless you are some kinda creep into that sorta thing. And, Tiffany—snooze—good luck with that. So, it looks like I'm all you got left!"

Mykelti takes her hand for the first time. She doesn't refuse. "It doesn't matter if there were a billion other women left on the planet," he whispers, as if the soft words will slip through her sarcastic self-defense.

"It's about time you said something. I know it's old-fashioned, but—Hell!—I want you to find me irresistible."

"Resistance is futile." He takes her into his arms. Her curves fall over his strong, angular body, like cream over a wedge of cake.

§ § §

As they lay in bed together, Sherbert asks, "Do we live in sin now?"

"Don't worry. God abandoned us long ago."

"At least we have each other," she says sarcastically. "Seriously, I've been teasing you for a long time." She pinches him. "I wanted you to chase me. But, heck, those were Old World rules. This is the New World. Who even knows what day it is?"

"April seventeenth. I've been counting," he laughs. "It's the scientist in me."

"That's just a name and number now. We should create a new system."

"I say every month has thirty days, and we just ignore the last five days of the year."

"Yeah. Five days of anything goes."

"I nominate today as the first of Sherbert."

"Why do you get the first month?"

"Because it's my idea. You scientists are always naming stuff after yourselves. Jeez." They laugh.

The western wall of the master bed and bath is a wall of glass, and they have lain long enough to trace the Sun's arc towards the horizon. The sky glows orange, and the old farm fields make a lovely pattern in the distance. Below, the Mississippi winds through the valley. And the prematurely rust-brown trees appear to hold the promise of an autumn harvest. "I haven't looked at the world and seen beauty for such a long time," he says, but as soon as he says this, the realization that the world will never be green again taints his vision.

"Not long ago people farmed this land. They lived and loved. Children laughed. Imagine how many children there must have been?" Sherbert chokes on her words.

"They'll be children again. Lots of children. You'll see."

"I wouldn't wish a child into this world. A life lived inside a spacesuit and tugging on plants to make them grow faster. What inheritance do we have to offer? Everything we've worked for our entire lives is gone: houses, heirlooms, traditions… It won't be much longer before the books have fallen to dust. All our history will be lost, and there won't be anywhere for our imaginations to escape. Think of all the dreams that will die in those books."

"Can you believe that we could fly through the air, walk on the Moon and send probes into intergalactic space? We created machines that could turn matter into energy and quantum computers that appeared sentient. How can a civilization this powerful destroy itself so completely? Where did we go wrong?" bemoans Mykelti.

"I think we—humanity—were lost the day the last gorilla died. Maybe we could have been forgiven for our arrogance—walking out of the Garden of Eden like we owned the place. But the day the last gorilla died, we lost hope. We were robbed of hope by our own culture. That was the real problem, Mykelti.

People no longer believed they could make their lives better."

"That is still our problem."

"Our arrogance destroyed the world; loss of hope destroyed humanity. So, here we are. The last of the not-so-great apes," says Sherbert.

"The hopeless humans."

"Desperadoes. Seriously, Mykelti, blaming yourself for destroying the world—that makes you the most arrogant person I have ever known." She laughs contagiously, "Good thing I'm so forgiving."

"Is this end-of-the-world pillow talk?" says Mykelti, and they laugh even harder.

In the quiet moment after the orgasm of a good laugh, a shooting star blazes across the horizon at a shallow angle. "Make a wish," Mykelti says.

Sherbert appears to dip into despair, as if there isn't anything left in the world to wish for, when, suddenly, inspiration transforms their previous conversation into an idea. "It's up to us now. There is no culture to feed us lies, or religion to tell us what is right and wrong, or governments to create imaginary laws, or police to enforce them. All our children will know is what we will teach them."

"Our children?"

"Not literally. I meant we mustn't let the next generation inherit a sense-less world, living for generations convinced that humans, flawed from birth to death, are doomed to repeat their mistakes. Our children need a reason to live. If we don't give them hope, they'll never find it… Not in this world. What if we teach them everything that we *never* had? Let's teach them how to set aside their animal nature. Let's teach them to be happy with the little things. Let's teach them that they are not alone in the world. That they are just one thread in the spider web of life. That no one person is any stronger than the weakest link. Let's teach them to cooperate. Let's teach them that their happiness comes from within. Most importantly, let's teach them that together, with a common purpose, they can create the miracle of civilization again."

"Yes," Mykelti agrees, "Without new traditions, the entire concept of hope will be lost with the last dictionary."

"Let's give them new rules to live by."

"You mean like Moses?"

"Not commandments. More like guidelines. The world isn't black and white anymore. While we are at it, should we leave greed out of our new dictionary?"

"No, what good will it be if our mistakes die with us? We will teach them that their ancestors chose to build machines of war instead of instruments of art and science."

"They will think we are monsters."

"Maybe it will inspire humanity to mature into adulthood." Mykelti looks across the dormant farm fields. "It is a beautiful night, you know. We haven't seen stars in months."

"You know, it really is," Sherbert says, squeezing his hand.

"It feels good to have a plan again—a purpose."

"You mean it feels good to have hope."

"Shouldn't we be heading back to camp? Benji can't cover for us forever."

"They'll be fine for a night."

"What if they leave without us?"

"What if they do?"

Rule #2: Contribute more than you take
The next morning

Sunlight pours through the glass walls. Mykelti had forgotten curtains existed, and for a few blissful hours, he had forgotten his problems. While Sherbert sleeps, he packs supplies and prepares breakfast. Afterwards, he tickles her feet, "C'mon, sleepyhead. The world waits for no one." It's how his mother used to wake him.

"That's what I'm afraid of," she moans.

Mykelti serves Sherbert breakfast: coffee and oatmeal. "What do you think?" he asks.

"You're right; it's the *hot* that's delicious." She holds her cup out. "Pour me another cup of that *hot.*"

Mykelti tops off her coffee. "I have one last surprise." He reveals a necklace with a flourish of his hands.

"Oh! You shouldn't have," Sherbert mocks, hand over heart.

"It's an emerald. You can't imagine how expensive it is."

"Henrick would say it's worthless. Just an instrument of trade in the Old World."

Mykelti holds it up to the windows. The necklace focuses the last of the Sun's rays before passing behind a cloud. "To me, its beauty is priceless. Like you. Like your emerald eyes." He wraps the necklace around her neck and secures the clasp. "A reminder of how green the world used to be."

"Now you're being ridiculous. Just because we slept together doesn't mean we're married, and I don't need you to be my he-man boyfriend."

"There's the old Sherbert. *Haha,*" he tries to laugh off the sting of her remarks. "We've been gone too long. Grab as many supplies as you can carry. We have to make it look like we're worthwhile citizens."

"You mean bribe the others to forgive our absence."

"You know my father. He'll be worried sick."

They laugh heartily.

Even though the house will probably fall to pieces before another human steps foot in it, Mykelti disconnects the water cracker, turns off the electrical devices and closes the curtains. He feels like he is giving thanks to the house. Is it a vestige of his upbringing or a tribal instinct? He's not sure.

As they head back to camp, mist is settling out of the clouds. Mykelti feels like he's soaked up enough warmth to last a month.

From afar, they can see that the camp is in chaos. Benji rushes over.

"We asked you not to breathe a word."

"I... No... It's Henrick. Heeee..." Benji wheezes. "Heeee..."

They rush to his side, pushing through the crowd. Lorenzo is kneeling beside Henrick, mumbling Spanish prayers. Out in the open, everyone is wearing their suits, shouting to be heard through their face masks, hands occasionally cranking the dynamos to charge the batteries on their water crackers—the whirring makes it even harder to hear.

Jonathan looks up from the argument. "We were about to leave you two behind."

Mykelti kneels down. "Henrick." He is pale blue. Henrick's eyes are glazed, and drool runs out of the corner of his mouth. "What happened?"

"We found him like this. He ran out of oxygen. His dynamo broke. Maybe. We don't know," says Benji.

"Where is Elizabeth?" asks Sherbert.

"Off crying in a corner. Turns out she's not a real doctor."

Mykelti picks up Henrick's hand, massaging life back into it. "Henrick. Can you hear me?"

"He's not making sense, I'm afraid," says Grant. "Circuits are fried."

"Henrick. Speak to me," Mykelti pleads.

Henrick's eyes flutter to life. He sees Mykelti and a dim awareness returns to him. "Myk... my... f... fri... end..." The effort is too much for him. His eyes roll back and he faints.

"We need to get him to the house," says Sherbert. "It has power."

"Power!? That's where you've been this whole time? Enjoying yourselves at our expense? At Henrick's expense?"

"Raymond, if you don't have anything useful to say, get the hell out of here," says Sherbert.

"Leave him," says Jonathan. "We're going back to the boats."

"Leave him to die?"

"His brains are scrambled. He's going to die anyway."

"But we need each other... Like you always said..."

"But we no longer need him."

"He's still alive."

"So, we take him back to the boat. Then what? Are you going to feed him and change his diapers? Let me remind you all," Jonathan says sternly, "rule number two: Everyone must contribute. If you are unwilling or unable, it makes no difference. We don't have the resources for anyone to be a burden to the group. You all agreed to the rules—"

"I never agree to this," says Raymond. A murmur of assent flows through the crowd.

"You expect the kid to contribute!?"

"Her time will come."

"Are we animals, now!?" asks Sherbert.

"We were always animals," corrects Jonathan. "It could have been any one of you. I'm sorry. But Henrick lost the lottery."

Mykelti stops tending his friend and stands to confront his father. "Do you even have a heart!?"

"We can't drag around his dead weight. You have to learn to set aside your feelings—"

"Emotions are what make us human."

"Emotions are what is going to get us killed. You don't think I care about Henrick? I *care*. I care about—" he gestures towards the crowd— "everyone here. I take responsibility for this ragtag group. But one weak link jeopardizes us all."

"This is inhumane. We can't leave him to die," says Mykelti.

"You're right. He deserves better." Jonathan turns to Gregory, "Finish him. Make it quick."

"But he's my friend," Gregory says, looking confused.

"Take him to the house. Give him a chance," repeats Sherbert.

"We're not giving or taking any more chances."

Mykelti puts himself between his father and Gregory. "I'll stay. Nurse him back to health," he says. "We'll catch up to you."

"We need you now more than ever. No one leaves. Not even the fake doctor."

Jonathan turns to Gregory, "Now! Give him mercy."

The tall man hesitates.

Jonathan points his gun at Gregory's head. "We don't need two pieces of dead weight. You're the muscle. Now! Do your job."

Mykelti shouts out all the air left in his lungs, "Stop!"

Jonathan looks at Mykelti with disdain. "There is no room in this world for disobedient children. We should have left you in Africa."

A long-lost memory comes flooding back to Mykelti about a troop of baboons near his village. The leader was a brute named Piggy, whose job was to protect the troop from danger. But the humans had driven the lions away, so there were no real dangers left for the baboons. Still, Piggy took the rewards: he hoarded food and females, and enjoyed harassing his competition. The rumor was that he even ate children. Mykelti's brothers liked to joke that Piggy was coming to get him. Later, Mykelti would learn that baboons really do eat the infants of their competition and attack pregnant females. *Apparently, human society is not any better,* Mykelti thinks. *Humans are animals.* He wants to strike back at his father with bitter words, but his lungs are drained of air.

"'There are too many humans in the world. Not enough resources,' I told my wife—the woman you presume to be your mother. 'We can't save everyone. It won't make a difference if there is one more orphan in the world,' I said. But she said, 'We can save this one. We can make a difference to this one. Do it for me if for no other reason.' I thought it was best to let Africa erase you from memory. Instead, I tried to make her happy. I tried to raise you right. I don't know where I went wrong," he shakes his head. "Now stand aside. There is still not enough room in this world for useless people."

"If mother were here—"

"Do you need your mommy to come rescue you again, Mykelti? Nothing was given to me. Unlike you, I earned it. Welcome to the New World. Everyone needs to earn their way—including you. Including Henrick."

"We owe it to him, and to everyone here."

"God guarantees nothing. All we have are my rules."

"Father—"

"Do we look related, Mykelti? I'm not your father. Not in blood, and certainly not in spirit. Now. Get out of my way." Jonathan sweeps Mykelti aside with his free arm.

Mykelti trips over some airplane debris and lands with a thump on his back. WHOOSH! The air escapes his lungs, and his mask falls askew. He can't breathe. *Is this what happened to Henrick?* Worse than the pain of suffocating is his emotional distress. It paralyzes him.

"I'm sorry, Henrick," Jonathan says. "When you meet our maker, tell him that he could have done a better job down here." *BANG!* The bullet plunges into Henrick's head, exposing the bloody womb of his soul.

"You're a barbarian!" cries Abigail, the first to overcome their shock.

"I'm sorry. I know—"

"Don't apologize to us!" Sherbert screams. "Apologize to him!" she gestures to Henrick's body.

"—it is a painful lesson. A close-up of how evolution works. Survival of the fittest. But you knew the rules. You want social security, you're going to have to earn it. Now pack up and head to the boats."

"Bastard!"

"When we all survive this, you will be thanking me."

"We didn't *all* survive *this*," says Sherbert.

Mykelti struggles to stand, struggles to breathe, struggles to understand what had just happened.

§ § §

Mykelti and Sherbert stay behind to lay Henrick to rest in the back of the airplane, despite Jonathan saying it was a waste of effort. The others had left for the boat. There were murmurs of dissent, but a consensus was formed when someone uttered, "Where else are we going to go?" Eddie lingers nearby with his dogs. In place of flowers, which no longer grow, and candles, which no longer burn, Mykelti takes a big swig of the fancy bourbon, offers the bottle to Sherbert, and then pours the rest over Henrick's head as if it can erase the damage. "If there is a better world, I hope you are in it, my friend," he says. Sherbert's crust of dry tears is washed away by more tears. Her grief deepens Mykelti's heavy despair. "Come—" he holds out his hand. *The boats are a trap now,* he thinks, but he echoes the deadly truth, "Where else are we gonna go?"

"Let's stay here in the house. Let's forget this apocalypse ever happened," she cries.

"If we stay, we'll die alone."

"I don't care. I don't care about the rest of the world anymore."

"Henrick, wouldn't have lived. Maybe it was easier this way," he says, trying to console her but immediately regrets his words, even before Sherbert reprimands him.

"You of all people!?"

"I'm sorry. I was trying to help."

"Like you helped, Henrick? Thanks, but no thanks. Fuck trying, Mykelti. We should have saved him. Look around. How many people are left?"

"I didn't know— I couldn't— My father—" He falters through explanations.

"Oh, grow up! You tried to save the world with words, too. How did that work out!? I'm not going to waste any words. I swear, I'm pushing your father overboard the first chance I get." She rips off her emerald necklace, throws it atop Henrick, "Rest in *pieces* thanks to Mykelti," and stomps away.

Her words cut deep. Not only did he fail, but it has revealed a character irredeemably flawed. After a moment of shock, he races to catch Sherbert, but not before he sees Eddie and his dogs going into the plane.

The Big Uneasy
Day 246–253

Though the Mississippi flows fast, the days are long and dull, both in color and flavor. Jonathan made Sherbert the new captain of the TOFU and Benji first mate, effectively isolating Mykelti on FUBAR with his least favorite people: Gregory, Eddie, Raymond and Sonja. Mykelti couldn't bear Sherbert's sad eyes, anyway. How could he ever bear disappointing the one person he loved—the one thing left in the world worth loving? With no one to talk to, his anger festers, especially with Eddie's dogs staring at him, licking their lips.

Why did Sherbert expect him to be the hero? Even if he wanted to be the hero and lead everyone to salvation, they all had a different idea of where to go. Hell! Only sixteen people are left in their group, and they can't even agree. Is living in peace and harmony a joke? It seems the best humanity can do is agree: "I'll leave you alone if you leave me alone." It was a far cry from the Golden Rule, more like the Aluminum Rule.

I could have saved Henrick. I know it, Mykelti thinks, the words shouting inside his head, *But then my father came along swinging his dick. Fuck! He's not even my real father.* He groans and rubs his face in his hands. *But he's the only father I've ever known.*

"Having a bad day?" asks Eddie sarcastically.

"Every day is a bad day. Give me the fishing pole."

"Here ya go! Better reel in a good one before my doggies get too hungry… if you know what I mean," he laughs.

Mykelti takes the pole and sits on the back of the boat as far away as he can get.

Eddie is an asshole, too. Is it the male curse to prove their dominance: to stick their dick in anything that moves, or piss in the snow and watch it turn yellow? Men are mere puppets running around thumping our chests and howling at the Moon. A primal scream: "Do you see me? I did that! It's mine now!" These primitive instincts to dominate the Earth nearly drove the human race to extinction. Is it an immature reaction to the first god of our known universe—our mothers? Deep down, men know they can never be a god to anyone. They can never give birth to life. They will never receive the true love a child has for its mother; or understand the love a mother has for her child as if it were still part of her own body—the love we lost when we grew from children to men. That is the curse of being male—to always be impotent and to always be second best. That must be why we find power intoxicating, and that is why we try to dominate the world—to dominate anything. We try to give birth to our ideas. If our energies are channeled, we can create great works of art or science, but if not, we create chaos. Chaos is readily available to prove to ourselves that we can make a difference in the world. Was this our fall from grace? Rather than wait for the apple to fall from the branches into our hands, mankind's greed and arrogance chopped the whole tree down!

Long ago, Mykelti saw this in his brothers, taunting him and others, creating joy out of other's misery. He vowed never to be like them. Still, he is the victim of men like them, like his father and Eddie. Even the good-hearted oaf, Gregory, blindly follows orders to torment others for praise.

The question is: are humans flawed on a genetic level, or are we inheriting bad ideas from our culture—is it our genes or our memes? If it's a bad idea, maybe we can change. But how do you kill an idea? An idea is a synaptic pathway in the brain; it's part of who we are, like an arm or a leg. And, even if we did, even if we all woke up tomorrow with amnesia and color blindness, wouldn't we sort ourselves into a new order? Wouldn't there still be leaders and followers? New definitions of beauty, and right and wrong? And wouldn't we still go to war over our differences? He sighs. *Maybe it's best if humanity and all our ideas go to the grave.*

Mykelti's thoughts continue to spin and churn like the muddy waters of the Mississippi until he exhausts himself.

§ § §

They must be getting close to New Orleans. The cities along the shore keep getting bigger and are home to loading docks and freighters. The river overflows the buildings near the shore. And some of the boats, still tied to the docks, have been drowned by the rising water. The SNAFU and TOFU have fallen behind. They should remain together, but Mykelti's tired of being ignored by Sherbert. He takes up pole position, as they jokingly refer to it, the closest thing to privacy he can get on the boat. He baits the line with some old catfish. Seems they don't have a problem with cannibalism. Catfish eating catfish, not much different than humanity, now.

Mykelti has been spending his spare time reading. He has a suitcase full of books from the Burlington library on every subject he thought might be useful. There was no shortage of books about the rise and fall of civilizations, but he has found no solution to humanity's greed and arrogance; quite the contrary, they seem an endemic characteristic of the species—every man for themselves.

"You're gonna hurt yourself if you keep thinking so much," says Raymond.

"Fishing and thinking. Thinking and fishing," says Gregory in a dimwitted yet poetic manner.

"Just leave me be," Mykelti says, not in the mood for their games.

"You better catch some fish today. My dogs are getting *really* hungry." Eddie slaps him on the back, hard enough to make him teeter on the edge.

It rekindles his anger in an instant. Mykelti drops his pole. The Mississippi catches and drags it under. "Did you defile Henrick's body? You heathen!" he yells.

Eddie laughs, "Watching you is better than television."

Mykelti grabs him by the collar. "He was your friend!"

"Get your hands off me." Eddie shrugs Mykelti away.

Mykelti grabs him again. Pushes him up against the railing. "You selfish, greedy pig. All we have left is our humanity. And you took it."

"My dogs were hungry—" Mykelti wraps his hands around his throat. "*Arrgh!* You'd do the same."

"I wouldn't."

"You would. We all have."

"It's not okay."

"None of us are innocent. Ask your girlfriend."

Mykelti doesn't know what he's talking about. Doesn't want to know. His rage boils up inside of him. His failed attempts, his father, Henrick, Sherbert— all bubbles in his boiling pot of rage. "People like you are poison. Infecting the rest of us with your ideas. Maybe I can't kill the idea. But I can kill the house it lives in. Maybe my father's way is the only way that works." He levers Eddie's body over the railing. "Maybe it *is* every man for himself."

"What are you doing?"

"I'm going to drown your bad ideas in the river and you along with them."

"No, don't. I was just joking."

"I'm not." With a mighty heave, Mykelti flips Eddie over the railing. "Good riddance."

Eddie, wearing his suit and tank, sinks fast. Within seconds, nothing but his flailing arms are visible in the brown and bubbling water. It's a vision of how Mykelti's brothers must have died in the bubbling Lake Nyos. Drowning. Suffocating. Mykelti suddenly remembers his birth mother, saying: "Mykelti, I know your brothers act like tough young men. But we are family. God cut you from the same cloth. Good or bad, you are who you are because of your brothers. Our family is what it is because of our tribe. And our tribe is what it is because of the world we live in. We cannot exist without each other. They cannot exist without you. We are all part of each other. When one person breathes out, another breathes in. We call this ubuntu." It's a piece of his heritage that had been lost when he had come to America.

Eddie is sinking quickly. His hands reaching up as helpless as a child. If he weren't wearing his air mask, he would have drowned already.

What have I done? Mykelti thinks. In a flash of insight, he realizes: *If I killed everyone that stood in my way, I would be no better than my father. In the end, even if I eliminated every greedy, arrogant, ignorant person, I'd have to turn the gun on myself. I would be the last place the bad ideas have left to hide.*

Eddie's hands are barely visible as Mykelti lurches forward onto his knees, reaching below the surface to grab him. "Gregory. Raymond. Help me."

It's a Herculean effort to drag him back on board.

"You are—" *Cough. Cough.* Eddie sputters. "An asshole!"

"It wasn't personal," says Mykelti.

"How the hell not!?"

"I was…" He tries to think of the right words. *I'm no better than Eddie. Hasn't God cut us all from the same cloth? Is there a sin I haven't committed? Well… Henrick wouldn't have called them sins. My anger serves a purpose—to right my father's wrongs—but I lost control. That was my true sin.* "I was temporarily angry."

"Temporarily!?"

"You are right. I am an asshole. We are both assholes. Hating you is tantamount to hating myself."

"Is your oxygen working? You're losing your shit, man."

Mykelti reaches out to Eddie, "Forgive me, brother."

Eddie takes his hand, and Mykelti helps him stand. "I needed a bath anyway," he says.

"You really did," says Mykelti, and everyone manages a tentative laugh.

They all resume their positions: Raymond at the prow watching for debris, Gregory on the bicycle, Sonja resting in the cabin, and Mykelti tending the remaining fishing pole. He may have earned Eddie's forgiveness, but his father will never bend. Despite his father's sense of honor and duty, he has grown into a threat. But how can Mykelti take control? How does one overthrow their dictator without becoming the dictator of right and wrong themselves? How does one defeat violence without even greater violence? 'The pen is mightier than the sword,' is the old adage, but are Mykelti's words mightier than his father's gun. His words have been counterproductive so far.

But survival of the fittest is a warlike mentality, pitting one individual against another, stealing their lifeblood to last one more day. Survival of the fittest only works so far as the individual is concerned. If this were the only truth, the only law of the natural world, there would never be a helping hand from a friend, the cry of a baby for its mother, the martyr that sacrifices themselves to win a war. Even animals help each other: prairie dogs take turns watching the skies for pending danger, deer wag their white tails as a warning to the herd, and bees build hives full of honey. An individual may be driven by selfishness, but a species must be driven by an even greater force. *Is cooperation a force of life?* He wonders.

Mykelti, feeling sudden compassion, gets his pet turtle, leans overboard and gently releases it into the Mississippi. Canary pokes his head around, seeming surprised, before disappearing under the muddy waters. "I hope you find a friend."

§ § §

The river had been growing higher, faster and wider as they moved south, overflowing cities and forests. They float through the Mississippi shipping lanes, past giant cargo ships run ashore, and railcar boxes toppled over like giant children's blocks. But now, it isn't the river that has overflowed its banks, it is the ocean. In the distance, the towers of New Orleans reach out of the water like the fingers of a drowning man.

Though their tiny boats are no longer contained by the banks of the river, the current still pushes them closer to the city center. They pass more cargo ships run aground on underwater obstacles and the tips of cranes poking out of the waters. As they near the city center, an overturned cruise ship is the only indication of the Port of New Orleans. No docks or piers are visible. No people, and no sign of rescue. After a brief discussion, every moment sweeping them further out to sea, Jonathan declares the hospital ship, or any nuclear-powered ship, must be anchored past the mud and debris. So, they turn their boats towards the city center, aiming for the tallest building to use as a lookout tower.

They backtrack through the remains of the French Quarter. The waters swirl around the submerged buildings in odd directions as the tide pushes back against the river. They use poles to push themselves forward like gondolas through the canals of Venice. Often they must row through deep water; even with three people rowing and one steering, they make slow progress. The tops of a few colorful buildings, with wrought iron balustrades and baskets of dead flowers, are all that remain of New Orleans charm. Most shutters have been ripped off, but some are shut fast, as if the houses can't bear the sight of the New World. On one balcony, an alligator tries to sun itself under a cloudy sky. It's the only living thing they have seen in weeks besides a catfish.

They reach a main road, which must be Canal Street. It is blocked on one side by a paddleboat that had drifted into the city and wedged itself sideways. Nearby is the business district with the tallest skyscrapers, but after further discussion, they conclude that the hotels have less security than the office buildings and easier access to the top floors. A few blocks away are two hotels, each about 40 to 50 stories tall. The Sheraton has easier access with its glass walls. They pull up their boats next to a mural of a giant blue dog standing in a swamp, shatter the window between the dog's legs, and tie off the boats to the window frames. Though only one person needs to reach the top, the entire group is anxious to get off the water, and being deprived of television and internet, they are wondering what happened to the world.

The building is in disarray and bodies dot the hallways. Evidently, the D-day storm was no kinder further south. The trek up the staircase bearing the extra weight of their oxygen tanks is almost more than the group can withstand. Their observation deck is the exclusive club lounge. The door is propped open by a former guest's body. Jonathan and Mykelti, the two with the most vested interest, arrive first.

Rule #1: Follow the leader
Day 253

They have a 360-degree view of New Orleans. As far as they can see, water is punctuated by buildings and cluttered with debris. Further out, the Gulf of Mexico looks like a ship graveyard. *This,* Mykelti thinks, *is the aftereffect of hu-*

manity's congenital greed, our lazy quest for the most rewards with the least effort. No boats, big or little, move. No planes or drones search the area. There are no lights or alarms. No sign of rescue. Dread weighs down Mykelti's face. His father appears unfazed. "Was there ever a boat?" Mykelti asks.

"What do you think would have happened if we stayed in the Midwest? You saw yourself. We wouldn't have survived another winter."

"So you took it upon yourself to *save* us by fabricating this story? Lie to us? What kind of leader does that make you? Do you think anybody will follow you now?"

"Mykelti, what do you think I did all those years in government? You can't rule by asking people to stop behaving poorly; you have to give them reasons, make them believe it is in their own best interest. And when that doesn't work—"

"We should have given them a choice. It's their life you are risking."

"I gave them a reason to live—hope. Isn't that what you always say we need? What have you given them? Ifs and maybes?"

"What's to prevent me from revealing your charade?"

"This is our best chance of rescue. If you want to spread more doubt, you'll be ruining your own transition to power. I've been grooming you to take leadership. I won't be around forever. Someday you will be all that remains to guide humanity out of the darkness. Until then, I suggest you play a game of father knows best."

"So, we are family again? I'm tired of your empty promises."

"It's not a promise. Who else but you is more qualified to lead the next generation?"

Mykelti thinks his father's sweet words are meant to manipulate him, just as he has been manipulating everybody. *Has he ever uttered a true or loving word?*

Raymond, Eddie and Gregory arrive, and after a cursory look out the window—"Big surprise!"—fix themselves a drink at the luxury bar. They are followed by Sherbert, Benji and Grant, who stare out the window dumbfounded. "I knew that New Orleans was sinking into the ocean, but—wow!"

"A runaway greenhouse effect must be melting the polar ice caps. All of the East Coast and Florida is probably underwater, or soon will be," Mykelti explains before turning to confront his father, "Where are you going to lead us now?"

"We stay. We'll keep lookouts posted and be ready to signal for help."

"Welcome to Hotel California," Raymond mocks.

"Cheers to that," toasts Eddie.

"Are you still trying to sell your story of a boat? Tell them. Tell them it was all a lie," says Mykelti. It feels good to say that. The apocalypse changed him. Instead of thinking and talking, it has forced him to take action despite his fears and doubts—it taught him courage.

"Did you expect the boat to be here the same day we arrived?" Jonathan rebukes. "We are not the last humans on the planet. Help will arrive. We can see for miles. What better location to wait for rescue? Until then, we are safe from marauders. We won't freeze to death. Plenty of food and drink in the nearby buildings. Plenty of work for idle hands. Once we hook up power, we'll even have entertainment." His last statement rings false and oversells his new plan.

"What makes you think there is anyone left capable of helping us?" Sherbert gestures to the panoramic view of the apocalypse.

"And conveniently, until help arrives, you get to make all the decisions," says Mykelti.

"What would you have us do?"

All the survivors have arrived, and Jonathan's question puts Mykelti to the test in front of his peers. "The world has changed..."

"Stop wasting air. Do you have a better solution? Or are you good for nothing?"

Jonathan's comments spark a memory: "You are good for nothing but eating the fish," his brothers used to tease. His birth mother explained, "Mykelti, you're different. Don't regret it. You have a big heart. But don't expect everyone to understand—your brothers won't—but those that do, they'll be friends for life. Your passion will be like a guiding light. You can do great things if you follow your heart and treat those that follow you with respect." His adoptive mother also encouraged him to be a leader, and Sherbert encouraged him to be a leader. Even his own father sees something of a leader in him. He had always thought they were wrong. He was no different than anyone else, as far as he could tell. He didn't want to be the leader, but his convictions wouldn't let him remain quiet either. Now, his mothers are dead. His father has disinherited him. And Sherbert lost her respect when Henrick died. It is time to live his own life—to face the consequences of his convictions.

He turns to confront his father. "Even if there is a boat, it's only going to take us back to the old way of doing things. We can't wait for the government—if governments still exist—to make a new law, or scientists to invent a new technology. Our past is filled with heavy baggage: money, religion, castes and culture. It's time we take salvation into our own hands. We need to erase our philosophy and start with new rules. The old ways must die. Greed must die. Arrogance must die."

His father counters, "Without rules, there will be nothing to keep the chaos at bay."

"Your rules are what caused this chaos," says Mykelti. "The problem isn't out there—" He points to the desolation of New Orleans. "It's in here—" he points to his head. "Your ideas are like a virus. You've been planting them in my head my whole life. And your cronies have been planting them in humanity. I've been trying to change the world my whole life—save it. But the world is a reflection of humanity's immaturity. The chaos isn't out there. It's in here—" he bangs his head painfully. "The world is not the problem. We are. Now is the time to change. Humanity is dying and taking the world with it. We have to start by saving ourselves. Our corner of the world."

"Governed by idiots!?" retorts Jonathan.

"I think he's talking about us," murmurs the crowd. "He's definitely talking about us."

"The Anthropocene Era—the era of man—is over. Humanity must find a new niche. Learn, grow, evolve. We must elevate humanity to a new level."

Eddie bursts out laughing, "I think he just said he's going to take being an idiot to a whole new level."

"Stay out of this. All of you. This is between me and my father. We're going to settle this."

More murmurs erupt. "It's about time… Here they go again… This should be fun… Get the popcorn… Eff them both…"

"What makes you think you know the mind of God?" says Jonathan.

"Perhaps God gives a man riches to watch him squander his fortune, or gives a fool knowledge only to burn his hands… That's not ours to know."

"What you mean is: shit happens," Jonathan says.

Mykelti admires his father's ability to boil life's conundrums down to simple sound bites. But simple answers give simple men an air of confidence; there is no brooding or pondering while they weigh evidence and arguments. But a doubtful man is a thoughtful man—that's how Mykelti sees himself now. But his father is a black and white man, a man of absolutes, a man who imagines there is only one right way of doing things and infinite wrong ways. "*What I mean is:* I believe God is watching and waiting for his children to grow up. It's time to make our own rules. Be responsible for our actions."

"These are fancy words, but how do you plan to survive? Or does your idealism not include such practicalities such as eating, shitting and fucking?"

"We go back inland and set up a permanent camp and recruit survivors."

"A brilliant solution. Why didn't I think of that!?"

"We tried your way."

"What makes your answer any better? Suddenly you are the judge of right and wrong?"

"No. Let them decide. Let them—" he gestures to the group— "be the judge."

Jonathan addresses the group. "I've brought you this far. You can trust that I will bring us home. If you follow him, you're starting over."

"You left half of us to die," says Sherbert.

"All we need to do is wait for help. We've done the hard work," Jonathan implores.

Murmurs, like ballots in a voting box, roll through the crowd. "If we leave, we'll never be rescued... We need to leave while we still can... Where would we even go?"

"If you take my place," Jonathan tells Mykelti, "you'll be knocked off the pedestal, too. Together, as father and son leading, we are stronger."

"I agree. Together, we are stronger. Everyone here is a leader in their own right."

The group gives no indication that they are the leaders Mykelti implies.

"There is a flaw in your plan, Mykelti. How will a society governed by idiots and weaklings ever rise to greatness?"

"The so-called elites have already risen to greatness, but their Ivory Tower rose so far above society that they have come crumbling down. Yes, they are flawed." Mykelti does not argue with his father as much as he argues with the crowd's disbelief in themselves. "We are all flawed. But it is who we are. We're only as strong as our ability to rise above our individual weaknesses and lend a helping hand—to heal the wounds of our neighbors, to educate the ignorant. As long as one person is downtrodden, that's one less person able to contribute, one more person eating away at the foundation of everything we're building. True, it may take generations for the old ways—the old ideas—to die, or it might take thousands of years for humans to evolve to the next level. But that's our only option. We must embrace who we are and strive to be better."

Jonathan laughs contemptuously, "We're on the verge of extinction, and your plan is to evolve!?"

"My plan is to kill the ideas that drove us to the edge of extinction. My plan is to rebuild civilization."

"With a snap of your fingers!?"

"Civilization begins with an idea—like cooperation and compassion. And that idea gets passed from one person to the next, one generation to the next. That's our legacy, not the monuments we build ourselves."

"News flash. Civilization still exists," says Jonathan, his temper peaking. "While you are reinventing the wheel, we will wait for civilization to rescue us."

"You have betrayed our trust." Mykelti breathes deeply, the vibration echoing in his face mask, and braces himself for a moment that he had been struggling to accept. "I'm not asking for your permission. This is going to be the way I do it." He addresses the group. They stand before him like a disheveled pack of angst-ridden teenagers wearing oversized, hand-me-down outfits. Their bodies are cannibalizing themselves in an anaerobic process to create the energy that oxygen would normally have provided. Hypoxia is causing chronic death on a cellular level, unnoticeable on any given day, but their bodies show telltale signs of diseases, accidents, and poor sanitation that could no longer be simply cured with a pill or some stitches. The biggest difference is their eyes. Some have a dim sparkle of hope, others are dull and drained, their lids heavy, waiting to sleep once more. The group has slowly been losing the will to live. Mykelti wonders if they ever had the will to rebuild society—the communal spirit. *Maybe I will be the only one. So be it.* "Anyone," he announces loudly, "who chooses to follow me is welcome. If you choose to stay, that is your decision, as well."

"I'll follow you," says Benji. Mykelti hears a few more murmurs of consent. But he has eyes only for Sherbert. She doesn't react. Most seem willing to follow whoever wins the argument, whoever is willing to do the work and bear the responsibility.

Jonathan's words flow unfiltered, "You want to put your fate in the hands of sheeple? We'd be better off without them. They're weak. There's not enough air in the world to placate all these sorry sobs." He turns to the crowd, his anger unchecked by logic, spittle flying from his mouth, "And you!? You want to follow him!? None of you would have survived without me. None of you even deserve to live—to populate the planet with your defective genes."

"Yes, we are weak," says Mykelti. "but together, we can build a new nation."

"I should have given you three strikes long ago. Despite myself, I have a soft spot in my heart for you. But... I've never met someone as ungrateful. So what if you knew the real problem all along! I am the one with the solutions. I am the one who took action. I'm the one who began preparing humanity for this decades ago. But what happened? You! This could have all been prevented. But you! In my home. Eating my food. Spending my dime. Complaining to your mother and tying my hands. Crying life is unfair in Congress and on the news. Lobbying. Rabble-rousing. Complaining. Telling people things they didn't need to know. The truth is overrated. Getting people to agree is overrated. You are right. This is the New World. Democracy is dead. It was a failed experiment, along with the rest of society. You want to rebuild civilization!? From now on, it is the Law of the Jungle. The only rights left are what a man can take for himself. Nobody makes the decisions anymore but me. Not your mother. Not you. Not anyone." He glares at the group, defying any challengers.

"I no longer believe leaders make the decisions," says Mykelti. "The people decide what is right and what is wrong. The leaders are simply administrators of the people's will. And you are not even that. You don't even listen."

Angered, Jonathan raises his arm, preparing to strike. "I'm going to teach you, once and for all, how the world works."

Mykelti's focus becomes sharp, moments become minutes as his mind races to find a way out. Another memory floods back, an image ingrained during his formative years as a child. His new parents thought taking him to see the elephants at the zoo would cure his homesickness. Upon seeing an elephant, Mykelti climbed the fence, teetering on the top with outstretched hand. "Hello, my friend," he said. He was so entranced he did not hear his father shout, "No!" His father yanked him down and slapped him across the face. "When I tell you to stop—you stop!" His mother chastised his father, but he merely said, "Next time, when he runs into the road without looking, do you want me to ask nicely?" and to Mykelti, "Pain is a powerful teacher. It will never leave your side. Someday, you will understand." Mykelti is overcome with sadness that fate had preordained he would collide with his father like matter and antimatter. He was a failed son, a failed scientist, a failed activist. He failed many things... As his father said many times, he was not born a practical man. It was his idealism that drove him to those unattainable goals. He could bear any pain if it led him even one step closer to a better world. As his memories solidify the truth of who he is, Mykelti's sadness transforms into a sense of righteousness. So, when his father brings his hand down in a violent swing, Mykelti chooses not to move. Jonathan slaps him across the face—*Crack!*—knocking his face mask askew. "Only the strong survive."

Mykelti gasps and readjusts his breathing apparatus. "You don't know your Charles Darwin. It is the most adaptable that survive."

"Then you'd better adapt." *SLAP!*

Mykelti falls on all fours, gasping for air. "Cooperation is the key."

"If you want to survive... If you want to be the leader... You will have to take control away from me!" says Jonathan.

He pushes himself upright and readjusts his mask. "I don't want to be the leader." He turns to the crowd. "You can follow him if you want—"

"This isn't a democracy."

"—I am leaving."

"No one leaves without my permission!" Jonathan backhands Mykelti across the face. His mask breaks and falls, spinning to the ground.

Without his mask, Mykelti's voice is loud and clear. "I make my own decisions. And those who decide to join me... are welcome." But without the mask, he has no shield. *Slap!* His flesh wobbles and snaps back into place. Blood trickles out of the corner of his mouth. But he stands his ground.

"Mykelti, what are you doing?" shouts Sherbert, the first words she has spoken to him since the day Henrick died.

"No one is leaving without my permission," Jonathan's enraged voice booms inside his face mask.

"I do not need permission!"

"The weak, like you, don't deserve to lead." *Slap!* Jonathans tortures Mykelti with slaps, wearing him down.

"We are not enemies."

Smack! The blows fall harder, but the pain is insignificant in a world where billions have died. All that matters is that his tribe survives.

"Defend yourself, Mykelti!" Benji calls out.

"Listen to your friends," Jonathan says. "Defend yourself."

"It's not you who I fight."

"Then what?"

"Your ideas."

"Can my ideas do this?" He slugs Mykelti in the gut and knocks the wind out of him.

Doubled over, Mykelti wipes his chin and inspects the blood on his hand. "They just did. They—" he coughs and gasps for air— "destroyed a world."

"You give me too much credit."

"I don't blame you. You are a victim of our culture."

"I'm tired of your disobedience and lack of respect." *SMACK!*

Mykelti falls to his knees. Lightheaded, he rests a moment to catch his breath.

"Look at you prostrating yourself before me," Jonathan's anger grows. "Is this the inspirational leader—the role model—you wanted to be?" His blows may land, but his threats miss their target.

"Are you?" Mykelti struggles to stand.

"Just stay down," Benji says.

"What are you trying to prove?" Raymond shouts.

"Please stay down," Sherbert pleads.

"Please," says Hannah, hiding the child's eyes. The others murmur assent.

"Listen to the bleating crowd, Mykelti. Are you waiting for them to rescue you? They will only suffer worse," he warns, patting the gun holstered to his side. His glare dares the crowd to interfere.

As Mykelti kneels, bleeding and panting, he looks at his friends—his new tribe. They are still cloaked in their old beliefs, their old way of doing things, like a protective shield, but they are as out of place as a poor African villager taking his first steps into Chicago. They look for an external solution, a leader, a savior. But this world has none of those things. Mykelti thinks, *They will die unless they find that leader within themselves, the courage to take responsibility for their own lives.* He rises to his feet, hunched over, hyperventilating. Dizzy.

"Defend yourself, Mykelti. Show them what you are made of. Show them the kind of man you are."

Mykelti gestures with open arms. "This is who I am." His voice growing thin like the air.

"I am losing my patience. Admit you are wrong. Or prove that you are right." Jonathan delivers a closed-fisted punch. It cracks Mykelti's cheek and brings him down to a knee.

Sherbert cries out. "You are a monster! What kind of person does this to his own son?"

"He is not a monster," Mykelti silences Sherbert with a wave, and to Jonathan, he says, "I don't blame you. Anger has made you weak. Irrational—"

Jonathan kicks him in the ribs. *Crack!*

"Argh!" Mykelti collapses onto the floor. Every breath burns. He would have suffocated already if it weren't for months of training.

Jonathan kneels before Mykelti and raises his fist. "Does this look like weakness to you?"

"We are all weak. *Huh... huh...* We need... *huh...* each other... I am... done..."

Jonathan gloats, "That wasn't so hard was—"

"Done... arguing... I am... leaving... Do... what... you will."

Jonathan stands. "If you can't defend yourself, then you are of no use to anyone." He cocks the gun. "This is your last chance." Sherbert and Benji surge forward to protect Mykelti. Jonathan fires a warning shot above their heads. "This is not your fight!"

Shocked, they freeze.

Jonathan throws the gun on the ground next to Mykelti's outstretched hand. "Take it. Use it, and you will become the leader."

Mykelti lays his hand on the cold, oily surface. His thoughts spin, *It would be easier. No one would blame me. I have the right to defend myself. Why not take what I want? Humanity has been doing it since time immemorial. What good does it do to die? I can go back to my ideals tomorrow.* He draws the gun closer. Mykelti thinks it is unfortunate that humanity wasn't born with the instinct of self-restraint; unlike animals with sharp tooth and claw that are born with weapons of destruction, mankind does not know its own strength.

"Go ahead," his father chides. "It will be Mykelti's New World order."

Mykelti curls his fingers around the gun. *The world has been ruled by fear-mongering and violence for too long.* Before he can doubt himself further, he slides the gun across the floor to his father's feet. "Where will it end?"

"Bah! What kind of leader can't defend themselves?"

"I am defending … my… self… *Huh…* My… *Huh…* Hu… humanity…" His deep breaths emphasize his words. "My ideas… My values."

Jonathan picks up the gun. "You are right. Bad ideas need to die. Starting with you."

"My ideas already have found new homes," he gestures to the crowd, afraid to implicate them, but also asking them to take stock of their own beliefs.

"Bah! You and your god-damned fucking ideas." His boot cracks Mykelti's protective arm and drives all the wind from his lungs. *Whoosh!* This time he punishes Mykelti with rage rather than the calm, indignant guise of teaching him a lesson.

Mykelti's body spasms trying to gulp air, but his chest muscles won't relax. Lying broken on the ground, lightheaded, almost euphoric with the lack of oxygen, Mykelti sees a mouse nibbling a cracker that Eddie has dropped. "Hello, my friend," he says, but there isn't enough air in his lungs to vibrate his vocal cords. *How has such a fragile creature survived? How have I survived?* Mykelti hadn't thought about his own inevitable death as much as he thought about the death of his species. Some think altruism doesn't exist, that it is just another form of selfishness. Perhaps that is true on an individual level, like Mykelti values his ideas more than his life. But humanity, as a whole, is like a beehive. It has bred into its workers the blood lust of a warrior. When threatened, the bees don't stop to debate whether their lives are more important than that of another bee or if the hive is worth saving. They fling themselves heedlessly into battle, even if that battle is to keep the queen warm during the winter. The bees on the outside edge slowly starving and freezing, peeling away, one by one, until spring.

As he watches the mouse calmly eat his lunch among giants, his field of vision grows smaller until it is like the Sun seen from the bottom of a pond. He reaches out. Trying to pull himself to the surface. *I am drowning. Will my father realize what he has done… rescue me, like I rescued Eddie? No. It is too late. I've gone too deep.* His arms grow tired of swimming forward. The light gets dimmer, smaller. *I did my best. That's all anyone can do.* The panic disappears, and his body floats in space. *I'm tired. I want to sleep.* Mykelti has never felt so calm. Far away, he hears Sherbert scream, but it doesn't bother him. *It is a new spring, Sherbert. It's your turn to be the queen.* The disc of light winks out.

The next thing he knows, Sherbert is holding a mask to his face. "Breathe,

Mykelti, just breathe." Tears stream down her face. The muscles in his chest relax and then flex violently as his lungs fill themselves in a painful gasp. A few more breaths and he pushes her away. "I'm okay."

"No! You are not okay!"

If Mykelti were being robbed of his land or gold, the robber would have won, and they would have left Mykelti to die. The altruistic gene would have died, and the selfish gene would have survived. But what his father wanted—cooperation, loyalty, respect, subservience—couldn't be stolen. Instead, his father is trying to mold Mykelti into his own image. What Jonathan doesn't understand is that Mykelti is everything he is and more. From the moment Mykelti came to America, he had observed his father and learned his ways, as all children do. And everything he learned added to who he was. He was no longer African, but he would never be an American either. Mykelti's dual perspective had caused him much doubt: Which was the right path? But now, he has learned that there is always a third path, some combination of the two, or even one unseen. Now he realizes he is a man of the New World. A man without labels. A man with choices.

Jonathan leans over and picks up the gun. "If you won't defend yourself, Mykelti, maybe you will defend your people." He points the gun at one person after another. "Eeny. Meeny. Miny. Moe."

The group's eyes are fearful and unwavering. No longer do they shield their eyes with cell phones to record the event, but the images are burned into their memory to be replayed for life.

"You see, the strong always win. They can take what they want. That's how the world works. That's how it has always worked and always will work. This is your last chance. Accept the brutal facts of life. Or else…"

Mykelti struggles to rise and protect his people, if only to shield them with his own body, but he is too weak to do anything but say, "You… *Huh*… are the one… *Huh*… who will have to… *Huh*… live… with this."

"Am I? I will make it easy for you. Just admit father knows best."

Mykelti's words have failed—again. There seems no limit to his father's ability for violence. It is a skill he learned, to take what he wants, and now that his blood boils, nothing but animal instincts rule. *He has won. There is no way to prevent the wicked from preying on the weak.*

"Do you doubt I will pull the trigger? One life is a small price to pay if we all learn to follow the party line. It's for the greater good, as you say. Now, say the words! Say *father knows best*."

Sherbert steps forward.

Jonathan aims his gun at her, expecting a loudmouthed reaction. Instead, she says calmly, "Are you going to kill us all?" The words hang heavy in the thin air. She removes her face mask. "Did you not hear me? Are you going to kill us all?"

"Are you volunteering to help teach Mykelti a lesson?"

"I am. Go ahead. Start with me."

"Another martyr for the cause. Fine. I will start with you—" Jonathan cocks his gun— "and end with you."

Mykelti's words are again useless. He tries to rise and physically intervene. But he can't. And, even if he could, wouldn't that be violence of a different kind? But now, there will be violence no matter what. *Maybe I should have chosen the lesser evil?* he thinks. *No, better to die than to live in this world.* Mykelti has lost, and his father has gone too far to turn back. In his father's mind, compromise is a sign of weakness. When Jonathan begins to pull the trigger. Mykelti screams with all his might, "Sherbert!" but his lungs are empty.

Before the hammer comes down, Sherbert turns her back, upstaging Jonathan. "Go ahead. I'm waiting," she says.

It takes a moment for Jonathan to judge the situation and regain control. "Do you think it matters if you die with a bullet in your front or your back? I will still get what I want."

"Not as long as Mykelti's ideas live," says Sherbert.

"Can't you see!?" He waives the gun maniacally. "His ideas can't protect you."

"Better his than yours."

"Have it your way." He raises his gun, taking aim at Sherbert—square in the back—until Benji steps forward.

He removes his mask. "Mykelti's ideas live in me, too." He pauses to be sure he has everyone's attention. "You're going to have to kill me next." He turns his back and stands alongside Sherbert.

The seconds grow long as everyone considers their next move.

Then Gregory steps forward. "Henrick was my friend." And he turns his back.

"He was my friend, too," Eddie says and turns his back.

"You abandoned my husband," Abigail says, turning her back.

"You can't be trusted," Grant says, as he turns his back.

"Cabrón," says Lorenzo.

One by one, Mykelti's friends air their grievances and turn their backs until Jonathan is effectively alone without an audience. To each one, Mykelti's actions had a different meaning. To some, it meant: *we are all equal.* To others, it meant: *I will no longer be a slave.* To another, it meant: *I can follow my heart.* And, to another: *My hope will live on without me.* The different points of view combined gave the group the will to live and prosper. But to his father, it meant loss, and with that loss came fear. Mykelti could see it in his eyes. Even if Jonathan made an example of Mykelti or Sherbert, even if the crowd followed him again, it would only be for a week or a day or until the next time Jonathan closed his eyes or turned his back.

Jonathan tries to salvage some authority. "Anyone that wants to live, come with me. Eddie, Gregory," he commands, but they don't move. He shoulders his way through the crowd, pushing them from behind. When he passes, they rotate like flags in a hot wind, keeping their backs to him. Only Mykelti, lying broken on the platform, watches his father walk away. When Jonathan is gone, Mykelti allows himself to relax and faints. The group rushes to his side. Sherbert is the first to arrive.

§ § §

The tribe finds the FUBAR and TOFU still docked outside the windows, but the SNAFU is adrift with Jonathan struggling to paddle. Without someone to steer, the boat spins in the wind and tide.

"What are we going to do?" asks Benji.

"Save him?" Grant asks doubtfully.

"Take the boat," says Gregory.

"Yeah, man. Throw him overboard," says Eddie.

"We're not like him. Give him a second chance," says Elizabeth. "We all make mistakes."

"You're kidding, right?" asks Sherbert.

Jonathon sees the group and gestures for help as the current drags his boat out to sea.

"He has made his choice," says Mykelti. "Let him go."

"We need that boat," says Raymond.

"We'll find another."

Part IV:
The End of Time

The eighth wave of deaths: The re-evolution of anaerobic life

Ongoing

Many frozen or dehydrated microorganisms are essentially immortal, lying dormant until the next job opportunity. When tomb raiders would open the coffins of ancient Egyptian kings seeking treasure, the actual surprise was that the coffins, pressurized by the decaying corpses and sealed from the hot desert air, would pop open like a balloon filled with dust and disease. The tomb raiders would return home, their arms filled with treasures and their moist lungs filled with newly hydrated diseases. Entire families died from what was thought to be the Mummy's Curse. Likewise, when the Siberian Traps erupted, it was like popping open the coffins of billions of animals, from reindeer to wooly mammoths and saber-tooth tigers. Eventually, even the ancient diseases locked in the Antarctic Ice since the days the dinosaurs roamed the continent would be freed.

In the years-long aftermath of the Doomsday Storm, the vortexes of hurricanes, tornadoes and dust devils vacuumed the reborn anaerobic bacteria and viruses into the upper atmosphere, where the jet streams transported them to mountain tops and valley bottoms and to every festering wound and gaping mouth. And so, microscopic forms of life that would have been oxidized and rendered harmless circulated the planet continuously and thrived in the hypoxic atmosphere like the good ol' primordial days. Modern plants and animals of all species were exposed to a plethora of diseases for which they had no built-in immunity.

Fortunately or unfortunately, depending on where one is in the food chain, the evolution of plants and animals never stops. What might seem like a problem to one species, inevitably benefits another. As the Earth's ecosystems changed and the oxygen continued to decrease, the aerobic forms of life lost their advantage, and the anaerobic forms of life rose to succession. It was a re-evolution of life on Earth. But it was not survival of the fittest; they did not compete with each other; they did not raise swords and battle for territory. The forms of life that were successful prior to Doomsday simply lost their footing, and the anaerobic life stepped in to fill the gap. Their success created microenvironments filled with their byproducts of gases and acids that further pushed the other out of existence. It was a similar process by which humans paved over fields and forests to build their cities; in turn, the city's heat and dead air drove away the birds and butterflies, leaving the vacant fields unpollinated and fallow.

The post-apocalyptic world gave anaerobic lifeforms a new lust for life. On the ground, insects, which can spawn generations of evolution in a few days—multiplying and evolving thousands of times faster than any mammal—developed enhanced anaerobic metabolic pathways. Free of mankind's pesticides, these superbugs proliferated and piggybacked diseases like anthrax and tuberculosis. In the rain forests, fungi infected plants with methanogens, microorganisms that produce even more methane, which further modified the atmosphere. In the sea, what was left of the coral reefs was overrun by anaerobic forms of life resembling primordial slime. In the air, many forms of anaerobic bacteria, like staphylococcus aureus, evolved to survive in the thick clouds, raining down on unsuspecting animals. And, though viruses are neither aerobic nor anaerobic, being deprived of their densely populated hosts, they also needed to evolve. Diseases like the highly infectious Ebola virus, formerly transferred by contact with bodily fluids, evolved to spray into the atmosphere like an aerosol can by the oozing wounds of the infected.

And so, the new forms of anaerobic life evolved, devolved and re-evolved and proliferated into every nook and cranny on Earth, seeking safe havens and new opportunities. Some being commensal and some being pathogenic. From the Earth's point of view, Homo sapiens were not much different than pathogenic bacteria, and they were going through their own evolution, devolution and re-evolution. But from the point of view of the Homo sapiens, they had long preferred to revolt rather than re-evolve. Most remained stuck in their mental niches; thus, most were slowly replaced by natural and unnatural selection. In some areas, their numbers dwindled below the minimum viable population, and though they would last several generations, these cultures were committed to extinction.

An ill wind
Year 7

They must venture further and further all the time for supplies. Mykelti has done three days of hard labor towing a makeshift wagon with fat bicycle tires that still get bogged down in the mud and bramble as he weaves around obstacles and up and down sidewalks and roads. The air continues to get harder to breathe. What little oxygen is left in the atmosphere, the Earth seems to be greedily sucking back in, slowly rotting and rusting things. Not even the strongest survivor can risk being outside without supplemental oxygen, and now they must use respirators to filter out the poisons. There are others better suited to gather supplies. After the fight with his father, Mykelti's left arm had healed at an odd angle, often a small movement pinches his funny bone. But he endures the pain and the thin air because these expeditions are all he has left of the Old World. If he's lucky, he will find a newspaper or magazine—they were relatively rare even before D-day—and pretend that he's reading it the same day it was printed. If he's really lucky, it will have been printed on D-day. Maybe it will give him clues about what happened to the rest of the world.

The atmosphere has gone from a turbulent series of deluges and blizzards to a doldrum of drizzles. Winter and spring seem like a thing of the past. The long-dead crops in the farm fields have disintegrated and blown away in the winds. A flurry of snow is like a white confetti atop the burnt sienna earth. Mykelti trundles down an old farm road. It's a difficult and uninviting path, but that means it is less likely to have been ransacked. His feet crush sticks into dust as he walks. There are a few wisps of green grass. He harvests the tender shoots and places them in a leather pouch. He can't eat the grass raw without wearing out his teeth and clogging his intestines. But if he doesn't find food ahead, he'll mash it up with a stone mortar and pestle to make a green energy drink. Who knew his days at the smoothie shop would have provided impromptu apocalypse training?

At the end of the road, Mykelti finds an old farmhouse standing under skeleton trees. Mushrooms grow from the limbs like lightbulbs. It reminds Mykelti of holiday decorations waiting for the flip of a switch. The trees creak in the wind. It's hazardous to walk underneath trees now. Branches snap off frequently, evidenced by punctured cars and houses. The old farmer's wisdom says that if you want to tear down a barn, just cut a hole in the roof and wait. The farmhouse appears intact; however, the disintegrating wood and paint, and rust on the hinges, are like festering wounds waiting to rip open the patient. Slime and fungus—it covers most everything now—start at the ground and grow up the sides of the building as if the Earth is hiding her mistakes under a blanket. The scene before him is framed by a greenish-orange sky, the colors being refracted by a different composition of gases. *I will never get used to the colors of this doomsday world,* Mykelti thinks.

He drops his cart handle—hopefully the cart will be full when he leaves—and walks up the stairs. Beetles scurry and hide. He is glad to see the door is closed. During the chaos of the first year, scavengers would break windows and rip doors off their hinges just for the hope of finding one can of food. It's surprising how fast humanity dismantled itself. The broken doors and windows left many buildings dissolving from the inside out. So, Mykelti insisted their scouts leave the homes as intact as possible. "You never know what we may need someday," he said. "And if we get any gangs looting our territory, a broken door will be an advanced warning."

Mykelti tests the door. It's locked. He knocks, and it echoes loudly into the apocalyptic emptiness. He'd hate to surprise someone, especially if that person was banished from their group. Mykelti had lost most of his faith in humanity and came to the conclusion: people are going to do what people are going to do. As a result, their tribe only has one rule, but it is an unforgiving rule: Do no harm. It is a rule that encompasses all other rules. Not only did it govern such obvious things as theft, it also governed neglect, like leaving a person to die of starvation or illness. Of course, there have been many disagreements regarding what is beneficial. Often what benefited one seemed to harm another. But that was when Sherbert came into play, who is now the arbitrator of such decisions. Mykelti welcomed the disagreements because they were cause to discuss the greater good in a world that had no guarantees.

Since the group, only threescore strong, did not have the resources to imprison anyone or the desire to punish them, Mykelti gave criminals an option: penance or banishment upon penalty of death. Most chose penance: double their workload. Mykelti feared retaliation from those he banished, but none had ever returned. He figured they were more like parasites than hardened criminals and had moved to a new host. There is one advantage to the apocalypse: the remaining people in the tribe are kind-hearted and cooperative. Even those of an argumentative nature realize that they need everyone to fulfill their roles in order to survive.

After a perfunctory knock, Mykelti breaks a windowpane as gently as possible with the butt of his gun and reaches inside to unlock the door. "Hello?" After a few moments without an answer, he must be safe, but it also means there are no survivors. If they had been friendlies, he would have put on his ambassador's hat and invited them to join their tribe. Encountering survivors becomes rarer and rarer. Their group grows old and tired, and the women seldom give birth.

Mykelti enters the kitchen, reluctant to expect much; there have been houses with nothing more edible than a rawhide bone. Right away, he finds an unopened jar of instant coffee. Bags of coffee beans had lost their flavor years ago. *It's going to be a good haul,* he thinks. It doesn't take long to sack the kitchen, pantry and bathroom of the staple items. He even finds an unopened package of razor blades. He would never have guessed that having a beard would be one of his major peeves of the end of the world. The soap is also sealed in a package. The owners here were very tidy. It's good luck because almost everything has gone bad. In a few more years, there will be no food, toiletries or medicine left. Ironically, the lack of oxygen in the atmosphere is helping to preserve food. In the cellar, he finds jars of pickled eggs, sauerkraut, jams, stewed tomatoes and the rest of the Earth's last bountiful harvest. It's more than he can carry. It's his best haul in over a year, and he hasn't even begun the search for tools. He'll have to mark the location on his map and send a team back. The farmhouses nearby are probably also untouched.

He packs his cart too full. A can of tuna falls out and gets dented. "Damn!" He was saving that for Sherbert, but after Abigail died of botulism, they can't risk a dented can. He'll have to eat it now before it goes bad. He carries his own utensils and pops open the can, drinks the juice and enjoys the chewy meat. Food texture is another thing lost in the apocalypse. Afterwards, he treats himself to a stick of banana bubble gum. It makes his saliva glands ache with pleasure. Not long ago, gum was for children to blow bubbles, and bananas had little more significance than a flavor he could choose for his smoothies. Now, if he were to find a banana, it would be a miracle. It would mean banana seeds for their greenhouses, little plant factories springing forth from the dust and producing sweet sugars, fragrant spices, vitamins, minerals and the other building blocks of life.

Mykelti rearranges the load on his cart but, on second thought, removes a few items and returns to the house. The group is also starved for entertainment. Besides work—which lasts from sunup to sundown—there's not much to do. No smoking. Tobacco has gone bad. No gambling. There is no money. People inclined to drink have drank so much they don't even enjoy it anymore. People hardly even have sex because personal hygiene is as rare as a hot shower. Maybe the razors and soap he found will help his cause.

He returns to the house and finds some games and puzzles. For Tommy, he finds a *Boy Scout Handbook*. Learning to tie knots should keep him busy, but

Mykelti is saddened by the now-useless chapter on how to build a fire. He also finds a self-help book, *The Power of Positive Thinking*. He laughs, "If I could just get people to go from negative thinking to neutral—that would be a win." He finds some candy in a desk drawer, which will make nice presents. As a practical joke, he wraps a can of gourmet dog food and puts a bow on top. Sherbet says she'd prefer to starve than eat dog food. Rummaging around the garage, he finds a box of children's toys. He sees a stuffed tiger. Rainbow loves stuffed animals. She has created a zoo of animals in her bedroom—animals that he doesn't have the heart to tell her no longer exist. The tiger is just out of reach. When Mykelti forces the boards and boxes apart, he scratches his arm on a nail.

Mykelti boards up the broken window and dates and signs his name. The tribe had unintentionally created a new calendar. In the Old World, the abbreviation AD meant *anno Domini,* which is Medieval Latin for *in the year of the Lord.* Now it means *After Doomsday.* It makes Mykelti laugh. 7 AD. Seven years of hell. It's an ironic fuck-you to God. He wonders how long his calendar will survive.

Once again, his cart is full, but it will never be enough. Their life is unsustainable. The scavenged supplies don't contain enough nutrition; the Old World prioritized flavor, and Mother Earth has little left to nourish her children. Even the plants in their greenhouse are sickly for no apparent reason. Maybe it was infertile soil. Had the earthworms died like everything else?

He made a note to send a team to look for worms. They can take nothing for granted anymore. The Earth is slowly dying, and life has fallen down to the bottom rung of evolution. Even the mold and the mushrooms will run out of food when the trees are gone. Time is running out. Years, certainly. Decades, maybe. A lifetime, doubtful. Generations, impossible. Often people lose hope, and if anyone asks too many questions, he reminds them to focus: "Do what you can do, when you can do it." It has become a mantra for the tribe. Thus, Mykelti carries the burden of their future. He wonders if there is a limit to his ability to give? And what would happen to the tribe without him? He feels guilty—very guilty—especially for Rainbow.

§ § §

Dragging the heavy cart home takes Mykelti twice as long, and it becomes increasingly difficult as the infection grows in his arm from what seemed like an innocuous scratch. When he crests the final hill, his arm is red and swollen, and his forehead feels feverish. Below, his new home sparkles in a rare ray of sunlight. It's an old biodiesel factory that they encased in a hermetically sealed, geodesic glass hemisphere, surrounded by windmills and solar panels. Gregory gave his life building that dome. Now instead of creating fuel, they use the algae to create oxygen and food. Mykelti's proud of what they have accomplished.

The group, everyone except Sonja, who retreated into her own mind, was lucky to survive the trip back north to Memphis, a place far from any potential floodwaters and known hazards. Along the way, they gathered survivors and, more importantly, the skills those survivors possessed. Once they established a home, the next chore, which took months, was to find an internet server. It took several more weeks to rig up a power system. Fortunately, as Mykelti suspected, the dummy terminal didn't require a password. Once again, albeit temporarily, they had access to the internet and the collective wisdom of humanity. After such a long absence, it was like having their own Oracle of Delphi at their fingertips. Still, it wasn't easy to apply the information to the New World. It required long expeditions to find the needed parts, and thousands of hours to teach themselves basic things, like how to weld steel (using precious tanks of oxygen to do so), and rewire circuit boards. It took an effort none of them had ever endured.

It seemed no one had enough hope left to sustain themselves, much less the tribe; however, as cliché as it sounds, the rallying cry to build a future for their children was enough to overcome the inertia of despair. Many women could no longer bear children, but everyone realized they needed children—young, strong hands—to survive. Bringing a child into this desolate world was the ultimate selfish act. The irony didn't escape Mykelti—that humanity's selfishness is what saved them from extinction. Thus, the survivors converted the biodiesel factory into a new home and filled it with supplies and every spare part they could find. Then they had the relatively leisurely job to collect the last vestiges of civilization. They used every ream of paper and cartridge of ink they could find to print out more survival manuals. They filled the biodome with thousands of books from nearby libraries and dozens of paintings from the museums—the French Impressionists line Mykelti's office. Children and dogs, once again, play in the yard.

The sight reinvigorates Mykelti. He's excited to share his presents, and his body aches for some fresh food from the garden. *What I wouldn't give for a tomato fat with rainwater, ripe with sunlight and inflated with fresh air.* But soon, his thoughts turn into a blur as his higher cognitive functions shut down, leaving his feet to automatically stumble forward.

Sherbert is the first to see Mykelti stumble home and rushes to his side. "Are you okay?"

Mykelti smiles. He is always happy to see Sherbert no matter the day's troubles. The relief of being home evaporates the last of his adrenaline. "I'm fine. I'm just… I'm just…" he says before dropping the cart handle, slumping to the ground and passing out.

One less breath
A week later

Voices echo in Mykelti's subconscious.

"Maybe we should amputate?"

"And how are we going to do that?"

"He's fine. He's going to be fine."

"How long are we going to let him drain our resources?"

"Excuse me? I didn't know Jonathan was back."

"You ungrateful bastards. We wouldn't have anything if it weren't for him. We wouldn't have even survived. Now one thing goes wrong, and all you can think of is your own starving asses?"

"What do you want us to do, Sherbert? We're just like everyone else trying to make the best out of a bad situation."

"Worst. You mean *the worst* situation."

Mykelti's eyes swim into focus at Sherbert's voice. He can barely breathe, less than usual, of course.

"All I'm saying is, our resources are stretched thin. I'm not sure we can save him, much less the rest of us."

"Then what do you suggest we do?"

"It may be for the greater good to—"

"To euthanize him!?"

"To *not* use all our medicine on one person."

"He's right." Mykelti's voice shocks everyone.

"Oh my God! Mykelti, you're okay." Sherbert wraps her arms too tightly around him. Her warm tears stream down his cheek. "I was so worried. We were all worried." She glares at the others.

"I just needed a rest." He tries to lever himself up.

Sherbert pushes him back down.

"Let me get up. There must be a million things that need talking about," Mykelti's vocal cords have stiffened, and his words crackle.

"Just relax," Sherbert instructs in her no-nonsense tone.

"Yes, ma'am." He manages a laugh.

"Mykelti, I don't know what to tell you. Everybody has been arguing about the right thing to do. This place falls apart without you."

"I just do what needs to be done."

"Yes. And everyone else avoids doing what needs to be done. Or argues about what needs to be done."

"Is Rainbow okay?"

"She's fine. Look, you just rest. I'll get Rainbow and prepare you something nice to eat."

"Gourmet dog food?"

"No, dog. Eddie runs the kitchen now," she laughs and gives him a pinch.

"Benji—"

"Don't worry. I'll take good care of him."

"As for the rest of you—" she gestures to the crowd gathering at the door. "Get out of here!"

"Yes, ma'am," they respond in varying tones of acceptance.

Benji hands Mykelti a bottle of water. "Drink up."

Mykelti coughs and sputters when the bubbles hit his dry throat.

"We discovered that the creek water still had some dissolved oxygen, unlike the stale water left in the tanks and reservoirs. Now we make our own oxygenated water. It'll give you a turbo boost."

"Is this a marketing pitch?" Mykelti laughs.

Benji returns the laugh. "It's all FDA approved. Oxygen is the new essential macronutrient."

"How is everyone doing?" Mykelti implores. "Really?"

Benji shrugs and reaches into his backpack. "I've brought you something to ease the pain."

"Is that—?"

"Bourbon. Honest-to-god Kentucky bourbon."

"Where have you been hiding that?"

"Are you accusing me of hoarding? I was *saving* it in case of emergency."

"Wow!" Mykelti admires the golden-brown liquid sparkling in the light. "Can you imagine a time when the Earth was so bountiful that we could let fields of corn rot into this?"

"Lucky, they did. Bourbon never goes bad." Benji hesitates to admit the truth, "Honestly, Mykelti. People are fine. Mostly running on automatic. Arguing about every little decision. Sherbert's right. Much longer without you and... Who knows?" Benji pours two measures. "We're running short on bourbon, but there must be millions of barrels just waiting for us in Kentucky."

"Road trip."

"Cheers to that."

The bourbon burns going down. Mykelti coughs. "Whew. That killed some bugs."

Their banter is lighthearted, but as Sherbert and Rainbow enter the room with a platter full of the tribe's finest food—Benji hurriedly hiding the bourbon—Mykelti passes out from exhaustion.

§ § §

Mykelti's eyes flutter open as he regains consciousness.

"Mykelti. Thank God. You're awake."

"Sherbert…" his voice trails off.

"She hasn't left your side in days," says Eddie, hand-delivering her meal.

"You can't waste all your time here. The tribe needs you," says Mykelti.

"I need you," she says. "We need you. Isn't that right, Rainbow?"

"Hello, daddy."

"Hello, Rainbow." His daughter takes his breath away and brings an instant smile to his face. "Aren't you the most beautiful young lady!?" She is as colorful as her name: a curly mop of hair that starts out dark and gets lighter as it tickles the sky; skin a mixture of Mykelti's purple-black and Sherbert's pink-cream; and she has one brown eye and one blue eye. Her personality is just as colorful. She has a hypnotic gaze and instant charisma. Mykelti has been amazed that the passion of one person could glue a whole group together, especially when that person is a child. If it wasn't for her love of life, many more would have walked off into the sunset.

"I'm the *only* young lady."

Mykelti can barely inflate his lungs to laugh. "Just like your mother."

"Rainbow, fetch Tommy to say hello." When she leaves, Sherbert confesses, "It hurts me to look at you this way."

"Do you think she would be as precocious if we had given her a different name?" Mykelti had joked that they should call her Rainbow Sherbert after her mother. "You do know my real name, don't you?" Sherbert had laughed, but the name stuck. He's grateful Sherbert survived childbirth. Most haven't. Humans are so ill-equipped to birth children through their pelvic bones. So ill-equipped that, unlike most other mammals that are born running, humans are like embryos living outside the womb for the first years of their lives, like marsupials. It's a miracle humans overpopulated the planet. Fortunately, the few children born had inherited an ability to survive in this low-oxygen environment. They are different in other ways, too. Tiffany had set up a school, but the children preferred to learn by working alongside the adults. They never questioned our plight, rarely argued. Mykelti wondered if they had absorbed the tribe's new culture or if the selfish gene was going extinct along with so many other things…

"She has never seen a rainbow," Sherbert says sadly. In this infertile world, Rainbow was a surprise. Given a choice, Sherbert would never have brought a child into this world; regardless, Rainbow was a product of love, and Sherbert lived for that love.

"It's best that she never knew the Before Time," says Mykelti. "The memory of what was never clouds her mind. She has nothing to regret. To her, everything is new. Endless possibilities. She lives for the future."

"What about your future, Mykelti?"

"Would you mind getting me something to eat?" he says as an excuse to close his eyes for a short time.

§ § §

Mykelti wakes to Sherbert force-feeding him soup. The surprise causes him to gag.

"Breathe, Mykelti. Just breathe."

"How long has it been?"

"It doesn't matter. You're here now." She bursts into tears.

"Is everything okay?"

"I thought we lost you."

"I mean, is everything okay with the tribe?"

"You should worry about yourself for a change." Sherbert sighs. "The arguing is getting worse. Some are refusing to work. Mykelti," Sherbert uses his name to emphasize the importance, "we're losing hope. Most of us never had hope in the first place. But that's one thing you have in abundance—a mindfulness that there is always a way. People get out of bed just because you tell them things will get better."

"When will they learn to motivate themselves?" he sighs.

Sherbert sees Elizabeth politely standing outside the doorway and rushes her words, "Mykelti, I know this isn't the world you imagined—hell, that sounds cliché—this isn't the world any of us imagined. I know you wanted to make a difference, that you had faith humanity was going to do the right thing." A wisp of wind ruffles her hair, giving the impression that there are still fresh breezes. "You can still fulfill your purpose. Maybe it isn't the utopia we all envisioned, but you can still help make the world a better place. Just start here with our small group."

"Haven't I been doing that?" he says, perplexed.

Elizabeth enters the room. "May I talk to Mykelti alone?"

Sherbert wipes tears from her eyes. "Yes, of course." Before she exits, she turns to Mykelti. "I'm begging you. People are counting on you."

Elizabeth sits beside Mykelti. Due to her charade of playing doctor, she had more medical knowledge than anyone left. So, despite not being able to save Henrick, the tribe promoted her to being an actual doctor. To Elizabeth, it was penance. "I have few instruments and know little more than I can read in books," she says. "But I can tell you, Mykelti, the prognosis is not encouraging." She holds a mirror before him. The veins on one side of his neck run black, even against his dark skin. Mykelti gasps, his body reflexly preparing to scream.

"The infection has spread," says Elizabeth. "The antibiotics we do have aren't working. You should, as they say, make peace with yourself and say goodbye. I know, easier said than—"

"So, this is what fate has had in store for me—a scratch. It seems like such an anticlimactic ending. Yet, it jeopardizes us all."

"Mykelti, I'm sorry. I really am."

"However swift a man, he may never outrun his shadow." He gives Elizabeth's hand a reassuring squeeze. "You did your best."

"I'll send for Sherbert."

"Tell her I'm resting." He doesn't want to say that he needs time to purge the doubts already raging in his mind: *How will the tribe survive without me if it can barely survive with me? What will happen to Rainbow?*

For the fourth time, he lay dying, like he did at his father's feet, and on the streets of Chicago, and before that, as a child in Cameroon. Except now there is no escape, and now it comes as a relief. He had done everything he could have done. Though he failed, no one can say he didn't try. As much as he wanted to quit, and as easy as it would have been to simply lie down and die, he didn't. And each time he rose, he brought others up with him—that is a success. In retrospect, he has lived a long and full life. Certainly, it is not a life anyone would have volunteered for, but no one can accuse him of not seeing the world, not doing things never done before, not caring. And he had lived long enough to see humanity's final dramatic act. Perhaps to God, this was a life well-lived. *Had I been the plaything of God all along? Did God set up humanity like dominoes to see how we would fall? If I were a god, I'd do the same. But what is the game now? Does God have the same dream as I do? A dream of humanity living in harmony with the Earth. Rising, once again, to form nations and build a future filled with wonder. A race of beings that could seed the galaxy with their creations.*

The dream still lived in him, breathing life into his spirit, but soon they would both be gone. For a moment, he mourns the death of his dream more than himself, but reviewing his failures and unrequited dreams causes a bitter, life-draining feeling to arise. The only people entitled to be bitter are their children, cursed as human placeholders waiting generations for the Earth to regenerate itself.

His mood spirals into depression. He wishes someone would hold his hand and comfort him, but he is no longer the one that needs comfort. Any energy the tribe may devote to him is less energy that they have for themselves. He must focus. He can't wallow in self-pity. His last act can't be greedily sucking up praise and sympathy.

A crowd outside his room has been discussing his fate. One sentence rings clear, "Everything is lost."

Mykelti's subconscious mind—his flickering ember of a dream that refuses to die—automatically whispers, "Not everything." What is a dream but an idea? Rags or riches, peace or war: they are all ideas. Suddenly, he realizes that this dream that he perpetuated among survivors, the hope to build a better life, was no longer a fantasy or will-o'-the-wisp, but as real as any other thing that was birthed and breathed. It is as real as he is—more real. It would outlive him, but for how long? He must use what remains of his life to give his tribe—his family—another dream that would pull them forward. He must inspire them. Mykelti almost laughs. *Inspiration* literally means *to inhale.* This dying man in a dying world must inspire them with his expiration—his last dying breath.

§ § §

"Stand back. Give him some room to breathe. You're sucking up all the air." Sherbert makes a dramatic entrance. A stream of people paying their last respects to Mykelti has grown into a crowd. "What's all the commotion about?"

"He refuses to nominate a replacement." As usual, the crowd takes on an anonymous voice of dissent.

"It's time for the old ways to die," says Mykelti.

"We need a leader."

"Everyone here is a leader," says Mykelti.

"We don't all agree and never will."

"Are we supposed to vote every time someone needs to take a shit?"

"Yeah, someone needs to make the tough decisions!"

"You don't even have to think," says Mykelti. "Let the rule do the thinking for you. Do no harm."

"You can't expect one rule to cover every situation."

"Form a council," says Mykelti. "Make new rules. Call it the Declaration of Inter-Dependence. Call it whatever you want. The point is that everyone here is the de facto leader of their own area of expertise. Trust me, I never wanted to be the leader—the taskmaster—and neither does anyone else. Nor do you need one; I remind you of my father."

"You expect us to reinvent civilization!?"

"Not only civilization, I expect you to reinvent yourselves. You're not animals. You can control your own destiny. You can evolve. And you can choose in which direction."

"That's far-fetched, don't you think?"

"Nothing else has worked. I will no longer be your scapegoat. You will have to find your own reasons to live. Consider yourselves a tribe of leaderless leaders. That is my final recommendation."

Mykelti looks at Sherbert with tired eyes, and she takes the hint. "Come on, everyone. Get out. Let him rest!" The crowd murmurs objections. "You heard him. It's time for everyone to be the leader of their own lives. Now, go figure it out for yourselves."

Mykelti feels guilty dismissing them, but he believes there is only one person in the tribe that holds the key to their future. "I'd like to speak to Rainbow."

"You need rest," says Sherbert.

"I will be getting plenty of rest all too soon."

Though Sherbert tries to hide her emotions, her eyes are overflowing with tears.

Mykelti reaches his good arm towards her. "Be grateful for what we had."

"It's not that. I mean, it is that. It's also Rainbow. She's missing so much already. And now… to lose her father…"

"Tell her stories about me. What we had, not what she lost."

Sherbert leaves, too choked up to speak. A few minutes later, Rainbow arrives.

"Well, look who's here," Mykelti says with a smile, but Rainbow is unusually serious.

"Are you going to be okay? Mommy says you might take the long nap."

"I am very tired."

"Do people ever wake from the long nap, daddy?"

He wants to cushion the truth, but there is no hiding the truth from her. But what to say? He answers quickly, before Rainbow can see the doubt in his eyes, but in doing so, his answer comes from his heart, "Yes, but in a different time, a different place." Mykelti had lost his faith long ago; now, he has no choice but to have faith. Had he answered differently, it would have robbed her of hope. "It's okay. It's my time… We all have our time."

Rainbow's eyes fill with tears like her mother's. "Mommy says that I have to say goodbye. I don't want to."

"Not everyone is as lucky as we are. Not everyone gets to say goodbye. I wanted to tell you something." He must choose his words wisely. Words carry weight, and the waves ripple through humanity like a stone thrown in a pond. Even when the stone sinks to the bottom and the waves dissipate, the pond is forevermore changed.

He has read—there's been lots of time for reading—that women, their charisma, temperance, and intuitive grasp of relationships honed from generations of raising children, have ruled society since the dawn of humanity. While the men were afield, hunting and foraging, women made the rules and governed the tribe. Their allegiance was to their children—not an individual—and they channeled the raw strength of men for the betterment of the tribe. Somehow at the dawn of Westernized religion, things changed. Men became jealous. It's easy for him to understand. Sherbert loves him, but she would save their daughter and leave him on a sinking ship. Even now, Sherbert listens at the door, ready to protect their daughter from the things he might say. Deep down, every man knows that they are replaceable. It is the men who risk a broken leg on the hunt. It is the men that go off to war and die alone. It is the men that sacrifice themselves for the love of a woman. One misconception of society is that men have few emotions; it is just the opposite. Our emotions rage inside us, each one a wild horse without name. If men appear cold, in part, it is because we fear the consequences of our own actions, whether that be raging at our impotence or giving away our hearts. Society, on some subconscious or unspoken level, has taught men to suppress their emotions, knowing that leaving men unchecked was like a ticking bomb—a bomb that had finally exploded.

Were these evolutionary truths or cultural lies? Mykelti didn't know. To make such polarizations seemed to doom one side to subservience. He is happy to let womankind rule once more. Rainbow, however, is different. She defied being put in a box. She is both soft and strong. Both accepting and opinionated. Both willing to work and to command others. At times, she seemed to disappear, just doing what needed to be done. Yet, other times, her personality shone so bright the shadows of doubt had nowhere to hide. Mykelti knew that Rainbow held the key, and it is his dying wish to help her unlock a better future. To help her lead humans back to their humanity. To show us how we are more similar than different.

"Daddy? Are you okay?"

Mykelti's having trouble keeping his eyes open. The cells in his body have already given up. They prolong his life simply by emptying their reserves of energy. He can feel his life draining away. He had but one try left. Would he fail again? He wouldn't live to see that. Maybe it is too late. Too late for the world.

Too late for more words. *No!* Faith. He needed to have faith. It is time to let humanity fend for itself. Rainbow is a beacon of hope. In comparison, his own attempts to cheer the tribe were disingenuous. Had he the wisdom and charisma of Rainbow, perhaps he could have saved the world. Still, he had one thing left to say, one piece of wisdom that took a lifetime to learn, one last try to save the world—a dream. It is his gift to the future… if it would be accepted. He wants to tell her it is important and not to forget, but he doesn't have that many words left. "Alone we live our life, but together we create our destiny."

Rainbow squeezes his hand. "Together."

§ § §

Mykelti's eyes flutter open. His family and friends stand vigil. Sherbert's eyes are as green and moist and full of life as our world ever was.

We only have so many breaths in a lifetime. It's an unknown amount, but finite. That being said, the quantity of breaths isn't as important as the quality. Did you use them to shout from mountain tops? Were they expelled in laughter or sorrow? Did your words fly on wings of love or hate? Who's to say if a breath was wasted and better saved for another day that may never come? The important thing is: Did you breathe life deep? Did it tickle your lungs until you had to let it out in a roar? Did you weep with joy? And run until you could run no further? Or did you hold your breath, afraid to move? Were your words caught in your throat afraid to be breathed?

Now, every breath Mykelti takes is one less breath he has left to live—like us all—but now he could count them on one hand. Inhale. A deep breath. It's hard to breathe. Harder than ever. Not because of lack of oxygen, but the lack of will to live. Exhale. One less breath left to live.

Inhale. Sherbert sandwiches his hands between hers as if she can imbue a healing power. Time to say goodbye if he can… Exhale. "I love you…" One less breath. One less sentence with the wind to carry its wings.

Inhale. Exhale. One less breath. One less soul illuminating the darkness.

Inhale. Exhale. One less breath. One less body owed to Mother Earth.

Inhale…

Exhale…

One…

Breath…

Less…

The children of Earth
The following millennia

It was the beginning of a new era, and it was time, once again, for the Earth to remake herself. The volcanic core of her heart still beat strong, but it would take time to heal. She shrugged her shoulders, roiled her shores, coughed a few times, and began to clean house.

Mankind's famous monuments and landmarks were erased like pencil marks. Even the Great Pyramids of Egypt, which outlasted written history, were nothing more to the Earth than a mother putting away her children's building blocks. Cities and entire nations were swept under the rug like dust. The land was scrubbed clean of mankind, like bacteria from dishes. When they were gone, the Earth blew the dust of mankind's bones and monuments—along with their poisons and plastics—across continents until it settled in lakes and oceans, where it was compressed into a sedimentary rock that would have made beautifully marbled countertops for future generations if it were not radioactive.

When the oceans ran fresh again, the phytoplankton blossomed and gradually filled the atmosphere with the product of their flatulence—oxygen. Many more millennia passed as the phytoplankton gradually replenished the atmosphere, giving rise to aerobic life once more. As mammals arose from between the toes of the dinosaurs, so did life rise again from the ashes of humanity. The few remaining species of birds reseeded the world, and the beetles pollinated what ancient species managed to grab hold. Plants flourished: their roots anchored the soil, and their leaves nourished the sky. Once again, the cycle of life was on the upswing. From the point of view of the Earth, species were more like individuals being born, maturing and dying.

Forests would walk from one ocean to another, reptiles would sprout wings and fly, and animals, in general, would metamorphose into all manners of shapes and sizes, trying to outwit and outbreed one another—but even more so to play and explore new possibilities, like plumbing the depths of the sea or flying into the stratosphere to see the stars. It was no longer an issue of survival of an individual or a species, but the entire web of life, which became more diverse, more intelligent and more empathic. The web of life took on a cooperative tone and formed new agreements: plants produced an abundance of fruit; animals understood they were playing a game of predator and prey, and when their time came, gave willingly of themselves with no more regret than a corpse gives itself to the worms; nothing took more than it needed; and, all respected their home.

As for humans, the culture of mankind had died, but isolated tribes of their species survived in a variety of ad hoc biodomes that were a testament to the robustness of the human spirit. The domes ranged from underground emergency bunkers that hoarded enough supplies to weather the changes; to refurbished, pressurized buildings; to makeshift greenhouses; to undersea research facilities that had already adapted to extracting oxygen from the ocean water; and even to ice caves in Antarctica, whose melting glaciers contained bubbles of oxygen. In addition, there were many more enclaves subsisting in dilapidated cities: some had a natural adaptation; many formed a symbiotic relationship with algae; and one group colonized the Dead Sea, a spot on land over 400 meters below sea level, where the oxygen pooled.

The drama that Mykelti's tribe faced had played out across the world. The male-dominated tribes rose up to subdue and enslave the weak, taking what they wanted and destroying what they could not. Though, without a buffer of law and order, individual bullies and warring tribes annihilated each other, like two cars that failed a game of chicken, subsequently purging themselves from the human race. So, eventually, tribal warfare ceased simply because those inclined to argue no longer existed, leaving the modest, patient and gentle people. It was one prophecy that did come true: the meek had inherited the Earth.

Mykelti's legacy fell to his daughter. Eventually, Rainbow, like her father, was erased from history because history would no longer exist; however, her genes and, more importantly, her ideas—Mykelti's ideas—would spread across the planet. This is what made humans truly different from animals: children do not just inherit genetic information, they inherit ideas—genes and memes—whether good or bad, whether sins or virtues.

It was the ideas that a person must do no harm and contribute more than they took that altered the course of humanity. It no longer mattered if an individual was the fittest, smartest, or the most adaptable, because no individual was capable of surviving alone. What governed evolution now was the intangible idea of benevolence, and it was an idea that only survived within like-minded groups. Those individuals that did not abide by this rule were ostracized and left to wander the barren and desolate environment until they consumed the last cans of food and then each other. After dozens of generations, Mykelti's rules no longer mattered; they had become embedded within the species as an instinct to cooperate for the greater good. The greater good did not mean humanity: it meant all life, even the planet itself.

Eventually, when the humans emerged from their safe havens, they discovered they were no longer the lone sentient species; they also discovered they were no longer entirely human. As time passed, the new humans wove themselves harmlessly into the fabric of the landscape. Buildings were molded from the Earth. Roads weaved through the trees. Rivers and canals transported cargo. Their classrooms were the world itself, and children worked and learned beside the adults and their sentient friends: descendants of the dolphins and octopi. The people were as diverse in appearance—truly a rainbow of color—as they were in their beliefs. Each individual's truth held to be a small part of the whole as seen from any one perspective. They cherished doing work by hand; if that were not possible, they used benign technologies, like plants that harvested metals from the ground. There was little need to go anywhere except for fun or curiosity. Their goal, as a species, was to become better and better creators in order to experience all that life could be, their God being creation itself, and their worship being a reverence for life in all its myriad forms and possibilities.

And, so, the new humans survived. If given a name, they would be called Homo superioris, and they would study their ancestors much like Homo sapiens studied neanderthals. Likewise, the Earth, having endured her mid-life crisis, entered middle age with grace, adorned in a new shawl of the most beautiful flora and fauna, which her visitors greatly admired.

Bonus material

For more information about this book and some fun bonus material, please visit the author's website:

ScottStoll.com/breathless/bonus/

Please leave a review

If you enjoyed this book, or even if you didn't, please leave a review online. It helps people find a book they might love. And it helps me write more and better books.

Acknowledgments

First, I'd like to thank you, my reader, for helping to bring this book to life. After all the feedback that I received from Falling Uphill, I learned that each reader brings a unique perspective to the book, giving it new depth and meaning.

Second, this book would never have blossomed into reality without the help of many people, including the books and articles of at least a thousand authors and scientists. You can't all know who you are, but thanks anyway for contributing to the inspiration, facts or structure of this novel.

Third, thanks to dozens of people, including friends and family, who gave me much-needed encouragement. Though I somehow rode a bicycle around the world, I am not sure I would have had the confidence to have written this book without the constant nudges. Most of you wish to remain anonymous, but you know who you are.

Finally, a shout-out to a few people: Thanks to Nikolas Everhart, Scott Macmann, Alex Vernik, Wendy Vogel, and everyone else in my author's club, Cincinnati Fiction Writers, for comments on my work in progress. We always joke that anyone who submits a chapter for review will end up rewriting the whole book. Thanks to filmmaker, Michael Cross, for help with plotting. Thanks to Mason Alexander for feedback on my rough draft and being the kind of fan you don't want to disappoint. Thanks to Cindy, who deserves credit for not letting Mykelti die in the first chapter. Finally, thanks to Steve Perry and Sara, who listened to me go on and on and on about this project for over ten years.

www.ingramcontent.com/pod-product-compliance
Lightning Source LLC
Chambersburg PA
CBHW020403120726
47904CB00002B/688